KREINDIA OF AMORIUM

D0967616

MORE NOVELS FROM BLUEBERRY LANE BOOKS

Books by

Irving A. Greenfield

ANCIENT OF DAYS

WHARF SINISTER

MASS FOR A DEAD WITCH

ONLY THE DEAD SPEAK RUSSIAN

A PLAY OF DARKNESS

SNOW GIANTS DANCING

BEYOND VALOR

Ben Parris

WADE OF AQUITAINE

MARS ARMOR FORGED

CREDS: THE IRS ADVENTURE

KREINDIA OF AMORIUM

Wade of Aquitaine

Book Two

Ben Parris

BLUEBERRY
LANE BOOKS

NEW YORK

WADE OF AQUITAINE, BOOK TWO:

KREINDIA OF AMORIUM

FIRST U.S. EDITION

Cover art by Roy Mauritsen

Library of Congress Cataloging In-Publication Data
has been applied for

ISBN 978-1-942183-05-1

www.Blueberrylanebooks.com

For Maggie Estep

Who we lost before

This ending was found

THEODERIC'S ITALE
500 A.D.

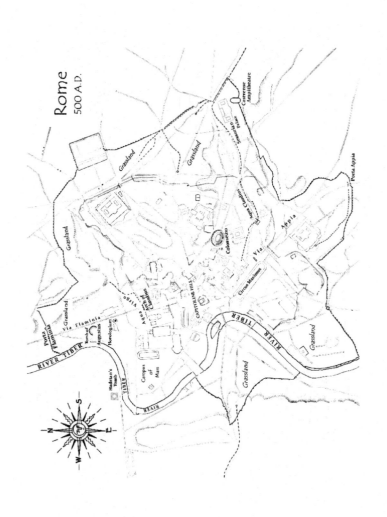

Rome
500 A.D.

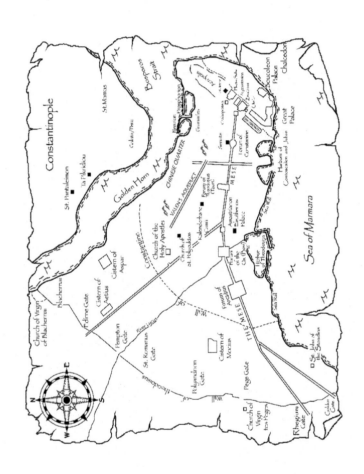

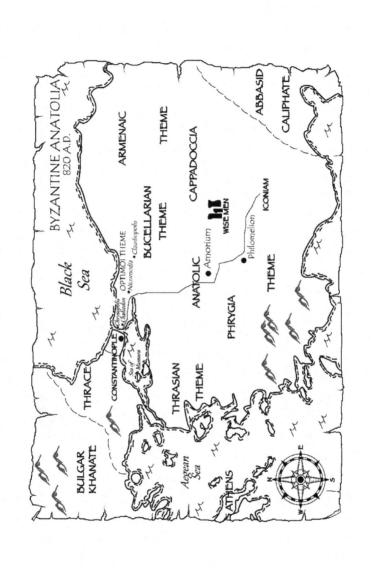

BYZANTINE ANATOLIA
820 A.D.

Black Sea

BULGAR KHANATE

THRACE

CONSTANTINOPLE
Chrysopolis
Chalcedon
Sea of Marmara

OPTIMOI THEME
Nicomedia · Chrysopolis

ARMENAIC THEME

BUCELLARIAN THEME

CAPPADOCIA THEME

ABBASID CALIPHATE

WISE MEN

ANATOLIC THEME
Amorium ·
Philomelion ·
ICONIAM

THRASIAN THEME

PHRYGIA

Aegean Sea

ATHENS

N E S W

CONTENTS

Part I

The Land of Descendants

"People who believe in physics know that the distinction between past, present, and future is only a stubbornly persistent illusion."

~Albert Einstein

PROLOGUE

*"In the Year of Our Lord 814, on the 29th day of
Pharmouthi, the lost legion of Rome took up arms against the traitor
Raginpert The Insolent, Prince of the Longobards, each force
garroting the other in mountains that swallowed their secrets."*

—Scriptor Kreindia of Amorium

<u>Brennii Pass, 814 A.D</u>

KREINDIA OF AMORIUM gazed across the battlefield to be, the Alps' Brenii Pass. Her high perch of stone behind the isolated tree provided her with a picturesque tableau. Her side, the resurrected Roman legion, sat in ambush while the invading army, tiny figures in the distance, trudged up the icy slope from Itale.

As the enemy closed in, surprising them would depend upon the perfect, most silent deception. In the hush, even the scratching of her pen on the parchment seemed intolerable, so she stopped her notes. The restless part of her mind was held in abeyance too, because history waited. In those moments of peace, she watched a nutcracker land to investigate a shattered pinecone; a sheet of snow wind-cleared from the ledge; and a golden eagle gliding high in the distance.

Then a future scene impinged upon the present, exposing a multitude of the dead and the dying in the smoldering aftermath of this same battle, bearded vultures descending to make of it a feasting field. In that flash of things to come, she knew that their ruse would hold long enough for the trap to spring shut. But the Holy Roman Empire would pay a staggeringly high price.

General Michael's niece was a synesthete, her mind drift-sampling dimensions wrapped within her own. At her gift's most functional, she spied through the tattered veil of time.

In the next blink, the legion's General Honoratus initiated the attack with iron-tipped missiles. When the enemy took losses and shrank from the assault, Honoratus used the hidden trenches to shift his forces in response to the enemy's new distribution. By his latest actions, history-to-come was refreshed and revealed to Kreindia anew. As her friends and allies took their new positions among the brass-helmeted troops, she flinched at flash after tragic flash of their fates—a thigh rupturing in a fountain of blood, an eye taken by a sword tip, the sinew of a strong neck cut deep—and had to keep these outcomes to herself. In ninth century Europe, her very nature constituted a crime, and by necessity none of the most central events could transpire differently. Her role in the present conflict was that of a scriptor, not a commander, not an advisor, and certainly not a soothsayer. Honoratus suffered her presence only because she could write and was schooled in history, and the neo-Roman legion wanted an accurate record of their long-hidden force and its glorious return.

Kreindia saw more than anyone intended. Under the new positioning, some participants would now get a reprieve as unfortunates died in their place. Still others' fates hinged upon their leader's next decision. Her prescience had never been so active and so clear. She'd never leaned this close to one of the great pivots of history. Position mattered. Timing mattered. Every rolling calculation that passed through the commander's mind tallied and showed her another result.

Her dear Wade of Aquitaine would suffer from the loss of his friends. From the moment Honoratus gave the signal to fall upon the Longobards, she knew that the enemy, Raginpert the Insolent, would be cut down... as would her side's Tankred and Snorri. She herself would be struck down, yet she was blind to her final fate. Only the faithful Saxon, Grimketil Forkbeard, survived by virtue of his enormous strength and skill, in each version of reality. Grimketil's grief at the losses, however, would be as expansive as the man himself. As much as Kreindia's gifts and responsibilities had made her stoic, this Pyrrhic victory was yet the hardest fate to bear in silence.

And as she saw by second sight, so it happened, with the triumph over Raginpert himself twice as sweet and the empire's losses twice as searing. Before the battle was fully done, however, Wade tried to rescue her with astral manipulation, and Kreindia ceased to exist in her era or any other.

In this void suspended, she left behind the cruel heat of conflict where her grievous head wound let copious volumes of her lifeblood, to face a harried exit with Wade of Aquitaine bound for the land of descendants, a place where she might survive. Wade, a twenty-first century native with his own synesthetic abilities, had breached the astral plane; without him, she could not.

For an unknowable interval, new memories would not form. Whatever she had witnessed in the world between, if anything, would remain a sealed box as she hurtled toward the next unknown. The war she left behind was the start of a conflagration that would have easily extended the ages of ignorance by half a millennium had the Longobard's plans succeeded. In the moment preceding her astral ascension, her prescience confirmed to her that the larger conflict had been favorably decided in the one great battle, putting a stop to the ambition of Raginpert the Insolent. That news gave her a moment's peace.

Then Kreindia felt a lurch of panic. Wade's link with her failed without warning. *What happened?*

She didn't know what to do. Her orientation shifted and blurred with a palpable wrench. A rapid tunneling to infinity left an ever-widening gap between Wade's road and the path before her. She floundered with no way to control her flight. The path she'd left had an established feel about it in which her synesthesia lent her the sensation of shoe padding conformed to its owner's foot. Her new path had the raw odors of sawdust stirred into the air with a grinding tool, blinding and choking her as she pressed forward.

With a flicker of hope, she saw that her mind had not been entirely severed from Wade's. As she plummeted toward some future Earth, Kreindia beheld the place in which Wade would come to rest, eyes open, kneeling in full armor as he had knelt before her, tending her wound prior to their departure. Cleaner and better furnished than her era's houses in the heart of Europe, though far from opulent, Wade's destination, his home, might have passed for a servant's quarters in the Great Palace.

The events within her scope compressed and stuttered. Some froze while others played out. In the clearest images, Wade rose and spun as though it dawned on him that Kreindia had veered out of his reach. The grime and blood of his battle gear flaked onto a plush blue rug as he searched the living area, raged, howled, and spent himself in agony. Shouting Kreindia's name, he seemed aged as though he had endured far worse than bloody battle. Wade, who she had summoned from across the centuries, the young man who had set right the ages, the very man she loved, was severed from her now.

And she saw, too, that the outcome of the Battle of Brenii Pass was no longer a settled matter, but had become a tarred morass of indecision. It was no longer success and still not failure. Even though she stood on the doorstep of the twenty-first century where the result of that ancient conflict should have been plain, the Fates showed her opposite results simultaneously, and she did not know how that duality could exist. Things in the past either were or they weren't. Happened or didn't. Events of an earlier sequence had to have gone one way or the other in order to get to the later point. Time did not cleave and get stuck. Yet now it was.

In the midst of that madness, she attempted to leave a trace of herself in the places that she had observed, a spoor for Wade to notice and follow. As she was unable to touch anything, it required enormous concentration.

Before she could reinforce her trail, her destination drew her away and the vision faded like a high-speed version of shadows melting to full dark with the loss of the sun. For her transit had ended, her new life... begun.

Life in a cage.

CHAPTER 1

The Richters

21st Century, Long Island, New York

DR. NESKY STUDIED the Richter family in the waiting room through smoked glass doors that favored posture over detail: the father waving his arms high and sharp in the manner of an authoritarian; mother bent, cowed by him; their daughter immobile in her wheelchair, head atilt like a machine shut down.

The youngster needed Nesky's help. He sighed quietly in his peaceful alcove. *A great deal of work awaits and we must begin now.*

The doctor did not operate his holistic psychiatry boutique as he used to run his medical practice, with patients shown to a second room for another round of waiting. Here he bounded through the reception doors and extended his palm in greeting. *Much better.*

"Come in. Come," said Nesky, opening the spring-loaded door and blocking it with his lanky frame. He had to do most of the reaching to complete his handshake with the reluctant father. "Good to see you again, Faron, Clara. How are you, Kreindel?" He always greeted the daughter brightly even though she could not respond.

Faron turned to his daughter and grated, "Kreindel, this way."

The young woman, a near-quadriplegic, had sufficient command of one finger to nudge a joystick with which she negotiated the doorway and the long hall that followed. Her short haircut allowed Nesky a view of her small, delicate ears on which he picked out potential acupuncture nodes that might ease her suffering when pierced.

The trio, clad in severe black and white, crowded the front part of Nesky's office in his wake while the doctor seated himself on the other side of his desk. Out of the corner of his eye, he saw Faron level an appraising look at him that teetered on the edge of contempt. His eyes were rimmed in red, the whites clear.

When they were seated amidst comfortable clutter, Faron glaring out the window at a blue-winged warbler in the pine tree, Clara fidgeting with a handkerchief, ready for tears, Nesky said, "I have not seen you in a while."

Faron said, "No, that's right. You haven't."

A charmer, that one. Trying another tack, Nesky smiled and said, "What brought you here today?" Nesky had been wondering why the couple had not returned with their daughter after her first appointment. They had canceled the second appointment and gone silent for weeks.

"You've had ample time to study her files, Dr. Nesky. We want a diagnosis and a treatment plan."

"Yes?" The doctor smiled. Gennadi Nesky, whose sensibilities were a throwback to those of pre-Bolshevik Russian intelligentsia, was not easily intimidated in the freer atmosphere of the modern-day United States. He would provide help for the sake of Kreindel and Clara. Not Faron.

The parents craned forward in expectation, the mother a bit further back, her eyes drifting to a wall diagram of an acupuncture body-map shot through with black pinpoints. The air conditioner hummed a steady one-note tune. Kreindel drooled.

The psychiatrist steepled his fingers, forming a little roof under which he could collect his thoughts. He had indeed studied her array of tests before and after his own examination. The results were disturbing. No one Dr.

Nesky knew in the medical profession liked to use the term "mystery illness."

Out loud.

It shattered the illusion Americans preferred to nurture in regard to their doctors. A failure to classify wasn't conducive to scientific thinking. It also implied to the patient that you were surrendering to the unknown. But a mystery illness was what Kreindel had. No diagnosis from previous caregivers had held up. Paralyzed for two years from the age of eighteen.

Nesky said, "We will talk at length, Mr. Richter. First, however, allow me to set your daughter up with an auricular treatment in the other room. You understand?" It would give them a chance to debate the case without upsetting the patient.

After a moment of consideration, Faron consented, and they all moved to the treatment room.

Donning a white lab coat to cover his jacket, Nesky drew Kreindel's chair next to the examination table and let her remain in it, dabbing at her moist chin with a sterile wipe. The girl could not converse, but he told her what he intended to do.

The parents watched with curious revulsion as he freed the individually wrapped acupuncture needles and placed them deftly in strategic positions on their daughter, with a gentle twirl to deepen each.

What Nesky visualized as he worked in her ears was a map of the entire body, the inverted fetus with its head in place of the earlobe. On the rim—the helix of her left ear—rested her theoretical right arm. The inner ridge, the antihelix, represented her spine. Her legs curled into the triangular fossa near the top. All received a needle treatment. To those, Nesky added the *Shen Men* point at the fossa's apex, the so-called "heavenly gate," for deep relaxation. When he was done, her ears bristled with tiny metal projectiles. To enhance the calming effect, he cued up *Pavane pour une infante défunte* by Ravel and set it on repeat.

As they cleared out, Clara covered her mouth with her fingertips as though the act she had witnessed was unspeakable.

By the time the parents returned with Nesky to his office, the blue-winged warbler had flown. A ruffled, mud-colored bird now took its place.

Faron said, "I want you to understand that I'm not the girl's biological father. If she inherited anything, it's from the Grunewald side." He glared at his wife. She kept quiet.

Nesky asked, "May I?"

"Go on."

"This is a tentative diagnosis, you understand, but I believe your daughter has conversion disorder."

Faron said, "You mean hysterical paralysis?"

"You've heard something of it then."

"Some nineteenth century quack's idea as an excuse for malingering."

"I assure you, Mr. Richter, that the collection of problems popularized in the nineteenth century as hysteria is actually an illness recognized as far back as the ancients. Emotional triggers can mutate into very serious physical ailments."

"We're not ancient. I think we can toss those notions."

Nesky persisted, "The recognition, if not the label, has endured because there is a basis for it."

"What about multiple sclerosis?" Faron asked. "That could affect her vocal cords too."

"My inclination is that it doesn't fit. Her paralysis was rapid onset."

"Marburg's Variant."

"You're going over old ground, argued out by other doctors." Nesky ran his fingers through his hair. "Marburg's is very rare. Your daughter's case wasn't preceded by fever, doesn't respond to any MS treatment, and hasn't advanced further. Also the MRI shows no characteristic lesions."

"How do you know?" Faron demanded.

"I'm quoting the specialist you saw. I double checked it too."

"Some kind of intermittent remission could explain why it hasn't advanced further," Faron offered.

"There would still be signs."

"Parkinson's?"

"Even less likely. Conversion disorder fits better."

"Hysterical nonsense."

Nesky sat back, signaling that he would not argue. "She may have experienced a particular trauma, as well as regular stress, and I see signs that she suffers from dissociative disorder. Her body has converted her stress into the current condition, although that doesn't rule out some organic element playing a role as well."

Faron snapped his eyes shut, and his breathing came with effort. In an instant, he appeared to lapse into troubled REM sleep, shrugging and then flailing. In this tumult of a nightmare he appeared to be managing a giant machine that required frantic adjustments.

Nesky cleared his throat. "Mr. Richter?"

Faron swung his arms so violently his wife had to shift her chair twice to avoid being struck. She did not move it closer again afterwards.

Clara said, "He's done this before."

"Does your husband suffer from seizures?" Nesky pursued. "Is he under care?"

Before she could answer, Faron grunted and opened his eyes. He said, "You think she's traumatized, Nesky? That's garbage." He behaved as though his turbulent interval never happened.

With a glance at Clara, Nesky replied, "I know she is."

"Then we have nothing to discuss," Faron declared. "My family is leaving."

Faron stormed into the examination room down the hall and pulled the needles from his daughter, casting them to the floor and stomping over them.

Nesky yelled, "Stop. You are not at home here."

Faron manhandled Kreindel's chair out of the room, chipping the doorway with one of its castor forks. Clara put her hands up, imploring him to wait. He showed her his rough knuckles, and she flinched and touched her jaw as though she knew what they felt like. As Faron pressed on, Kreindel rolled through the hallway ahead of him, smiling in oblivious serenity.

Dr. Nesky shouted after him, "What is it you wanted to hear, Mr. Richter?"

He watched as the trio found the elevator waiting and cleared out quickly. The glass waiting room door inched shut, providing a soft counterpoint to the turbulent scene. Extraordinary. Never had Nesky succumbed to an outburst by a patient's parent before by raising his voice to match.

Though upset to the point of distraction, his custom was to document the visit immediately. After a moment's delay to recall where he had left his laptop, he retired to his office and went at it with zeal, writing:

K was highly responsive even to an abbreviated auricular acupuncture session. Though her father cut it short in an abrupt, somewhat violent fashion, she had no immediate reaction to the disturbance.

Instead of using the abbreviation "pt." for "patient" he journaled her as "K" in the old European manner, at once denoting both intimacy and discretion. Laptop user or not, he was an admirer of the old ways. He wrote:

F's behavior provides a more- than- sufficient stress trigger for a diagnosis of conversion disorder in his daughter. F has a peculiar condition as well, exhibiting in a similar manner to a narcoleptic seizure. Rather than the accelerated REM sleep of narcolepsy however, his lapse appeared to be instantaneous in both onset and remission with signs of REM sleep behavior disorder in between. These are, perhaps, the result of particularly intense hallucinations. I have not had the opportunity to examine him.

As a burst of wind swayed the white fir outside his window, Nesky stopped typing. He realized there was no avoiding it. His responsibility was to call Social Services to curtail the domestic violence. The situation wouldn't be easy to explain because Faron was smart enough not to hit his wife or child in sight of him. The abuser would probably hit Clara in the elevator and save the rest for home.

Nesky had just lifted the receiver when he heard a fresh commotion in the outer office. This time the raised voices were not those of the Richters.

CHAPTER 2

Time Blind

<u>814 A.D.</u>

WADE LINWOOD, KNOWN to the Roman legion as Wade of Aquitaine, needed to shut out the thrum of battle around him and harness his full resources to pull Kreindia of Amorium through time and space with him. Though victory was assured, her head wound seemed grave. She required a twenty-first century hospital to ensure that she would survive.

As Wade closed his eyes, his other senses heightened in a rush. The hot sun baking the skin under his metal garments, the stench of mingled blood and filth, and even the solid security of the rocks beneath his feet needed to be closed off one at a time to reach the required level of concentration. Perhaps Wade should have heeded the centurion's advice and kept Kreindia far from the conflict no matter what she wanted. In compromise, she had taken the role of one of their scriptors behind the lines. That decision had put her within harm's reach, notwithstanding the sword at her side. But Wade would not have been the man she fell in love with if he kept her from life's responsibilities.

In any case, decisions before the clash with Raginpert's rebels seemed as distant as another lifetime. The arc of a single stone that struck her head marked the dividing line between that life and this. The old reality was the one in which he fulfilled a promise to the world by helping the two remnants of empire preserve the peace of Nicephoros. The new one concerned the two halves of his soul.

Wade drew the serpent's fang bracelet from his tunic and checked that the points were true. As the rarest of synesthetes, he possessed a unique gift of space-time manipulation made possible by stimulating acupuncture nodes. It had only worked properly a couple of times— only once across the centuries—and the first time was by means of a piece of glass that left him with damage he couldn't afford. But if previous experience held, he had only to exert the correct pressure on a precise point on his ankle. At the proper depth and concentration, he would ascend the astral plane, cleave vast swaths of time, and fold the yawning distance.

The synesthetic mechanisms that applied to him, however, would not work for both of them, a problem he'd long suspected. Having gone to great lengths to visit Taoist Lord Du Sian for his opinion, Wade now had the idea that if her ankle was not the key for her, her ear more likely would be. That was the reason he'd had his fang bracelet designed with points on opposite sides. He had to have faith in this approach because it was the only option he knew. Breathing deeply and slowly to control his breath so as not to disturb his precise movements, he linked himself to his soul mate, ankle to ear, and set his sights on home.

Given his flawless kinesthetic memory, Wade had no problem triggering the initial pathways. He moved close so that the fang points pressed home on both sides, and the color sequence and associated feelings supplied by his crossed senses provided a sort of countdown:

Purple, tainted with the uneasy rolling of a ship's deck, which Wade suspected to be a whiff of prescience.

Honey, a promise or a trap.

Rust, an antidote that corroded fear.

Though each stage was fraught with emotion, the sequence usually calmed his anxieties. This time the sedative effect had many layers of worry through which to cut. What torments was Kreindia experiencing on her end as she lay insensate from her injuries? What could he do to ensure that they both exited simultaneously?

The battle had gone silent, and dimly he registered an urgent cry. It may have even been his own. Before he could worry about that, the higher plane gathered the pair to its bosom, as nature knows its kin.

As the two vanished, a curious new sensation raged through Wade's left hand—not at the wrist where he had once been plagued by carpal tunnel syndrome, but in his fingers and sliding somewhere beyond them. Where each finger pointed, he could feel the null space filling up, as if his digits were growing to grotesque proportions. In his mind's eye, his new hand lacked only the webbing needed to form a bat's wing. He had never experienced this symptom as a part of astral travel before. The bizarre deviation should have been his first clue that something had gone terribly wrong.

$\sim W \sim$

WITH Wade's return to his twenty-first century apartment came the flood of synesthetic reactions that he had rarely experienced in the ninth century. Seeing the Egyptian Blue of his plush carpet awoke the auditory hallucination of a thousand tiny bells from his crossed senses; only the vivid, medium-dark calcium copper silicate dye in the fibers could accomplish that. The spalted maple finish on his coffee table felt to him like a light caress on his scalp, and the birdcage finials on his curtain rods lowered his blood pressure as effectively as a display of swimming fish might do. Having collected his furnishings for their harmonious result on his peculiar gifts, he could count on them to produce the same reaction at each approach. This time they were scant comfort for he could not counter a gathering sense of dread that he had arrived alone.

He spun around, armor clanking, searching for Kreindia first in the living room, then the bedroom and the rest of the apartment. Each area suffered collisions with his hard shell. He tore outside and screamed raw, ignoring the neighbors, until he realized the futility of his search. She could be a house away or in a galaxy two billion light years distant. For the first time, he had no memory of what had transpired in the passage. His greatest fear was that he had left her to die on the battlefield. He had to go back to the ninth century and see for himself. Crouching to use the bracelet again and pressing the point home, he waited for the color change sequence that would presage his return to the astral plane.

To his dread, the tooth had no effect on his acupuncture point. Pain yes, a wash of red in his mind, but nothing of the familiar pattern. Varying the angle of entry, his back braced on the sofa, his next dozen attempts produced nothing more substantial. His head sank between his shoulders. This failure meant there would be no retracing his steps through space-time. Like a frantic junkie, he had destroyed the injection site through abuse, and he had no other.

Then his eyes alit on his laptop, triggering a floating image of fine blue powder on an objectoid surface of ice that carried his gaze to infinity. *Impossible.* Her synesthetic marker did not belong here.

He'd left his computer open to a dark screen, which he now approached with hope and trepidation. Blue powder on ice was the unique personal signature triggered by Kreindia of Amorium when he was face to face with her. Unlike a personal encounter with the general's niece, this effect faded with his increasing proximity to the laptop in the way that a normal person discards the illusion of a mirage. Curiosity drew him on, however, and he booted the computer up, doing his best to clear dirt from his eyes with repeated swipes as he waited.

When the desktop appeared, an alarm went off: a series of beeps and the flashing words, "REMINDER. YOU HAVE AN APPOINTMENT." The current date stamp in the corner gave him a Wednesday, 09/09/19. His entire scalp reared up. That made it four weeks since his last visit to Dr. Nesky's office, before his travels began—"YOU HAVE AN APPOINTMENT"—the day he met the crippled girl Kreindel, who he called Del.

"IT IS NOW 5 PM. YOU HAVE TWO HOURS." That was right. His previous appointment had begun at 7 PM when hers ended. He hadn't known at the time that Del and Kreindia would prove to be a synesthetic match, the fine-blue-powder-on-ice signal, which should have been proof of their linkage. Would Del's appointment be the same this week? Was that where he needed to go?

"YOU HAVE TWO HOURS."

Wade sat at his computer for a moment to think about how he might manage the encounter, prove the connection between the two women as the tantalizing blue powder signal told him he must. The similarity of their names was coincidence, but was the modern girl a human portal? Was the synesthetic tag a long-distance message to Wade from Kreindia? Was the computer itself another message?

He glanced at the screen, shocked to notice the clock had leapt from 5:01 to 5:23 PM. He couldn't find his phone and it wouldn't be charged anyway so he checked a date-and-time website to confirm it. The sources matched at 5:26 PM. Yet when he closed the browser, the time at the corner of his screen jumped to 5:44 PM, and he had to check the site once more. How had he been contemplating this curiosity for nearly twenty minutes without realizing? Even as he worried about the loss of control and how it would make him late, he found the clock had advanced to 5:53 PM.

No, 6:04 PM. Every time he stopped to think about the problem, the situation deteriorated further.

Perceived seconds could equal minutes, and the relationship mutated in an unpredictable fashion.

As he verified the random clock changes on one website after another, he satisfied himself that he had done nothing tangible to cause these jumps but pausing to think. Finally, struggling into his street clothes and bursting out the door, he recognized and acknowledged his ailment because Kreindia herself suffered from it.

He had become time blind.

~*W*~

WADE charged up the stairs and stumbled into the doctor's waiting room. He was late. The third floor receptionist, Estela, who was somewhere in her sixties, wrinkled her nose at his grimy and rank appearance. He'd changed into whatever shirt and jeans were in the hamper. She had never liked him to begin with and must have assumed he was there for psychiatric help. Wade's matted hair whipped around as he looked for a friendlier face and failed to find one. He hadn't had a much-needed scrubbing in perhaps six weeks of ninth century time.

Estela reared back at his closer approach.

"The girl," he said, "The one who finishes her appointment at this hour—is she still in a wheelchair?"

Stunned, Estela reached for a telephone, probably wanting to consult with Dr. Nesky about how to handle him.

"The young woman! Answer me!" Wade shouted. He was desperate with fear that time blindness would rob him of a chance to find Kreindia if he stood still. If the conversation was a long one, or if she made him wait...

"Of course she is!" Estela sqawked, her hand frozen on the phone.

Wade tried to imagine what he must seem like to her. His sensibilities had adjusted to what he thought of as The City—Constantinople—a part of that other world, now fading and nonsensical, where casual violence and terror mixed easily with the highest vestiges of civilization.

He strained to lower his voice. "Is she still here?"

"She just went down in the elevator with her family. You missed her," Estela said with triumph, then jumped back as he quickly turned.

Wade plunged down the three flights of stairs, and raced outside and across the parking lot to the van where he spotted Kreindel and her family. Her parents did not look pleased to see a maniac coming towards them, trailing blood from crusty re-opened wounds. The father hastened to usher his brood to the safety of his car.

CHAPTER 3

This Vessel of Flesh

"A thousand years in Your sight are but as yesterday"

(Psalm 90:4)

THE HORROR BEGAN before Kreindia opened her eyes. A second mind crowded the confines of her skull, manifesting at first in a throbbing pressure, an otherness sharing and dividing, surrounding and smothering. She wasn't privy to the other's thoughts, a vague, primitive wash. They resonated and rippled, turned, struggled and ran aground like a hull scraping rock. Kreindia jostled and asserted, screamed inward and let a storm flare out, feeling her countenance crinkle and flatten against bone in gross reflection of her internal flexing.

Finding a path, the Second darted free, sought a corner and shrank to quiescence, retreating through millions of years of evolution, down and down to the lizard brain, where it lodged. It seemed the Second could go nowhere else. The general's niece would have to endure its presence.

The situation worsened when Kreindia regained her sight in a large box flooded with an unnatural bluish glow. She found herself sitting in dreamy paralysis, arms and legs denying her will—feet, hands, neck, and vocal cords likewise useless. She had materialized in the wrong place with no means of escape.

What she would have told her legs was to lift her from the chair. What she would have told her arms was to pound the walls that hemmed her in. And what she would have bid her neck was to raise her head and scream. Instead she moaned like a dog twitching through a nightmare, and that unintelligible sound frightened her even more.

Kreindia's eyes tracked right and left like a narcoleptic buried alive, awaiting the last clump of dirt. That minor freedom of movement, however, gave her bad news greater substance. A man and woman, each dressed in black and white, stood to either side of her, a placement reminiscent of palace guards.

After a glance at Kreindia, the two at her sides regarded each other in a fleeting clash. When the woman shrank in self-loathing, the man offered her a cruel smile with lips as thin as any Kreindia had ever seen. In a face that must have been nearly handsome once, his pebble eyes were splashed in red and seemed to have recessed from a lifetime of asking for trouble and getting it. His head was hairless but for grizzled brows and a bit of similarly peppered stubble. Not otherwise plagued by wrinkles, twin wattles of flesh traced his Adam's apple, making his age as much a puzzle as his unbridled hostility toward his companion.

Kreindia wondered if the presence of the pair meant she faced a threat more potent than the trap of her body and the trap of the box. No matter how the fear clamped down on Kreindia's gut she could not rouse her muscles to stand and bolt. Though she cried out for Wade, no more than a dog moan escaped her throat. *Could this be Hades? Did the devil possess this surfeit of imagination?*

She squeezed her eyes shut and opened them again. The general's niece could not be governed by fear. If this were not Hades, there had to be a solution amenable even to her reduced circumstances. Wade would not have sent her to this location of his own volition.

Despite her restrictions and the close air that conspired to throttle her, a shapeless something nagged, awakened from the presence of the man. He had robbed her of something vital. She felt she had possessed a hint of the answers she sought just a moment ago. She'd known more than that just two precious moments ago on the astral plane. Another glance at the man clouded her thoughts further and she decided her separation from Wade might account for her unease. The Aquitanian—wherever he was—stood alone as well, and his potential course of action worried her.

"You didn't press the damn button," the man said.

Kreindia saw that indeed the wall held a set of button-like discs with thick black numbers on them. If the tableau were meant for use in divination, Kreindia had never seen the method. Furthermore, the buttons had not been holed for sewing and she had no idea why someone would press one.

The woman poked at one of the numbered surfaces and a tiny lamp awoke inside it. At the same time came a small jolt and a sense of movement. Downward? Unless there were men outside with levers, Kreindia's sense of direction must have been utterly useless. These numerologists or diviners did not seem alarmed that they might be lowered into the ground.

Along with the buttons, the astral traveler saw unfamiliar writing on the wall. It shifted in and out of focus at the edge of understanding. Under better circumstances she would have enjoyed the opportunity to decipher it.

The man said, "My family consists of two idiot women."

After another small jolt and a pause, the box cracked. Though no one on either side appeared to have pulled or pried at the vertical lid, it slid in two directions, like a puzzle made to collapse upon itself in hollow layers.

"Kreindel, let's go," the man barked.

*Krein*del *rather than Kreindia?* This then was the girl's body to which she had once before been summoned.

23

Now the general's niece had some idea of where she was, and why another mind resided in the same skull. Kreindia realized that she was the guest and the other the host. She sat in a horse-bereft chariot, peering out of the eyes of the girl Kreindel, who she thought of as Del. It explained the sensation of being bound into an immobilizing form-fitting cage but for some imperfect movement above her shoulders and in her hand. For the most part, this vessel of flesh could not move. Kreindia could no more explain this summoning than she could the last brief time it had happened. The current arrangement felt far more permanent as she had not settled so deep before.

Fortunately, she could compel the finger that controlled the tiny magic wand. She pushed it forward like the world's smallest lever and her chariot lurched ahead, passing through the opening with a small bump, and into a corridor beyond.

"To the left, you dolt. You've been here before. How do you get stupider every day? You'd like me to believe the doctor's diagnosis of hysterical paralysis, wouldn't you?"

Kreindia could take little solace in being free of the diviner's box when she remained a captive in every other way. Her female jailer said nothing. In fact she tried to stay out of sight to the rear, but Kreindia got a glimpse of her as she swung the chariot around, and another as she straightened out. Much younger than the man, the woman retained a plain beauty beneath some blemishes on her cheeks and chin. Few locks escaped her pulled-back dark brown hair, which was shot through with light streaks above her widow's peak. Her eyes seemed gray one moment and muddy blue the next as though they didn't dare decide what color to be. Her eyebrows had been frightened away entirely. The tip of her nose flared with a ruby shine against fair skin and one cheek was patched red in the shape of a large hand. This was a fellow slave.

They passed into sunlight and through a remarkable

translucent door that reminded Kreindia of the one she had seen Wade crash through in a vision. *Amazing. They make doors out of glass!* Birdsong shared the air with an unfamiliar rushing sound. As she listened, the horrible man beside her struck a smarting blow to her head saying, "Look where you're going." She found her thwarted impulse to strike back added to a growing store of anger and the resolve to find a way out.

In the open air, a machine raced by without benefit of mules, as though demon impelled, with a roar and a foul odor. A long shadow sped alongside in the minutes before sunset. She gaped after the phenomonon in astonishment.

When she put herself back in motion, the other mind in her skull opened up and she found herself drawn to it in a trickle of commingling. With the mix came the tantalizing gift of knowledge.

I'm sharing, it said. *To keep us sane*, it said.

Us.

Based on that entreaty, and knowing the other's identity, Kreindia cooperated. They were mentally migrating to a place nearer the middle. What began as a gentle tug enveloped her and then seized her like the madness she'd hoped to avoid. Too late she realized it was lunacy to abandon one mind to accomodate the mind of another. Sharing was not the correct term. Surrender was more like it. Once committed, however, she had no choice. As the new mind absorbed her, her own memories reluctantly slipped from her grasp. She retained little more than her sense of self and her perspective of the situation. It was as if the two linked side by side in the manner of connected twins with uneven control.

Painful as the transition was, most of what Kreindia wanted to know came within reach. With a gasp, she suddenly knew that the man and woman were Faron and Clara, apparently the mother and stepfather of this Del, her host.

The self-propelled vehicle was a fuel-burning machine,

its name shortened to "car." The time period was the twenty-first century. How many years had passed since her era was something she should have easily been able to calculate, but it eluded her. Losing contact with her memories meant losing the questions that related to the solution of her plight. She feared now that these new facts were the acquisition of trivia. The claustrophobic imposition of "sharing" came with the nightmarish sense that if their combination lasted too long it would become permanent. To calm her a bit, the other girl let Kreindia keep physical control, such as it was.

Deceptively quiet now, Faron said, "Don't head that way, Kreindel. Use the ramp. If you could move those scrawny arms, mark my words, you'd be in a chair that ran on your own power. But you choose to be useless. The doctor said so." Like Kreindia, Del thought of her stepfather as a jailer and her mother as a fellow slave. From Del: *Thank you, Daddy. I so appreciate my mobile prison.*

Faron's remark seemed to have awakened Clara's curiosity. "But a few minutes ago, you said—"

He glanced around to make sure no one watched, and then dealt Clara's cheek an efficient clip that snapped her face askew.

Kreindia had already taken off on the sloping route, grateful that it led in a different direction and disappointed when it made a complete turn back to meet her putative parents at the foot of the stairs.

Together they crossed a black expanse paved with ripe asphalt cooking in the sun. At a spot marked out in blue— a handicapped space—they halted. At that same moment she heard a buzz along with a muffled tinkle of music. Faron brought out a cell phone (Del's term for it), and said, "Yes?"

The caller spoke loudly enough for the words to leak out. "Sir, this is the receptionist from upstairs. There's a crazy man on his way down to you. I don't know what he

26

wants, but I couldn't stop him. The doctor didn't want me to call the police, but I did anyway."

Faron said, "You did the right thing, warning me." Without another word, he threw the phone back in his pocket and retrieved a set of keys and a fob that he used to elicit a chirp to unlock the white van parked in front of them.

Before they got any further, a shambling apparition approached them, dirty, bleeding and disheveled. Faron started at the sight of the man, almost as if he knew him, and hastened to operate the van's lift gate.

The tall, thin upstart closed quickly on the small family group in his disarrayed pullover shirt, jeans and sneakers. Crossing a loose shoelace, he stumbled and recovered without taking notice. The missed stride revealed bare ankles and his freshly torn wound. When Faron began to push his daughter onto the lift gate, the grimy intruder stopped the chair and swiveled her to face him.

Both of the merged young women needed only the twenty-first century memories to realize that they had seen him at least once before, at Del's last visit to Dr. Nesky. *And in dreams.* His face could not have been gentler or sadder. With a sigh, he seemed to buckle at the knees to land in front of them.

This relative stranger crooned, "It's me, sweetheart, it's me. Is it you?" Tears welled over the rims of his eyes. Distraught beyond reason, this fellow was oblivious to the scene he had caused.

Faron snarled, "What the hell are you doing to my daughter?"

Father's remark and its daggered tone could not divert the poor man. He pleaded, "Sweetheart, can you move? Please speak to me, please move for me." He came out with it in a voice so choked with emotion that it tugged at their collective heart, even though they didn't know what he hoped to gain by accosting them.

As Kreindia and Del struggled to make sense of the mysterious figure before them, the girl's will retreated, causing everything to blur. The Second pulled back enough to give Kreindia's psyche a chance to emerge for a turn at dominance along with access to her memories. Once again she fought to hold onto both sets of information to no avail.

Herself again, Kreindia felt as though a curtain had been torn aside. Wade of Aquitaine had stood before her the whole time. She knew all would be well, and they could be together if she could only muster the proper reaction.

She committed the fingers of her right hand to the joystick, thinking she might waggle the chair back and forth, or forward and back. With little more than a touch—the effort required to quirk the chair an inch—her last strength failed her. Her collapse was mental as well as physical. She'd suffered the exhaustion of trying to merge the two minds. Darkness encroached on the fringes of her vision.

Faron shouted at Wade, "She can't move, or even speak, you idiot. She's a total cripple quad nothing. What do you want from her?"

Tenderly, Wade took her limp left hand in his own and kissed her palm, his eyelashes brushing the insides of her fingers.

"I'm calling the police," said Faron.

After her brief respite, Kreindia tried using the fingers of her right hand again to operate the controls, then hesitated and changed the plan, her palm leaving the very spot it had rested for years. *How?*

Almost of its own accord... But no, this was her will. She almost didn't recognize the idea that her thoughts might control her unused muscles. The movement was so slight that no one had yet noticed but her.

At once she saw the truth of her life. All of those gathered had come together in this manner for a reason. Somehow she had long ago been fractured into two women. That's what the joining had to mean. Fractured, and the pieces brought side by side to bond again, just as she and Wade were reunited.

For the first time since illness struck this body, she found that she could raise her trembling hand and her arm with it. It left the armrest with only a slight hesitation to ascend way in the air. Her stepfather dropped his jaw in astonishment. She fully extended her arm, and touched all five fingertips to Wade's cheek. Now she was able to cry too. As Faron's protests grew louder, she tilted her head and looked deep into his brown eyes. A teardrop ran the length of her nose.

"Oh, Wade, we made it," she sobbed.

If she were wrong about what her new abilities meant, about having been fractured, she must not be far wrong. The alternative was that she had been born a creation of fragments, an idea she found even harder to accept. The conundrum of why she remained two people in one body had to wait.

Kreindia murmured, "We made it, we made it, we made it," until the atrophied muscles in her arms could hold no longer. Her right arm slipped first, with her hand making a clutching spasm, briefly grabbing hold of Wade's shirt. Her left arm dropped like a bird dying in flight. Now she cried tears of frustration, wondering if the cage would return, limiting her to moving this chariot with her tiny magic wand, and luring the unwary to take her place in the manner of a heartless Siren.

Then she colored in shame for worrying about her condition, followed by a rush of thankfulness for being alive and with Wade. "We made it," she repeated, this time in clarity and confirmation.

Wade pulled back and brushed the dark hair away from her eyes. He laughed, "Can you say anything else?"

"I love you, Aquitainian," she whispered, using his ninth century name to demonstrate her identity through special knowledge of his. The declaration made her cry even more in great heaving breaths. Her tears flowed not as drops, but in a continual torrent of relief, coating her flushed skin.

A shadow came over them. Faron put his rough hand on Wade's shoulder and squeezed as though his sharp fingers were digging for bone. Kreindia could not imagine a captive or servant anywhere in the empire subjected to more mental suffering than the girl and her mother endured at the hands of her unlikely father. Now Wade had been dragged into it.

"Young man, I warned you to stay away from her when you showed up at the doctor's office last time," Faron said. "Soon you'll see the price."

CHAPTER 4

Separation

DEL'S FACE TRANSFORMED as it had the very first time Wade saw her, that sense of temporarily breaking free from a narcotic, the burgeoning recognition charging the air between them with synesthetic flakes of blue powder. This, together with her words, gave the confirmation Wade had waited for that his Kreindia at least held some claim here. And on top of that, the warning from Faron.

Soon you'll see the price.

The voice of Del's father triggered a primitive state of hyper-awareness in Wade. The pungent asphalt that roughed up his knees; the red-patched face of Del's mother, her features swallowed in a mask of confusion; the sun gleaming off the wheelchair's push handles; the rocking branch behind it vacated by a startled dove; and those fingers of her father's, that gruesome claw aiming to excavate his shoulder. Wade reacted with a twisting shrug that turned into a shudder. The confrontation may have lasted seconds or minutes, but he sensed they had an audience behind him before anyone else looked up. When they did see the new arrival, Kreindia's and Clara's faces showed fear. Yet Faron looked expectant.

Their visitor commanded, "Hold it right there." Wade made no sudden moves, knowing that the parking lot bordered on residential houses. Anyone could have taken offense at the activities below. He half-turned to see a young, pale man with a large caliber gun leveled at him.

Dark street clothes, early thirties, long face accentuated by receding black hair and scraggly beard. His eyes drooped unevenly and his ears were mangled and healed as though he used to tear at them. His neck bore the tattoo of a Celtic design twisted into the shape of a long-winged bat.

Dr. Nesky, dressed in business casual, trailed at a reassuring distance. No one else moved. Nesky, in his faint Russian accent, said, "Henry? Henry, what are you doing?"

Over his shoulder, Henry replied, "I heard your secretary talking about calling the police on this guy. It's not necessary. I never told you, Doc, but I'm Secret Service. I'm taking charge."

Using his clinical tone now, Dr. Nesky said, "I don't doubt you, Henry, but there is no need for a gun."

"I'm here to protect the President." His voice was tight and urgent.

"The President is not here, Henry. He won't be coming. He's canceled."

"Don't try to confuse me. I'm— I have to do law enforcement wherever I go."

"You're missing your appointment upstairs. It's an important session. We were making progress, remember?"

But the spectacle was attracting even more attention. To Wade's horror, a boy of no more than twelve-years-old, slid over to them to see what was going on, expertly riding the little wheels on the backs of his sneakers. He had that suburban naiveté that made him act younger than a city kid would, melting into a crowd of adults with the assumption they would do him no harm. Yet he was drawn to trouble.

Wade had been afraid of this. While Faron was accosting him, he had noticed the boy briefly at the window of the house that bordered the parking lot. Though the window glass confused the matter with its obscuring reflections, the young face behind it seemed for a moment animated with a cocktail of curiosity and arrested compulsion. He had bolted from the window as though being jerked aside by an unseen force. When he arrived, however, there was nothing puppet-like about him. The boy stopped by dropping his feet flat, allowing him to settle his gaze first on Wade, and then peering over at the armed arrival, his eyes going wide.

Del's father got Henry's attention, saying, "I'm the one who called the authorities. Get that troublemaker out of here." He pointed at Wade.

Henry flinched at the voice as though duty-bound and ashamed of being derelict. He shouted at Wade, "Turn around, mister. Lace your fingers behind your head, step backwards towards me, and drop to your knees." He raised the muzzle so that Wade could see it dead on.

Newly emerged from primitive times, it was a novelty for Wade to encounter an automatic weapon, as though the clever Byzantines had hurried up and invented one. Unlike ninth century inhabitants, however, Wade knew very well what a firearm could do.

The passing kid who had melted into the family cooed, "Wickit." It took Wade a beat to figure out he was saying "wicked," something the Dark Age Franks and many generations afterward would have associated with witches or wiccans. "Wickit-cool," the youngster elaborated, and went on to say, "That's ossum." He meant "awesome."

If a trigger-happy mental patient in front of a defenseless crowd was exciting, then Wade guessed this occasion qualified as ossum and then some.

Wade felt responsible for the boy and prayed no one else would run in and add to the parade of innocents. Slowly and carefully, he faced away from the gunman and raised his hands, stepping backward and clearing his mind. He'd never fully understood how time blindness worked. Everyone believes they have only five senses because the time sense is taken for granted. Now he saw that in the absence of time sense, his mind reacted by creating a false sense of certainty about time's passage. Even as the turmoil and adjustment to his new condition churned away precious minutes, those gaps appeared to him to be seconds. Unable to trust any perception, he now counted each breath to keep track of time. He would have counted his heartbeats but there were too many of them.

Henry braced for recoil with two hands on the weapon and his legs in a wide crouch as if his thirty-eight might turn into a howitzer at any time. His own breath became ragged in the course of repeating his commands in nervous panic every time Wade threw a peripheral glance over his shoulder.

Meanwhile, Dr. Nesky advanced on Henry like one of those small animals that could scoot across a pond so long as they didn't break the surface tension of the water. Advance and wait, in patterns that predators would find hard to recognize. A few delicate steps later, Wade remembered that he'd seen the movement pattern on a nature show: Gennadi Nesky looked like a basilisk, the so-called Jesus Lizard, treading on little cups of air.

"Do not hurt this man," said Nesky. "His name is Wade Linwood. He's in my care."

"Psychiatric case," said Henry with a lilt of professional curiosity in his voice. "Is he dangerous?"

"Not at all," Nesky said.

When Henry looked at Nesky and heard the reassuring words, his elbows began to bend with the melting of his tensions.

Before Henry could cede control, the father pointed at Wade. "I told you to arrest this man."

Henry stiffened up, restoring his shooting position.

The boy could contain himself no longer. Pointing at Henry, he said, "Bullshit. There's no way you're Secret Service. Those are the good guys." Henry swung his gun toward the kid.

"No!" The word was not so much spoken as torn from Del's throat. Nesky raised his eyebrows at her in surprise.

Henry lowered his pistol slightly, more in confusion

than decision. He glanced at Nesky and back at the crowd. Finally, Henry seemed to fixate on Del's father, even as he asked Nesky, "What do I do, Doc?"

Making sure Nesky wasn't looking, the father mouthed at Henry, *Shoot Wade.*

"Faron!" his wife cautioned, not daring to go further.

Nesky said, "Henry, the family will leave and there will be no more trouble. Then you can release Wade on his own recognizance. What you do you, say?"

"Do your job," Faron growled softly at Henry. "Are you a public servant or not?"

Henry frowned into the long pause that followed.

Wade felt sweat rise on his brow. One of the few times in Wade's childhood when he had seen his father, they had gone to the circus, and the only part of that trip Wade could remember was the high wire act. Father and son ate their popcorn in the cheap seats, an elevation uniquely suited to witnessing performers at the top of the tent. The spotlit man on the platform bore the weight of a long pole he held crossways to the trail ahead of him, a rope extending into the unforgiving dark. Once they absorbed his plight, a second spotlight revealed a thin filament of netting far below. This bit of stagecraft made the safety precaution seem irresponsibly inadequate.

To an endless drum roll, the acrobat ventured out over the drop, his soft shoes placed one directly in front of the other in a measured pace. When his feet didn't square properly, toe and heel dipped so that the rope filled his arches while his knees trembled. Wade had wondered what the pole was for—baggage so big and heavy that it drooped at the ends—more like a cruel additional challenge than a balance aid. *Which was it really?* Wade had turned to his father as children do, imagining that the world that so puzzles kids makes all kinds of sense to adults. Dad simply shrugged and the mystery remained.

Henry asked, "Do I shoot him or release him?" He scrutinized Wade as if considering that a bullet to put him out of his misery might not be a bad idea. Probing Wade with those sagging, remorseless eyes. "I can't just let him go, doc. That would be irresponsible."

Nesky said, "You can put him in my hands though. No one could blame you for that."

"I suppose," said Henry, wavering, "if anything bad happens, the Secret Service can hold you accountable. And we will too!"

Nesky said, "That's right, Henry. You're doing well." At the same time, the doctor held out a placating hand to Wade. "Now, Wade, all you have to do is walk away from Kreindel and over to me."

Del's father added, "You'll never get near my daughter again, Aquitaine. I promise you that."

Wade's name in Faron's mouth hit like a kick to the stomach. To come close enough to touch the woman he loved, believing as he did that she resided in a different body twelve centuries removed from the day they met. If Wade had not lost his mind entirely, then sanity was running three doors down and taking a left turn, waving its hat in the style of an old Vaudevillian rascal leaving the stage. He wasn't sure if he could pick up his marbles, such as they were, and separate from Kreindia at this point.

Dr. Nesky said softly to Wade, "We'll get this all straightened out." The words came out flat, unlike a promise, but then Dr. Nesky was not the sort to jab a recalcitrant patient in the neck with a sedative. All Wade had to do was abandon the woman he loved, the one who just declared her love for him as well.

He shifted tentatively and the gun followed him.

Kreindia must have tapped some hidden reserve of energy, for she reached toward Wade just then, her fingers splayed like an exploring baby for all things put beyond her reach. That got Henry paranoid again. He pointed the gun at her as though obligated to shoot anything that moved. Young Wheelie was struck dumb, edging back, afraid to skate away.

The frightening prospect of a bullet tearing into Kreindia crystallized the tightrope puzzle for Wade. It was a matter of Newtonian physics. He realized that the tightrope walker's pole must not have been a burden, but a balance aide after all. The fact that it went crosswise was the key.

Moving along the line of fire as he had done so far with Henry was dangerous, akin to keeping your center of mass narrow, increasing the possibility of reaching the tipping point. Outstretched arms or a long pole stabilized you by spreading out your center of mass. In the current situation, a sidewise movement would be analogous to spreading out the gunman's attention. For that reason, a real law enforcement officer would not allow the deviation from his instructions, but Nesky had provided Wade the opening.

Wade crossed in front of and beyond Kreindia, drawing the gun's muzzle away from her in his wake. With his chest tight, he came to rest standing beside Dr. Nesky. Nesky, to his credit, then moved in front of Wade. With his original target invisible, Henry remembered his gun and gradually lowered it toward his holster. Wade watched Kreindia in mute witness as her host's parents closed in on her. In a moment he might have his opening.

Before the sidearm was secured, Faron shook his head vigorously. Henry twitched as though in response and the muzzle exploded. The unexpected discharge did sound like a howitzer in the still air. Henry dropped the gun and stared at his empty palm in puzzlement as though awareness had just returned to him.

Nesky located the mark on the ground where the errant bullet had ricocheted, saw the damage to the lower corner of his jacket, and glanced behind him where the fence had a new hole. Wade moved forward, but Henry quickly grabbed up the gun, put it in his holster and kept his hand on top in pensive repose. Wheelie boy evacuated himself to his home next door. Nesky and Wade remained wary of what the still-armed Henry might do next.

Police sirens warped the air in the distance as Faron fled with his wife and what he supposed to be his daughter.

With a hand on Wade's shoulder reminding him to stand by, Nesky said, "Henry, you have to come upstairs with me."

"Why?"

"You need to let local law enforcement take over here. Those are the rules, aren't they?"

"Yes," said Henry in a distant voice. "Those are the rules. You have to have rules."

CHAPTER 5

Wade and Nesky

WADE'S HEART RIOTED with trepidation as steam rose from the basin to clog the clinic's bathroom mirror. At least he couldn't see himself, only the foul runoff that drained away as he washed. His hands shook and skin tingled in recall of the last time he reached into a vapor cloud: his trial in the ninth century. Being subjected to the Ordeal of Boiling Water where he had to force his arms into unimaginable heat had been the worst day of his existence up until this one. If he were tempted to dismiss his experiences in the Dark Ages as mere illusion, the blotchy pink scar tissue served as a potent reality check.

None of that mattered compared to his separation from Kreindia. To find her again, he would have to somehow convince Nesky to violate patient confidentiality and give him Faron's address.

"Wade?"

"Coming out." Making sure his disfigured limbs were as well concealed as possible, Wade followed the sound of Nesky's voice into the Serenity Room under the skylight's muted glow.

"I've never seen you so agitated," said Nesky, inviting Wade to rest on one of the red cedar benches by the fountain. He didn't mention the stunning visual impression Wade must have created earlier.

"That's because I've never—"

"You've never what?"

Wade glanced around to make sure no one else had entered. Reminding himself that Henry had been safely packed off to observation, he watched mist paint the fountain's shale boundaries, and wondered at the patterns of wetness in the dappled fading light. They'd known each other for five years, Nesky his client at Wheelwright Insurance, Wade a beneficiary of Nesky's flawless acupuncture skills.

Wade had never come to him for psychiatry, but he could see the qualities that made the doctor so popular. Nesky had a way of uttering a single statement that rendered all prying questions superfluous, and his knowing expression bespoke intellectual curiosity without being smug or pitying. Wade could almost believe Nesky would understand his every natural and supernatural experience if he dared reveal them. But the whole truth was far more challenging to credulity than Henry's claims of being in the Secret Service.

"What do you know about synesthesia?" Wade began.

Nesky smiled. "It's rare. Multiple cognitive pathways. What others experience through one sense, the synesthete experiences through two or more. A scent may be associated with touch, a sight may be tinged with sound. Or a second sight may overlay the first. Any combination. But each experience is permanently paired, entangled from its inception."

Wade appreciated that Nesky did not trot out the word "hallucination" as his teachers in school used to do. "Entangled," said Wade. "That's the best short explanation I've heard. If you know that much, you also know the exception to the singular experience rule where one action gives only one result."

Nesky smiled more broadly. "Yes, it's part of my job. Acupuncture. Each micro-movement of the needle brings a further perception to the synesthete."

40

And there it was as Wade first heard it five years ago. Nesky's Russian accent on the word "needle" triggered a synesthetic experience, delivering the tang of grapefruit and the sight of charcoal tinted forest-green. As with all synesthetic groupings, the linkage made little or no conscious sense.

Wade had spent his young lifetime training himself to ignore the duality of experience. The things that came at him that no one else saw were a distraction. Voiced to others, it invoked either dismissiveness or fear for his sanity. He once believed that his second sight was a random miswiring with no significance. Acupuncture, and the experiences that followed showed him otherwise.

"What are you thinking, Wade?"

"I'm thinking there's still a lot about my situation that I don't understand."

"Are you a grapheme synesthete? That's what most synesthetes are."

"Yes, letters of the alphabet wear their own clothes. Color and texture. And numbers have a personality. A photographic memory comes with it. Do I sound crazy yet?"

Still smiling, Nesky said, "The second description is ordinal linguistic personification. There was a time not very long ago when you would have been considered delusional like Henry. Today, synesthesia is clinically documented. It's hard to fake, and easy to prove. How many synesthetic characteristics do you have?"

"Most of them. Sound-to-color, sensations-to-color— whatever those are called—and some kind of lexeme synesthesia that sometimes comes out when…well, when you speak to me."

Nesky laughed, delighted. "Then you are among the rarest. The one-in-a-hundred thousand case or better."

"Actually," said Wade choosing his words with great care, "I may be rarer than that."

The doctor knit his brow for the first time. "What actually happened to you on my table last month? During your carpal tunnel treatment?" Nesky's face had darkened and tinged orange with the sunset. Their talk reminded Wade of late-night, sleep deprived discussions in college, spooky metaphysical musings where no one wanted to turn on the lights and break the spell.

Wade said, "I didn't know what was going to happen. I had four responses—an enriched color sequence for three of them. I'd never before had three reactions to a single act."

"We'll get back to that," said Nesky. "What happened next?"

"The fourth response was even more surprising."

"Show me." Without waiting for Wade's assent, Nesky led the way to the examination room, donning his white lab coat as they entered.

Wade followed, but said, "It's not working anymore. The site is damaged."

"We'll see about that. I have a preparation that will help."

Nesky tore the old paper from the treatment table and disposed of it. He pulled down and across on the roll holder and secured the continuous sheeting on the bottom, after which he invited Wade to alight.

Kicking off his shoes and climbing onto the crinkling symphony, Wade said, "Does anyone know why a needle treatment breaks the rules of synesthesia, why it gives a layered response?"

Nesky switched on the LED, uncapped a pungent bottle of rubbing alcohol and turned Wade's foot to clean behind the bulge formed by the base of his fibula. He said, "That's because acupuncture is far more complex than a single act. Through acupuncture, you unblock energy distribution channels called meridians. In *Jing Luo* theory, there are four depths to reach the parallel paths. Nothing in current science can reconcile the mechanism because the ancient descriptions don't correspond to anything we know about physiology."

"But it works," said Wade. "My neurologist used a nerve conduction test before the treatment you gave me, to confirm that my carpel tunnel existed. His test after your treatment showed that the condition was nearly eliminated. Then I managed to re-injure myself."

Mixing a minty concoction on the rolling side table, Nesky said, "It worked on you. Everyone is different."

"Nate?"

"Yes?"

"Do you know anyone credible who believes in past lives?"

Not smiling anymore, Nesky thought for a moment and said, "Plato believed in pre-existence. He taught that all learning is recollection. Several Indian religions have similar concepts. Do you believe you've recollected something disturbing?"

Before Wade could answer, Estela put herself through on the intercom. "Doctor?"

"Estela, please," said the doctor. "We cannot be interrupted."

"I think I have to though. You have an urgent call from Faron Richter. He says he's trying to reach someone named Aquitaine?"

"We'll take it," said Nesky. "Yes, Mr. Richter?"

The voice on the phone grated, "Dr. Nesky? Is that kid with you?"

With a guarded glance at Wade, Nesky said, "Yes. What do you need?"

"It's about Kreindel. She's gone."

CHAPTER 6

Instability

FOLLOWING FARON'S DIRECTIONS, Wade joined evening traffic on Long Island's Route 106/107 artery north, where everything once familiar to him looked awry. The too-flat terrain, the cars gliding under artificial lights, and the absence of humanity in the streets, underscored the fact that nearly everyone he knew in the ninth century had passed to bones at the stroke of his serpent's tooth. Kreindia belonged to that era and now her twinned version may have vanished from both sets of space-time. Struggling to keep an open mind, Wade feared the worst for her. And then something happened to deepen his apprehension.

As he passed a certain Chase Bank branch on North Broadway, a shiver charged with static rippled through him. He slowed a bit to stare at the strip mall that housed the location. Just a month ago, he'd learned from *The New York Times* that in modernity the unassuming building had been used to hide the second century's Codex Tchacos— the lost Gospel of Judas—in one of its safe deposit boxes. The document wasn't there anymore, but every item of significance left synesthetic residue. This one, perhaps because of its age, generated and left behind an enormous surplus.

Though every original copy from the Gnostics had been destroyed thousands of years ago by rivals, part of the Coptic translation survived in a leather-bound papyrus in Egypt. Once discovered, the book was carved up and passed in secret to private collectors over several decades. A crumbling thirteen pages remained.

Wade wondered how many times history had been manipulated through targeted destruction. And who was responsible for preserving the genuine article? Kreindia's answer would have been: she and Wade. At least they'd made it so when they prevented a war between Byzantium and the Holy Roman Empire. They'd marshaled the force of the hibernating legion to counter Raginpert's false flag attack.

Although Wade originally assumed the Gospel of Judas had nothing to do with his tribulations, he began to get suspicious of the timing of its emergence in modern day Hicksville, New York. The English translation carried a message that might as well have been just for him. It warned that two kinds of human beings exist: "mortals," and "those from the eternal realms who will abide there always." Wade was a hyper-synesthete who was capable of straddling the millennia, and didn't want to spend his life on the astral plane. He was far better off when he didn't know his capability. But if he had a linkage to the Gospel of Judas, that investigation would have to wait.

Merging into the turnpike cloverleaf, foot heavy on adrenalin, he found himself in Jericho, one of New York's last bastions of unsullied middle class. He passed the sky-blue water tower and turned into a residential plot, nodding at a dog walker because the man nodded at him. Befitting the gateway to the Gold Coast, the hamlet of Jericho parceled a sea of split-level brick ranches around islands of private communities. After another two turns, he found a middling section where most of the houses had grown to two stories clothed in aluminum siding. Portable basketball systems—the new suburban tree—sprouted three to a block.

The pre-War redwood and stone-faced house caught Wade's eye before he confirmed its number. The bay window had a copper roof, and the section over the door swept to a high point topped with mismatched tile. Faron's house was a patchwork of contractor's scraps: odd, dark, and charmless.

Wade parked next to a silver maple that had buckled the sidewalk, and emerged under the wash of a streetlight. Two different pairs of planters painted black met visitors to the Richter residence at both the bottom and top of the short set of steps. Their flowers, brown whorls in winter-rot, had not been replaced. He took a deep breath. Faron had sounded conciliatory on the phone. Maybe this meeting would heal their rift. The curtain fluttered, and the oak and wrought iron door swung in. The man he had come to see filled the open space.

"Thank you for coming, Aquitaine."

"Linwood," he corrected. "And it's Wade. What happened?"

"She vanished."

"Where have you looked so far?"

Faron snorted at that. "I won't run around aimlessly, if that's what you mean. I've talked to the police. They say they'll keep an eye out because of Kreindel's condition."

"Meaning what?"

"They'll put it into the system in case her name pops up at the hospital or something. But they let me know they can't spare manpower for an adult who left on her own and isn't missing long."

Still wary of the man, Wade asked, "Left on her own?"

"That's the assumption."

"Just tell me what I can do."

"I called you here to get some insight on her thinking. I suppose you went to school with her in the years before she became—"

"I did. We called her Del." Wade hoped Faron wouldn't challenge him by asking which school he supposedly attended with her. As he avoided Faron's gaze, he noticed the wheelchair ramp to his right concealed behind a row of holly, thorns grown deep through the railing.

"Don't worry, Wade," said Faron. "It's not an ambush. On the contrary, I realize I owe you an apology."

"I appreciate that," said Wade, keeping his reservations about this startling turn-around to himself.

"I guess you did her some good back there in the parking lot, but after two years of her illness and one charlatan after another coming at me, I just overreacted to someone trying to perk her up. I was under the impression she didn't have any friends."

"That's all right. Del has always been secretive like that. I didn't want to betray her confidence. May I come in?"

"My wife doesn't want any company. You can understand she's hysterical over this." Faron reached back and pulled the door shut, crowding Wade on the landing, his breath a fetid salad. "Listen, I last saw Kreindel when she went to her room. When she didn't answer our call for dinner, we discovered she wasn't in that room or any other."

Wade said, "What do you think happened?"

"She's too weak to get up and walk away, but with her newfound abilities—"

"What abilities?"

Faron's gaze sharpened for a moment. "Her movement and the independent attitude that came with it. She could have called a car service."

"Why would she do that?"

"Rebellion," said Faron, irritation creeping back into his voice. "My wife's daughter never grew up."

Wade noticed the choice of words, but decided not to ask what he meant by it. "Did she say anything before she disappeared?"

Faron scratched at the edge of what might once have been his hairline. "I'm embarrassed to say she babbled some nonsense about instability, and not being able to hold onto this time frame. Forgive me if I sound incredulous. I don't mean to mock her, but that's garbage."

Trying to hide his excitement, Wade said, "Instability? That was the word she used?"

"Yes, among other things. With all that drivel I thought she was going to wear herself out and fall asleep."

"What else did... Del say?"

Faron sighed. "She said she was afraid she would end up back where she came from. I guess she meant paralyzed."

Wade's heart drummed in his chest. "She didn't mention a place?"

"I don't understand."

"Did she say anything more specific?"

"This is a waste of time. What could you possibly do with this information, anyway? Was she talking about a video game or an arcade you two used to frequent?"

"No, it doesn't mean anything to me either." Wade almost smiled at the triviality of a video game after what they had been through. "I have no idea where she would have gone."

"Really? Nothing to say to me?" Faron seemed irritated that contacting Wade and being nice to him hadn't panned out.

Wade gazed into the dark. Distraught or not, Kreindia wouldn't have made any reference to astral travel in front of Faron unless she counted on him repeating it to Wade. What Wade wanted to do at this very moment was to follow her lead into space-time, disappear into "the eternal realms," as the gospel put it. He wasn't sure that he could.

Before he had left the doctor's office, however, Nesky had molded a homeopathic mint oil dressing on the ankle injury that kept Wade time-bound. The last time someone did him that favor, the trick had worked very quickly to reactivate his astral pressure point. Wade muttered an apology to Faron as he ran under the sodium-vapor light to his car.

"Call me immediately if you find her or hear from her," Faron yelled after him.

Wade's skin prickled. He didn't expect to hear from her. The obvious message Kreindia wanted to pass on was that she had gone back to the battle with Raginpert in the Brenii Pass in 814 A.D. Whether she wanted to or not.

~ *W* ~

WADE returned to his apartment to change and he collapsed from exhaustion, legs spilled off the bed. His last coherent thoughts were that he would just sleep for a few minutes. Theoretically, he could wait years and still go back to the point he needed. Intuition told him not to take that chance, though.

Five hours later, he woke with a start, his stare trying to penetrate the inky darkness. Groping at his bedside, he found the button light on his solar powered clock, and then the lamp. For a breakfast, he hastily downed a can of tuna fish.

Pulling on the sweat encrusted linen tunic of his ninth century light armor, he realized he had been away from it long enough to be disgusted by the smell. Still, it beat having the hundreds of small lamellar plates with their leather lacing directly raking his skin.

After the metal vest and shoulder plates, he fastened the flexible skirt, which consisted of two offset rows of metal-studded leather paddles. The open sandal-boots left him access to the acupuncture point, and his custom designed wrist guards incorporated the fang bracelet he needed for precision.

With pride, he looped on the dual scabbards and filled them with his prized gladius and spatha. The short and long swords were not standard Eastern Empire issue, but rather what his friend Grimketil had trained him on. Old Roman tools of war. He gratefully added the red cape, another layer of protection, attaching it to the vest. Lastly, he donned the simple riveted helmet and pulled the chinstrap until it left just enough give to move his jaw half an inch if he let it bite flesh.

Crouching to access the base of his right leg's fibula, he fixed the destination in his mind, picturing the gore-stained battle as he last saw it, including the shouted commands that marked the moment of departure. If all went as planned, he would go there and watch himself and Kreindia disappearing from the observation rock, and witness her reappearance alone soon after.

Pressing the tooth through the mint oil sheen, he achieved the first level, blanking his surroundings in a wash of royal purple. A textured color. It was working.

The second level showed him honey, fresh and translucent as the coating in a beehive. Each layer contained a beauty of its own.

Then came rust, which he savored despite his urgency, because the deep *Jing Luo* channel brought serenity.

With one final nudge, he achieved the fourth level, which bought him his cherished passage to the astral plane. A state outside himself. Not whole, yet present.

With a jolt, he passed into a new zone on the plane, which presented him an astonishing choice. The space-time fabric divided into two uneven lanes of traffic, the function of which was a puzzle. Before him churned a narrow passage winding shut. He could make it through if he tried. The further lane was a much broader upwelling beside it, expanding as it crowded the smaller one to nothing. Shuddering at the claustrophobic option, Wade chose the broad path. Once committed, he immediately regretted it as he found no link to his intended destination.

After a giddy moment of shifting and solidification, he saw no pitched battle in the frozen Alps but a fire-warmed monastery sick room much like the one in which he himself once convalesced. There, his old ally, Grimketil Forkbeard lay dying. It was the last thing Wade expected to see. How did this time and place relate to Kreindia?

Wade crept to the bedside, his shadow dancing on the floor. The Saxon had been his adversary before they were friends—and in Wade's mind—as good as family, the elder crossing the countryside as the novitiate's protector. This Grimketil was a decade older than when Wade knew him. His hair fully white, he wore the impoverished clothes and sunken features of a land long in famine. Missing were his jewelry and his trademark chalmys, the short cape that characterized the barbarian-born's affect for the symbols of high civilization, an article he would never have surrendered willingly. His labored breath competed with the crackling embers.

Grimketil, a self-taught man of letters who had been like a father to Wade, leapt from his deathbed when he saw his visitor, and Wade braced for the big man's hug. Grimketil grabbed Wade by the throat and squeezed.

"I'll kill you," he said, his thick fingers hard at work.

Wade tried to fight him off and a monk in brown robes reluctantly came to his assistance. As Wade tried to protect his airway, pulling the hands outward, the attendant encircled the aggressor's waist to draw him backward. Had the Saxon been anywhere near his peak, Wade would have been dead already.

When they had Grimketil back in bed, no small matter for the two of them, the robed figure enthused, "Very impressive. Who would have known this dying giant still possessed so much strength? You have been a boon to him, rousing his ire like that. Why has the abbot not introduced us? I am Cluny of Pavia. Forgive me for speaking at length." A Benedictine monk, bound to all things in moderation, Cluny may have used up his word allotment for a month.

Around heavy breaths and intense concentration, Grimketil said, "I hate you, Aquitainian. I have never hated a man more… in my life. Give me back your neck so that I may squeeze it closed with my last breath, and die happy."

"Why?" said Wade, holding down a bile-raising sense of dread. "What happened?"

Grimketil gazed at him in shock. "You know what happened. You abandoned us."

"I had to because of Kreindia's injury."

"I saw no injury. What I saw was that we lost to Raginpert at the Brenii Pass because the Roman legion you had us depend on was undermanned and incompetent."

"It didn't look that way to me."

"No, because you conveniently left us to die, and the lands of Charlemagne and Byzantium both fell into a chaos darker than any in history. The price of our friends' lives was wasted. There is no excuse and no redemption for you after that."

Wade reflected that the criticism would be fair if only it were true.

At first Wade took the look on Grimketil's face to be one of pure revulsion, and the panting and sweating a result of an aged man's exertions. When Grimketil clutched his chest as though he couldn't bear recounting the story, Wade noticed before Cluny did that it wasn't an attempt at drama. Thinking Grimketil's heart had stopped, Wade tried what he had seen of CPR, intending to start with chest compression; but Grimketil fulfilled his promise to grab Wade's throat again, valuing revenge over survival.

Cluny jumped in to separate them, warning, "Do not fight a dying man."

Strangled by Grimketil and yanked at the waist by Cluny, Wade managed just two shallow pumps at a time, mostly warding off Grimketil's battle-hardened thumbs while trying to stay on target. Cluny's interference grew more urgent as Grimketil's grew weaker.

The old warrior lashed out like an uncoiling spring and lay still in a disarray of hair and beard that encircled his countenance like a fatal frost.

Wade checked the stricken man's pulse. Finding none, he went at the CPR in earnest. The Saxon had saved

Wade's life many times.

Cluny said, "Whatever you're trying to do for him, it's too late. He's with our Lord."

That was when Wade realized there would be no ambulance, no modern hospital, no resuscitation paddles to take over. This was the ninth century. He stood back and let Cluny draw the covers.

Despite the circumstances of his aged friend's death under the dank arched ceilings, Wade grieved for him, bowing his head and joining in Cluny's prayers. But this could not be the Grimketil Wade knew, for this version of the Saxon had everything wrong. The legion Wade remembered when he fought with them had been close to full strength, their strategy and tactics flawless, their victory assured. Wade felt a sinking in his chest. The only way Forkbeard could have an entirely different account of the battle and its participants was if Wade had been diverted to an altered timeline, pinched off as a separate universe. *But how could that have happened?*

Only one way. Wade had never discovered the author of the earlier assault on the natural course of events, the intervention that set Count Raginpert in motion on his treasonous course in the Alps. The Longobard was never cunning enough to devise that plan on his own. Now, someone Wade dubbed "the Interloper" had apparently succeeded in disrupting the legion in an earlier era so that Raginpert would be victorious when he engaged a depleted force of hidden Romans in the ninth century.

Given Wade's modest skill level, he would never get back to his own universe in his own era. His only chance was to find the point where the two realities branched and repair it there.

Mindless of whether Cluny of Pavia saw his actions in the timeline he would abandon, Wade knelt to access the astral plane a second time. The walls continued to echo the monk's soft prayers. Wade added a last brief one of his own, and tried his ankle again.

Employing the bracelet, he found that the difficulty had increased, each step drained by agonizing doubt. The purple wash appeared tie-dyed, the honey sour, and the rust mundane and corrosive. Employing the keenest of visualizations to guide him, honed all the way down to the last clang of steel in the battle and his last ninth century breath, he persevered until he broke through.

In this visit to the plane, space-time was not warped. He encountered only the usual downstream course, ever piling toward the twenty-first century in a chaotic mass, and the upstream route as part of the same astral river, thin but straight, and struggling to the past and the further past.

He had more decisions to make and more work to do before he could be on his way in earnest. Poised to jump, Wade remembered what Centurion Honoratus had said at the Brenii Pass about the secret legion's formation being many generations ago. That would mean well before the ninth century, back to the only time that could provide a continuous link to the bygone empire.

Given that calculation, Wade dived upstream toward Rome's collapse, praying that Kreindia would make the same logical connection and find her way there to join him. Permanently, if need be. That conceptual jump and commitment would be a lot to ask, sorely testing her connection to him. Until Wade set things straight, however, one thing Kreindia would never find was any place the two of them had ever been.

CHAPTER 7

Five Hundred

"When Roman citizen Theoderic the Great led Ostrogoth and Visigoth to slay the Scirians, he gained the confidence of the One True Empire. Made viceroy for Constantinople's basileus, he recruited old empire soldiers from Roma to Ravenna to resettle in secret in the Brenii Pass, and thence to form a reserve against the barbarian Clovis and his ilk in the dark generations to come."

—Scriptor Kreindia of Amorium

(Undated parchment)

WADE SWAM THE temporal transition, fighting to keep his emotions from drawing him off course. Targeted astral travel was an all-consuming discipline. The very first time he'd jumped, he unconsciously guided himself in on Kreindia's beacon.

Her guidance was absent now.

Subsequent times left on his own, he'd had less success, and those travels centered on familiar things or more concrete ideas. His present options were wider and his ideas of direction less definite. Nevertheless, he took the visualizations he witnessed on the plane as a cue that he might be ready to take greater control. On intuition, he over-jumped toward more distant history. Once there, he forced his mind to relax, allowing himself to drift in retrograde on the current until the outlines of the time stream he sought unfolded rapidly beneath him.

He watched infant Rome grow from a city-state to a nation that battled to the ends of the Italian peninsula; saw it spread to the islands as well as south across the Mediterranean in its titan clash with Carthage and acquire the empire-building trade routes that the scourge of conquest opened through Africa; the long wars of Rome on the Iberian peninsula; then the thrill of seeing Julius Caesar himself breaching the barbaricum of Gaul and eventually Britain, Celtic domain invasions that included payback for their attacks on early Rome. The frenetic expansion of the empire was dizzying at this rate of observation.

Slowing as much as he dared, Wade followed the completed encirclement of the Mediterranean Basin via Greece. It was at this point that Rome conquered the Middle East as far as the Jordan River. Now Wade caught a glimpse of Governor Varus, Pontius Pilate's role model, marching into Jerusalem, and heard him ordering "two thousand crosses to punish the families of the rebels.

After the Roman devastation of Palestine, they shifted their seat of power to the East, and all of the Imperium would come to see this far reach of soil as their inseparable Holy Land. Ironic that the territory they absorbed, in turn absorbed them, for in the end, the place that Rome made suffer most would be the only country that impressed and humbled this solitary superpower. It wasn't long before the emperors split the ungovernable giant empire in two.

Wade slowed further to witness in amazement the rapid dismantlement of the increasingly remote Western portion as it fell prey to the comforts of its own success, orgies of brutality and lust, as well as mismanagement and corruption. Meanwhile he saw the invaders crouching at the fringes, waiting for Rome's moments of weakness and then pouncing. And when the western empire was merely Itale again, one last spectacular act of power-hunger by an underling was all it took to spike the remainder.

A manipulator of the timeline could find a useful point of attack anywhere in that period of the Late Roman Empire through the turbulent centuries to follow. Given what Wade had learned from Grimketil, he decided that the Interloper's target must be the very inception of the secret Roman legion's formation, a group left hidden in the mountains after all else was swept away, to train and grow to defend the remnants of civilization in the event of dire emergency. Though the plan and its consequences had somehow been concealed and lost to history, Wade surmised that it began with Theoderic's documented visit to Rome from Ravenna in AD 500, by which time he and his Ostrogoths had already reconquered Itale for Constantinople.

Wade had no Kreindia, no Grimketil, no other ally to back him up, but he had to proceed to this particular year somewhere in the region and somehow find a way to shore up Theoderic's clandestine mission in the Brennii Pass. The devil was in the details, and the details were Wade's destination.

~*W*~

WADE arrived in the sixth century on a warm day in the middle of a well-paved Roman highway, the air sweet with wildflowers, their scent magnified by heavy humidity. As a guidepost to his landing, he had imagined spring with all its signs. The small, fresh leaves on the trees told him he had found it. With the yellow-tinged Tiber River taking its sinuous course on his right and the Aurelian Walls of Rome rising majestically ahead, he knew he faced south. Opposite the river, mist rose to a sky streaked pink with sunrise—lighting the dominion of Theoderic the Great, if

Wade reckoned correctly, in the season of armies on the move.

Despite the Germanic name, Theoderic was as legitimate as a Roman Emperor of the latter day could be. Bristling with righteous energy, the semi-barbarian was sent by Constantinople after having trained there for a lifetime to restore Rome's greatness. This western leader at mid-millennium would resemble the longhaired and whiskered mid-thirtyish monarch struck forcefully on his country's coins.

Wade made his way toward the walls thinking that any plan by the Interloper to shatter the original reality would have drawn in Theoderic's brother-in-law Clovis as well. From his base in post-Roman Gaul, Clovis, whose name meant "glory by combat," was the most feared man in Europe. Killing members of his own family to absorb the other tribes helped make him the first King of all Franks. His later conquests won him what would one day be northern and southwestern France while he harried and nipped at the rest of the Germanic territories and collapsed the last of the Gallo-Roman spaces that had survived the fall of Rome.

So Wade braced himself to meet one or the other of these titans sooner or later and hoped it would be Theoderic.

While surveying the path behind him, Wade was startled by the noise of an approach at the road's bend and someone addressing him in Latin. "This road is closed, general. Whose army do you command, and how did you slip past my advance men?" At that, Wade unconsciously touched his red cloak, surmising that only a general should be wearing one in the sixth century. It had not been so in the Ninth.

The man facing him astride a regal horse—a vigorous rider for someone who must have been seventy years old—wore the purple and held his ground while his guards advanced a few paces further in Wade's direction.

Astonishing. The head of state was neither Theoderic nor Clovis.

This man had one of his irises so deep brown as to be nearly indistinguishable from black, the other a beacon of electric blue. Complete heterochromia, a mismatch of pigmentation. With those famous eyes, he had to be the Eastern Emperor Anastasius. Yet, in 500, Anastasius should have been engaged in governing Constantinople, twelve hundred miles distant by sea. He should have, in fact, been enjoying a peaceful interval between wars. His presence on the peninsula was evidence of yet another affront to recorded history—a crisis immeasurably worse than Wade had predicted, perhaps an alteration great enough to sire another universe on its own.

"Speak," Anastasius commanded.

Wade drew a deep breath, keeping watch on that one blue eye all-giving, the other all-taking. The jarring quality must have provided the emperor a distinct advantage in questioning his lessers, which included everyone. Even the emperor's courteous tone carried a threat, so Wade had to take care. Who would dare lie to eyes like that?

Bowing, Wade said, "I am Wade of Aquitaine. I work for Theoderic, therefore I work for his Roman masters, and ergo, for you, my lord. I am at your service." In Wade's first visit to Europe's past, he had been easily mistaken for one of the Aquitainians of southwestern Gaul, given his superior height and all-around foreign appearance before the Swabians. He saw no advantage in groping for a new identity while trying to sell the rest of his unlikely story.

"Charming," said Anastasius. "Come, what proof do you offer? Speak the truth and I'll know it so you may live." Anastasius' entourage seemed eager to enforce any negative outcome.

As with those Wade had met in previous travels, the basileus had no difficulty understanding Wade's words. Barely conscious of how he'd spoken, Wade had answered the king in Latin. Wade once read that those who heard multiple languages in their infancy could more easily learn a variety of tongues. If so, all the world's languages must have whispered to Wade across the eons from the day he was born. When he crossed the banks of time, he found no language impenetrable to him provided the other party spoke first.

Wade said, "May I speak of confidential matters in front of those assembled?" He hoped not. It was easier to convince one man than a crowd.

Gesturing at the two beside him, Anastasius said, "This is the heart of my war council. Proceed."

Having gotten in this deep, Wade could not fail to offer proof, though he carried no documents to support his claim. Wade looked at the sullen men who bracketed the emperor, one with the bearing and build of a starving intellectual, the other large and smoldering like those schooled in the brutal arts. Thinking it best to paint Anastasius' opponent in dark terms, Wade said, "The villain Clovis marches against my lord Theoderic." Or so Wade hoped.

Anastasius gave him a mocking yawn. "This is known to me for a month, Aquitaine, and known more recently to the general populace. You might have heard it anywhere."

Wade leaned in and lowered his voice. "There's more. Clovis marches to stop the formation of the hidden reserve legion. His spies have given him Theoderic's plan."

Anastasius exchanged grim looks with his entourage and said to Wade, "*My* plan actually. But the information you offer is true...and entirely too much on target. You may have come by it from the wrong direction. How am I to know that you're not one of Clovis' spies yourself?"

"You'll know it," said Wade, "when I gut him like a Cappadocian boar and present you his foul smelling head."

Anastasius laughed heartily. "Spoken like a true Aquitainian general. You are too conspicuous to be a spy, and too likeable to work for Clovis. And yet… we can't afford a mistake. If you had a letter of introduction you'd have given it to me. And since you're an Aquitainian, I don't know if you're a Frankish subject or a rebel."

"No, that's right," said Wade without rancor or apology. "I have no papers with me, nor did I bring my army to ride at the head of it. I did not expect to meet you at this time."

"Very well. Before we take you into our confidence, go with Egan into Rome. He'll devise a more clever test for you than I can."

Egan nodded his agreement, his lips pressed tightly together.

"And if you have lied to me Aquitainian," Anastasius shouted after them, "you shall leave this world with more tears than the day you entered."

Not again. As he took the proffered horse and went with Egan, Wade couldn't help but wonder, *Does this road of woe lead to Kreindia? If not, where is she?*

CHAPTER 8

The Contemplation Forest

THE DEADLY METAL tube, which Kreindia likened to a Nubian poison dart reed, swung toward the little boy. Suddenly Kreindia came wide awake, jolted like a lightning strike that sent all of its power to her lungs. She screamed, "No!" and the raking discharge inside of her felt powerful enough to cleave the assailant on its own. It didn't, but it got the man's attention.

Up until then, Kreindia had watched Wade's parking lot standoff in disbelief, or rather, in muted belief. In this unpredictable world with the madness it demanded, events flowed distant and dream-like. Her own fatigue had fed the morass.

Who was the inept soldier with the Celtic bat tattoo who threatened Wade? She thought of her time's excubitors, forever on call to protect the royal palace. If this one was a latter day guard, who did he answer to? Not the tall fellow who intervened, else the older man would not have resorted to persuasion. No, his actions couldn't have been directed by anyone in authority. She decided that, even in the far future, people occasionally went crazy. But why would a Celt have a Nubian reed?

When she cried out, Wade looked at her and she read his resolve. The message she found in Wade's battle scarred eyes was that he would just as soon die than abandon her.

Together with the other tall man, he tricked and

disarmed the Celt.

With a last lingering glance, Wade withdrew so that their tormentors might withdraw as well.

Del's parents seemed to hold their breath while the site cleared. The foul smelling courtyard grew ever more noxious in the intensifying sun. The ersatz excubitor gone, Kreindia marshaled the strength of her right index finger to nudge the tiny magic wand to follow Wade. With a lurch, her conveyance moved backward instead of forward!

Faron loomed, gripping the handles. "Where do you think you're going?" he said softly. "Did today's adventure put crazy ideas in your head?"

Though she tried to rise, to run to Wade, her desire had no more effect than willing a stranger's body to move. *I'm still too weak.*

Faron swung her to face a wooden fence that bounded the lot. From the corner of her eye, she could see him making obscure preparations. With no choice but to submit to those who thought her their property, Kreindia managed a shudder.

Faron hefted her withered body like a sack of turnips and landed her in the tall car, wasting no more words. Kreindel's mother, eyes circled by dark rings on blood-drained skin, assisted in the cumbersome transfer of the weighty chariot itself. To keep Del's body upright, Faron had to fasten her in another type of chair, a smaller one, on top of the long bench.

Before Faron went to secure the chariot wheels in place with the focus of a thorough jailer, a curious scrap of something fluttered from his pocket to land on Kreindia's lap. Something flat and neat. It wasn't papyrus, parchment, or refined Chinese paper, but clearly some kind of bleached fiber cut to a small rectangle. She'd seen a flash of ink before it flipped face down.

Before she could investigate, Faron withdrew, shutting the door with a whump and a latch click that hit Kreindia like the pain of a wasp sting. She cried out though she knew full well she had not been caught in the door. Her crossed senses delivered the illusion. It did not linger.

The coach rolled backwards, turned as it did, and then dove forward in a remarkably smooth manner, the scenery blurring past. A soft growl accompanied their progress. Some things about this world she had learned from Wade. The surging force at the heart of the coaches had not been one of them. In the royal court, she had seen shows staged to impress barbarians, technology dressed as divine intervention. The current century could conceivably hold wonders beyond her imagining. She was not ready to believe that she played the role of ingenuous barbarian now. Not when there was a far more manageable mystery to investigate.

Kreindia worked towards the scrap, taking measured breaths, her exertions ventured on the exhale. The task was made easier when the coach hit a small bump, which caused her arm to fall from the armrest and land in her lap. Her anger flared at the feebleness imposed on her as a prisoner in the depleted body.

You have to be strong for both of us, Del reminded her.

Kreindia thought of her patron saint, the Empress Irene, the one she looked to for strength. One day Kreindia would tell her children that this was the very moment she swore to the empress that she would overcome these limitations, return to Wade, and drive a sword into anything that stood between them.

Faron focused on his driving, which kept his back turned to her but for a few head movements that preceded a turn of the wheel. In Kreindia's next attempt, she concentrated on what it would be like to curl her fingers—they curled faithfully in her mind's eye—and letting that notion roll back as though her arm were a catapult ratcheted to firing position at high tension. Loyal troops manned the grips, gathering her sinew to the reel. *Now pull free the catch to release the spring.*

Outside of her visualization, she felt blessed movement. When she opened her eyes, the paper had come within reach. From there she picked at an edge and nudged it over with her fingernail. Allowing her head to sag down to see it was the easy part.

At first glance, the writing looked like gibberish. Then her gift of language took over. The letters were akin to Latin, but she knitted her brow at the curious combination of Latin with English, Germanic, and Gallic all at once. She extended her finger toward the fine print. Some of it was easy, with the—

When her skin touched the paper, the point of contact coursed with synesthetic fire,…

…and she experienced……an interval…of…

…nothing.

Her eyelids held fast like crusted portals sealed by Hynos for enforced sleep. *But I wasn't asleep!*

For the first time in her life, Kreindia, oracle of the Imperium Romanum, emerged from a vision unable to retain any image or message but for a foreboding that invaded every level of her existence. Knowing that the scene might never repeat, and certain at first that the information it carried was vital, she tried to reconstruct something of it before her body shook off her vision state. It had to do with her trip to the astral plane. *Take a piece and hold it until the next floats by,* she told herself, *and add that one to the growing picture.* She and Wade traveled as a trio, but that made no sense. Her immediate effort, like the fragmented bits she clutched at, fell to pieces.

She reached and gathered and slipped, and began again.

And failed. And it seemed the pieces were fewer now.

But she must *not* fail.

Indisposed as she was, she wasn't entirely bereft of tools. She abandoned her useless groping and fell backward to what she called her contemplation forest, a mental refuge she'd fashioned for problem solving. There the gentle hills were preternaturally green and manicured with synesthetic precision, the bark of trees perpetually darkened to a burnt umber from recent rain. In her visits, the rain was always something she'd just missed, a touch that made the leaves glisten and droop in vibrant wetness. Together with the shrubs and cobbled ways, these features met in a harmony of nature and art more pleasing than any noble's estate she'd ever seen. Any of her most vexing troubles could be resolved in this remote place. Cities—if they existed—could not be found, as the branches, each pruned with flawless artistry, ran to infinity. And somewhere in that infinity, this time, obscured by the intervening woods, Kreindia sensed a beast drawn forth in her wake.

As a pure invention of her mind, there had never been another entity in her contemplation forest. She wasn't mistaking Del for the intruder. In fact, she had once made a supreme effort to invite her best friend Verina to mentally join her there, and it couldn't be done.

This creature that had done the impossible and gotten in, was nominally male, and truly a beast. A thing dedicated to devouring. Wherever it was from, it could obscure its visage here but not its hideous nature. She hoped to sneak up from cover before it realized where it was in relation to her.

So began a pursuit between the trees. At the outset, she managed to project a marker on the beast's essence. As soon as it fled deeper, it left a dark, zigzagging streak. She ran after the tag at a break-neck pace, ducking and dodging around obstacles she could no longer control. She faced limbs and trunks arranged initially by her mind's whim, yet the beast designed to shift them into her path as it went.

Changing her strategy, she took on the clothes of the landscape and moved like the wind, rolling in a circuitous route to flank the creature. This trespasser, who crafted illusions of its own, was not at all fooled, or short on devices. When she caught up to the tail of the streak, it dissolved into motes of dust rising in shafts of sunlight. All along the criss-crossing length it came undone, leaving her gasping. The missing trace of its changing location would leave her vulnerable should the beast turn on her.

Already an indistinct figure, only a suggestion of shape and motion could be seen now. With a backwards rotation of its extremities, her vital memories were drawn to the devourer as though they were a taut rope it could coil onto a spool. She abandoned her disguise and ran toward the fiend to slacken the rope, but all it had to do was stand still and she could not equal the speed at which it robbed her.

A noise matched its coiling movements, grinding like mechanical cicadas, and a dull sense of alarm pounded her head. It was only a matter of moments before it erased her memory of the fact that it once existed, and when it had done that how would she be able to respond to the threat it represented? She had to get out of there. But it was too late. The beast filled the spool until the last of the line of her thoughts was wrenched free of her.

In the manner she usually perceived them, her recollections could be classified by weight and solidity. Facts were heavy and hard as brick, dreams ethereal and pliant as rose petals. Though she now sensed nothing more substantial than the impression of a feather on wet clay, she felt certain that something disturbing had transpired in the missing interval. A pursuit among the tree trunks. *What tree trunks?* Playing the scene over from the beginning yielded ever less information no matter how many times she tried.

Instead, two words rose in her mind's eye and hung in space:

TABULA RASA

Latin for a tablet erased. That's what Kreindia was now.

Kreindia came fully alert in the moving coach, assailed by its unfamiliar, cloying odors. Faron and Clara were silent in the front seats, acceleration pressing them left as Faron spun the wheel to the right. A gull flew out of the way and left a feather on the glass. All she could gather was that the feather had something to do with her and the quality of memories lost. No, a vision lost. How her recall might have been blocked, she did not know, but a synesthetic smell sprinkled the air in her compartment. Almonds, like cyanide, overriding all else. The more she breathed, the more confused she became. When she tried to peer back in time, her heart raced and a rash of sweat rose on her skin.

It was as if someone had planted a hidden fear to consume her from within if she dared attempt to remember. This anomaly, unsettling as it was, had to be a nightmare. Had to be. But she knew better. True prophecies retained their potency, while rose-petal products of sleep had never troubled her afterwards. Her fingertips trembled, then they settled down. Then everything was fine again.

Part II

From Whence She Came

"Happy is the one who has broken the chains which hurt the mind."

~Ovid

CHAPTER 9

Up the Water's Pout

THERE WAS A reason time was measured out as grains in the chambers of an hourglass. The trickling sand inexorably lost, told of its true quality, a slippery thing even at a chokepoint. Kreindia could only ever see the upper or the lower part of the glass, where time either ran out or filled a new space, and even that she witnessed only for an instant. Her time blindness prevented her from quantifying the intervals, so she had no idea how long she'd been a guest of the Richters. Without the ability to move, she could not keep a journal.

Riding in the coach once again, Kreindia, along with Del and her family, were rushing to a kind of hospital at a speed that blurred the scenery. Sometimes, though, her eyes caught up and Kreindia could make out streets, trees, people, and an astonishing number of these coaches. It was easier to imagine that the cars were rolling downhill than to picture the equivalent of minute horses under the hood (Del's attempt at explanation), but neither illusion lasted long as other conveyances flashed by them in the opposite direction at double their rate.

Kreindia assembled an understanding of her situation from pieces of conversations around her. Dr. Nesky had told her new doctor, Royce Cealwin, of the sudden change in her condition, some authorities intervened, and Dr. Cealwin insisted Faron bring her in for what he called "physical therapy." Faron seemed motivated by the idea of keeping up appearances. The sly bastard thought, and he calculated, and in the end he decided, yes, she must go.

The blast of a nearby horn made her cringe with apprehension. As Faron drove the car's invisible beasts toward the appointed destination, Kreindia considered the idea that she might be under a profound curse to have ended up so helpless. And the way Faron had treated her thus far racked her frayed senses:

"Kreindel, get over here."

"Kreindel, go back."

"Kreindel, you disgust me."

Faron spoke like the crack of a whip. Although Kreindia had previously visited this young woman's body on one brief occasion, she knew nothing of how insidious her counterpart's circumstances truly were. No wonder Del's cynicism was rampant. As yet, fortunately, Del—and Kreindia for that matter—had experienced little of the violence of which Faron was likely capable. Del's mother had probably not been so lucky.

The car's sudden swerve tossed her sideways and she struggled to adjust. Even without Faron's badgering, every slight movement exhausted her. She'd grown into a painful awareness of tiny muscles that one would never expect to become sore, like those in her little finger. The small movements felt like triumph; her failures like a cocktail of ash and tonic. She thought that some of the muscles may have shrunk to a point of no return. How did the real Del manage, spending her whole life this way? *And worse.* Yes, she had it worse.

They arrived at a pale building, turning neatly into an open slot marked off in blue, and Faron conducted them inside with his usual alacrity. He managed to instigate some argument with the officials that Kreindia could not fathom. Her keepers, as she now thought of them, Faron and Clara, were politely ordered to leave even though the therapist had not yet arrived. Kreindia sighed with relief.

Here was her chance to gain the strength she needed for escape and the venue from which to do it.

She immersed herself in the new environment, peering every which way. The denizens of the gymnasium were all engaged in one activity or another, save for one remarkably small girl who commanded her own chariot, which Kreindia reminded herself was called a wheelchair. The child had full movement from the waist up, and was surprisingly cheerful and communicative with the adults. She might have been five years old.

When the outgoing little one saw her, she rolled by to introduce herself. "Hi, I'm Lorraine."

In the absence of Faron's oppression, Kreindia's senses rallied, showing her a flash of a highly unusual synesthetic signature. Lorraine's entire body appeared to briefly alternate between transparent and opaque, including her tiny and twisted legs. The effect must have been triggered by something she wore.

Kreindia offered, "I'm Del."

"Don't cry, Del," said Lorraine, only it sounded more like "cwy."

Kreindia's inherent sadness must have been obvious, even to a child. There had been no sign of Wade so far, and her powers were muted in this world to the point where she could not reach out to him with her mind. Moreover, she knew that Faron would have prevented Wade from visiting her in person. If Wade only knew how her mangled psyche echoed her mangled body, how her time blindness warped her perceptions, he would, without a doubt, find a way to communicate. It almost seemed as though Wade had disappeared off the face of the globe or had traveled back to an age where the world no longer included her. Her eyes stung with tears at the thought. *Could that happen?* Would Wade think she was only an alternate version of herself, and go searching for the "real" Kreindia of Amorium? If so, wouldn't he at least have given her some indication of his intent? Need one notify a duplicate?

Very seriously, Lorraine said, "Wade's not here."

A shock went through Kreindia. "Wade?" she asked through unsteady lips. "How do you know?"

Lorraine gave a baby-sized shrug. "Sometimes I just know who's here and who's not."

"You met him?"

"No, I felt like you asked me, and then I told you."

With fresh trepidation, Kreindia asked, "What do you mean by 'here'?"

"Here. Where the Everything is." Her eyes were wide.

"Do you know any more? Do you know where Wade went?"

Lorraine's brow darkened as she though about it, then pinched. The question plainly terrified her, and Kreindia could see that the girl couldn't talk about it through her trembling and shouldn't be forced to.

"Don't worry about it," said Kreindia.

"When I'm sad, the spider helps me," said Lorraine.

"You have a spider?"

She brightened. "I don't *have* it. I *do* it. I could teach you. Would you like that? You'll see it will help."

Kreindia managed to twitch a weak smile. She did not mind the company of this tiny spirit with her visions that implied there was so much more to her than the little broken body. "Yes. Teach me."

"Do hands like this." The girl made waggling gestures in the manner that a lute player might warm up her fingers in preparation for a concert.

Without expecting Kreindia to catch up, the girl with the Gallic name began to sing while acting out a sort of play with only her miniscule arms and hands.

She lent a high, clear voice to an eerie melody:

"The itsy-bitsy spider went up the water's pout.
Down came Lorraine and washed the spider's house.
Out came the Sun, and wiped up for Lorraine,

And the itsy-bitsy spider spun up the pout again."

Then the girl applauded herself, fluttering her delicate hands like a butterfly.

Lorraine's song seemed to carry a hint of eldritch power that made Kreindia shiver at the plight of the spider. It was as vulnerable as she to the greater forces of the world. In real life, before the Sun could wipe up for Lorraine, there could easily be another storm larger than the first. She considered mentioning to the child that itsy-bitsy spiders didn't have easy lives. The very idea that this hardship occurred to her meant that she wasn't quite ready to cheer up. Instead she smiled at Lorraine and said, "Solidus for a happy ending. I liked it."

"You're strange," said the child with honest certainty.

"I know." Kreindia patted Lorraine's tiny hand and gasped. For one searing moment, she saw Wade dressed for battle. And then she saw only his outline, a transition manifesting the fear that Lorraine had felt. The words pierced her again. *Wade's not here.* Her companion was a small girl though, and an adult's absence could scare her. It didn't have to mean more than that. But all of these connections meant that the girl was some manner of synesthete.

"Kreindel?" An able-bodied woman entered their area with a light step and now smiled warmly at her. "Sorry to interrupt. I'm Cynthia Marks, your therapist." Cynthia was as fit as an Amazon though not nearly as well protected. She was dressed in thin, form-fitting exercise clothes like those worn in the bath houses of Zeuxippus, though this outfit was even tighter and shined in a pleasing way Kreindia had never seen before.

The lady had an expectant smile. Kreindia could not muster a great deal of optimism to match. Duplicating that child's routine in song and gestures, if that was what they taught here, would have been a valedictorian performance for anyone who had long been paralyzed.

Somewhat daunted, Kreindia spit out a scratchy, "Hello. Call me Del."

"How do you feel today, Del?"

"Like a donkey. Tied under a heavy load and then beaten with a stick."

Cynthia laughed. "You're going to feel like that a lot for a while. Are you familiar with our exercise equipment?"

Kreindia took in what she could of the room without moving her neck. Many things, such as the medicine ball, were comfortingly Greek in nature. She saw a man struggling on a set of parallel bars, and that, too, came from her era. At the same time, though, a woman plodded shakily on a moving platform with no one there to crank it. *I wonder how that's done.*

"Some," she said, bringing a brilliant smile to the therapist's face.

"You'll have the run of this gymnasium in no time," Cynthia said.

Lorraine brought her hands together in a single clap to get everyone's attention, and then solemnly informed Cynthia, "I taught Spider."

Cynthia bent down to the girl, palms on knees. "You are my number one and best assistant, sweetie."

Lorraine giggled.

Cynthia said to Del, "According to Dr. Nesky's records, in the two years he saw you, your only capacity was movement of your right index finger, and in a single day, he saw you move your whole arm, and begin to speak. Can you move your arm for me now?"

Kreindia took a deep breath, more from anxiety than need. She slowly raised her right arm six inches, paused there, and managed another eight. She could not keep it from wavering to the left and then to the right before settling it back on the armrest.

"That is wonderful," said Cynthia with a wink. "Even better than I thought. We'll have you on the treadmill by the end of the week."

Kreindia felt a little better. Isolated as she was, she had learned that Del's house was filled with marvels as impressive as those in the gym. Lights sprang up by remote command and burned steadily like miniature suns. Distant peoples and events were conjured on sheets of crystal fitted into flat, square tablets. Boxes played music so odd it could have come from any of the hidden realms. In this age, perhaps everyone was a witch. The visitors to the gym looked so confident. Maybe she could do this. Here was opportunity, she reminded herself. *Wellness and escape.*

With or without Faron's hindrance.

Consulting her clipboard, Cynthia asked, "Your father doesn't seem sold on the idea of having you here, but it's on the best of advice. Do you have any idea why he changed your doctor in the first place?"

"Yes," Kreindia said distantly. "He said he'd been betrayed."

~*W*~

WHEN Faron returned to collect Del, he was in the foulest mood Kreindia had yet observed. He stayed that way, if not worse, for the entire trip home. By the time they reached Jericho, he'd accomplished a vigorous one-sided argument with his wife, even though she was careful to speak only when asked a question.

Back in the house, pushing her along, he brought Kreindia into her room and shut the door behind him. It was just the two of them alone, causing her breath to quicken. If Clara hovered at eavesdropping distance, cowed as she was, her presence would not help Kreindia at all. The room shimmered ever so slightly. She hadn't been conscious of it before because the impression was weak, but Faron generated a personal synesthetic signature. In his case, it could best be descried as foam—miniscule bubbles *en masse* under the surface of everything she saw in his presence—as though his projection laid bare the fundamental construction of all things in every direction. Wade and a very few other people had a personal signature, and Kreindia wasn't sure why. Was Faron allowing her to see it? While she was thinking about it, Lorraine had displayed one of these signatures too. *Hadn't she?*

Shattering her contemplation, Faron said, "They tell me you did some extraordinary things in the gym today. Already."

Kreindia did not know how to respond to his accusing tone. As ever, he made no sense. Did he want her less dependent, or more?

Faron slapped her cheek hard with his meaty palm. "I already got rid of your holistic miracle worker Nesky. What did you do now?" he shouted.

The second time, he gave her a swipe in the other direction with his knuckles. Her head lolled to the side, unable to recover. She felt warm liquid flow from one nostril. Faron took her face in his hands, lifting it upright to meet his eyes.

Kreindia needed no vision state to realize that Faron's next move might make the first strikes seem like caresses. In the silence, her cheeks burned and her eyes darted like trapped beasts. She thought of her uncle, General Michael, and tried to summon some of his courage. In her helpless state, her mind was as empty as it had been when...when what?

On the verge of being unable to bear any more, when she thought she must scream or else expire from fear in his grip, Faron said, "Now that you can speak, tell me true, girl. It's vitally important. Life or death. Are you my wife's Kriendel? Or are you possessed by someone else?"

$\sim W \sim$

POSSESSED. So that was Faron's problem. He

77

believed in possession. Two minds in Del's body would qualify, so in that sense he was right. She hadn't been prepared in any way to address such a question, and she was afraid of how he would respond to any answer she could muster. Eventually, he had given up and left her alone to "think about it without dinner."

What an odd and disproportionate thing to say to someone who might be possessed and just took a thrashing for it. His bizarre transitions puzzled her, but more than that, they engendered an overwhelming and unfulfillable urge to flee from his reach, a feeling that clouded analysis of his foibles. That, together with all the ways in which he muddled her mind made her suspicious that the effect was intentional. Why did she feel so detached sometimes?

She began to search for clues in the living room. Something in particular had to have happened to set him off. She should have known it without synesthetic indicators this time, on pure intuition. But what? Trying to cut through her misted thoughts, she considered the limited field of facts. She suspected that what set Faron off was the one circumstance that would have bothered him most. Clearly Faron's "hot button" (another Del term) was encountering Wade. Is that what actually happened?

Wheeling over to her front door, she grazed her fingers across the doorframe and gasped at the signature it raised—the dancing reflection of fire on ripples of water. Wade had been there. Been to this very house. He'd touched the casing or something in close proximity at some earlier date. How long ago?

Her gasp brought over Faron who had slipped into the room when she was distracted.

"Kreindel? If you're trying to get out by that door, you can't."

She tried telling him, "I'm not possessed. I'm recovering and confused. I don't know why you ask me such strange questions."

Chewing his lip, Faron gave a short, non-committal nod, and did not leave.

"You never really thought I was possessed, did you?" she accused.

"I overreacted." That was as close as he came to an apology. Beginning with the words "I have something to tell you," he belied his matter-of-fact tone and level voice by striding the living room like a panther patrolling the bounds of his cage. Here and there he found small matters to tend to, such as aligning a shelved soldier figurine or a decorative bowl. "While you were out trying to be a hero of the gymnasium," he said, reseating the wire base of a lampshade on its socket, "your friend Wade Linwood was here. The one you call Aquitaine."

He noticed her flustered reaction and quelled it with raised palms. "I only tell you this by way of explaining why I will never allow him here again." Faron paused with a smirk as though he found the subject mildly amusing. "Wade was trying to sell me some nonsense about your 'Uncle' Michael. I told him, of course, that you have no Uncle Michael. As your father, I would know, wouldn't I?" He smiled at her, and then frowned at a blemish on the switch plate. When his thumb's ministrations didn't satisfy, he polished it with a handkerchief. Then he folded the material and used a corner, rubbing with increased vigor.

At the mention of her uncle, Michael of Amorium, on top of this visit from Wade, Kreindia couldn't contain herself. "What did Wade say?"

"Ah, you can speak well enough when you choose to. When it's about something you want to hear, yes?"

"Please. What exactly did he say?"

"You know what? I'm going to tell you just so you can see once and for all how completely crazy this Wade Linwood is. Maybe it will work that poor judgment out of your system."

He gave her a chance to speak again, turning to her to

show his full attention, but she waited him out. "No comment?" he asked. "Well, when I told Wade he was wrong, he said he meant Michael *the Greek*. Among his Greek friends, the guy is called Uncle. He said to tell you that this Michael would be in serious trouble by 8:20 on Christmas Day, if he couldn't bail him out. 8:20? What is that? Ridiculous." Pointing a warning finger at her, Faron said, "Don't you dare go anywhere with Wade whether it's Christmas or not. Don't go anywhere, period." With that, he walked out, slammed the door and shot the bolt, locking her in the living room.

Faron's words filled her with a contradiction of dread and hope as Kreindia stared after him at the closed door. In a cold sweat, her eyes retraced the path he'd taken around the room, reviewing the information he provided, hoping to gather every scrap of meaning from it. Accuracy was essential, and his story bothered her. It seemed odd that Wade would come and speak so bluntly to Faron of ninth century matters. He risked arousing the man's suspicions. How could Wade be sure that Faron would repeat what he said? Yet if Wade hadn't been the source, how would Faron have known anything about her real uncle?

Then again, what choice did Wade have? He'd obscured the message as much as he dared.

Kreindia closed her eyes to concentrate. *Wade is not here.* Faron's description of Michael's situation matched a vision she'd had about her uncle in Constantinople, a sudden transition from darkness to blinding sun. Captivity to freedom. 8:20 wasn't a time. Eight hundred twenty was the year he would be imprisoned by rivals, and from that cell General Michael Psellus would either die in ignominy or escape his sentence and take the purple. She had been under the impression her uncle and his allies could manage without her, but perhaps her intervention was always meant to be.

Moreover, rescuing Michael created the perfect

opportunity to set everything right. She could reunite with Wade by meeting him in another space and time, and perhaps even become whole again. If she could achieve astral travel, bolted doors would never stop her.

But she didn't know if she could make that transition without Wade. What he did to travel between planes wasn't her path. Wade had learned from Taoist lord Du Sian that no two *méiyǒuguó rén* are alike. China had known synesthetes as well.

Where did Wade place the point of his shark's tooth in order to transport her? How did he steer himself where he needed to go? Though she hadn't been conscious when he swept her from the battlefield, she felt certain the information resided somewhere within her, a flawless kinesthetic imprint, just waiting for the proper ministration. Now she realized she would need a way to access that information, some sort of trigger to call it into service.

If she could mentally retrace their last trip to the astral plane during the Battle of Brenii Pass, ill-fated though it was...

As she focused on that memory, traces of it came into focus and she realized that something outlandish had happened in her transit. She and Wade had been joined by a third entity—

The smell of almonds invaded her train of thought. And then mechanical cicadas grinding on a spool.

The hot rash that bloomed on her skin seemed familiar. *Is this the first time I've begun to remember or one of many?*

Her mind blanked.

When she opened her eyes again, the air held a residue that led directly to the soldier figurine Faron had adjusted. When her gaze alit on that object, it resonated with foam, confirming that Faron had touched it. She moved to the stout, hand-span-height warrior as efficiently as one driven by profound hunger. Although it must have been crafted from a page in history, she'd never seen anything quite like it. At first blush, she saw a red-bearded Norseman bearing a long-hafted Danish axe with a crescent edge. On his head rode a leather and iron-plated *spangenhelm* with spectacle guards like great eyebrows, and an extended nose block. The strange part was not so much the Byzantine chain mail from his chin to his hips—anyone with a large enough purse could have obtained that—but the splint limb armor, which seemed to identify him as a palace guard. She remembered no such personnel from her time at court. While the statuette's knife and sword were sheathed, the axe pole angled to form a prominent point at the top. The metal man tantalized Kreindia within arm's reach. Could this statuette take her to her imprisoned Uncle Michael? More importantly, could it also bring her to Wade? *I must visit Michael first.*

Again she wondered if something wasn't right. In the back of her mind, she detected a gap such that a mistaken chain of logic can produce. Or—she chided herself— perhaps her hesitance to use the only way out was the reluctance that arises from fear of the unknown and sends the insecure searching for craven excuses.

As she edged close enough to examine the figure's neatly painted eyes welcoming her in, she decided it was the risk that she feared; the feeling that the action she contemplated was irrevocable. Yet Wade faced it all the time and dealt with it squarely.

With a suddenness of decision and motion that nearly terrified her, she tipped a chair to block the room's entrance, snatched the little Norseman, and aimed the axe point at her ear. Instantly, she knew the precise placement, triggered by the object in her hand and the touch-memory of Wade's fang bracelet. The last thing she remembered of the room was the door flying partway open to jam against the chair barricade and Faron shouting, "No!"

Then she was awash in a synesthetic haze of amaranth,

the chalky red flowers used in her time to staunch the flow of blood. That color was the symbol for her first *Jing Luo* level.

Unhindered, she nudged the axe point deeper to change her space to a sea of feathery icterine, the soft yellow bird color. With it, she heard the beating and flurry of wings.

She could not tarry here but went deeper still to the grainy light brown of plowed land sitting fallow. Tied to that imagery and earthy feeling was a sense of pure joy where she almost lost herself, and might have done so if her mission hadn't been so crucial.

In that clear image of fallow soil, she planted a thought-anchor, an image of her great capital city just a few years hence from when she had left it. Where Michael was then imprisoned. Hers was the land of the highest civilization and the most confounding intrigues. One last push and she found sunlight.

CHAPTER 10

Michael of Amorium

MICHAEL, LATE OF Amorium, in the worst days of his life spent in the Constantinople prison, could not stop reviewing the ill-conceived trip that had put him there. A day seventeen years past in Phrygia. Even before he adopted his dear, missing Kreindia. Leo and Thomas were with him that day under that damned sky.

All three of the companions had witnessed the dark seam of indigo clouds when they freed the dove to reveal their destination. It beat its wings vigorously, a smooth beast colored like the gradations of sand dunes, and for a while Michael could still make out its thick, black collar-marking trimmed in frayed white. He could no longer see their message tied to its foot. Their horses trotted in place, eager to flee from a place that made their riders so nervous.

"I hated the idea of buying that bird," Michael grumbled. "It was a dangerous gamble."

Leo the Armenian said, "The monk uses a fleet of these for messengers. I was assured that this is one of his. It will find him."

"Yes, but this way someone knows we were looking."

"A mere merchant," said Leo. "It's better than wandering the outskirts of Philomelion until the three of us get caught."

Their third member, Thomas the Slav, watched the

heavens and remained unusually quiet with anticipation. In his district he had the common touch with his followers, offering a slippery smile and a flattering memory for everyone's business. On a personal level, he could wax moody and dark.

The dove climbed high into a section of sky bracketed by fast-moving clouds, and as they watched spellbound, the wind scrambled the billows into a curious wreath formation before the shape tore up in the winds.

"That part of the sky within the clouds was dragged with purple," observed Leo. "Like a fresh scar."

The feature had held Michael's rapt attention as well. The spot he had thought of as an indigo stripe seemed to bleed and then heal in a lumpy mass so that it did resemble a scar. Leo spoke in a hushed and humbled tone, unnatural for him among friends, and didn't mention the wreath itself. Some powers are so potent they are dangerous to speak of, as bad as an incantation in the hands of a madman. Though the bird was long out of sight, the trio couldn't stop staring at the place it had been. The scar somehow lingered in that windy sky.

"What does it mean?" Michael asked.

"You're asking me?" asked Leo.

"You released it."

Leo said, "Nothing. Forget that I brought it up."

The Slav, who called himself Thomas of Pontus, burst out, "It does mean something! Everything means something, especially as it relates to birds."

The other two examined their pale friend with curiosity and concern. Michael said, "I didn't know that you felt so strongly about divination."

"They commune with the Heavens," Thomas said. "I can't explain it. I'm anxious to hear what this monk, Solon, has to say."

"Very well. We'll ride in the direction it flew," said Leo, and at last they started after the homing bird.

The three staff officers had slipped away from the

Byzantine army of Bardanes Tourkos—no small matter because they were the *monostrategos'* three most important men on the eve of a decision that would overturn the empire if the conspirators so chose. "We strike when Nikephoros' reign is young," Bardanes had said. "Before his power is consolidated. Are you with me?"

And of course in his presence they had sworn yes, they were with him. But they persuaded him to wait a week. Their intentions towards his plan actually depended on what Solon of Philomelion had to say. Bardanes did not believe in oracles at all so they dared not consult a local one. Being an oracle constituted a crime, in conflict as it was with Christian beliefs, and those who sought them out were criminals thereby.

With brittle resolve, the trio passed to the east on the Roman pavement until all signs of habitation vanished and the streams ran dry. Up until then, the trickles from which they gathered water had required an increasing number of distant side trips. A buzzard navigated the air drafts above them and Michael said, "Maybe this route wasn't the best idea."

"So we should go back and... do what?" asked Leo.

"Go back and not ride through the desert, find another way around." Michael reflected that they hadn't supplied themselves for a journey of this length. They had already begun to ration their stores. He pulled out his gourd and took a small sip, getting thirsty at the very thought of the shortage. "Let's at least find the lake that's on our map."

"That will leave us with no guide back here," said Leo.

"There it is!" cried Thomas, pointing into the sky. The sandy bird that had flown into the purple wreath, or a bird identical to it, came back to them, drawing nearer until they could see the paper attached to its foot.

"That's a different tag than ours," Thomas said to Leo. "It's a reply."

"How do you know?"

"It's tied to the other foot."

Tense and excited, Thomas detached the tiny parchment and passed it over.

"It's in Aramaic. Can you read it?" Leo asked Michael.

"Yes, it says, 'Halfway and ten stadia on the road to Iconium'—that's almost where we are now—'go north to the Rocks of the Wise Men.'"

"North?" asked Thomas. "My map says there's no road to the north of that point."

"Then we go where there is no road," said Leo in a voice hardened by command.

They pushed east as far as the quickening night permitted, and continued the next morning, striking out on the sun-baked desert plain.

After about two hours of not seeing their goal in the dry wavering distance, Michael said, "We're all out of water. Now we'll have to detour west to the lake."

"Agreed," said Leo.

"But the bird may never find us again," said Thomas disconsolately. "The monk may withdraw his offer."

"It's either that," said Leo, "or give up and head back to Constantinople."

Thomas said, "Never."

"Why not?" Michael asked. "It's not as if we have a choice."

"Wait," said Thomas, lifting a blanket flap. "I may, uh, I may have some more water in some other gourds."

"You've kept it to yourself?" Leo flared.

"I've carried the extra load for you and I'm sharing it when it counts," Thomas shot back.

The matter settled as far as it could be, they traveled half again the distance they'd gone from Philomelion before spying the long shadows of the Rocks of the Wise Men. These were three pillars of stone, high as any palace, which stood guard with boulders atop them like turbaned heads. The columns themselves looked natural. The bulging capstones that surmounted them, however, were said to have been mislaid there by giants. How the large heads stayed balanced defied reason, as they looked precarious enough to tumble in any strong wind. Although Thomas had come with them on a non-Christian errand, he nervously made the sign of the cross before moving forward.

The stony ground rose in the approach and they rode up to the base of the first tower and then around to the second, a shorter one. On the third, a fat one, flat-topped, a dove waited, just as they had hoped, and it fluttered off momentarily.

"We follow," Leo commanded.

The band of brothers plodded on to the north and east until the bird drew them to the green brush in the folds of conical rock formations, whereupon it disappeared. When they closed on the spot, they could see dark gaps where they supposed the mouth of a concealed cavern peeked. At this juncture, Thomas dismounted and led the way. Before inspecting the murky hole, he hesitated so that Michael bumped into his back.

"What's wrong?" Michael asked. "You were the one who urged us here."

Thomas said softly, "It wasn't signed."

"What wasn't signed?" Leo demanded.

"His note to us."

"Ours to him wasn't signed either," said Leo. "It's better that way. I'm sure we'll meet with Solon himself." To Michael, he said, "You're a Phrygian. What is this place?"

Michael scrutinized the landscape anew. "I've never journeyed this way but I've heard of the area. These hollows are said to be all over Cappadocia, though hard to find. The rock is soft enough to carve, so Christians used to hide here in the days when the empire was less hospitable to them. The caverns are underground ghost cities now."

"There you go," said Leo to Thomas with an easy confidence. "Who else but an oracle would live in a place like this?"

Michael grunted. Where once there was Delphi with its magnificent splendor and its thousand-year support system, oracles now hid in the ground. If either of the others saw the irony of a seer living in a Christian refuge to hide from Christians, none saw fit to mention it at the moment.

Lighting torches, they clambered down to find themselves in part of a great hidden city, rough-hewn and rounded at each opening and each pillar as if the path had been chewed out by innumerable ants. Most of the steps within, however, were cut level, giving way to passages and channels, rooms and chasms apparently abandoned to the spirits.

They heard a humming sound, the only sign of activity, and proceeded to trace it. The search led to one particular chamber where the walls dripped with a thin film of constantly running water. Michael touched the cool stream, placed his fingers to the tip of his tongue and found the liquid had a sharp nip to it that made him sneer with disgust. But for a capering salamander that ducked into a crack, the space was unoccupied.

"This was the wrong way," said Michael. Although the acoustics had played a trick on them, the humming continued, giving them a means to seek further. Now they could tell that the drone issued from an entirely different direction that seemed obvious in hindsight.

"Do you know where we've gone?" Leo asked Michael.

He smiled as best he could. "I couldn't say for sure, but I think we're almost where we need to be."

En route to the final point, a blast of wind doused their torches and they flinched at what the dark revealed. The next entranceway flowed with sparks such as a hammer and anvil over a forge can produce. Instead of the burning mist that rose and fell under the blacksmith's metered strike, the flow sprayed in an uncanny constant, as might be seen in a workshop of the gods.

"I guess this is it," said Leo bravely. "If I catch fire, put me out."

When he didn't actually go forward in the next few moments, a harsh voice from the other side bid, "Come." Leo moved first and Michael hurriedly made sure he did not look like he was the one hesitating. Thomas lagged, indifferent to what his present company thought of him. When they proceeded through, however, the light show around the arch did not prove flammable.

Inside they came upon a sole occupant, a ragged old man. He crouched by the dim light of a giant ornate burner over which he heated red incense poles as thick as a man's arm. Ablaze at the edges, they produced white winding sheets of smoke in pungent gouts. These were not the source of the sparks, which appeared to flow on their own.

Each of the visitors dropped a clinking sack at the side of the chamber and stood back expectantly.

"Army fugitives from Bardanes' elite," Solon pronounced with his ill-used throat.

"Your eyes are used to the d-dark," observed Michael, stuttering now because the man was a stranger and held power over he and his friends. "We w-wish to know whether the emperor Nikephoros will live a long life."

"—or be cut short by three wretched Byzantine schemers," Solon finished for him with a croaking laugh. "Three come so far to figure out who to double-cross next."

The trio touched the hilts of their swords but waited when he spoke sharply. "What business do you think I have with your coins?"

Leo said, "I don't know, but our offering wasn't easy to scrape together. We haven't been paid for a while. I'll take the gold back if it offends you."

At the mention of gold, the monk hissed, "Leave it. The gods demand a cost, and this will be a part."

"If it's settled, then, can you help us?"

For long moments they heard nothing but the chattering screech of a distant bat distorted to pitiful wails by the intervening chambers. Leo raised a cautious finger to keep the patience of the other two.

"In your future," Solon wheezed in his cloud of incense, "you all get what you deserve. That much I know."

"Which would be what?" Leo pressed boldly.

Solon breathed the fumes as they all did, but he engaged in it by habit, and now he placed his head directly over the cauldron. Surfacing with a deeper rasp than before, he said, "As to your main question, Bardanes Tourkos' revolt will fail. Nikephoros will survive."

Thomas gasped.

Leo snapped, "We didn't ask you that."

"But it's what you wanted to know." And hadn't they already realized that this prediction of failure was so, thought Michael, from the scar inside the laurel wreath and the bird that pointed to that area of the sky? The message in that heavenly tableau seemed clear enough. Royalty would be injured but would heal. Yet those who were not expert at reading signs distrusted their own eyes.

The sparks in the doorway flashed with ire as though responding to Leo's affront.

"We should leave," said Michael.

"Not yet," said Leo with a hard edge. Of Solon, he asked, "And about us? Tell us our fates."

Solon consulted the smoke again, drew it into his lungs. When his head rose, he coughed out enough soot to supply a year's dust to an old rug. "Leo the Armenian... and... Michael of Amorium—Michael Psellus, I dub you... will become emperors."

Both of us? thought Michael, reeling at the implications. Leo and Michael stared at each other, momentarily distrustful of who would one day kill whom, for surely that act would be necessary for ascension.

"When—" Leo began.

"There is no more to know. You are exceedingly lucky that this prophecy has come to me so clearly. Like no other."

When Thomas opened his mouth ask, Solon continued, "And Thomas of Pontus, for his part, will be acclaimed emperor, and then immediately be killed. That is also clear."

This time only Thomas started forward with his sword. He drew it halfway before the others stayed him.

Solon cried, "I've underestimated my visitors. Two emperors and an emperor's corpse came calling!" His cackling filled the subterranean city with raucous echoes.

"I don't think he's right," Thomas shouted in complaint. "He's insane. This is nonsense." Seeing the cold expressions of the other two he amended, "The part about me." He bared his sword to the full, starting forward again. "We need to kill him anyway."

The mysterious sparks burst with fury then and it made the officers turn to look behind them. The center was thick, the filaments long, projecting starbursts far from the origin. A rumble filled the city and Michael thought he saw a shape forming in the dust. Bravery on the battlefield was one thing... fighting ghosts, however...

Michael quickly put himself between Thomas and Solon, surprising even Leo. "No we don't, Thomas," he said. "Leave Solon, leave the gold, and let's go. Now."

Thomas was slow to put his sword away, and from the look in his eyes, he seemed to consider using the blade on Michael.

The story later went around that Bardanes had accompanied them to visit the augur. That wasn't true. *If Bardanes had gone along with us and gotten the correct advice,* Michael reflected in his stone cell, *he never would have led the rebellion.* But he did. Whereupon Leo and Michael defected to the imperial side, staunchly defending Nikephoros. Thomas, who was too frightened to trust anything Solon had told them, stayed put and fought on the side of the usurper Bardanes, who was forced to surrender, forfeit his property, and flee to a monastery where he later had his eyes put out.

Nikephoros rewarded Leo and Michael for their loyalty with their own palaces. Thomas, whose life was spared only by his immense popularity, managed to slink away with a total loss of property and a backwater posting. Nikephoros seethed with unfulfilled rage, commanding Thomas, "I never want to see you in Constantinople again."

But this was Byzantium, where the Fates threw dice instead of spinning threads. The half score and seven years that followed included a day in July 813 when, by means of a suspiciously arranged military disaster, Nikephoros lost his throne, and Leo the Armenian did indeed take the purple as predicted. Fearless and comfortable now, Leo promptly promoted his old companion, giving him sway over elite military forces. Michael received the *tagma* of the Excubitors, the most crucial of the professional guard cavalry regiments posted around Constantinople for it protected the emperor's palace. "How do you like being *Domestikos*?" Leo had asked.

"I appreciate your confidence in me," answered Michael gratefully, and he meant it. Considering that Solon had predicted the ascension of three emperors, the idea that Leo would put a rival in charge of his personal safety seemed like an unorthodox decision to say the least. This appointment of his was followed by an even stranger one regarding the third presumptive emperor.

Leo, apparently feeling indebted to Thomas—who had kept his secret about visiting oracles and considering rebellion—recalled the Slav from his penance in the outlands and put him in charge of a *tourma*, a regiment-sized division of the *Foederati*, stationed in the Anatolic Theme.

That opening was all that the ruthless staff officer needed. By 820, several more turns of the screw saw Thomas rise to control of all of Anatolia and become a close confidant of Leo's—serving as an ear-whispering poison dripper—while Michael sat chained to the rocks under the palace and wasn't sure how he got there.

Score two out of five predictions for Solon of Philomelion. He got it right regarding Bardanes' and Leo's respective fates. Possibly three or four correct if Thomas' highs and lows were any indication. The Slav could easily be on his way to becoming emperor and then courting disaster. The prophesy of greatness regarding Michael, however, coming from the first man to dare tag him Psellus, the Stutterer, seemed entirely without merit. *I should have let Thomas kill that cave-dwelling gold grubber.*

Now Michael sat in the dark musing that none of the events from Nikephoros' mysterious defeat by the Bulgars onward had made any sense to him at the time they happened. But with all of his days given over to thinking, he was beginning to discern the cold gray hand of truth.

CHAPTER 11

The Mese

<u>Constantinople, 820 A.D.</u>

A T FIRST ALL seemed well, extraordinary in its perfection. Her ascendance to the astral plane was the most beautiful thing Kreindia had ever experienced. Her consciousness unfolded like an opening flower, and she had the sensation of floating toward emancipating light. The lifting began with a gently increasing tug, first in one direction, and then another. It felt supportive, as though she were being guided by a guardian angel. Then the guiding force reached into her and found the part that was not meant to leave.

Suddenly, the conflicted pull increased in a rapid snap that made her gut clamp in violent spasms. Every fiber of her being split the way wool separates when drawn in two directions, a tapering filament of destruction and creation. The torture of forced decisions continued, sorting her filaments one way or the other among dwindling choices until that which was Del parted from that which remained. Profound pain racked Kreindia while her rising essence sorted and reassembled into an end product—a self that felt inexplicably hollow. She'd never known or recognized such emptiness before...

Amidst a cold rush of wind, the great avenue of Constantinople wrapped around her, leaving her shivering on the Mese, the main street west of the Senate houses, in what she hoped was the year 820. The day was young, the air thick with the myriad odors of a city trapped in humidity and yet sweet in proximity to the pastry vendors. There in the Eastern version of Rome, where Latin melted into Greek, where continuous civilization in a hostile world was only defensible from a walled peninsula with a secret weapon, a sense of self came back to her—the familiarity of what she had been for her entire conscious life, in the century to which she was accustomed.

Because she stood still, the people of her time buffeted her on all sides, clogging the way as thickly as the native fog cluttered the air. And there it was…the subtle tremor that swept the ground, the very hallmark of her home on the Black Sea, earthquakes big and small, the price of the city's greatness on the edge of two worlds.

She'd made it! On her own. Tears streamed from her eyes as she crossed her arms and slapped herself on the shoulders with joy. She *stood* there grateful, possessed of her own functioning limbs, albeit somewhat unsteady. No sooner did she put away the Norse figurine, than a woman burdened by a sack on one shoulder dealt her a glancing blow with the heavy load while trying to avoid a head-on collision.

The contact shook something loose in her mind. Kreindia suddenly remembered and her breath caught. The sprinkling of almonds. Mechanical cicadas spooling up her perceptions. Those were the blocks she had dealt with in the twenty-first century. They began to fall away now but for a lingering association. Or were there more blocks hidden? What sort of monster would steal her thoughts? *Who had the power?*

And the black box of memory opened and spilled…

~ *W* ~

"NO woman fights in my army," said commander Lucius Sergius Honoratus, glaring at the lady who dared recommend herself to him. Kreindia of Amorium was neither in charge here, nor could she take over by Byzantine law and bluff as she had once done on the deck of the dromon Delias. General's niece or not, in the Brenii Pass, the word of Honoratus held supreme. As the wind kicked up a snowdrift on the other side of the pass, she was one step from being cast in irons for persisting in disagreement.

Kreindia observed her Wade Linwood of Aquitaine frowning at Honoratus, sizing up his opposition. She wondered if Wade realized the danger he had called down in waking the sleeping Roman legion for a kind of warfare they'd never seen firsthand. She decided he did. While they shivered in the Tyrolean Alps, exposed to potential fire from an unseen enemy, in Wade she saw bravery, respect for her and her mission, and a myriad of tantalizing facets she had scant time to ponder. Without conscious communication between them, she was certain he thought as she did, that this uneven battle might come down to the last man and she would not want to be unarmed in such a circumstance.

Honoratus signaled one of his men for the promised shackles.

"No, wait!" Wade faced the commander. "Don't your forces include positions other than fighting troops?"

"Yes," said Honoratus, sounding impatient and distracted. "Some soldiers are exempt. Surveyors, medical orderlies, huntsmen, horse trainers, water engineers, swordcutlers…"

"What about scribes?"

The commander's eyes glimmered with comprehension. "Going into battle, we will need more than the one we have, in order to observe the different points of reference." As a piece of living history himself, he obviously cared about how he and his troops were represented.

"Kreindia is a scribe by profession," Wade offered.

Nodding slightly in acquiescence, Honoratus called out

a man with the gentle build of a scholar. He bore a sack of parchments and a pouch of quills from which he dispensed one each.

Kreindia took them as though they were sacred relics. These were riches anywhere, and far more precious outside of Constantinople. To Honoratus, who was already on the move, she said, "You do me a great honor, which I proudly accept."

Spotting the hilt of the scribe's field weapon, a wispy smile came to her lips, and she added quietly, "Still, I will fight if it comes to it."

As Wade must have known when he made the suggestion, the legion's record maker was a noncombatant, but armed due to his proximity to battle. Kreindia scanned the field for a supply master, and bit her lip hoping she could find one in time.

"Ready the ambush," shouted centurion Pansa, causing the signal bearers to respond with yellow triangular flags. A third of the force mobilized at Pansa's word. In this isolated conclave, no discipline had been lost in the Roman army as they awaited the opportunity to forge a re-united Europe.

At that moment, a great wall of a man arrived panting horse-sized gouts of steaming breath. A cleft beard framed his face and formed twin icicles below. Kreindia nearly swooned. She recognized him from her visions. Saxon born, barbarian raised, and then reborn as a loyal warrior-scholar under Charlemagne. The most extraordinary puzzle of a man after Wade himself—her first look at Grimketil Forkbeard in the flesh, resettling the drapery of his woolen mantle, an incongruous Roman chlamys over his foreign vest of mail.

Behind him, two more from her visions came to life. The infamous Snorri, looking dry and wiry, half-carried a hobbled Tankred who'd slowed the party sufficiently for the armed Roman escort to keep up. Tankred's bowed and tonsured head looked almost like the roundel of a shield. It bobbed up just once, and she could see him wincing in pain. Someone supplied fresh bandages for the oblate of Sintlas Ow and found a place for him to lean.

Kreindia noticed Wade regarding Grimketil with the sort of twitchy smile a son might offer to a father who would not suffer trifling emotions. His expression sobered when he caught the concern in the senior man's face, a battle mindset that would not allow for much else.

Grimketil advised Honoratus, "You will have no time to make an ambush. Raginpert's men are less than a tenth of a day behind us."

A scout arriving in Snorri's wake grudgingly confirmed to Honoratus that the front of the enemy line had been spotted at a short distance. The commander made quiet calculations and looked to his centurion while the scout squinted at the suspicious newcomers.

Wade glanced at Kreindia for some assurance, and then grasped Grimketil's hand, embraced the valiant yet ghostly oblate, and retreated from Snorri, who had raised his chin to ward off all contact. While Wade got through the introductions swiftly, he took care to say "Grimketil of Lowestoft," rather than risking a volatile reaction by calling him "The Saxon," or "Grimketil Forkbeard." Snorri, though also a Saxon, and duly introduced, would not trouble himself to speak no matter what he was called. To Kreindia's surprise, Wade also remembered the full titles and names of the recently met commander Lucius Sergius Honoratus, and centurion princeps, Gneaus Horatius Armiger. Centurion Pansa had left them, but she suspected Wade would have recited his sizable appellation as well.

Only when the formalities had been put right did Centurion Armiger answer Grimketil with undaunted pride, "You are wrong to think that our options are so limited. We have drilled for this eventuality and prepared this ground for three hundred years." He addressed them all. "We have our attacks coordinated. Do not join the fight until we give you the signal." With a murmur of agreement, the group broke up to find their places.

For his part, Wade sneezed three times in a row, confirming the wisdom of the last statement. He pinched his nose as though he would stop a fourth.

The group had scarcely separated when a savage pain in the head jolted the general's niece. She saw herself toppling sideward in what must have been the near future, the disarrayed battlefield in red, her eyes covered in blood. She lost her quill and reached for her sword, but her hand fell away limp. Undefended and injured, her life fluids drained until she felt like a soap bubble that could float to the heavens. With that, her mind's image of the field froze as though there would never be anything more to see.

As the vision retreated, she solidified, her vessel of flesh filled and her ordinary sight returned. Whatever she had done during the vision somehow got Wade's attention. He stared at her in alarm, and she realized she was digging her fingers into his arm through the tunic.

Kreindia said, "Wade, I just saw…something. We need to get out of here when the battle is almost won. Someone else can finish the treaty. Promise me we'll go."

Wade regarded her tenderly with his rich brown eyes while the Roman camp swirled with activity around them. From previous conversations with her, he would have understood that she was asking for passage on the astral plane from her time and place to that of his origin. Though a creature of crossed senses himself, a fellow synesthete, he did not yet experience the visions Kreindia had, if he ever would. Nonetheless, he apparently came to a decision not to question her, and said, "I promise."

They kissed and held each other a moment longer than they had a right to under the impending war, and then they hurried to their separate tasks.

The armicustos found Kreindia before she found him. From the girth of his biceps, he must have doubled as the army's sword cutler, which made sense since the doling out of weapons would have been a slow business while the growing legion lay hidden from the world in the passing centuries.

"By order of the commander, I am to issue you a temporary field weapon." His flat tone and hard stare made it clear he did not approve of this favor, and he added, "You are to use it only if the enemy advances to your position and you cannot retreat." When she acknowledged the conditions, he suffered the release of a sword and sheath that were together as long as her arm with hand outstretched. That was the short sword known as the gladius, and she found much to be admired in its sturdy design. The latter day legion did not skimp on craftsmanship. The ornate scabbard of the Children of Romulus bore the image of the final imperator, a mere adolescent himself when overthrown by Odoacer.

The armicustos made her sign for it.

Kreindia climbed mounds of dirt and rock until she claimed an unobstructed view into the valley. She situated herself behind an irregular outcrop that would serve as a stadium seat after the surprise attack was sprung.

Inking her quill, she began her notes with a somber assessment on the impending clash. The legacy of the Roman Empire—the fragment before her—consisted of a single legion of descendants, barely legion-sized, and it was a miracle to have that. The tattered refugees lasted only in secret and grew to fighting strength with the passage of more than four hundred years. Though her mind rejected math, her work as a historian sometimes made the attempt necessary. If the defenders had created for themselves a five to one advantage by surprise and terrain, then wiping out an enemy equal to their number would cost them one thousand men. If, however, Raginpert's army were eight thousand as expected, that could put Roman losses at sixteen hundred or more. It would be a crippling price to pay even if they won. The legion could not afford decimation; they had no source of replacements should they need to fight again, and this would be more than thrice decimation, a commitment that could end their history. Though the legion had never operated under battle conditions, this conflict had to be decisive if nothing else.

At stake was the *Pax Nicephori*, the peace treaty between two out of three of the world's superpowers—the Holy Roman Empire and Byzantium—standing against Persia and the barbarian hoards. When Prince Raginpert had kidnapped Kreindia, she discovered his intention to attack Louis, the unready son of Charlemagne, under banners and regimental decoration that would look to anyone to be that of Byzantium. Once shattering the treaty Nicephoros had brokered, Raginpert would allow the two outraged nations to deplete each other, after which he hoped to have the only viable military. According to her vision, she and Wade would not be there to see it through—

~ *W* ~

THE trance broke before retracing their astral escape. Kreindia was left wondering who had interfered with her transition to the twenty-first century.

"Pardon me," the lady who'd bumped into her said with some irritation, "I didn't see you there." The woman hurried away on the stone path with only one glance back, to be reclaimed by the ordinary. In this city like no other, no one questioned surprises too closely. Kreindia had to trust that the unfurling memory would return and that Wade would, as well. Meanwhile she had her uncle to deal with.

Although her view was partially blocked by the marbled Senate complex, by the great column in the Forum of Constantine, and by the jostling crowds, she knew that the palaces and everything that she sought lay ahead of her in the rolling fog to the east. She would pass through the forum and gaze down the hill at the hippodrome and her beloved, tragic Hagia Sofia beyond. There in the church, a more serious earthquake had claimed her best friend Verina. Kreindia shuddered and took off at a brisk walk. Unused to astral travel, it seemed as though she'd been away forever. In a sense, she had been. Twelve hundred years, and then looped back to a time knocked slightly out of joint by the seven year span between her departure from the capital and now. As though the world had swept inside out only to be reversed again, the worse for wear.

Rubbing her bruised shoulder, she found that the many changes she observed on the Mese made her queasy. In this exclusive district, some of the best shops had been boarded shut on their sheltering porticos. She recognized a footwear store behind a column where she saw weeds merging with the shrubbery. Copious dirt and refuse sullied the walk. She'd found the city in hard times.

But the broad street teemed with harried bargain hunters, and sun pierced the cold air. How she relished being back, and the prize of her freedom. And most of all, she had her body! Using her own two feet seemed to put her at a startling height after the wheelchair. She had the exquisite pleasure of being able to stand, to be able to take a step—

Something slammed into her from behind, knocking her into the foliage and trash. "Hide!" a harsh whisper urged in her ear. "What's the matter with you?" the voice demanded.

Stunned, she put up ineffective resistance as she was yanked to her feet and hauled inside the derelict building. Door shut, the sudden dark twinkled with pinpricks. Streaky light from shuttered windows illuminated dust and random corners of a musty, unfurnished room strewn with rubbish.

A man spun her to face his murky silhouette. "Are you insane, traipsing around in public?"

She squinted to try to see something. He seemed familiar. "I don't—"

"Descriptions of you are everywhere. Dark hair,

powder blue eyes, Phrygian features, mmph. You are the most wanted woman in the world. I could get rich off you…"

"There must be some mistake."

"Are you Amorian?"

"Yes."

"Are you Kreindia of Amorium?" he demanded.

"Yes!"

"Then there is no mistake…my lady." His last words came spiked with sarcasm. What could have happened to spoil her reputation during her seven-year absence?

Kreindia teased a glimmer of recognition out of the darkness now that the high-strung voice had turned ugly. She knew this man from the court at Constantinople. Keyx was a lowly cousin to a count, a peon who tried not to be noticed lest someone put him to work. The elaborate silver stickpin at his throat today seemed to suggest he'd grown far more prosperous since she'd known him. She had a feeling that his latest good fortune did not stem from honest labor.

"I've done nothing," she informed him coldly. "I've been away in the Frankish kingdom a long time."

"Away a long time," he echoed with a bitter laugh. "Michael of Amorium's niece. You can be put to death for that."

"*General* Michael—" she bristled.

"General Worthless. He's a traitor."

She said, "Nonsense. Michael's like a brother to Leo. He loves him."

"Please! They uncovered your uncle's plot to take the throne from Leo."

"He had no such plans."

He stared narrow-eyed at her for a moment. "Your Aunt Thekla put him up to it when Leo divorced her sister, Theodosia. I guess it's possible you didn't know. It's a whole different world to the west of us, isn't it? No one there knows anything."

104

"But if my uncle is out of favor, then you're a traitor as well for shielding me."

His cheeks rounded with amusement. "That I am, a regular outlaw, I suppose. You're lucky I was here." The gathering light resolved his spreading smile, turning wolfish. He wasn't a big man, rather a small one, but they were alone.

"Don't get any ideas," she warned. "I have a knife in my hand."

"No," he countered, "No, you don't. I can see that well enough."

"I have worse than a knife on me if you care to find out. A Chinese weapon from the Taoist lord."

"I'll bet, but you don't have to worry," he said with his eye to a chink in the window boards. "I'm not the emperor's man…" The light illuminated a stripe of his face, making his darting eye appear to be mounted on the middle of a stick. "They have him, you know."

"My uncle?"

"In the dungeon, sentenced to death," he said cheerfully.

She also took to watching the street, to see what he saw, some boys playing irresponsibly with a pole and a ball. The ball ricocheted off a store's doorframe as a customer was exiting, and then the lady storekeeper chased them. The woman got hold of the pole and kept it but slipped on the ball to fall on her rump. During that mishap, the kids got away. No one seemed to take notice that she and Keyx had disappeared into an abandoned building. Kreindia said, "If that's true, why haven't they done it then?"

"Done what?" he asked absently.

"Why haven't they executed him?"

Keyx rounded on her. "Because of you. And for the same reason, Michael's kept his eyes. The emperor wants you slain in front of Michael before he can die." Keyx seemed entirely too gleeful about the prospect. "I guess the pressure finally flushed you out. Where have you been hiding—no, don't tell me—just go slink back there before the end of Christmas. That's their deadline. I can't help you."

"In that case, I'll take my chances."

He blocked her from going out, saying, "I only meant I cannot help you unless you have access to gold...or can pay me another way." With that, he reached to caress her hip.

Suddenly she had the metal Norseman balled in her hand, exposing only the pike, which she lodged under his chin. "I didn't ask for your help, Keyx," she said, grabbing him by his tunic, his chest hairs bound into her fist. "But mark me, you lowlife filth, if my uncle dies, you die." She'd been raised by her uncle, in front of his troops, and had the tone of command that men found arresting, especially when it issued from her. The instincts with which she acted were all her own.

Keyx paled at this rare behavior by a woman. He must have thought her a demon spawn. "What has possessed you?" he gasped. "I told you I have nothing to do with it."

She twisted harder, eliciting a yelp from him, and said, "Did you think you could let Michael rot while the rest of your conspirators waited for a more convenient time? Then who would become emperor? You?"

"There...uh."

She pushed the little axe point into his soft flesh to draw a syrupy trickle.

"Ow, okay! There may have been a few more people involved in the plot. Maybe even me. But what would you have me do?"

"I want your loyalty."

"For what?"

"Get me into the palace or I'll get myself in. If I have to do it on my own—unseat Leo at the head of my own force—I will. Then you'll be less than welcome in Michael's court, and you'll have your own eyes to worry about."

When understanding dawned on his features and he said, "You have my word," she released him.

Taking a step back, Keyx checked to see if his stickpin was all right as he smoothed his tunic. "If you want to visit him in the dungeon, you'll need a better disguise than those strange clothes you wear. But they do call you Kreindia the Strange, don't they?" Seeing her reaction, he added sourly, "I said you have my oath, woman. I'll serve you, for what it's worth."

With a cutting stare, she said, "You lead me to the general. I'll worry about the rest. Now hand over that impressive padded cloak, and I'll start dressing better right now."

Reluctantly, he shed the cloak and then headed for the door.

"Stop!" she said.

"Oh what do you want from me now?"

"There are soldiers!" She had her eye to the window. "Only two of them. No, four."

"Let's go out the back."

"No, wait." Kreindia watched the soldiers talking to the shopkeeper who was now animated. With a furtive shift of her robe, the merchant accepted a small pouch. Kreindia stiffened in shock as the woman used the kids' pole to point in their direction. "So she *was* watching us."

"The back!"

"No, they'll have that covered. There's a side exit that connects to an adjoining store. Find it. Go."

From the rubble she selected something to bar the front door. The bolt had been robbed from its slide, but she looped and tied the leather straps of a broken boot around the hooks, and then crouched to work on the lower part of the frame where a nail protruded. Outside, someone collided with a mess of bottles in the weeds.

Keyx rattled the side exit. "It's stuck," he complained with rising fear.

"Put your shoulder to it," she hissed as the front door abruptly swung a finger's width to creak against the leather. The shouted orders from outside came through clearly, covering Kreindia's efforts to shore up their defenses, and the sound of the soldier's first shuddering blow covered Keyx' last shoulder slam. At the same time as the leather bindings holding the main entrance strained to a hand's width, Keyx tumbled through to a lit area of the neighboring store. Kreindia followed him, both of them blundering into a stack of boxes on the other side.

Resealing the passage, she heard the soldier break through and go down in a clatter of armor as she knew he would, given the tripwire she'd left behind. "He'll be disoriented by the dark," she said, helping Keyx replace the boxes against the entrance. "For a while, they won't be sure we were even there. There could have been vagrants holed up in that store for all they know."

They turned to face an astonished old woman and her customers. These occupants had been in the middle of passing a large wheel of amber-colored wool, and both parties remained holding it in mid-pass.

Kreindia strode forward, gave the wrinkled cheek a kiss, and said, "Cover me, Eudokia. I need a way out of here."

Still rigid with surprise, Eudokia said, "Sure. Why not, Kreindia? Happens all the time. Come again."

Keyx said to Kreindia, "You must be one heck of a customer here."

"I used to be."

The fugitives continued to the next exit, hurrying through the back streets. A tan mutt, aroused by their urgency, broke its leash to trot alongside them and bark. Its owner appeared, also at a run, yelling, "Fallow, get back here!"

Kreindia assured Keyx, "She'll do it for us. Eudokia will be fine."

"Why did you make us wait to stare at the guards for so

long?" Keyx asked. "What was it you wanted to see out there so badly?"

"Did you make out their red sashes?"

"No."

"Those were Anatolian Foederati," she said harshly.

With an elusive shrug, he looked away and said, "I don't know anything about that."

"Answer me, damn you. What were they doing here?"

"The Amorians are Anatolian," he said with care as though working out a puzzle. "Officials in your home town were accused of hiding you. They probably want to show that they are looking."

"The Anatolian Foederati are run by Thomas the Slav," she shot back. "He's obviously the one who betrayed Michael."

"Yes, there is that. Ironic, isn't it, that Thomas has more power over your homeland than Michael and you do."

She stopped. "Do you have an illness of the mind?"

"Well, I've been told—"

"While you are in my service I don't want to hear what you think is ironic. If Thomas is involved, that's two forces we're fighting."

"Yes, and Thomas doesn't like your family one bit."

She closed her eyes in exasperation. "I don't want to hear *anything* of what you think."

CHAPTER 12

Loss and Loss

MICHAEL FOUND HIMSELF roused from sleep by keen hunger. No one had left him food and drink for a long time. He would have smelled it. He half-stood and stopped with a jolt, having forgotten that his chains would not allow him to fully rise. He crawled forward to check the slot, finding it empty and frantically sweeping the filthy surface to make sure. There was a spot in his cell that Michael was well acquainted with and he made his way over to it now as it dripped continually to form beneath it a small pool of brackish water. The acid bite in the darkness reminded him again of the caves of Solon of Philomelion. Only this time, he reflected that the self-same event—his support of Nikephoros over Bardanes—had led to both the world's greatest triumph and his greatest personal losses. Moreover, they were all ineluctably tied together in the fallout from the Avar wars. So complicated, so Byzantine...

Michael's aid to Nikephoros, who had recently overthrown Irene of Athens, generated the one source of friction between himself and his niece Kreindia, who had worshipped Irene as a saint. She and the former queen-basileus were both of the icon-loving camp in a dispute that oscillated to extremes with each new ruler, and that vicissitude was undoubtedly one of the factors that felled the Athenian. Irene was doomed no matter what.

But of all the pretenders, Michael supported Nikephoros again and again. Without Nikephoros there would have been no *Pax Nicephori*, halting the hostilities between the Franks and the Byzantines. The trouble had been instigated in the days of Irene when Charlemagne defeated the Avars and rewarded himself with some territory that technically belonged to the Imperium. Irene, whose proposed marriage to Charlemagne had fallen through, could not have settled a peace treaty with him after that. And the preservation of the *Pax Nicephori*, of course, was the very reason that Michael had sent Kreindia to the war zone in the West, and the reason she was never heard from again. He closed his eyes in pain, regretting every one of his calculations now.

"If I send you to the West," Michael had warned Kreindia seven years earlier, "you will get no assistance whatsoever from the Imperium. Our enemies mustn't be tipped off as to the true nature and import of your mission." They were strolling along the sea wall from the main palace to the harbor palace of Boucoleon at twilight the day before she was to board a ship bound for Venezia. He was giving her one last chance to change her mind, and secretly wishing she would take it.

"Don't worry," said Kreindia, her blue eyes solemn, "Just like you, I'm an Amorian, a Phrygian, an Athinganoi—"

"—and my closest living relative." Since her father had died, Michael had kept her with him on his military campaigns and revealed to her their unusual heritage.

"Yes, Uncle. That's how I know that an Amorian would rather die than surrender, a Phrygian is the stock of legendary kings—Gordian, Midas, and Mygdon—and the Athinganoi, the Untouchables, are the warrior class of Byzantium. You see, I've learned."

"Recitation is not practice."

"You need to trust—"

"I'm trusting you with everything!" he burst out. "Based on visions!"

"You said yourself that Malki Tsadek's visions are the reason our people exist. And Wade of Aquitaine, whom I will depend upon, is the most powerful synesthete since Malki Tsadek." Tsadek was the putative founder of their Melchisedechian faith.

"So you tell me. You place a great deal of trust in this Wade of Aquitaine that you've never met."

"You would too if you could see what I've seen and what's at stake." Kreindia had reported to him that the frustrated Longobard prince, Raginpert the Insolent, would raise a great army to savage the peace between the world's two superpowers. She did not know how he would go about it or how to prevent him from acting. Her plan was to get close and enlist as much surreptitious aid as possible.

"I hope you're right," said Michael.

"You've risked everything before, and you did it on the word of Solon the monk," she accused.

Michael snorted, "If he's right about more than Leo, it's a long time coming."

"I never vouched for him, did I?" It was a rhetorical question. Unlike the Solons of the world, whose visions could be paid for and tapped on demand, hers did not work that way. She had a deep distrust of those who managed the convenient trick.

Presently, they came to the Terrace of the Pharos, and were obliged to follow its detour around the three-tiered lighthouse column. In that spot, which extended over the strait, they paused, listening to the ocean gnashing its teeth on the base of the wall. A spread of night-darkened clouds loomed and grew as the wind drove them into the city. Behind those came an endless supply.

Michael was thoughtful. "This Wade of yours, does he suffer visions like the ones you have?"

Kreindia said, "I don't think so…maybe he will

someday."

"He's unaware of you, then?"

"For the most part."

"He's unaware that you are the voice that calls him here," Michael pressed.

"I know him from my dreams. He would want to help."

"He doesn't know the risks."

Her eyes glistened with incipient tears that she had to fight back. "I've told you," she continued, "certain things have to happen, the good along with the horrible. I don't control the Fates."

"The Fates..." He searched the unsettled ocean for an answer, and then faced her. "You find that reason enough to worship icons of Christ and carry one of Irene?"

"I don't worship them. I favor them to heal our people's rifts. The powers of the civilized world are Christian, and in the long run, Christians will never accept the destruction of icons. I've seen it. That's future history."

"And your current peril."

Michael grew restless and walked on. Kreindia kept up as the seawall led them to the gargantuan pair of terrifying statues—the bull and lion—that gave the Boucoleon palace its name. Each beast hunched in powerful triangular repose, the broad-shouldered bull representing irresistible strength and vitality. The bovine had enormous hooves and haunches and a painfully compact face that stared a challenge to all who approached.

The lion, a classical guardian in every known culture, had gigantic paws, legs like columns up to its flowing mane, and a neckless, upturned face with bulging eyes that alternately seemed to look remorselessly down its nose or peer to the Heavens for strength. Kreindia had told her uncle that just the sight of the lion's peculiar set of shapes alit on her tongue like cold, bitter steel. Such an odd young woman she was, even to Michael.

A duplicate pair of statues, even larger, faced the sea so that foreign ships and visiting dignitaries could understand what they would be up against if they were so foolish as to become adversaries to the Imperium. Each of the figures, short-faced like Chinese Fu Dogs and invested with extraordinary power in their limbs, scared the city's residents nearly as much as their enemies. The Boucoleon statues were the reason that he and Kreindia could have their privacy on the wall. Starkos, the priest, had once told him, "In the year 1000 when all the Western world is Christian, these blasphemies must be hauled away and destroyed." The clergy didn't want them gone any sooner because they seemed to be working against the heathens.

Kreindia said, "I love these beasts even as I fear them."

"Where are they from, do you suppose? We've never conquered the Far East. At least, I don't believe so."

She smiled. "They're actually Syrian neo-Hittite designs from north of Damascus two thousand years ago. Their heads are small and their bodies gigantic to issue the threat that they will set aside all reason in the pursuit of conquering an enemy."

"Ever my scholar," Michael laughed. "But you and I know that's not the truth of it. The day that the world sets aside all reason, even our Boucoleon fortress will fall."

They almost missed it near the looming entrance. A shooting star, come early in the twilight, appeared to plunk right into the thrashing sea in front of them. Michael was about to ask Kreindia if that event meant anything, but as they passed under the palace arch, something must have alarmed her—perhaps a twinkle in her peripheral vision—and made her back up to look again. "Signal flashes," she cried. "We're under attack."

Michael studied the hills near Chalcedon and confirmed that partially obscured lights flashed a coded blinking pattern. The blood drained from his face. "You're right. This part of the message seems to say that Anatolia is beset by Abbasids. Dammit, I can't see well enough from this angle."

"Why isn't our own beam swiveled inward to spread the alarm to the city?"

They bolted to the lighthouse to find out. Breaching the entrance, they took the four flights of winding steps to the very top. Behind an unlocked door they found the beacon unmanned, every corner abandoned, the furnace growing weak.

Trying to catch her breath, Kreindia gasped, "Something is very wrong here."

Given the greater view to the opposite shore, Michael read off the bad news, "Amorium itself is besieged!"

With a straining shift of the levers, they swung the great barrel around and Michael worked the shutters to repeat the warning from across the channel to the next inland station.

"That's all we can do from here," said Michael. "Let's go find out what's gone wrong on our side of the channel."

They pounded their way back down the stairs and ran straight into Thomas. He and eight of his elite, red-sashed *Foederati*-at-arms ranged across the terrace like a forbidding wall.

Michael had heard of Thomas' recall from exile among the Arabs, but this was the first he'd seen of the outcast since the Bardanes uprising. The Slav's cheekbones crowded his eyes under close-cropped black hair, his chin crowded his curly lips, and his pinched nose dipped like a hawk's beak. How did Leo trust such a face, and what right did Thomas have to bar his way? The Slav looked pleased with himself too.

"P-p-p-Pontus," said Michael, his old stuttering habit acting up.

"You can clamp off the lantern and belay the warning," said Thomas to Michael. "It won't be necessary." When Michael didn't move to obey him, Thomas turned and shouted, "Brygos, see to it!"

A soldier brushed roughly past them and bounded up the lighthouse stairs.

"What are you talking about?" Michael demanded. "What in hell is going on, Thomas?"

"There is no attack. I had the flares lit and the lighthouse keepers relieved as a test, a war game. You seem to have run afoul of it."

Michael darkened. "You s-should have told me about this. You'll be sent packing before daybreak for this incompetence."

"Maybe and maybe not. For some reason I can't fathom," said Thomas too calmly, "Leo doesn't entirely trust you, Michael. I don't think he'll listen to a word of criticism about me."

"That's crazy."

"Is it? Don't you suppose he's brought me back to Constantiniple in order to balance the potential threat to him from you? That's what any reasonable person would think."

Michael wouldn't admit it, but this was the unavoidable conclusion that he had begun to suspect. Although Leo appeared to have entrusted him with his personal safety, the basileus had set everything up with what he saw as checks and balances, starting with giving Michael a low rank at court even though he held the second highest rank in the military. The double system had never been used so. But bringing back the questionable person of Thomas and giving him the elite *Foederati* was the worst idea Leo ever had.

"Excuse us," Michael said bitterly. To cut short their unpleasant encounter, he ushered Kreindia back towards Boucoleon, and the soldiers stepped aside to allow their retreat. As they hurried along the sea boundary, the lights on the horizon extinguished, the city-facing lighthouse on the other shore closed down. The sun had set by then, and darkness seemed to wholly envelop them before they could see the small guttering of sconces along their path.

"What are you going to do?" Kreindia asked the general. "You can't let him get away with this."

"If I can, I'm going to find a way to lock Thomas out of the court."

From that point forward, however, Kreindia traveled under a cloud. Michael managed to hinder Thomas for a long time, but locking the *Foederati* commander out would prove impossible...

Seven years hence, Michael sat up at the long echoes of approaching footsteps in the dungeon corridors. The sound of a latch giving way rang through the chamber. His stomach awakened and growled.

"It's about time you brought my food," he yelled.

When the door swung open, there stood Thomas the Slav in the harsh light of two torchbearers. Since their Boucoleon encounter, the man had thinned and matured still further, leaving his features incised on a skin canvas of lines and bumps. Although he'd lost little of his bristle of hair, his curly lips had hardened into a permanent sneer, and his nose ran even sharper. He wore the clasp of the *Domestikos*, which had been Michael's title, and retained the badge of his *Foederati* command as well. "Stand up out of the mud," he commanded Michael.

"If you are man enough to remove these chains, I will. Or you can step closer and I'll wrap them around your traitorous throat."

"I never liked you," said Thomas, accepting the passed food and drink from the tray keeper and then tossing it in Michael's general direction so that it hit the stone floor and sprayed out.

Michael looked at the mess and swallowed involuntarily, but made no move toward it. "By coming here," he said, "you confirm your role in my imprisonment for all to see." This was now the third time Thomas had intersected his life, and the first in undisguised conflict.

Thomas said, "Yes, I suppose that's true, and that's all

right now. To be honest, I was afraid that our plans for you and your kin had been spoiled. Not to worry though, old friend. Kreindia the Strange has been spotted and we know her intentions. That will make her easy to catch."

Michael went cold. "You lie."

"You will see for yourself soon enough. With my manpower, her capture is assured."

"Does Leo know what you've done?"

Thomas' wretched mouth made for an ugly smile. "He knows. It looks like you will be dead by Christmas after all. We'll throw you in the furnace and we'll have your icon-worshipping niece there as witness."

CHAPTER 13

Her Past in the Future

"I'M NOT LETTING you out of my sight until this is over, Keyx."

"Then you will be watching me relieve myself," he quipped.

"Turn here," she said at the crux of the corridor. They had been secreted by Kreindia's friends in a back room in the dank mausoleum of Constantine at the Church of the Holy Apostles. The oldest holy site in the city, the repository was begun and dedicated by Constantine himself, and rebuilt by Justinian. Kreindia found life under the giant turret with the bones of five hundred years of emperors oppressive. She and Keyx escaped that section, both of them hooded, to stretch their legs in the church proper. Their footsteps echoed under the arches and columns in the long Western arm of the cruciform.

"What is your plan?" Keyx asked. "And will it mesh with your uncle's plan? The general's design will be a more brutal one, I would imagine."

"You don't know him as I do." If Kreindia truly understood her uncle, the only person now living who would end up a permanent resident in the mausoleum—and only if necessary—would be Leo himself. Michael would want a bloodless coup to keep governmental disruption at a minimum and make the outcome more certain. The sole path to a bloodless coup was to acquire allies in the three unofficial branches of government—the clergy, the military, and the bureaucracy. Some of those offices overlapped handily with the Senate nobles. That meant that Michael must have lined up such a group.

Kreindia's options were narrow. The only way to break someone out of a Byzantine prison was to appeal to the people on the directory of the disaffected, and the only one she could imagine in possession of such a register was Michael, who was trapped and guarded under a thousand tons of stone. If she somehow got past this enormous problem and worked from the list in question, the only way to impress the conspirators with her leadership was to show them power. She didn't have the stomach or even the will to take anyone's eyes, so she would have to find another way. It would be a delicate balance. She said, "Whatever we do has to happen very fast."

"That's not a plan."

"My plan, Keyx, is for you to know what little you need to know and no more than that. Your activities will be the ones I proscribe and nothing else. I'll have someone watching you."

He looked hurt. "Do you think I'm the sort of person who would sell you out?"

"Let's just say I don't want to put you in a tempting position. You can get your rewards when we win."

"All I ask," he said with a careless gesture and a sigh, "is that you make me a wealthy man."

At a touch from Keyx, the same spot as her glancing contact with the woman on the Mese, Kreindia replicated the earlier sense of a box that spilled hidden memories ...

~ *W* ~

FROM her perch behind a screen of branches, Kreindia spied the whole of Honoratus' plan—Roman in its methods, barbarian in its inspiration. It was a variation on the strategy used by Arminius at the battle of

Teutoburg Forest to wrest the new province of Germania back from the Romans. The Germanic-born leader had used both natural barriers and prepared walls along constricted escape routes to spread their opponents thin and provide cover for the ambush.

In the Brenii Pass, the legionnaires commanded a sweeping view into the valley from their high ground on two sides of their enemy from which they planned to lay down crossfire and surround them in combat. With the Longobards forced into a narrow file, they could not use their numerical advantage to overwhelm the legion, though they could still win a war of attrition. It would take enormous discipline and good fortune for the kind of triumph either side needed.

With the advance preparation complete, Honoratus' army vanished and went silent. So skilled were they from their many years of hiding, that the mountain fauna resumed their business as though the human presence were no threat to them.

The Romans waited until the first of Raginpert's army reached the mid-point of the mountain's saddle. Kreindia could see the lines of men stretching into the distance. She could not see the camouflaged Romans that shadowed and hemmed them in.

Raginpert's men were fully armed and decorated for war, though not in battle formation. Although they were supposed to be loyal subjects of the Holy Roman Empire, the Longobards moved under a false flag of green with the crescent-moon and sheltered star of Kreindia's homeland. The strategy fooled no one here.

At the call of a hawk, the first wave of Roman soldiers fell on the long line, visiting total surprise and abject confusion on the front fifth of Raginpert's army. Behind that wave, soldiers bearing shovels found their predetermined trench lines, and shifted the dirt to reveal the foundation of a wall. A second row of builders levered pre-positioned stones on top, allowing their fortifications to accumulate at a staggering rate. Archers stood ready behind the new defensive lines appearing in the notches.

A few of the Longobards must have been ill-recruited for they broke down in uselessness from their terror. Most however, appeared enraged at the ambush so far from where they expected to fight. They could not have guessed at the nature and scope of the forces that awaited them in the passage from Itale to Swabia. The Longobards surged forward, probably thinking that they outnumbered the local attackers by hundreds to one, and could win easily if they could reach their tormentors. Prince Raginpert, his long hair flying loose to show rank, rode forward to instill discipline. At three lengths from the enemy he stopped and took his mount into a full-turn rollback, apparently confused when he did not encounter angry provincials but this strange anachronistic force in Roman armor instead. On his next attempt to advance, his horse stumbled on the piles of dead and dying men in its path, dragging him down to the morass.

The Roman trench diggers had left gaps so that their survivors of the first wave could fall back to fight from behind the defensive works. They took that option in the instant, vacating the lower field of battle as another fifth of Raginpert's army struggled forward. This group of Longobards was less shaken by the surprise visited on the first to come into range and was encouraged to see what they imagined to be a retreat.

As the Longobards gave chase, Honoratus himself rose out of hiding and dropped his hand, shouting, "Now." A cloud of arrows darkened the air, reached down and struck true. He had reversed the conventional order of attack in which missiles came first! Few of the enemy archers were prepared to answer. Another rank was decimated. Many more were injured.

Each group of legionnaires remained secreted until they joined the action. Honoratus had grouped Wade and his friends in the elite second wave, those who would have the more difficult task of hand-to-hand combat after the initial surprise wore off. Grimketil and Snorri, bringing Tankred, had slipped forward to position themselves at the very edge of prepared hiding places. Following the artillery barrage, all three of them got out ahead, running down slope to strike their early blows. Kreindia could see Wade rushing to catch up.

Tankred preserved his energy by launching two throwing axes at those who had ventured close thinking him an easy target. He could never have grappled with anyone in his condition but managed to fell the pair before a single slash of a blade from another attacker cleaved his ribs, knocking him on his back. His assailant stepped in and hacked at his face a few times as Tankred answered blindly with knife jabs. Kreindia made special note of the oblate's bravery in the face of certain death. She had to hold onto her battle resolve with an iron will to keep from breaking down.

Grimketil skewered Tankred's killer through the neck, slung the oblate over his shoulder, and fought his way to the earthen and stone walls one-handed.

Suffering despite her façade, Kreindia located Snorri, who led a charge that was overzealous even for his reputation. Leaving support behind, he struck deep within enemy lines as though he needed a place to swing only at foes. Kreindia realized that it might have been his intention to strike at the leadership and end the conflict quickly. If so, he'd attracted too much attention. Now he had the misfortune of engaging in desperate battle with an elite ring of foes, including Raginpert himself. While Snorri dispatched one opponent and ended the career of another, the rebel prince stuck a sword deep in the Saxon's shoulder, hobbling his formidable arm.

Then Wade was in the thick of it himself, fighting his way in the direction of Raginpert. At the speed of battle, it seemed that too many people stood in the way for him to aid Snorri in time.

As Snorri suffered harrying attacks from all sides at Raginpert's direction, Kreindia witnessed the Longobard leader open his windpipe in one clean blow. Though obliged to observe and record history, she reflexively turned away for a moment and could not hold back a sob. She did not avert her gaze long enough though, for Raginpert was diligently hacking his way through the rest of the neck. When the prince raised the head of Grimketil's companion by its hair as a war trophy, Kreindia felt bile rise in her throat.

Her apprehension doubled when Wade, with two Roman soldiers beside him, reached Raginpert. She could not hear what Wade said to the escorts, but the two attacked Raginpert's support. Wade could now deal with the rebel leader alone.

Kreindia shivered, remembering well the endless period when Raginpert kept her like an animal in a cage, twice attempting to violate her when he let her emerge. She knew that Wade desired payback for what Raginpert had done. Yet Wade had no more than his keen reflexes, the swordsmanship he had learned in Constantinople, and two prior battles. As a ward of the royal court in Pavia, Raginpert would likely be familiar with every move Wade had been trained in. Her heart raced and she realized that her cheeks were covered in helpless tears. Given that the prince had prepared since boyhood, Wade stood no rational chance. Unless he could pull off a complete surprise...

In the moment it took Raginpert to discard Snorri's head, Wade struck, springing an entirely new set of tactics. Curiously, he met Raginpert's sword before it could move again, and set his other hand, fist inverted, at his right hip so that his blade pointed straight out from his side. When his left arm drew back, his right fist advanced toward his opponent's jaw in a counterclockwise spin. He essentially used his limbs as though he were not bearing swords at all. Nonetheless, the sword spun in front of him. With the rotational power of the martial artist, his attack took Raginpert in a rapid combination of face, midsection, and groin in alternate-handed strikes. The effect was devastating. Each time Raginpert reflexively moved to defend against Wade's turning sword, while Wade connected not with the blade or his fists, but with the metal hilt. When the prince doubled over at the third blow, Wade paused to look at his friend's severed head among the rocks, accumulating battle dirt, and then used his gladius and spatha together to run the would-be usurper through.

Seeing their leader fall, and spreading the word, the Longobards attempted retreat led by a skilled second in command who had a face like a wedge. They had a long way to back out. The well-prepared Romans launched heavy artillery to the Longobard's rear, building a wall of fire that cut off the road to Itale. As with Arminius' strategy in the German province, the Romans had also left narrow side channels through which the enemy then "escaped" to face a secondary ambush.

In their desperation, the Longobards became increasingly dangerous and began to turn the tide, causing more casualties than they themselves suffered. By now however, when Roman reserves were released, the empire achieved approximate parity of troop numbers to add to their positional advantage. In the late phase of battle, some of the Longobards who had used up their throwing weapons took up rocks to avoid the close combat slaughter.

Victory was assured, though at what cost? Tankred, who gave up his earlier career as a wine merchant sacrificed himself as much out of desire for service to God, county, and friendship as for fulfillment of Carolingian law. He had essentially given his life in the earlier battle with Khan Krum but held on for one more valiant act. And Snorri, who dedicated himself to the service of one hero, served everyone this day. It didn't seem right that neither could see the outcome.

Wade, who likely suffered wounds of his own, made his way back to Kreindia's side fighting diehards as he went. Moving upslope, the population of Raginpert's men in opposition to him grew fewer until there were none. Kreindia watched Wade's return thinking that this man of the far future must have experienced a great shock discovering his destiny in the past—her present—where he forged a bond with battle comrades and suffered their loss. Here he was buffeted by fate, yet he shouldered however much responsibility was required. In the fighting's lull, she dared look away, inspired to write of the victory and what it meant for peace. She took up her parchment and quill, and lowered her gaze to the task.

Something hard and sharp-edged struck her head with a pop, and the quill flew from her hand. As she toppled, she felt a hot wetness pour into her eyes and across her face. Instinctively, she reached out for her gladius as she fell. She was unable to feel herself hit the ground as her mind had already begun to drift from her body. As in her vision, the sense of emptying, of hollowing, appeared to draw her upward like a soap bubble departing a heated bath.

When she felt Wade's presence, she rallied. Kreindia floated outside of herself and tried to observe, dimly aware of Wade's ministrations. Cradling her gently, Wade touched two fingers to her neck. Though he judged her unconscious, her outer senses had a fleeting window through which she could operate.

Time to go, she thought, time to leave this world for Wade's. When he originally came from the twenty first century to the ninth, it was Kreindia who helped guide him from afar. She longed to aid him again. To reinforce the promise she had extracted from Wade prior to the battle, she attempted to fill his mind with the assurance to trust his abilities.

She'd scarcely begun that task when the blood loss

weakened her so that she could no longer use her mind's eye to see him. Her confidence in Wade would have to substitute. She knew he possessed a character primed by a lifetime of being a synesthete, a mind of crossed senses. He was the witch of his time.

Use the shark's tooth, she pleaded. *Use it now.* It surprised her when he said aloud, "Let me be able to do this one last time and do it right." After a pause he added, "Please God." Kreindia added her prayers via Irene, the former empress and now her patron saint.

She could tell when he commenced and connected. The purple of royalty briefly blanked out all volition. The color sharing meant that their thoughts were merging; this sequence of hues was unique to Wade. With the purple still present, Kreindia now experienced a flood of chalky amaranth, and she supposed that Wade had made contact with her own synesthetic trigger.

The melee continued unmistakably around them, the clatter threatening to disrupt their delicate concentration. She could hear Wade thinking that centurion Armiger had fallen nearby, and there was no way to help. *Go further*, she urged him.

Honey, fresh in a bee's hive, replaced the purple. The new color meant Wade had pressed deeper on the acupuncture site. At almost the same instant, icterine laid its feathery carpet, and this signal would be the second level for Kreindia.

She struggled to remain sensate in the slightest degree to help Wade in any way she could, even though she had no experience of astral travel. Fleetingly, in her vision-sight, all she could see was the battlefield's blood from both friend and foe, dried and fresh, concentrated in one place, forming a shock of black. Then that darkness gave way to gray, and then to lighter gray by degrees on the journey that brought her to near-white. She knew she was slipping away.

Wade rescued her once again with the next stage,

blissful rust. Close on its heels came the tan soil of a field in dormancy. But the last step, crossing the void of millennia, would be the most difficult of all. Wade had to undam a passage in his unique mind and open it widely enough for her to enter with him. The fourth level did not and would not yield until Wade made one more intuitive leap: he blended the rust and tan. With one more subtle push, the astral plane welcomed them.

Then a dark ripple crossed the pure expanse of her fading essence, and she perceived it as a new entity, a third soul joining them. A creature as well disguised as that which had invaded her contemplation forest. Did Wade notice too? Before she could alert him, the sentient ripple bore them up and—

$\sim W \sim$

THE vision wrenched away and her eyes flew open to expose a sheen of doubt coating everything that had previously made sense to her. Which of her decisions since that time had been her own ideas and which had been suggestions planted by someone else? How was she to rescue her uncle if she couldn't even trust her own actions?

What's more, Keyx was gone.

CHAPTER 14

Thomas and Leo

"IS YOUR MEMORY long?" asked the *basileus* from his throne, as if this were nothing but an idle question.

"My memory?" Given recent events, Thomas had a feeling he knew exactly what Leo was going to ask him. It would be about the singular occurrence of seventeen years ago that had tied them with a bond stronger than they'd had as comrades-in-arms prior to the events of that day.

Thomas had to look up at him. His appointment with the basileus unfortunately came on the heels of a session where Leo had settled several disputes from his elevated platform and did not see fit to change the venue now. With Michael's imprisonment, Leo must have been feeling secure enough to dominate everyone around him. Therefore Thomas stood before the old soldier with his exalted regalia like a penitent come for judgment rather than the coequal he thought himself.

"Yes, your memory, Thomas."

In answer, the *Domestikos* simply shrugged.

With no particular need to be sensitive, Leo plunged ahead and asked, "Considering how history played out with Bardanes' defeat and the consequences to you, do you place any stock at all in what Solon of Philomelion had to say?"

"You mean how I feel today?" asked Thomas.

"I mean in regard to what we're dealing with now—with Michael. I need a blunt assessment of his disposition. Speak freely."

Thomas, the senior member of the trio, waved it off as though he didn't bear a grudge over his years in exile, didn't mind that he was the only one who paid a heavy price for his role in the revolt, and most of all didn't resent that Leo looked as handsome at forty-five as Thomas looked cunning at sixty. How had Leo advanced so far ahead of his companions? On those looks of his, obviously. The most bold and forceful of the three had a dark brow that sat low on his hazel eyes under a square forehead that was now offset by a mixed-white beard on his square chin. The slightly uneven teeth and the stray black hair or two on the bridge of his nose did nothing to hinder his appeal when he would but smile a fraction to crinkle his penetrating gaze at his swooning women. Even his scars, just nicks really, on his handsome forehead and cheek, provided the right window dressing to go with his crown. Visual charm was the secret of Leo's inexplicable success. Anyone could have predicted that much.

Michael, too, had been a successful younger man at fifty, but he was being dealt with for now.

Thomas answered, "That so-called prophecy from Solon still makes no sense. How could the three of us, in a normal lifetime, and starting so late, each become emperor? Why would I be proclaimed to that high station and then immediately killed? And we know for certain that Michael will never rise to the office once we finish with him. So no, I never believed the old crackpot. In fact, I sent someone back to silence him from spreading that nonsense soon after we left."

Leo pursed his lips. "I thought you might."

"The dangerous part is that Michael believed everything Solon said."

"As did I at the time."

And you were a pissant, thought Thomas. Forging ahead,

Thomas told him, "Michael stirred others to join his course of sedition, and now we have to root them out from here to Amorium. I thought we should have executed Michael immediately, and that it was a bad idea to wait for his niece—with all due respect to you, of course—but you were proved right. She couldn't stay away, and now we can remove her threat at the same time."

"So, it's true then? Kreindia has actually been spotted in the city?"

"Yes," said Thomas.

"Those gemstone blue eyes of hers... Is she still fetching?"

"So my agents tell me."

"Youthful?"

"The years have been kind to the traitor," said Thomas darkly. "I won't be."

With a sharp finger, Leo said, "You'll be what I tell you to be."

"I mean to say, I will know how to proceed with your permission once you've reviewed all the facts." Leo had tossed out Michael's sister-in-law, Theodosia, for his current wife on Thomas' previous advice. Now Thomas wanted to immediately squash any flicker of an idea Leo might have of overthrowing his current marriage in favor of wedding Kreindia, whose popularity would be an asset to him. Ticking off the reasons on his fingers, Thomas said, "Kreindia's an idol worshiper; thinks it's proper for a woman to be basileus of the Imperium; is loyal to your enemy Michael—why else would she turn up now—and she's an oracle! I leave it to you to distinguish which of those crimes is worst."

Leo sighed. "Do what you have to do. As long as I don't need to hear about it."

Thomas turned away and smiled, attending to the large codex on the podium that recorded decisions. He knew he'd been a hair's breadth from Leo's acquiescence even if the course was radical. This Armenian had a knack for making the bloody choices. After all, it was he who had castrated the four sons of Rhangabe to remove any possible threat from their legitimate claims to the throne.

Though Michael of Amorium had no sons to avenge him, and therefore none for Thomas to rob, Thomas coveted Thekla's property and that of Michael's other female relatives. Thekla held the inheritance of Bardanes and her treasures would be forfeit; when the head of a household was convicted, the entire family was destroyed with him.

And when the Amorian general was no longer a rival, Thomas could finally settle up with Leo himself.

"Anything else on the agenda?" Leo sighed. "It's been a long day."

"A moment."

The *Domestikos* was scarcely finished penning the verdict convicting Kreindia the Strange *in absentia* from the court, and was in fact blowing a light sheen of dust on the wet ink when they heard a pounding at the heavy door. Since they were in a private meeting, there was no one else to handle the traffic. At a nod from Leo, Thomas had to put his back into slowly easing the portal open by its iron ring. "I'm too old for this," he moaned.

A sweaty captain of the guard pressed in, prompting Leo to stand and shout, "Explain this disturbance."

"Pardon me," the captain said, turning to Thomas, to whom he was loyal, "but you said you wanted to know immediately, no matter where you were, or whom you were with."

Thomas replied, "I had forgotten, but I might have said that, yes."

"To know what?" demanded Leo.

The captain bowed to the emperor belatedly. "It's good news, my lord. We've captured Kreindia the Strange."

CHAPTER 15

Under the Palace

KEYX WAS GONE and Kriendia tried to tell herself that his unexplained absence was not necessarily cause for alarm. She had never been part of a conspiracy before and did not like the feelings that came with being in that position now: the ant-crawl on her scalp that made her turn and search for the cause; the perpetual knots that tortured her shoulders; the sour gut that could betray her with every breath.

She rushed from place to place, searching the arms of the cruciform and interrogating friends of theirs that she came across, but none of them had seen Keyx. She didn't want to think about what might happen if he left the grounds without supervision.

Finally, she found him in the back room counting the funds the church had lent them, separating the gain into piles of coins and baubles. He had replaced his fine cloak with a heavyweight version for the cooling weather. It was the happiest she'd seen him. Of course. Swimming in money. If he weren't so distracted, he'd likely have noticed her relief.

"I know how much is in the collection, Keyx," she warned. "Right down to the solidus."

"Just a pleasurable activity," he said, finishing up by packing away a thick gold bracelet that featured a bust of the Virgin on the clasp's disc. "Practicing counting treasure for the day when our enterprise makes me rich."

"Where were you today?" she asked. "Aside from here?"

"I took a walk. I almost went to the public bakery, but Agenor said he would bring me something back. Hey, you don't expect me to stand around while you're catatonic, do you?"

"What do you mean?"

"You were transfixed," he smiled. "I'd heard you were subject to visions because Thamar told everyone at court about it. The power that must give you... What did you dream this time?"

His reference to Thamar gave her pause. Thomas' daughter had too many allies and Keyx seemed to delight in bringing her up. Through her teeth, she said, "That's right. Never overlook my powers. Whatever Thamar could pay you, it wouldn't be worth my revenge. You see how difficult I've been to kill."

He looked wounded. "I may have done a favor or two for Thamar but I know better than to trust her."

"My vision was nothing you could profit from. But it confirmed that we have to visit Michael immediately."

"Visit him? He's not being squired in a nunnery, you know."

She gave him an icy stare. "We need to know what Michael knows, and that information can't be obtained second-hand."

"Okay, okay, but I only have one contact in the bottom level of the dungeons, and you don't want Tiro."

"Why not?"

"Because he's not one of our conspirators," said Keyx. "Tiro demands large bribes for small risks. And he's not very bright."

"Then he's exactly who I want."

"There has to be an easier way than sneaking in there."

She was loath to admit it, but part of her motivation in taking the risk of going to the year 820 was to flee Faron's grip. Continued use of astral travel could bring unpredictable, dangerous results. She wasn't about to use her new ability to attempt a jump to the palace prison. Now that her vision had alerted her to the menace on the astral plane, her bad feeling about using Faron's Norse figure, or any other proffered implement for that matter, more than doubled.

She said, "There is no easier way."

"I'll send Tiro a note. You can carry it to him."

"No, you'll be leading the team that goes in."

Keyx threw his hands up. "Perfect. Think how convenient that will be for Thomas. He can clap us all in the dungeon directly."

The door of their chamber shook to the rap of a distinctive triple knock: one strike left, one high, one right. With Kreindia's consent, the painfully thin priest named Agenor stuck his head in. "Do you have the traveling sacks ready?" he asked.

"What's going on?" Kreindia demanded.

"I forgot to tell you—" said Keyx, scratching the back of his head.

"The search for Kreindia is coming here next," Agenor finished for him. "So our informants say."

Keyx said, "I've packed us up." To Kreindia, he grumbled, "We have no choice. We can always return after the *Foederati* make their rounds."

She nodded, more than happy to get out of the mausoleum's pall and onto some forward momentum. Although they could probably come back to the church shortly, she didn't like not knowing what was happening in the power centers of the city, way on the other side.

"Oh, one more thing," said Agenor with a sly grin. He tossed them each a package redolent of fresh baked goods, which Keyx immediately held to his nose for a deep, smiling breath. "Free bread for you from the distribution house. Courtesy of Leo."

~ *W* ~

"ARE you a Green or a Blue?" asked the big man entering Michael's cell with a stool tucked under his arm and a large case he pulled along on wheels, yanking it up and over the door saddle. He slammed the door behind him with reverberating finality. "Green or Blue?"

"Neither," answered Michael. Although he had been secured to a cumbersome metal chair several hours in advance of the newcomer's entrance, he managed a tone as businesslike as that of his inquisitor. At least for now. Even he would have to admit that anticipation was choking him, not to mention the tight clamps on his wrists and ankles. He knew what they wanted from him. The list.

"Apolitical, Michael? That's unfortunate," said the visitor as he brought out and tested a horsewhip with a long shaft and lash, cracking it on the far wall. "Earth or sky, spring or autumn, your faction in the circus says a lot about a man. To me, the thrill of life is in the swift and decisive chariot race, not the marathon. With some vicious cheating of course. Did you know that chariots were the first event in the Olympics? I've won a race or two myself at the hippodrome," he said, cracking the horsewhip again. Michael was keenly aware of the susurration of the first stroke set-up, and the sharp splash of the denouement. "This one is called a lunge whip. My name is Brygos, by the way. I think we met once on the Terrace of the Pharos by the lighthouse."

"Thomas' war games," Michael said soberly. "He sent you up to douse the light."

"After that, you used your influence to have me reassigned."

"I did not. Who told you that?"

"It was a real setback for me. I felt like Sisyphus for a while, rolling that career boulder up the hill. That's why I had to learn this ugly trade."

"You're awfully erudite for an intimidator, Brygos. At any rate, you've misjudged me. I won't fall for a bluff."

"I'm actually an assistant sub-commander in secret operations. I do a little bit of everything. But I'm sorry if I didn't make myself clear, Michael. I'm not here to judge you. I'm here to hurt you."

"No," said Michael. "Leo wouldn't allow that. He was saving that part. He wanted me to have my wits about me when Kreindia was captured."

"You're right. It was Thomas who sent me and he wanted you to know why. Kreindia has been apprehended along with her team of assassins... I think I'll begin with something sharp instead." He rummaged in the case.

"I d-don't believe you. Kreindia never returned safely from the West, and in 814 when she disappeared, she had no reason to come back and hide."

"Believe me, it's true. Furthermore, Leo has told Thomas to do whatever he wishes with her. I expect to get in on that entertainment."

"Go to Hades."

"Be reasonable. Give us the list now before someone else does. It will ease the pain you have to go through. At least a little. This is the part of my job that I'm not very good at. They say I'm too hasty and bloody. Thomas doesn't mind though. He told me that you were apolitical. He doesn't even think there is a list." Brygos laughed. "That would mean that the torture you are about to endure is for nothing."

"Shut up and do what you came for."

"Very well," Brygos smiled. "Let's have ourselves a chariot race." He got to work with his sharp implements, and Michael screamed.

~ W ~

EVEN though they had easy access to the Mese from the church, Kreindia and Keyx descended the hill on the east side to follow a dreary access road in the shadow of Valen's Aqueduct. Drawing fresh water from the east-west hills to the valley, the structure fed pipes headed north and south.

"This way," she said. "We'll follow the last of the north lines to avoid the nymphaion rotunda and its gardens." Large weddings were held there with many socialites who could recognize Kreindia. Down the slope and through the crunch of leaves, they had to emerge on a commercial street near a northern harbor before they could trace east again by their painfully circuitous detour.

When a small group of soldiers rode up the street, she and Keyx were obliged to step to the side like everyone else. "Keep moving," she whispered to Keyx. As the soldiers dismounted and crowded them further, her hood snagged on a nail from the awning of a fish stand, and it pulled back the heavy cloth to expose her face. They were barely more than a horse-width away. Instead of running, she tilted her chin down slightly, stood still, and held her breath.

The soldiers laughed, slapped each other on the back, and walked into the tavern without a glance at her.

Keyx commented, "They really do want their liquor, don't they? They didn't notice you at all."

"Keyx!" she said with restrained urgency.

"Must be a blow to your womanly ego."

"Keyx! They didn't even question us. They've stopped looking for me entirely. What's going on?"

"Oh yes, it makes sense now that you put it that way," he said with fascination. "They must have stopped seeking because they've found her."

"Found who? What else have you been holding back?"

"The other Kreindia."

"What?" she gasped.

"For the original plan to work, our conspiracy called for a woman who resembled you to cause a distraction. Now that I see you in the flesh again, the Syrian looked

138

even more like you than you do," he laughed. "She looked the right age, you see, and you yourself look too young. Don't you get it? They think they found you! Considering how well it worked out, I wish I could claim credit for letting them capture her."

"So you're telling me that they have this Syrian woman who volunteered to help us. And she's suffering in my place?"

He heard her anger building and said, "Hold on. Don't get any crazy ideas."

"If you're proud of this, you're an idiot. If I'd known about her, we could have used her resemblance to better advantage than to toss her in like a lamb. No matter what else happens, I'm not sacrificing her."

"That's the kind of crazy idea I meant. We can't help her."

Kreindia took a deep breath. Del flickered through her thoughts. "What's this Syrian woman's name?" she asked.

"I don't know."

"We'll break her out when we rescue Michael." Kreindia restored her hood just in case she might be recognized by accident. The cold day justified it.

Keyx sighed. "Another terrible idea. One Kreindia of Amorium rescuing the other."

She'd given up trying to train him to hold back his opinions. "Keyx, if you are half this unstoppable in the face of our enemies, I shall have you talk them to death."

"Oh I'll be sure to try it, if the mission you've sent me on doesn't kill me first."

~ *W* ~

"WAIT, who?" Thamar sputtered in groggy indignation.

"I'm talking about Kreindia, my dear Thamar," said Thomas, trying to avert his gaze, as he usually had to when visiting her bedchamber. But these days she could hardly be found anywhere else. "Kreindia of Amorium," he reminded her. "Michael's neice?"

Thamar sat up and shook her head, making one ill-secured earring fly off. "Why are you bringing her up now? I'm having my recreation."

Thomas sighed. "It looks like you've worn him out." The young Bulgar slave lay on the covers in a sleep of brutish exhaustion.

"So I'll have another. And another after that if I please. Dead witches can wait."

"I told you, she's been captured alive. This is urgent."

"No, that can't be. She went west, taking her idols with her. None of my assassins did the job, but I prayed for her death all those years ago and it worked."

"Pray the other way now. Some people are saying we don't really have her in the cell."

"You don't. She died in the battle with Raginpert. My spies reported it to me."

"Well you knew Kreindia best when she lived at court. You have to come down and identify whoever it is we have. I don't want anything to go wrong with Michael's execution. Do you?"

She grimaced at the thought. "No. I'll get ready."

"Prepare yourself to meet her then, but please close the door now and in the future. I don't want to see this... activity."

She saw his wrinkled nose and laughed.

Thomas had lined up four respectable men from the clergy, the bureaucracy, the military, and the senate, two Greens and two Blues. He located them now and asked them to meet him under the palace to witness his daughter's testimony. The factions had been threatening a revolt, and as usual their reasons were various and impenetrable. But they agreed on one thing. All had heard Thamar's tale that Kreindia was dead and most held that the trial of a dead woman or the execution of her stand-in was pagan blasphemy. Only Thamar herself could undo the damage. It never occurred to Thomas that the woman he saw in the cell might not be Kreindia.

Thomas came back to his daughter's door only to find it still closed so he called out, "What are you doing in there now, Thamar?"

"Don't worry. It's not going to be her."

"So why are you taking so long?"

"Just in case."

"What does that mean?"

"On the very thin, impossible chance that I'm wrong, I have to look good for our locked up Amorian." She stuck her head out and added, "Because she can't."

"You fixed your make-up and you're dressed up. What else could you possibly need?"

"Accessories?" She shook her head and drew out the word as if any fool would know how crucial that element was to a proper wardrobe.

"You have enough." He dragged her out by the wrist. They headed for the stairs, acquiring a jailer and a torchbearer along the way. The temperature cooled as they traveled downward, with Thamar lagging and fixing her hair or dress at every step.

Deep under the palace, Thamar whined, "Dad-ee, it smells like poverty in here!"

"I know. All the more reason for you to hurry up."

Bringing out a large white cloth to hold to her face, she obeyed, with only muffled complaints thereafter. Soon they came to the group of four witnesses standing by.

"Is this her cell?" asked Thomas.

The guard accompanying them nodded.

"Finally," Thamar sighed. "Have you got this beast properly chained up?"

"Yes," the guard reported, "and the length is short."

"Then I shall go in. Wait here for a bit," she commanded the others.

Thamar entered the deep shadows by herself with an easy stride. "Light, please," she called out impatiently.

The torchbearer rushed in after her. Within a moment she screamed, refilled her lungs, and screamed again, fairly scrubbing the stones with her hysteria.

Whatever she had seen in that cell made her knock over the servant and his flame, jump back out and cringe against her father. "That's her, that's her, that's her. Why isn't she dead? Get me away from here fast."

~ *W* ~

KEYX and the hooded monk entered the palace separately, timing their appearance to the beginning of Tiro's shift. They could come no sooner and dared not arrive any later. Before Keyx could prepare and proceed to his appointed place, he was intercepted by his cousin Codros, a portly teenager with a lopsided bowl cut. Keyx gnashed his teeth in irritation. *Why did I have to cross this particular marbled floor right in the center corridor?*

"Keyx," the teen greeted him with impudent ease, "I was wondering where you'd been. Not that you're missed around here, just that I know you're ducking out on something on your way to the flesh pots."

Keyx could ill afford to be thrown off his coordinated plan by the inveterate troublemaker. Changing direction, he said, "Codros, I think I hear Zeus calling. He says he's in the mood for your special sense of low intellect humor."

"Ah, the old gods," said Codros, sticking close as they circled the great fountain. "I'll bet Zeus is fat and useless like you now." Codros, who looked like his face was continually pressed against a glass plate and spoke like he had a mouthful of marbles, was the most repulsive creature living at the court. He relieved part of his self-loathing by projecting it onto others.

"Well now, Codros, you may be right. I think you should go see if that's true."

"Cousin Bethania says you're in a lot of trouble."

Keyx was amused. "*Does* she?"

142

"She says you need to see her right away."

"That's where I was going."

"Liar. That's where *I'm* going—to tell her where you're *not* going." Codros took off in another direction with studious determination.

Thankful that his cousin was remarkably gullible, Keyx went to his room to pick up some supplies. He was surprised that the monk did not upbraid him for his lateness when they finally joined up again. Keyx led the way down to the lower levels past a lone man attempting to mop the floors. The custodian made no attempt to stop them, saying only, "If you've come to see the conspirators, you'd best stand clear of the splashing blood."

Keyx glanced at the hooded figure and swallowed hard. Proceeding with fresh urgency, they came to the first guard station where the commander informed them, "You can't pass any further."

Keyx didn't miss a step. He said softly, "The password is *Golgotha*."

The guard moved aside, whispering, "You're lucky. You just missed Thomas and Thamar."

The monk hesitated slightly as though surprised, but still said nothing.

After passing the second door on the next lower level, they heard a man screaming. Although the universal sound of anguish might have issued from anyone, one of the guards had assured them that this was Michael's cell.

Immediately outside of the cell, they encountered Tiro, a jolly little man who seemed inured to the noise that soaked the stones as he sat in his chair picking his teeth. When he saw them his eyes narrowed with calculation. "Ah Keyx, my friend. You've come to visit me, and you've brought a monk with you?"

"A monk to see Michael, yes. He's entitled."

"Not according to Thomas, he isn't. You know that Michael's in for suspicion of conspiracy, right? Those people never get visitors. Except for visitors like Brygos," he laughed while stabbing his thumb over his shoulder to indicate the man at work inside.

"A solidus says otherwise."

"Absolutely not, Keyx. I see how well you dress, how prosperous you are." He opened his fingers and his eyes wide. I want *five* solidus."

"That's outrageous."

"If you find a better deal, take it," Tiro laughed.

Keyx snorted with dissatisfaction and counted out the coins one handed, holding the shovel in casual concealment on the far side of his body. Tiro, however, was used to people trying to smuggle things into the dungeons.

"What do you have there?" asked Tiro, reaching out. "Let me see it. A shovel?"

"It's for Michael," Keyx said, bringing it into full view.

"But he's alive! Didn't you understand me? The torturer is applying his craft right now."

"Exactly. A shovel just in case."

Tiro burst into laughter and lounged back against the wall. "Okay, take it in, no extra charge."

Keyx leaned toward him and said, "Don't just stand there. You're paid to disappear."

"Of course," Tiro said, standing up. "Just catching my breath. Don't interrupt Brygos too long. It's a big night for him with more conspirators on his waiting list." Laughing all over again, he walked up and out, with a shake of his head.

Once they heard the second door above them slam, Keyx pounded the iron knocker against its plate over the reinforced wood and then hid behind the swing of the hinges.

After a few moments, Brygos opened the door a crack and called out, "Who comes?"

"Brygos, step out here," the monk rasped with difficulty.

The door swung wider and the assistant sub-commander leaned halfway out. "What are you interrupting me for? I'm in the middle of something urgent. For Thomas."

Behind the door, and thus out of Brygos' sight, Keyx made frantic motions, urging his compatriot to draw the man out of the chamber, and into his range.

The monk backed up and managed to duplicate the same raspy tone. "I thought you'd like to know that the palace has made a terrible mistake."

Supremely irritated, Brygos asked, "And what's that?"

Tossing back the cowl to reveal her face, Kreindia explained, "They've arrested the wrong woman."

When Brygos stepped forward to examine her in shock, Keyx swung the shovel. It hit the back of the torturer's head edge-on with a "chok," so that a section of his loosened scalp pushed up under the black hair like a dog raising one ear in curiosity, before the big man fell heavily.

"I think you bashed his head in permanently," said Kreindia, leaning over him to obtain a large ring of rusting keys.

"There's plenty where he came from. He won't be missed."

"I hope you're right. When he fails to report, it could cut into our schedule considerably."

"What would it have done to our schedule if he'd sounded the alarm?" he asked reasonably. "Oh, don't look at me that way. I'm leaving empty liquor bottles. They'll think he went to sleep off a binge."

Unsure whether he was kidding, she said. "Stay out here."

"No problem. I've got work to do."

Kreindia watched Keyx cross Brygos' arms across his body and then get hold of the tunic at the shoulders. As he dragged the torturer away, she took a deep breath and entered the chamber, unready even for what the shadows told.

The stench was overwhelming. For a moment, Michael

didn't react, and she couldn't either.

How long had it been? She had left Europe in 814 but it was in 813 that they'd last seen each other, and 820 now. Seven years in a blink. His usual round smiling face had a ghastly pallor and was visited with welts above the gray beard line. His dark curly hair was matted, and one of his generous eyebrows showed a stripe of skin through it.

"What's going on?" Michael said. "They sent me a monk?"

This was never the reunion she intended. Time was short and she needed to get him out of there. She turned and moved so that the light from the hall fell on her. Michael's face filled with instant and painful recognition. She laid a finger across her lips to keep him in check.

"Wh-w-where?" he screamed at her, emotion tearing a stammering fit out of him. "Where have you been?"

"You look awful," she gasped.

"I'd have looked better if you'd come here sooner!"

"Keep quiet," she warned.

"Why?" he said bitterly. "I've been screaming since before you got here. It will seem strange if I stop now."

"All the same. Wait until I've gone."

"You're leaving me here?"

"Brygos is dead. I have to wait until Leo is subdued or there'll be no way to get you past the gate."

He laughed. "So what did you come for? I thought I was safe, that you'd never show up after all these years. They said they had you for leverage. I knew it was a lie. Brygos or no Brygos, if you fall into their hands, that's the end of both of us."

"Neither you nor I are getting executed."

"Why not?"

"A list of your conspirators will work wonders."

A light went on behind his sad eyes. "I think I know what you're up to. It's a trick. Thomas sent you, didn't he? Who are you? Who *are* you?"

"Quiet, please! I'm your niece."

146

"All these years. She must be dead," he despaired, staring into nowhere.

"No. Stay with me. Do you remember what we talked about, on the day when we saw Thomas return?"

"Brygos mentioned that day, too. You're in league!"

"No, I'm sure he didn't mention what I said about the statues outside of the Boucoleon Palace. Do you remember that?"

"Yes," he said cautiously.

"And you never heard anyone else say the same? And you never told anyone?"

"No, but you tell me. Go on."

"I told you that the lion and bull were Syrian neo-Hittite, two thousand years old. They were bitter steel on my tongue."

"Yes, yes! That's what you said. Kreindia, you *are* alive! My dearest."

"We don't have much time. If I know who is with you, I can pressure them and come back here in force."

"Come close, please."

She moved in and freed him from the bonds of his chair. None of Brygos' keys fit the chains that still held him, but neither could she leave any obvious sign that she'd been there so it was just as well. No one would have unchained him.

"I have no list with me," he whispered when he had her ear. "You must find the Studite."

Kreindia understood. Theodore of Studion had been flogged and exiled the last time icon worshipping was outlawed. It stood to reason that the same would recur under Leo, and that Theodore would become the chief opposition among the clergy.

"But he must be over sixty years old," she marveled.

"His back is stronger than you think. Thomas is almost the same age, and look how much trouble he can cause."

"How did you get yourself into this? Why did you

want to usurp Leo?"

"I didn't. That's why the Studite has the only list. It was never my idea. One of his people came to see me after I was imprisoned, and he rallied the opposition to free me. Then the rabble got cold feet. I had no idea why I was locked up in the first place, but I've had plenty of time to review. I believe Thomas set his plan in motion by getting rid of my sister-in-law as a first step. Eliminate family ties between me and Leo."

"You suspected right."

"Where have you been? And who is it they have that looks like you in the other cell?"

"It's a long story."

"If you can come back to life, my dear, maybe everything will work out after all."

"We'll see about that," she said, patting his shoulder carefully. "It's going to be close."

$\sim W \sim$

"WHAT did Michael say?" asked Keyx.

They were tracing a circular route on the perimeter of the baths to mingle with the crowds and make sure they weren't followed. The wall beside them was incised with a wide array of available pampering services and Kreindia pretended to be studying them. "He said we have to go right now to The Princes' Islands."

"The Islands of Exile. That makes sense. That's where the emperor's noble opposition is banished to. Well, we'll need to go by way of the Philoxenos Cistern near Julian Harbor."

"For what purpose?"

"A messenger waits for us there."

"To confirm our Alpha Team?"

"That's what we're going to find out."

She made no attempt to argue with him. For the first time Kreindia felt hope. She had no new visions, saw no disaster on the horizon. With several days to go before the Christmas deadline, Michael was still alive, and she was beginning to devise the details of the plan to get him out. They even had some thoughts on how to detain Leo on the day of Michael's execution.

As they walked past the cathedral-sized landmark, a man brushed past Keyx seemingly by accident. A few intersections later, Keyx lifted the note in his hand and read it. He looked crushed.

Kreindia examined him. "What?"

"Bad news. Team Alpha has been captured. They were supposed to secure Leo, the first critical step."

"How is that possible? Thomas doesn't have the list."

"The palace must have ferreted out their identities by their own investigations. I think we're done."

They took another half dozen silent steps before Kreindia announced, "No. The operation goes ahead. And everything I warned you about still stands."

"How do you propose to continue?"

"I have other confederates that no one knows about."

"Whoever it is, you haven't seen them in years and they're probably still untrained whelps."

"Untrained in assassination maybe. There is one thoroughly trained in the art of war, a Saxon."

"One?"

"But I want our target alive."

"If you take my advice, you want him any way you can get him. Dead is safest."

"Alive. Do you understand?"

"Yes, if we must. And his family?"

"Exile." She walked on as though fully confident, and didn't even glance to the side. The bad news about the alpha team still shook her, but they had the prospect of the Studite and the considerable resources he might bring. And if her messages got through to that one Saxon she had in mind, Grimketil Forkbeard of Lowestoft, she would at least have someone she could trust with her life.

"Oh by the way," said Keyx, "Without that team in place we no longer have a way to know where Leo is going to be on Christmas night. That's what makes me think our precious plans have gone to hell."

"You'd better hope not. Because we're crashing that execution no matter what."

CHAPTER 16

Read the Random

KREINDIA TOLD KEYX where she wanted to be and they made their way beyond the palace complex past the grain storehouse to arrive breathless at the edge of the docks, there to evaluate the challenge they faced.

The harbor of Julian was one of five deep scallops carved into the peninsula, one of the largest hubs for worldwide shipping, rivaled only by its sister-ports in the same city. Even with a third of the vessels in December dry-dock, the seaside swarmed with excess activity. A good part of it consisted of naval personnel on alert from the threat posed by possible Michael sympathizers, and particularly the search for Kreindia, who would be capable of leading those sympathizers, if not her own force. A message about Kreindia's supposed capture had apparently reached the command here because a large portion was in the process of standing down. As they demobilized, a double-wide column of soldiers formed along the arch-supported stone walls to march back to the interior. More of them gradually joined the formation from the towers and bridges, leaving a smaller contingent behind. Watching the soldiers drain off in such a disciplined fashion, Keyx marveled, "They take us more seriously than I do, don't they? Or at least they did. I would hate to have been here before they grabbed the Syrian girl. Even now, I think we should wait, put our heads down, let them forget us."

Surveying the ship-littered sea, Kreindia said quietly, "I want a dromon."

"A dromon?" Keyx squawked. "You want us to steal a warship from the Byzantine navy to sail off to an island-prison? Are you out of your mind?"

"I know how to run them."

"Perfect," he said sarcastically. "You can sail them. Maybe the royal treasury will render up to me because I know how to count."

"Maybe we won't do it just yet. But soon."

"But never. From where I'm standing, it's the might of the Imperium versus the two of us. What we need in order to get out of here is a small cog. Nice flat bottom, square sail, hire three deckhands and we'll be set."

"If we go that way, we'll take on one deckhand plus myself, and I'll show you what you have to do."

"It sounds like a lot of hard work for me," sniffed Keyx, "just because you don't trust people."

"Honest work in the salt air will do you good."

"Umm," he said distractedly.

"What is it?"

"That man is staring at us," Keyx noted with unease.

She followed his gaze. They were under scrutiny from a merchant marine, silver-bearded but sturdy.

"That's all right. Don't try to evade him. The one who's interested is the one we want." With Keyx trailing behind, Kreindia walked up to the sailor, enduring his uncomfortable stare for fifty paces, and then said to him, "Do you have a ship for hire?"

"Sometimes." He measured her with the sort of apprehension he would use to approximate a high and threatening wave. "It depends on who's asking."

"We want passage to the Princes' Islands."

The marine gave both of them a dark look. "That's too bad for you."

"And what is your name?"

"Davilos. But my name won't help you. No one is sailing where you wish to go."

"Why not?"

"In addition to the fact that it's illegal? You can't sail there in winter."

"Winter has scarcely begun. The sea is relatively calm."

"And the other matter?" asked Davilos, coming back to its illegality.

"Money changes everything."

"Now you want me to take a bribe in front of the royal navy?" Addressing them singly, he added, "You and *you* are trouble. I could smell it festering since you stepped on the dock."

Kreindia's supreme confidence was undimmed, as though she dickered with merchant marines on a daily basis. "It's not a bribe, Davilos. The islands need supply ships."

"All taken care of. The authorities do that in late spring and again in late autumn."

"That's not the kind of supply I'm talking about." She glanced at Keyx for a moment and he nodded ever so slightly as though giving permission. With a broader look around, she addressed Davilos again. "Are you someone we can trust?"

Davilos' nose twitched as though he smelled an interesting tale and serious money. "Yes, of course."

"Am I supposed to accept your word alone?"

"You can ask anyone. Ask at the four other harbors if you like. Ask a Venetian. Ask an Indian. That's how far and how widely I'm known for integrity."

Kreindia paused, as if to consider him, and said, "I'm Korinna, and this is Helgesippos. My colleague and I are in the business of filling special requests. We represent an exile of means who wants certain things that are not on the proscribed lists."

Davilos lit up. "That's different. Who is this exile with exotic tastes?"

"Let's just say he is a resident of Halki."

"In the Princes…"

"That's what I told you."

"Very interesting. Do you understand the sort of premium required for a venture like this?"

"We do.

"I have to consult with my superiors," he cautioned.

"Please do."

"I'm not promising anything," Davilos added as he went up the gangplank and disappeared into a ship.

Motioning Kreindia outside of the traffic stream, Keyx cried in a mild fit of pique, "Helgesippos?"

"That's the only name I could think of."

"What happened to hiring a single deckhand on a small cog?"

"Change of plans," she said, walking quickly.

"Your plan could swallow almost every solidus we have."

"That's what the money is for. We're going to go get the funds right now. I thought you'd be happy that you don't have to do anything."

"Yes, one would suppose so, but somehow I feel like you'll have me doing a lot more, and none of it be easy."

~ *W* ~

KREINDIA and Keyx held tight to the flimsy crisscross folding chairs beneath them, planning their next steps on the deck of the *Diantha*. One shore faded and another grew, with the winter Sea of Marmora rippling between. They watched a busy crew of nine manage through the chop.

"As I predicted," said Keyx despondently, "We're left with nothing." It had taken both time and money for the contents of several smaller shipments of slaves and liquor to "go missing" and find their way to the large cog. The crew, the diversion from the *Diantha*'s schedule, and the "premium" were tallied as separate fees. And lastly they had to pay an enormous deposit in case the entire ship went down.

"At least the fee covers a round trip, and you seem to be enjoying these chairs," said Kreindia.

"Which we had to pay for and lash to the mast ourselves. They're still shifting. And I'm sick."

"Rough seas are the quickest way to get your sea legs. It's a short trip."

"If there was any room below deck I wouldn't be up here looking at the water. I think we're overloaded with cargo," said Keyx, his normal witty and biting tone subdued with nausea. The whole state of affairs made him oblivious to her teasing.

Kreindia surprised and alarmed him by replying, "Yes. Maybe a bit."

Keyx started to get up as though he wanted to exercise his anxiety, but she said, "Just in case, it's best if you don't walk around. They have the ballast properly balanced for you to stay right where you are."

He believed her, sank down, and stayed put the rest of the trip.

As the sun tracked west across the southern sky, the wind picked up and the deck rolled in the swells. The ship came about to avoid swamping. One of the sailors flipped over the railing and managed to hold on. His companions had him halfway pulled in when an unsecured bucket went flying, struck him in the back and he went over again.

When land finally loomed, Kreindia stood up and held directly to the mast while a green-tinged Keyx attempted to do the same.

"See?" Kreindia told him. "It was nothing."

"That's Proti," shouted Davilos, pointing at the land in front of them. "You said you wanted Halki. That will be the third one."

After passing tiny Proti, they had to steer around the larger Chalke Island and then swing to the south side of

Halki in a heavy spray to find safe harbor. For the big island, it took a few more minutes to come about and dock. In the sheltered zone, the water was relatively calm, but Keyx still lurched and finally surrendered his stomach contents before he could make it to the starboard rail.

Davilos cleared his throat and smiled, "If you and Helgesippos are in a hurry, go on ahead. We'll clean up here and unload your supplies for you."

Kreindia thanked Davilos for his kindness and they went on. Keyx was happy to put some distance between himself and the ship. "Did that sailor who went overboard ever come up again?" he asked.

"Of course he did."

From the shore they made their way up the steep rocky hill to a small villa where a lone old man stood outside. The wind fluttered his thin beige wrap adorned only with small illustrations of crosses on each shoulder.

"I knew you would come," he said with stolid assurance.

"Do you know who we are?" Kreindia asked in surprise.

The Studite wore his advanced age with style. His beard flowed from the wild confluence of his sideburns, moustache and cheeks, and combined to tight curls down his chest. It gapped to a bare wisp at his chin so that the tributaries appeared to form long white tusks. In a clear and steady timbre, he said, "No need. You've come here because you know me. I am the most exiled man in history. To the outlands and back with each change of emperor and each change in sentiment over icons. It was only a matter of time before the next one wished for my return."

Kreindia had never heard anyone sound so certain yet so absent of pride.

"The emperor is not changed yet," said Keyx. "We'll need your help to do it."

Ignoring him, Theodore squinted at her. "Would you

be Michael of Amorium's niece?"

"Kreindia. Have we met?"

"Come," said Theodore.

They passed through the atrium and into an airy sitting room. An alcove in the wall with its own small door stood open to reveal a dazzling mosaic of a fish representing Christ rather than the far more common image of a man, or that of a crucifix.

Following their gaze, Theodore explained, "Even here they persecute me. This is the reduction of my monastery—a corner to worship in."

Keyx said, "Still pretty nice for the home of a pariah."

In his first flash of anger, Theodore snapped, "You wouldn't think it so nice if they flogged you and covered you with rats and lice before the trip here."

Keyx had no answer for that.

They sat around three sides of a square table with their legs folded in the low space. Kreindia very carefully explained what they wanted—a large-scale undertaking culminating in her objective to unseat Leo and free her uncle.

Theodore scrutinized her with disapproval as though she had come to sell him a horse with a cracked hoof. Michael had warned her of the Studite's reluctance. She gave him a chance to think it through as he gazed at a ray of light from the vented ceiling.

Eventually, he said, "There is only one issue for me. What will be Michael's policy toward icon veneration?"

"I'll be honest with you. If I remain to influence him, I will try to make his administration progressive like the reign of Irene. But I can never be sure what will happen to me."

"No one can," he allowed. "You've discussed it with him, though?"

"No, but I know my uncle. He won't rock the boat in this transition. He'll stake out a middle ground to avoid antagonizing Leo's iconoclasts… even if Leo is gone."

"How will Michael govern in regard to my concerns?"

"No more icon destruction. The Imperium will be neutral in public and support your cause in private. You can come home."

"I won't come home. I've been cast out so many times that I'll cast myself out." His warm smile belied his serious intent. "At my age, I'll never survive the beatings if the decision is reversed again."

Kreindia tried to imagine the unthinkable pain and injustice Theodore must have gone through. How he held on with such grace was a tribute to the finest in human endurance. "I understand," she told him. "And I can assure you that your practice of writing letters to the Pope will not be punished." She sat back and hoped he wouldn't shrink from his supplying assistance the way his flock in Constantinople had already done. She wasn't promising him everything he might have expected.

Theodore stared at her for an eternity. She thought she could see the lines in his forehead deepening and his tusks growing. Keyx sat back and frowned in infectious worry. At length, the Studite said, "I have a list for you."

He stood and went over to the mosaic, pausing there as though in further contemplation. With a nudge of his thumb against the fish's tail, the panel opened to an inner alcove. From this recess he retrieved the parchment, and Kreindia breathed easier and wiped away a tear.

When she had the full list of conspirators in her hand and had committed it to memory, she let Theodore walk them back to the beach. He'd also given them several letters he'd prepared in advance if a suitable messenger ever came. Kreindia could sense the new possibilities that had opened up to them, but instead of providing comfort to her, they multiplied the uncertainties.

Being a seer had taught her to read the random. Or that which seemed patternless to others. The heavy clouds that shadowed them were holed so that the late sun drove six shafts of light, all in different directions. The sounds of the ocean battered their senses from everywhere. Kreindia paid attention to these signs and found a troubling pattern emerging that she couldn't yet grasp, let alone vocalize. Trouble was imminent.

On the high ground, none of them had to go far to see the problem. They kept moving forward anyway at an ever-quickening pace as the land slid toward the water.

Kreindia was thunderstruck to find the harbor empty but for hundreds of sea birds going about their business in the air and on the land undisturbed. Dozens of small brown sandpipers hopped like pieces moving around a game board, while a large gray heron stood supreme at the pinnacle of an upended piece of driftwood.

"The *Diantha* is gone," breathed Kreindia.

Theodore, no stranger to every manner of treachery, said, "If it's any consolation, they probably left immediately."

"And they didn't unload anything," Keyx groaned, his shoulders sagging. "They've kept it all."

"I don't care about any of that," Kreindia said, "We have no way back, and time is running out."

"We've been abandoned here," said Keyx as though he was just beginning to realize the stunning immensity of the crime.

"Yes," said Theodore, standing like a banner in the wind. "You get used to it."

After another moment's contemplation, Keyx said, "No one will come until spring at best, and that will be too late for Michael. Makes you wonder why we ever thought we could do this, doesn't it Kreindia? Why did we?"

Surveying the small island and surrounding ocean that formed the exile's trap—and now hers, too—she felt the heat rise in her cheeks, and she reminded herself that her people deserved better than Leo the Armenian. He had ascended to the throne through one of the most dangerous acts of treason Byzantium had ever seen. He'd withdrawn his troops from a major battle with the Bulgars in order to destabilize his own government, watched the slaughter of his people from the safety of a hill, and when Rhangabe abdicated, took over and killed his heirs. If Kreindia didn't stop him now, Leo was going to throw her uncle into the large furnace under the Great Palace.

Standing tall and rock solid as Theodore, Kreindia announced, "We're going to build a raft and hazard a return to the city."

"A raft?" Keyx blubbered. "You saw what happened in the large cog. How are we going to survive some lousy raft in winter?"

"The beginning of winter," she corrected. "That's why the sooner we go, the better. Theodore, if we can coordinate an offensive, can you find a way to fund us?"

"I don't doubt it. I used to be the Count of the Sacred Largess for all Byzantium. In fact, I've plenty of money to give you right here, but I don't think any of those coins will ever leave this demesne."

"What do you mean?"

"You've seen the harbor on the south side. That's the only one. From there, even in summer, at the mercy of the current without a proper ship, you can only end up at Prinkipo."

Keyx drooped. "Another island of exile. They've planned this miserable prison well."

"And on the northern half?" Kreindia asked Theodore.

"On the north, there is nowhere safe to launch."

"But if we did try it?"

"If the rocks and surf didn't conspire to destroy you, you'd either be caught by another current that goes to Prinkipo or one that rides north and east to Anatolia. You can never get back to the Thracian mainland either way."

"That chance is good enough for me."

"What chance?" Keyx asked, his arms spread in incredulity. "I didn't hear any."

"Help me build the raft and you'll see."

Keyx said, "Whatever we build, I can't guarantee I'll be

willing to get aboard. We could have used the slaves from the ship. Where are your slaves, Theodore?"

"I've none. I don't believe in them. There are several other Studites here that assist me voluntarily."

"They're better off than me then," Keyx grumbled. "I'm certainly not doing this voluntarily."

With the help of the Studite followers under Kreindia's direction, they sealed and tested four barrels individually. Once they aligned and affixed them to a long waterline frame with cannibalized planking, they had the outline of a workable raft in a day. Despite the time limits, Kreindia insisted on attaching a steer board as well as outriggers for stabilizers, an arrangement they approximated after a few days of trial and error.

Keyx was impressed, though still immensely skeptical. "Will that steer board really work in the winter current?"

"Only if you help by paddling like your life depends on it. Which it does."

The least technical part of the construction, held for last, were seat, hand, and footholds to brace for shock. Finally, she pronounced, "That's it. We're out of time."

Keyx said, "We can't properly test the finished work. It may sink halfway over."

Kreindia agreed. "No maybe about it. We'll be sinking almost from the moment we leave. The barrels won't stay sealed. And if there's a storm, we'll capsize even with the stabilizers. We either get there fast or we won't get there at all. You can spend your life right here if you like."

"Oh no. Your luck has been uncanny. If I stay behind I'll probably die in a one-man earthquake or something."

Having had a friend who died in a similar freak occurrence at the Hagia Sofia, Kreindia didn't laugh.

They chose the closest thing to a harbor on the northern coastline, a tiny notch that would never serve a normal sized ship. She was glad they didn't have to build the raft on the shore. The strip of beach was narrower than the raft itself. Even with four people to haul the fruit of their labors over the stony slope and through the shrubs they lost control setting it down and barely missed dashing it on the black rocks that protruded from the water.

Climbing aboard, they sat one behind the other, Keyx in front so that Kreindia could steer. While one assistant steadied them, the best swimmer among the Studites carried a rope out to an old wreck and then dove under.

"What's he doing?" Keyx asked.

"Saving us a lot of trouble. The more we sit and paddle, the more we sink. I asked him to find the anchor and tie us in. It may be the only way out of here."

The swimmer surfaced and waved them on. Keyx and Kreindia began to pull themselves and the raft along the rope to overcome the confining waves hitting the shore. Keyx turned back and asked, "Are you pulling too? We're barely moving."

"I'm pulling. If you find this hard, imagine how it would have been without the rope."

Once they were at the wreck, Keyx manned the paddle oar and Kreindia took the steering oar.

In the waters beyond Halki they could see their target to their north, a wide gray-brown expanse. To the east they could see the rocky promontories of Prinkipo Island—which were swathed in a spectacular tidal spray—even better.

"Now you can tell me the details of your plan," said Keyx, glancing over his shoulder.

"No, I can't."

"I have no one to repeat it to out here," he pleaded.

"I have no plan. I move on intuition."

"So tell me your intuition."

"I can't."

"Tell me your life story then. What sort of man are you doing all this for?"

She looked at him for a moment thinking he knew something more and then decided he didn't. "I act for an infinite number of men."

"There's a word for that."

"Do you happen to know how quickly you can drown after being hit in the head with an oar?"

He swallowed. "I'll try not to cause that to happen."

At that moment they drifted into a spot where the raft bobbed a little higher on a wave, and they felt the tug of the east-moving current that would take them to Prinkipo, an outcome that was one of her greatest fears. She grabbed the control stick for the steering board and yelled, "Row!"

Keyx dug in hard with the two-headed oar, first dragging the left side and then the right. The raft moved sideways towards Prinkipo as though he'd done nothing.

She called, "Faster, or we're dead," and he responded with a burst of speed in a left-right rhythm. At first the craft continued sideways and then began to wobble along in the direction of the mainland as she fought to hold the control steady. They only needed to go a little way to work their way past this branch of the current according to the charts, but it was impossible to see just where that border was or to measure their lost ground.

Twenty-five frantic strokes in, he paused and she screamed, "No." Another twenty strokes and she called for more to be safe.

Keyx cried, "I can't." He slumped forward, spent, and they continued on a steady course, now taken by the new current in the desired direction. Although it wasn't due north as Kreindia would have liked—but rather northeast, which was further from their goal—they could not miss Anatolia if nothing else changed.

The sea was remarkably rough as they rode so close to its surface, but the outrigging did its job, and the sky, while ragged with clouds, was in no condition to produce a storm before they got there.

They'd fashioned the raft with large gaps for the water to flow through, which was possible because they rode high on the barrels. As sea washed over them and let them continue unimpeded, Keyx, with his eyes still closed, mumured, "I'm sorry."

"No, no, we're fine," she said working the steering oar.

By the time Keyx gathered himself to look up again, the shore had grown significantly, and he marveled, "That's not Prinkipo. Are we as close to salvation as we seem?"

"I told you it was a short trip to the mainland," she said, trying to pretend she wasn't shivering and coughing water. "I hope you're well rested and can swim like a dolphin."

"I'm exhausted thanks to you."

"I had to save my energy to carry the burden of the Studite's gold."

"I would gladly have done that part."

Once they reached the coastal zone, the wind was at their backs and her improvised rudder was working serviceably for minor changes. She tried to steer for a spot where the waves were high and the sea splashed and resolved to a white trace on the beach rather than the place where it crashed and made vertical spikes.

This is the dangerous part. "Brace!" she shouted.

They both held tight while the wave bore them to its crest. From the new height, they rolled toward a juncture on the beach where a bald headed man made a hasty appearance, churning mightily through the sand. He seemed to be well aware of them but with the entire coast open to him he still wasn't getting out of the way. She was sure they were going to collide with the bystander though she could no longer do anything about it.

Either they weren't exactly aligned or the force of the water wasn't. The imbalance caused them to turn, and in the next moment, they began to spin. Now their landing point would be unpredictable.

They closed fast, and the stubborn man, what Kreindia could see of him when the rotation came around, hovered close and then finally jumped clear. Kreindia's design stayed faithful until the very end where its structure failed and dumped them in the shallows.

When they tumbled to a stop on the Anatolian mainland, the man helped them struggle up, aiding first Keyx, who was closer, and then her. At that point she saw that the man wasn't a man. *It was Anthimos!*

Upon deciphering that it was Kreindia under her wet slop of black hair, the eunuch screamed with surprise.

Grabbing him in a tight hug, she said, "What are you doing here, Anthimos?"

"Can it really be you, Kreindia? And Keyx, is it?" The presence of the court's second most notorious lecher seemed to amaze him almost as much as the long lost general's niece. "I got a message to be here at this place and time, and bring three horses and two soldier's uniforms."

"A message from whom?" Kreindia asked.

"I don't know."

"Why did you listen to it?"

"For Michael's sake. The entreaty said it was from a friend of yours. He actually called himself your defender. That person knew things that only you and I knew. But he didn't seem to know that you were dead, or more accurately I didn't know that you were alive. I had hoped." His voice remained loud and ran fast, presumably from a still-quickened pulse.

The message must be from Wade, she thought. *He finally came. For some reason he has to move anonymously.* She wouldn't give him away, even to the most powerful of the eunuch staffers at court, her dear, sweet friend.

She asked, "How did you afford the horses?" Knowing of Anthimos' access to the palace, acquiring the uniforms was the easy part.

"Borrowed money. I was also told that the person I was meeting would have sufficient wealth to reimburse me and proceed from there."

"That's true. I have money with me."

"I want to join you, wherever you're going."

"Sometimes I think you're in the business of saving my life, Anthimos."

"You exaggerate," he said with an amused and modest smile. "These rescues are only a sideline. Now, who do you suppose sent that note to me?"

"I have no idea."

He examined her in mild reproach like he didn't believe that was possible. He probably also suspected that the messenger was Wade yet he kept his mouth shut in front of Keyx. "But what are *you two* doing here?"

"This is part of upending Leo," she said.

"Leo is a monster," Anthimos told Keyx in case he didn't know.

Keyx said, "All emperors are monsters. He thinks of himself as rather decent."

"You should have seen what he did to the Paulicians for believing that Christ was the adopted Son of God rather than born so. Where have you been all these years, Kreindia?"

She stared at the air as though her gaze might bore a hole through the sky. There was so much she wanted to say to him it was overwhelming. Any start to the telling seemed wholly inadequate, especially where it involved astral travel, something she could not even begin to explain and would not wish to attempt in mixed company. As far as Keyx was concerned, she had not even tried to describe where she went during a vision state, one of which was skirting the edge of her perception even as they spoke. "Nowhere at all. And everywhere," she found herself whispering.

Anthimos, who'd seen her in the throes of a vision before said, "It's scary when you get like that."

"I agree," said Keyx with sincere wonder.

Her eyes suddenly cleared and she said, "We have to get to Chrysopolis. Immediately."

They mounted up without argument, though Keyx

could not stop looking at her, and Anthimos wore a wistful smile. Soon they rode hard through the region of Bithynia to get to the city of Chrysopolis, which was along the Bosporus in view of Constantinople across the strait. Once they were in the business district, Kreindia purchased a very expensive dress and jewelry, and put them on *en route* to the lighthouse. Anthimos and Keyx donned their uniforms as Keyx expressed surprise at the flawless fit of his, even with all the accoutrements.

"Your sizes were given to me," Anthimos explained, which only baffled Keyx further.

By sundown they were at the lighthouse itself, which was almost as grand as the one at Boucoleon. There were two guards in evidence but there would be more nearby. At a glance from Kreindia, Anthimos commanded the pair, "Stand aside for the emperor's niece."

The hefty guards took in Kreindia's splendor and were properly impressed. Besides the emperor himself, only the emperor's family, who had an indeterminate but powerful unofficial status, could interfere with the running of a city.

"What's going on?" one asked without ceding any ground.

She informed them, "Nicomedia is under attack from the Caliphate. We barely got out of there in time."

"Why didn't we get a signal from their station?"

"They were overrun too quickly."

"We'll notify the tower," he said, turning away.

"No," she ordered, breezing past them. "I have to send my personal signature to Leo so that he understands the seriousness of the situation."

Uncertain of the protocol for this unusual circumstance, they started to join her and her companions at the entrance. She whipped around with steel in her eyes and barked, "Why are you coming in with us? Imperial communications are private."

"But—"

"You're to stand by until I call for you. Allow no one

else to come in."

Without waiting to see what the guards would do, the soldiers that accompanied her—Anthimos and Keyx—drew their weapons to enforce her message, and the guards stepped away quickly.

Kreindia used the same procedure on the personnel inside through several floors until they reached the top. "Bind and gag the men on this level," she advised Anthimos, "and we'll call the rest back in for the same as we go down."

In the lantern room, Kreindia set up the signal beacon.

Keyx followed her like a puppy. "You know how to send false signals?"

"I learned this trick from Thomas himself. The signal code I got from my uncle."

Grasping the two-handed control sticks, she worked the shutters, opening and closing them at silent intervals to tell a harrowing tale.

"Are you warning them of this supposed Arab attack?" asked Anthimos rejoining them.

"No," she said with a tense smile. "I served up that version strictly for the Chrysopolitans. It's what they expect to hear. Thomas knows the Arabs too well to buy that story. With his network and contacts in that world, he'll probably know exactly where they are at any given time. The message I'm sending him is different, the only thing that Thomas will find believable."

CHAPTER 17

Embattled

THOMAS DECIDED THAT he and the emperor were fortunate to get the beacon warning when they did. The bright signal lights from Chrysopolis beamed to the Pharos lighthouse at Boucoleon in the early dark of winter, and in turn the personnel there relayed the alert directly to the throne room's reflection system. A runner from the lighthouse would be along shortly as a redundancy measure, but Thomas signaled back, "Message received," simple words that belied the rising panic he felt. His heart sank when his response generated one more confirmation from across the Strait of Bosporus, a precautionary procedure he'd put into place years ago. The full protocol meant that the bad news was very real.

"It's the warning beacon from Chrysopolis," Thomas called to Leo with alarm.

Leo was busy reviewing the decision codex for something that would get him out of the trivial schedule that had been prepared for the next day. "The Arabs?"

"No, it's a civil insurrection."

"Then let them handle it in Chrysopolis with the contingent I gave them."

Thomas approached him. "The trouble is much more than a street fight and it's not in Chrysopolis proper. They say the Optimatoi Theme has put the mob down, but the unrest that started inland at Claudiopolis has reached east to Ancyra and probably further."

The news hung in the air as though Leo were processing it with an entirely differently grasp than he first had. "Michael?"

"This isn't Michael," Thomas admitted. *More like something I would do.* "He hasn't the imagination for this. If he were directing it, he'd go straight for Constantinople. He wouldn't start in Claudiopolis and head away from us after that."

"We'll have to take care of it before it gets any worse."

"Yes."

"Then take care of it! I'll join you in a while," said Leo.

Thomas was deep in thought and reluctant to leave when he noticed Leo step up to his throne and sit down heavily. "Is something else wrong, my Lord?"

Leo studied him briefly, and said, "I was reading an illuminated book of divination the other day."

Thomas, whose pagan roots had stayed intact as well, did not remind his sovereign that such books were outlawed by his own decree.

"I wanted to see what we should do with Michael," Leo continued.

"By divination? That's ridiculous. We know what to do with him."

"I opened the codex at random… and there was a picture of a lion."

"A Leo."

"Right," said Leo. "And the lion had its throat transfixed by a sword. It stood between the letters *Chi* and *Phi.*"

"And?"

"Don't you see? *Chi* represents Christmas and *Phi* the Epiphany."

"We don't know what it means," Thomas said quickly.

Leo scowled at him. "Is not that sword impalement an unmistakable prediction of my death between those two feasts?"

Thomas feigned horror and denial while inside his

blood pulsed with excitement. *That's correct,* thought Thomas, *only it won't be Michael killing you. It will be me.*

"First I suffer Michael's disloyalty," Leo wailed. "And now Claudiopolis rises and my life is in danger? Why is this happening to me? I've been through everything as a ruler. I had to swear on a dead dog to conclude a peace with Omurtag."

Thomas remembered. Omurtag was the son of the Bulgar leader Khan Krum who took over upon his father's sudden death. Omurtag and Leo had each agreed to adopt the other's customs for the ceremony to end hostilities.

Leo said, "I put one hand on my heart and the other on a stinking, fly-swarmed cur they had slaughtered earlier in the day to grow putrid in the sun, while the Bulgar only had to swear on a Bible!"

Thomas considered reminding him that the Bulgar threat to Byzantium at that point was entirely because of Leo's manipulations, allowing Krum to exterminate an entire Macedonian regiment for Leo's own gain, but thought better of it. "Those were also difficult times," he mumbled in agreement.

"I have to go myself to Anatolia," Leo concluded. Almost every Byzantine emperor was an active commander-in-chief. Leading from the front was the norm and the only way to hold their complicated people's respect.

"No, you don't," said Thomas, rushing over to him. "This was not the plan."

"Maybe I shouldn't be here in the capital though. Supose I stay and get slain in the palace?"

"Or maybe you get killed when you charge recklessly off to Anatolia. That's more likely what the prophecy is warning us about. A chance to assault the palace in your absence is exactly the sort of opportunity the conspirators want. All of Byzantium would fall. Maybe we should both stay here."

Leo shook his head. "No. You, at least, have to go and

quell the unrest, Thomas."

"I can't desert you."

Thomas' uncertainty seemed to make Leo more certain. "Anatolia is your primary responsibility. You can leave Zoticus behind with a contingent here. But you're going. I want you to leave now."

Considering Leo's state of mind, all Thomas could say was, "Yes, my lord." And as he went out to gather his *Foederati*, he considered which route to take. He would go to assess the situation and come right back. Nothing was going to keep him from the pleasure of executing Michael and Leo.

~ *W* ~

FROM the lighthouse at Crysopolis, Kreindia and company rode along the steep coast to Chalcedon, a port city to the south. Upon reaching its outskirts, Keyx asked Kreindia, "Why do you believe Thomas will come through here when he could go anywhere?"

Kreindia said, "I'm a general's niece. I've seen both land and sea battles up close."

Anthimos nodded in agreement. "That she has."

"In case you haven't noticed," Keyx grumbled, "I'm not a general's niece, so just run through the scenarios for me. Please."

With a long look at him, she said, "Firstly, Chalcedon is closer port to Claudiopolis, where the riots supposedly began. It's especially convenient if he leaves either from the palace port at Boucoleon or the Port of Julian. He'll also consider that the local troops have already moved inland, leaving no one to gather at Chrysopolis."

"What about ports further east? That will put him in the right direction."

Kreindia shook her head. "Along the way, he'll want to pick up reserves and check on Nicomedia, but strategically—and especially on a rough sea—he'll want to leave the warships at the mouth of the Bosporus. I repeated the alert to Chalcedon, so no will contradict us there."

"That's all very convincing to me, but suppose he likes the roads that run from Chrysopolis better. What happens if Thomas goes out of his way a bit to make a landing at Chrysopolis and gets a description of who sent him that message?"

"I know Thomas. If he believes my alert in the first place, he won't second guess himself to check it further."

"But if he does?"

"Then we're finished."

They left the horses in the care of a stable as close to the docks as possible and walked on from there. Kreindia had considered selling them, but wanted to keep their options open. "We still have plenty of cash from the Studites," she told her companions. "While Thomas is on his way here, we'll hire a ship to sail us back to Constantinople."

"Like that last one we hired?" Keyx sniped.

"Unlike the last one, this destination is legal."

Anthimos said, "I think the *Foederati* have responded to your ruse. Look."

The triangular lateen sails made one side of the small port look like a sea of sharks gathering under a bloody night sky. Kreindia bit her lip in contemplation. "This must be the number of vessels Thomas already had mobilized."

"Why do you look worried?" Anthimos asked.

She caught the strain in his voice and shrugged, moving away from the water. "Thomas' response came sooner than I thought, that's all." Until she had a plan she didn't want to vocalize the fact that the troops' speedy arrival might cause enormous complications for them.

With the trio clothed as they had been at landfall, they went to the other side of the harbor to secure a merchant vessel from among those that stood apart.

Keyx took in the busy scene in front of them where dockhands were hastily tying spring lines to jam cleats, and scowled, "There's an unusual amount of activity after dark in this village."

Anthimos said, "Ports of call always jump when the ships come in. They do seem unusually rushed though."

At the next pontoon over, Kreindia saw a merchant mariner giving orders to a crew on the planking. His men moved with urgency, shifting crates into a cellar on land and tossing them in roughly without proper stacking. Other crews down the row were doing the same. She said to the merchant, "Pardon me, I know it's late, but we'll pay you double if you have any sort of vessel to take us across."

With a frown, he said, "Ha, I would love to, but I can't. All the boats and ships are locked down under a strict travel ban because of the civil unrest in Claudiopolis. That's why we're all still awake, and that's why I'm having my men secure everything. I could use a couple more hands to hide our supplies if you can spare them."

"No thanks," she said, returning to her friends.

"Perfect," Keyx muttered. "We did this to ourselves. There'll be no getting across now."

"Come this way," said Kreindia. She led them to higher ground above the docks to survey the sea of sharks in the hazy night. It was no accident of design that lent the dromons the impression of predators.

Keyx rubbed his eyes. "Are we on our way to turn ourselves in?"

"This isn't over, Keyx. I want one of those dromons."

"Please, not that again."

"New plan: We take the small one on the west end, closest to our route of escape."

"Just a small one, eh? How in the world are you going to wrest a ship away from the *Foederati*? It's not the same as bluffing your way into a lighthouse."

"The *Foederati* are army, not navy."

"So they're no match for you."

"Right."

"I was joking," he protested. "There's nothing right about it."

"Kreindia can do it," said Anthimos. "I don't know how, but she'll get it done."

"We saw most of the dromon crews walking the streets on shore leave," she pointed out, deep in thought.

Keyx said, "Sure, that helps. If they leave ten men guarding each position and have twenty ships, we just have to fight through four hundred of the Imperium's best soldiers."

"Once again, the guards left behind are army, not navy. They'll have some disadvantages ship-board. Aside from that, we may be able to enlist some help." Kreindia began to walk them further up the hill, back to the bustle of the city.

"None of the people on this route look idle," Anthimos observed. "I don't think they'll be anxious to help us."

"They don't have to. As an historian who used to live abroad, I've documented an isolated community of Galician Celts still living in this area."

"I've never heard of Celts over here," said Anthimos.

"You wouldn't. Their numbers continue to dwindle as they hear of wars and join mercenary groups abroad."

"Why would they help us?" Keyx asked.

"If they're true to their ancestry, it's considered the height of dishonor when they have an opportunity to get into a scrap and don't do it."

"So they fight for no particular reason?"

"For reasons that make sense to them. When they win, they take whatever they find."

"Now it makes sense to *me*," said Keyx. "Where do you look for people like that?"

"We start with a tavern."

"That's where the dromon crews will be," Keyx complained.

"Not the tavern I'm thinking of."

After they retrieved their horses, she led them past the outskirts of town through dark, branching roads, none of which resembled a Roman highway.

"How do you know where you're going in this forest?" Anthimos asked.

"I don't exactly. The roads have changed. But I have a perfect memory for direction."

After a couple of dead ends, they decided to notch the route they chose with sword slashes even though it made their path a blazing beacon to anyone who might want to follow them.

Finally they saw a peek of stone that turned out to be a public house fashioned like a minor fortress. The lower windows, warmly lit, were filled with iron bars topped by triple-headed spikes. On the upper tier, however, was a row of arched windows framed in wood and extending artfully from a painted façade, a design that was not remotely Byzantine. It stood alone by a dirt road with the forest pressing close.

"No Roman settled this parcel. Are you certain we're still in Chalcedon?" Keyx asked.

"Not exactly." The wild pockets of Anatolia beyond the pilgrim trails were many, and the niches held remnants of the numerous conquered tribes bypassed by imperium settlement.

"How does a lady of the court know of such a place?" Anthimos wondered with a smile.

"You used to tell me I don't know my way around the court," Kreindia laughed. "That's because I know my way around here."

Before they could enter the tavern, a stocky red haired man went flying out the door to land in the dirt. They had barely gotten a look at him on the ground when he got up and plunged back in. A few moments later, two other men went sailing out. These two didn't get up.

Kreindia said, "The man we just saw is the one we want."

"Which one?" said Anthimos.

"The first one."

Keyx fidgeted with the saddlebags. "Should we put on the army uniforms before we go in?"

"Not if you want to get out alive."

On the inside, the smell of liquor was strong, as though it had been used to mop the floor. Here the stones were evident again, a rougher cut with each corner and turn accented by heavy wooden beams. The busy service area was styled with a finely carved wooden awning and lamps. At the bar itself, the red haired man with an even brighter red beard, sat drinking as though he had not just been in an altercation. When they were but a few steps in, he immediately sprung up and spun, ready to meet any challenge.

When he saw Kreindia his blue eyes sparkled. "I thought I'd survived that last beating but I see now that I've fought my way through to the angels. "Well, one angel with two slugs in tow. I'm Fedelmid."

"And I'm surprised to find you here," she said, recapturing his gaze with redoubled curiosity, "when there's better fighting to be done elsewhere."

This amused him too. She gave him silver for a few moments of his time and the four of them occupied a table.

Once she had explained her intentions and showed him that more silver was available, Fedelmid said with a grin, "I can assemble a crew. There are only eight of us left in shape for war, but I would pit these men against the Army of the Damned."

"Eight are all we need," said Kreindia.

Keyx looked at her in disbelief, but said nothing.

"They will have to come with us immediately," Kreindia added, "and be ready to sail, drunk or not."

Fedelmid smiled, "Immediately is the very best way to get their Celtic blood up. Especially drunk."

~ *W* ~

KREINDIA worried that her emergence from the night in her noble's dress accompanied by two soldiers with two rows of prisoners in tow had to have been an alarming sight for the men on the deck of the dromon.

A low ranking officer came to the fore to challenge them, looking as if he did not have much stomach for this sort of confrontation. "I'm the decamarch, Phaedo, senior officer on board. What business brings you?"

Kreindia considered that a decamarch commands ten. So ten to contend with at most. "I'm the emperor's niece, Korinna. I need to commandeer this ship."

Phaedo raised his chin in reflexive opposition. "Thomas of Pontus ordered that we keep it here."

"He's not navy."

"But he's the *tourmarch*."

She struck a tone of impatience giving over to spoiled petulance. "His authority is temporarily superseded by mine, which covers the entire empire, and all I want is one ship."

With a nervous lick of his lips, he said, "What would you do with the ship, Korinna?"

"We have to ferry these prisoners back for questioning."

Phaedo acknowledged the eight fair-haired men linked by chain for the first time. He stepped forward and wrinkled his nose at them. "Prisoners, you say? They're not Arabs."

"Precisely. They're mercenary Celts enlisted by the Arabs to fight behind our lines. That's why Constantinople has to know." Her shipboard stance was broad and unyielding with her fists planted at her hips.

"Why are there so many of the filthy barbarians?"

She glanced at Fedelmid and the others before answering. "Our problem exactly. Each primitive knows so little, you practically have to question a battalion to get the whole story."

The explanation resonated with the decamarch, though by the skeptical set of his lips, he still wondered what indulging her would cost him. "Why *this* ship?"

"You've seized everything in Chalcedon, and this small warship is the only appropriate vessel for enemy transport. The dromon will be back in your control for days before Thomas returns. No one will be inconvenienced."

"That all sounds reasonable," said Phaedo. "There's only one problem. I don't know if you're the emperor's niece Korinna, as you say. You'll all have to wait here until I can find someone in my chain of command that can verify who you are."

That argument froze her blood. It was the most difficult of all to address since of course her story would not hold up. Phaedo had already turned his back. She was concerned that the decamarch, never having been senior enough to deal with orders outside of his own command, would consider himself in an untenable position if she boxed him in further. Yet the threat of his leaving could not go unanswered and a rash reply was all she had left. In a loud voice, she raised her hands and announced, "We're under a state of emergency and I have been warned of spies. I forbid any of you from stepping off this vessel."

"Then I can't let you hazard the crossing." Phaedo reddened as he strode up to the prisoners. "You've got these shifty, rat-eating barbarians to guard and not enough sailors here," he protested angrily, letting his spittle fly in Fedelmid's face. "How would you run the ship properly?"

Fedelmid said, "With we barbarians at the helm, that's how." In continuous motion, he dropped his chains, heaved off his winter covering as he drew his sword, and slashed the decamarch's throat. Phaedo crumpled to the deck.

As the rest of the Celts took up their arms and all of them rushed the remaining crew, Kreindia shouted angrily at Fedelmid, "I told you that we don't take over until we're out to sea!"

Fedelmid replied over his shoulder, "You promised us the ship. I grew tired of his excuses."

"Now we have to ready the fire," Kreindia said with resignation.

They took over swiftly, using their surprise to good advantage. The decamarch's unit turned out to be undermanned, with just seven in total, and most of them were not *Foederati*. But they fought and died well, which made Fedelmid happy.

Against Kreindia and her ten, albeit with Keyx of little help, the Imperium lost another two at the cost of a badly drunken Celt who had the misfortune of getting his belt caught on a belaying pin and dying on the ropes. Kreindia herself slashed two soldiers who tried to board from the docks and they fell back to seek help.

In the end, four slightly wounded marines surrendered. *Good,* Kreindia breathed, putting her sword away. *We need the extra manpower.* She assembled everyone on deck, climbed above, and pointedly asked the survivors, "Will you take my orders now?"

A quiet settled in as both attackers and defenders listened carefully for the other's answer. By the way the Celts watched her every smallest move, she got the distinct impression that Fedelmid and his people were ready to make an independent decision.

"Are you actually the emperor's niece?" a dromon sailor called out.

She came down from the upper deck to speak to that man nose-to-nose, so that each could see the other's sweat. Then she shouted, "You already know that Byzantium is rising. The insurrection is our doing. I am Kreindia of

Amorium, General Michael of Amorium's niece, and I say Michael is emperor now. By tomorrow, no one will say otherwise!"

She would run and hide no more, and it felt magnificent.

The sailor piped up, "Then I say, 'Aye!'" A broad cheer erupted from the small assembly, and Kreindia welcomed their allegiance with pride.

"Anthimos," she called, "You know what to do."

"Aye."

They untied the mooring lines and pushed off, preparing both for sea and for battle. But as they culled the Greek fire from the xylokastron one of the sailors at the task stood frozen in fear. A simple, silver cross dangled from around his neck. It was similar to the one Kreindia wore on her own necklace, and she touched it briefly now as she treaded lightly in her approach.

"What is your name?" As she got closer, her heart twisted within her. *He looks practically a child*, she thought. *Of course he's afraid to carry out these orders.* She had never wanted to fight her fellow Byzantines. Why would he?

"I'm Sosthenes," he said into the empty air before his eyes.

With a hand on his shoulder, she assured him, "Everything is going to be okay, Sosthenes. Do you believe that the Christian god is the only god, and that he protects us?"

He nodded vigorously, closed his eyes tight, and asked, "Are those barbarians with you Christians?"

"No, but I am. Have you changed your mind about following me and our new emperor?"

Softly, he said, "No."

"The church is uniting behind us. Anything else will be treason. Do you choose the path of treason?"

He opened his eyes wide and shook his head.

"Then your duty is clear. Get to those sails and do your job. If this is your first trip to war, we'll make it a good one."

"To the rigging then, aye, my Lady. Thank you… By the way, it's *Phaidra*."

"What is?"

"The name of the ship, the *Phaidra*. You can't sail her to safety without knowing the name of the ship."

"Thank you," she said.

Their drift away from the other ships and the commotion on board did not go unnoticed. Although none seemed to believe they were under attack from the tiny force, the military police were scrambling for what they must have thought were drunken sailors gotten out of hand, and the dromon's flagship ran signals to order them to stop. Like the *Phaidra*, the other ships were mostly empty and unprepared to sail in pursuit. But it would not take an entire fleet to stop them.

"Hoses," she commanded, calling for the channels that would spray liquid fire. Anthimos conveyed the order to the old crew, as they were the ones familiar with the equipment.

Sosthenes, who stood near the rigging, was petrified. It was one thing to prepare for war and another to actually participate. "Are we really going to fire at other Christians?"

Kreindia shook her head. "Step aside." Taking over one of the stations to show them what she meant, she laid down a line of fire in the water between the *Phaidra* and the rest of the dromons. The oily tar-like material that launched kept the fire sitting on top well fueled, forming a prohibitive wall that would force any pursuers into a long detour around the burn zone.

Fedelmid and his men were agog at the might held at bay. Kreindia brought them back to reality, warning, "That barrier won't be enough. If they add any oars, they'll outrun us." She ordered, "Spray the docks too so that reinforcements can't reach their ships."

They set the docks aflame. And ran a course for

Constantinople.

A merchant ship that had been out to sea and on its way into Chalcedon harbor reversed direction to make for the open water again. They would have had to do that anyway to avoid the flame wall, but Kreindia noticed that the ship scrambled to move along with them. In a short time, the single sail with the square rigging came close enough for her to see the captain and for him to identify her.

Davilos! It was the *Diantha* that dogged them. Probably looking for a reward for locating her or seeing where they went. After the close look, it pulled away from them.

"Make sure you strike that ship, and hurry" she instructed Anthimos. "A small burst to the bow."

"But it's only a merchant ship," he pleaded. "One that we need."

"I know exactly what it is. Do it."

"Aye," he said sadly.

Manning a hose, Anthimos carefully painted the bow with their fiery tar, and the *Diantha* ignited, spreading the flames along the hull. Kreindia saw Davilos emerge and leap overboard with the rest of the crew. One brought along a loose plank and a dozen fought a savage battle for possession, a fight that ended in mutual disaster.

Keyx went up to Kreindia as she peered over the sheer strake to see the dishonest ferry masters thrashing in the water. Sounding mournful, he said, "You just burned up our money."

She patted him on the back.

Now the Celts cheered the destruction as the merchant vessel flared from stem to stern. With a glance at their glowing faces, Keyx asked her, "You don't feel bad about giving the Celts a warship?"

"There's only eight of them," she said, trying to sound confident. "How much trouble can they get into?"

$\sim W \sim$

THEY had only this one night left to go before Michael's execution and Kreindia was determined to see things go otherwise. Having returned to the Thracian peninsula, she had distributed the Studite's messages to their designated recipients.

All of the churches were open late on Christmas Eve. Michael's Studite clergy and their allies went from church to church *en masse*. To aid their endeavor, they had freed a famous giant slave named Pammon who had not been treated well. The enormous, angry man was all the muscle they needed. With him leading the way, they put their uncooperative peers in chains for the duration.

Having witnessed one such spectacle at the Hagia Irene, Anthimos asked Kreindia, "Is this support going to be enough to take control?"

Her eyes were dark. "It's the beginning. Until Michael is in power, nothing will be enough. And even then, Thomas won't go down easily."

"How much time do we have?"

"Maybe none. Assume that Thomas will realize our deception long before he gets to Claudiopolis."

"That means he could be back tonight. And then what?"

"We'll contend with him when we have to."

~ *W* ~

ON Christmas Day, long after the sun had set on the Sea of Marmora, the *Foederati* assembled in a building close to the docks in the Chalcedonian port to prepare for the race back to Constantinople. It seemed to Thomas that cooperation among his troops was lacking.

He lamented to his inner circle, "I don't know how Michael's supporters did it, but the attack was false. We've had conflicting reports from every quarter and there were no refugees from battle. If they lured us over here, it means the conspirators are on the move in the capital."

Commander Dardanes stirred, restive.

"Yes?" Thomas demanded.

"My lord, I'm not certain it was a trick. There is talk of unrest everywhere, and there has been for a while. We need to move *Foederati* troops to the interior before the outbreak of hostilities."

"And if I say otherwise?"

Dardanes' eyes flicked to the side as though he had surreptitiously discussed this very matter with others in the room beforehand. "Then we will move them just the same."

Thomas could have spit enough nails to build another fleet of ships. Most of his troops came from this region and were set to defend their homes. If he opposed them going inland, Thomas could expect an open insurrection. He closed his eyes and frowned while he got himself under control. When he opened them, he said, "Do it then. I don't care. But I'm going back with my household troops. Is everything ready yet?"

"No, my lord, the damage done by whoever burned the docks—"

"I don't want to hear it again, Dardanes. Just do what you have to and let me go."

There was a swift rapping at the door. Thomas turned to face it in annoyance and distrust. "Come in." *No one could have gotten this close without being vetted.* Thomas had been warned that a fleet ship with a dispatch would presently appear to meet them before they left. *Could they be here already?*

The door swung open, and in strode an uncommonly tall, thin man with sunken, depraved eyes and stringy black hair. Thomas's chair clattered backwards as he jumped to his feet. "Zoticus," he breathed, aghast. "What are you doing here?"

Zoticus Macroducas stood menacingly in the doorway, glaring suspiciously about the room. He was once Thomas' bodyguard, now risen to his second in command.

"I didn't trust our communications," said Zoticus with his gravely voice at its deepest. He glanced around carefully at the faces of those present before stepping into the room. "I needed to see you personally."

"Do we have the names?" Thomas asked. "The list from Michael?"

"No. That's the problem. The task was assigned to Brygos and he passed along nothing."

"Why is he not in front of me? I want to question him."

"Someone's murdered him."

"How?"

"We don't know, but we began an inquiry, and then Tiro slipped away."

"Tiro?"

"He was the one assigned to Michael's door."

"Brygos is dead, eh? That's more than a shame. I had great plans for that man." Thomas had carefully cultivated Brygos. He had reassigned him under Michael's signature as though he was being punished by the Amorian, and it had embittered Brygos, shaping him into the perfect revenge tool. *How could this have happened?* "Michael is still in our custody, right?"

"Why wouldn't he be?"

"You said his jail keeper was missing, though."

Zoticus shrugged. "It s suspicious, but his running off could have been over anything."

"Are you with them?" Thomas yelled.

"My lord?"

"The conspirators. Are you with the conspirators, Zoticus? Is that why you've abandoned your post?"

"You're getting paranoid, my lord."

Dardanes and the other men looked at each other and shook their heads sadly.

Thomas sneered, trying to control himself. "Get on that fast ship of yours, Zoticus. You find out what happened to Brygos or don't come back."

~ *W* ~

"THE next steps have to happen nearly simultaneously," Kreindia announced back at the mainland. Assembled in the private house with Kreindia were Anthimos, Keyx, and Agenor the priest, along with several others. With her synesthesia-boosted memory, Kreindia had recalled the entire list of conspirators, key figures from every walk of life. They joined her now.

One of the esteemed, the magistrate in charge of prisons, called to her, "What if we don't want to take the risk?"

"It's too late for that. You can stand with me or be exposed. As long as you don't stand in my way, you'll be safe."

He swallowed. "I can do that."

Kreindia continued in a loud voice, "We leave here, we grab Leo, reveal his treasonous acts, and show him that his supporters have withdrawn. Like Rhangabe before him, he'll be forced to abdicate. Another group of us will free Michael and get him to the throne room with the patriarch presiding, and have Leo transfer his power. I will be in the second group."

Senator Blathyllos, who was with them now and giddy to help, grabbed her arm and told her, "I was entirely in favor of Michael as emperor and just waiting for you to join our numbers."

She leveled a look of contempt at the senator and shook him off. "If not for my intervention, you politicians would have done nothing."

As for the others, the atmosphere in the meeting was dangerously near that of a celebration. She addressed them again from atop a stool she placed in their midst, "Look at yourselves! Too many of you look like you're fitting yourselves for new togas. This isn't a party. The stakes are high—the highest possible. We don't accomplish *anything* unless we accomplish everything."

"Don't worry, Kreindia," said Anthimos. "I think we have it all organized now. There are no more loose ends."

Addressing the group, Agenor interrupted, "You're all to be commended on what you've all done, of course, but does anyone know where Leo is going to be tonight? Anyone?"

CHAPTER 18

The Purple

S O, THE STRANGE *dyed her hair blonde,* thought Thomas as the dromon bore him steadily across the strait in the dead of night. Thamar had positively identified the prisoner as Kreindia. But what could be the purpose of such a thin disguise? Such a bizarre choice for posing as a Syrian woman. And yet it had to have been Kreindia that came up with the Chrysopolis ruse. She could easily have transmitted instructions to confederates. What's more, she had to have wanted to be apprehended. Maybe because it put her in proximity to Michael. *The point is that Kreindia did fool me after all.*

Soon enough, though, none of that would matter. He could see the Thracian mainland coming up fast, marked by the powerful lighthouse lamps of the coast and supplemented by the lesser lights behind them. He would do without Michael's list of conspirators because now he traveled with a select group consisting of only the people he trusted best. His household staff included soldiers. The uncle and the niece were doomed even if Leo were dead by now—especially if Leo were dead now. The night would close. The day would begin anew.

Thomas would claim his throne.

~ *W* ~

WELL past midnight after Christmas Day, wet snow

filled the wide windowsill that faced the interior courtyard at the Palace of Daphne. A soft glow burned above that ledge unseen. Attending the one-on-one matins service within the disused and unheated chapel of St. Stephen was the basileus himself, Leo V the Armenian. He had no expectation of an untroubled sleep until every crucial task was done. Like Thomas, he remembered their fate-drenched journey to Cappadocia in sharp detail. The messenger bird flying into the unnerving formation in the clouds, the configuration so like a wreath-crown, a diadem. How fragile it was. Like the life of an emperor. Gritting his teeth, he tried to clear his mind of the final image, the lion transfixed by the sword.

He should be safe here and now, kneeling in the cold. No one else knew he was at Daphne except for the priest who was with him. Dressed as meanly as the lowest members of his court, he'd moved about freely by the low light of candles rather than lamps or torches. In fact, he was expected in Boucoleon Palace where such services were customarily held for the past two centuries. But until Thomas could round up all of Michael's co-conspirators, or Michael lay dead and unable to inspire anyone to insurrection, the precautions were more than necessary. He was here to pray that everything would go smoothly at Michael's dawn execution, which was to be his very next stop.

The priest had just completed the lengthy psalmody and was now beginning his homily, "We repent with fervor on this day because the Resurrection is nigh. We do not know when Christ will come. It may be in the middle of the night. It may—for all we know—be in the middle of this *very* night."

Just then, the doors flew open with a bang. The volume of air was warm from the interior room. The priest shouted, "Oh my Lord!"

Leo stood as a group of five brown-robed and winter-cloaked monks trod rudely into the chamber. And then stepped aside for a giant.

Aghast, Leo backed away from them. He recognized the man and his colossal strides from his games in the Hippodrome. It was the slave called Pammon, the One and a Half. His gigantic square jaw could have served as the keel of a ship. "What do you want here?" said Leo in ripening confusion.

Pammon boomed, "We want to put a tyrant outside the wall." At his words, a rough paraphrase of the city's ordinance on cemeteries, the false monks suddenly threw off their cloaks, revealing a glittering array of weapons. With swords and knives out they set upon the officiating priest in his finery of white and gold, apparently mistaking him for the Emperor in the dim light, especially as both men wore fur caps against the cold.

Doffing the hat, the clergyman blurted, "I'm with you, you asses. It's him right there!"

Meanwhile, Leo went scrambling for the great cross to defend himself with—he'd need an outsized weapon against the giant—and then remembered. He'd been convinced that military losses of the past three decades meant that God had been displeased by imperial support of the iconophiles. In a dreadful mistake, he'd had his men scour the chapels and strip them of anything that smacked of icon veneration, including the massive wooden cross that he might have defended himself with in this dire moment. He looked around wildly. He had to be satisfied with a candelabrum. He lifted the burning brass holder and swung at those nearest.

The men ducked, either in fear of catching fire or of losing the light. The feeble gambit could only hold them off for so long.

"Guards! Guards!" Leo called out, pausing only when he noticed that the door had been securely barred with two-man beams. *No! They must have done it while I searched for the cross.* Trapped, he could do nothing but pray as the attackers came towards him. "Stay away from me!"

Encouraged by someone pounding on the other side in apparent response to his call, Leo threw the guttering tree of candles at his assailants. They jumped clear and the decoration hit the stone floor. One candle rolled and sparks scattered, setting a bottom edge of the drapes on fire. The diversion allowed Leo to race his attackers to the exit while they tore down the hangings and stomped the flames to stop the smoke. Seeing that the lock itself stood open, Leo began to slide the heavy beam out of its rings, spurred by fright-fueled strength. With excruciating sluggishness, the beam scraped with a grating cacophony through all three supports to fall with a clunk onto the floor.

His triumph turned to ashes as his time ran out. A second beam remained on the upper portion of the door and the drapery fire that had occupied them was out. The robed men spun him around while the shaft above held fast against the outside assault. Within a few moments, a sword stroke sliced his defending hand, and a second cut opened his biceps. He dashed back through the men who surrounded him like a gauntlet. Off balance in the flurry of swings that followed, he fell across the broad communion table, whereupon the One and a Half commenced to hack him to pieces. Pammon underestimated Leo's writhing desperation, for the first shot was meant for the emperor's shoulder and only took a hand. After a couple more tries and a plea of "Hold still, my lord," the giant got the hang of it and diced him like a salad.

They carried out the royal remains, one or two parts for each of them, and made a bloody mess of the courtyard snow before rushing off to the dungeons to assist in freeing Michael.

~ *W* ~

THOMAS' household troops, including Zoticus, swarmed the dock at Constantinople and mounted the horses that stood ready for them. A unit of *Foederati* that had been left on the home front stood by to join them.

"Hold," said Thomas to the second group. "Any news?"

A young commander named Vanoush answered him. "Michael's execution is on schedule. We can get to the palace on time to witness it if we hurry."

"That's well. Are you looking forward to the event?"

"Very much so, my lord."

As Thomas approached him, he said, "Vanoush, aren't you a distant relative of Leo's?" He broke eye contact to brush his horse gently. It was time to winnow down his select group still further.

"Yes," Vanoush said cautiously as though he scented the tone of suspicion. "What about it? I thought we were going after Michael."

"We are. I need someone I can trust to take command of the docks. That will be you."

He wished he could kill Vanoush right now, but that might disturb his remaining supporters, who were nervous enough. Without waiting for an answer, he pointed forward and the group took off, leaving a bewildered Vanoush behind.

Although they had but a short distance to go, Thomas drove the horses hard and their hooves took a beating on the city stones. As the first rays of sun hit, they ran over one of the hard-working people of Constantinople, who had been setting up his fruit stand for the new day.

"Zoticus," Thomas called out, "we'll split up now. You go to the Boucoleon, I'll go to the Great Palace."

"You can trust me," yelled Zoticus.

"I know," Thomas replied. "I was crazy to think otherwise."

The loyalty of Thomas' core troops—his elite—and the passion they held for him would bring the bold victory he sought. Leo would never expect him back so soon.

~ *W* ~

WHEN the group wearing the monk disguises came rushing into Michael's cell under the palace, Kreindia pointed her sword to the gut of the first man through the door. He gasped and stopped short. Then she noticed his great height and moved the tip above her head, bringing it just under his chin.

"Leave him," said Keyx, hurrying from Michael's side to hers. "The giant is ours. That's Pammon."

She released him, realizing she'd seen the One and a Half before.

Pammon smiled crookedly to show he was still of good cheer. "We did it," he shouted, holding up a severed hand for inspection.

"No, no, no! I said head!" Keyx admonished him. "Not hand! Head!"

"It wears his ring," said Pammon with a gathering of his great brow. "That should be proof enough."

"I'm working with amateurs!" Keyx screamed in complaint.

"We already disposed of him. We can't go back for other parts."

"One of you had damned well better try." He slapped one of the monks on the shoulder and pointed out the door. "You! Go!" The man bolted through, grateful to get beyond Keyx' ire for the moment.

Now Keyx turned to face Kreindia's fury. "I told you I wanted Leo alive," she yelled.

"And that would never have worked, my dear," he explained in a calming, buttery tone. "No one follows a new emperor when there is still an old one hanging around. That's why I added the One and a Half to your group. I thought of him when you mentioned that one Saxon you had in mind."

"What about the keys?" Kreindia interrupted for anyone who could answer.

194

"What keys?" Pammon asked.

"The ones you need to unlock me," Michael cried. "How could you not think of it?"

Pammon frowned. "I searched the corpse. Leo didn't have them."

Keyx snapped his fingers. "We'll get a blacksmith."

"Do you know where one lives?" Kreindia demanded. "Because it's the middle of the night."

"Right. No blacksmith."

"Where did you hide that shovel?" she asked.

"You can't break chains with a shovel," said Keyx. "Are you feeling all right?"

Kreindia knew she must look far away. She wasn't quite having a vision, though—simply remembering one from long ago. She'd explained some of it to Anthimos when they were together on the rolling deck of the *Delius* before they faced the pirates. What she hadn't told him was that she'd seen small details of how events regarding Michael on this particular day were supposed to unfold... *enormous hands on the shaft and socket of a shovel... bursting the chain link... men carrying her uncle on the shield... dubbing him "Michael II"* ...and now she said with certainly, "Pammon can do it."

"I suppose it's worth a try," said Keyx.

They retrieved the shovel and Pammon looped the first length of chain over the chair's metal arm. Michael advised, "Try not to kill me, you gigantic fool."

"All right." Pammon raised the shovel high, leveled two strikes of enormous arc and loud clangs, and stopped to examine the hot metal. With a giant's wounded confidence, he said, "That should have done it. Why didn't that do it?"

Kreindia said, "Once more, and make sure you use the edge."

Pammon scowled at the digging tool in his expansive hands and made a slight adjustment. With the very next strike, the first chain snapped under the blade and dropped away. The small group cheered.

When they had done away with the other bindings, Kreindia said to Michael and the others, "You go ahead to the throne room. I have to take care of something here. Pammon, come with me."

Kreindia hadn't forgotten the other captive. The Syrian's incarceration on her behalf still haunted her, and she feared that the woman might have been tortured.

They ran along the filthy corridor and came to a turn where a well-muscled guard snarled, "I was wondering when in Hades someone would come to relieve me."

With one great arm, Pammon swept him away to crash against the wall. "Done," he said.

With the watchman's keys, Kreindia began to investigate every dark cell in the section just in case. The first two held members of her original team that never made it to Leo. She freed them. In the third one, she found the woman. "Are you all right?" Kreindia asked.

When the captive calmly turned to her and smiled, Kreindia regarded her in shock. She'd heard of the resemblance, but...

The woman had ash blonde hair and a slightly gaunt air of battle about her. Yet she had the same eyes of blue and the same face as Kreindia but for a scar on her cheek; gazing at her was like examining a brass reflection of herself with a scratch on it.

"Who—?"

"They call me Amynta." *Defender.* That was the word Anthimos used when she thought he was talking about Wade. She was the one who'd sent Anthimos to the Anatolian shore.

"By the saints," gasped Kreindia. "I can't believe it. You *do* look like me."

Amynta leaned forward and whispered, "I *am* you."

At the tickle of breath against her ear, Kreindia experienced dancing blue powder on a sheet of infinite ice. She witnessed only the local part of it, the rest stretching into darkness. The ice and powder stood as elements rather than objects—the very same synesthetic signature that Wade registered every time he encountered Kreindia. Amynta wasn't an image in a mirrored surface. She wasn't a missing part of the general's niece like Del who had fragmented away from her. She was a downstream Kreindia standing on a part of the arrow of time that had doubled back like a serpent swallowing its tail.

Kreindia shivered, grew weak, and dropped to her knees, thinking she could feel the universe twist inside of her.

"What are you doing?" Pammon shouted. "Come on! We have to go."

"He's right," said Amynta.

"What about you?" Kreindia whispered with one hand reaching out and not quite touching.

"I was only here for you. Go."

$\sim W \sim$

AT the gates of the Great Palace, Thomas encountered a small provisional force that had been mustered in favor of Michael. Standing firm, they formed a shield wall that filled the great archway with too few men to shore it up from the incomplete second rank behind. Thomas and fifteen of his householders with another twelve *Foederati* came thundering up to them intending to climb the stairs, but the horses balked at the rise, coming up short so that several men fell off. The rest had to dismount and launch the attack on foot.

The defenders, standing higher, easily absorbed the momentum of the first clash, but proved immediately outnumbered and outclassed. The foolish skirmish stretched on, with every blow in defense another excuse to cheer. Nonetheless, Michael's followers dwindled and surrendered their lives to the delaying action.

Towards the end, Thomas' force was down by a third.

"I should have brought a larger group," he remonstrated to no one in particular. "This hindrance is intolerable."

When the opposition cleared down to the holdouts in an incomplete single rank, Thomas broke through. He paused the carnage to grab a bloodied survivor and shake him. "Are there any more of you?"

Gasping, and closing his eyes against the coming blow, the man had only the pitiful answer, "I don't know."

~ *W* ~

KREINDIA scooted up the stairs while Pammon's stride took him over several steps for each of hers. They crossed the building to the sumptuous throne room, and caught up to Michael's ceremony just in time. She entered and stopped near Keyx. He cleared a space for her beside him along the aisle and closer to the platform.

Even as her mind churned through the possibilities entangled in worlds of "now," "then," and "to be," the spectacle in front of her under the mosaics of the saints did not fail to hold a part of her attention. Since Michael had lost so much weight in the prison, his followers easily hoisted him upon one of their rectangular curved shields of red and gold. With his legs astride the silver metal boss, his iron chains rattling, they carried him up the steps along the purple carpet and set him in front of Constantinople's Patriarch Theodotos I.

While the patriarch hurried his assistant to bring the coronation adornments, Kreindia's thoughts swam. *If it was Amynta and not Wade who had reached out to Anthimos, then what has happened to him?*

In her mind Kreindia saw a skull. She took the opportunity to turn to Keyx and asked him, "Back at the dungeons, when we met the first guard, and you said—"

"The password, *Golgotha?* It means—"

"Place of a Skull, the mount where Jesus was crucified."

"Yes," he mused. "That guard was a good man, my one and only personal recruit. Look at us now, all that work coming to fruition."

"But you said that Tiro—"

"I said that Tiro was my only contact in the *lower* dungeons."

She wondered if that new piece of information about *Golgotha* fit anywhere, and why she thought of it in the context of Wade.

Saying a hasty prayer, Theodotos adorned Michael with the purple drape known as the paludamentum. In classic fashion, the priest started it on his right shoulder, wrapped it around his back and front, fastened the shoulder clasp at the starting point and then threw the remaining tasseled length once more around his back and over his left shoulder.

Finally, two young priests helped an unsteady Michael to the ivory throne itself. He was smiling broadly. Theodotos crowned the matted curly hair with a golden laurel wreath saying, "You shall be Michael II."

Just as in Kreindia's vision.

What she had not foreseen was the very next moment when Thomas and his troops burst into the chamber, the Slav shouting, "Hold." They spread out, and then froze in apprehension, finding a new reality to absorb. The householders and *Foederati* looked about in the great chamber, apparently trying to figure out if they had a mission here or were absolutely too late.

Seeing Leo's snow-capped head on the side table, Michael already in the paludamentum and diadem, and the Patriarch himself presiding at the ceremony, with a giant and other armed men for witness, Thomas' loyalists submitted to the new emperor, each dropping to a knee, tossing their weapons aside, and dipping their heads in subservience. Those few who had remained beyond the open doorway did the same.

"Michael II," Theodotos repeated for their benefit.

"Michael II," they answered in subjugated unison.

Thomas did not acquiesce. He alone stayed upright in the throne room, and a long keening noise escaped his curled lips. Taking a sword in each hand, he thundered through the ranks of kneeling men toward Michael.

Pammon simply stood up in Thomas' path. The *tourmarch* collided with one side of the giant and went spinning away. Once an able soldier, long a crafty general, Thomas' age and the fight at the gates had slowed and weakened him. He rose slowly and seemed as though he was in great pain, but upon rising made a new decision and bolted for the door, only to find that Kreindia had beaten him there.

Kreindia had not surrendered her sword like the others. She lifted it against him. Never breaking stride, he batted her blade away with the two of his. Before she could recover, Thomas launched himself through the door.

As she made to follow him, Michael shouted, "Kreindia, stay here."

"I can catch him though."

"No, he's more unpredictable than you can imagine. The rest of you, go after him. Anthimos, see that they do it!"

The combined troops, led by Anthimos, rose to retrieve their weapons, ran around Kreindia and her uncle, and flowed out the exit.

Even as the last of the soldiers could be seen clattering down the hall beyond, commander Zoticus filled the doorway, his sunken black eyes bloodshot, and leveled a left handed swipe at the first person he saw, which was Kreindia. Although he took her unawares, she struck the weapon aside, marveling at the state of her own reflexes when it counted.

As Michael went back to arm himself with Keyx's weapon, Kreindia thought of the role Zoticus had played in the death of her friend Verina. Yes, by chance a piece of the ceiling of the Hagia Sofia had come loose in an earthquake, but where would Verina have been standing if Zoticus had not delayed her? "Stand clear," she shrieked. "This one is mine!" Kreindia blocked Zoticus' next shot and launched a strike of her own as he reared back. It sliced through one of the tall man's nostrils.

He touched the spot, looked at the smear of blood on his fingers and growled. Holding the blade flat, Zoticus went for her middle. She moved aside just in time but felt the shallow cut as his entire arm slid past her on the right.

Enraged, Michael stabbed Zoticus in the belly, withdrew the point, and set about smacking him in the face with his blade. One of those strikes cut the high commander's neck and drove him finally to the floor where he clutched his midsection and moaned. Michael raised his head to the sound of pounding feet.

Behind Zoticus came a group of six *Feoderati*, presumably part of the contingent of men he led. They barreled into the room as though they were being chased. Ushering the priest ahead of her for his safety, Kreindia mounted the platform steps to get the height she needed and put her back to the podium. Michael quickly joined her there and they both prepared to face the onslaught.

Behind the imperials came the Saxon, Grimketil Forkbeard, the barrel-built half-barbarian, grinning fiercely in his battle rage. He led a single companion, smaller than himself and still large in his own right. From their red blades and blood splashed faces, the gore that colored them was not likely their own. As a battle cry, Grimketil bellowed, "For the Athinganoi!"

At the prospect of being cornered by the vicious duo— despite what they'd seen the Saxons do before—the soldiers rallied. Three men charged after Michael and his niece in hopes of ending the objects of the conflict. Using one of his axes to point to Michael and Kreindia, the Saxon shouted, "Beorhtric, defend them."

Grimketil's countryman would not have gotten there in time but for the vigilant defensive moves of the royals-to-be. For his part, Beorhtric centered his axe in between the shoulder blades of the first attacker, kicked down the second and put steel into the jaw of the third as he turned to the ongoing assault. They were all quick and shallow strikes to change the flow of battle. The first man was arrested by Boerhtric's strike but the axe head had not gone far past his armor. He turned to fight. The second got up, and the third crawled for his dropped weapon as Michael came down and finished him. Kreindia, already weary and struggling, made sure she kept her blade up to discourage another reckless charge. Boerhtric now faced only two, one of whom was wounded.

Grimketil, who faced the other three, was practiced to the point of wielding his axes with figure-eight fluidity. Being a long veteran of war, he slowed to a workmanlike pace to put calm to his opponent's desperation. His uncommon strength and skill quickly made three opponents into one. Grimketil and Beorhtric, with Michael's help, laid about and the finish was a slaughter.

In the aftermath, Kreindia examined her right side where Zoticus had struck her. Her dress was cut open to the skin and her blood ran in a thin line. Although the injury was glancing, it was unaccountably painful, the way a cut from parchment could be. She examined his blade's edge and saw that it was ragged.

Zoticus lay still and Michael had the bodies ejected.

"Thomas is going to be trouble for me," Michael said, coming back to Kreindia. "Very serious trouble."

Pinching her wound, she asked, "With the divided loyalties of his householders, can you trust them as your own to go after Thomas?"

Michael, whose savaged face was softened with concern, took her hand and said, "Don't you worry about Thomas anymore, Kreindia. You've done more than your share."

She looked over at the side table where Leo's handsome face adorned his freshly severed head, and shuddered at the thought of the consequences she'd helped bring about.

Michael reminded her sternly, "Whatever happens now, Thomas is my problem. Promise me you'll leave it alone."

She blinked and dutifully said, "I will," even though she was no longer sure of what she might do. She turned to Grimketil, who was cleaning his sword in preparation to sheathe it. "Have you seen Wade?"

"Wade of Aquitaine? I've not seen him in as many years as I've not seen you." He gave her a measuring and altogether wise look that she was too distracted to fully process.

"Grimketil has knowledge of our arts and is formally bound to us," Michael explained.

"And have always been," Grimketil admitted. The Athinganoi had in common not only a religion but also a warrior caste with far-flung agents.

Kreindia scrutinized him. "Always? It didn't seem that way when you arrested Wade in Swabia."

Michael intervened. "That wasn't Grimketil's fault. My messenger reached him late. For your own safety, I couldn't let you know that your undertaking with Wade had any support in the West."

But Kreindia had greater concerns at the moment. *My mission here is accomplished,* she thought, *so where is Wade now?* She'd expected him the whole time, but most of all she thought he would appear at the end. If the palace coup wasn't the completion of what she needed to do, then what was?

"We're not finished," said the strict patriarch.

"Of course, Theodotos," Michael acknowledged, gathering himself up again. Those few remaining attended as witness for the close of ceremonies. They were joined now by several palace functionaries.

As Kreindia watched, suffering the beginnings of a furious headache in addition to the pulsing fire in her side, the patriarch took the podium. Rather short in stature,

Theodotos stood high as though he had ascended two steps instead of one. At first, she regarded the difference as a mark of the occasion and its majesty. If the effect were more than just her perception, but a physical reality, the priest could not be blamed for adding an extra step behind the podium.

Adjusting a large tome in front of him, however, Theodotos seemed to grow still further so that the great codex appeared to rapidly shrink to an ordinary size. Looking around as though ensuring silence as he worked a stiffness out of his neck and spine, he stretched unevenly in all dimensions until he was bigger than Pammon. His reader could easily have disappeared into a crease of his monstrous palm. At the same time, the great room warped around him, and then broke into a rough sort of froth before it solidified again.

Kreindia grew dizzy and the pain in her side flared. The last disturbance blurred and passed as quickly as a fallen eyelash can be blinked away. Theodotos now assumed his usual proportion, looking tiny by comparison.

She examined the kneeling men who now included Keyx in their number. They exhibited no more or less than the proper respect for the occasion. Michael, the center of attention, looked on expectantly. Still reeling from her meeting with Amynta and the fierce battle just past, Kreindia was apparently the only one who had witnessed the visual disturbance. *What did Zoticus do to me?*

When Theodotos was supposed to be giving Michael the final blessing, he began a most unusual speech. "Here we stand," the Patriarch said, "one hundred eighty years from the End of Everything when sinning is done and Creation undone. Heaven will close and Hell will open."

Nothing is right about this, Kreindia realized. Those were not the words of the ceremony. Not remotely correct. And unlike any blessing she had ever heard!

The visual disturbance arose again, dismantling the room, and this time her mind withdrew and crossed the centuries the way it once had to seek Wade, only unbidden, and much faster. She hadn't had a vision since she'd returned to the ninth century and her temples flared in screaming pain before going silent.

She was gazing over the shoulder of the body she had once shared with Del, and a part of her was there still. They were in the physical therapy center in Long Island. It had to have been a day she'd never seen because Del was in control and doing an exercise with finger cups. When Kreindia appeared, Del seemed to acknowledge the change. She interrupted herself to call out to the tiny girl who shared her crippled plight.

Upon seeing Del and bringing one wheelchair to meet the other, Lorraine said to her solemnly, "You're nice, but you're not her. You're only a fraction, and not even half."

Then the vision began to draw away and Kreindia heard the rest as an echo down a twelve hundred-year corridor. The child's eerie, frail voice was singing, "Row, row, row your boat gently down this dream..."

Dimly, as though she were at the bottom of a thundering river and her Byzantine friends were at the top, Kreindia heard someone calling for a sledgehammer and chisel for the remainder of Michael's chains. Even more distant was a warped voice saying that they would reconvene at the Hagia Sofia. She hadn't fully returned to the present, or hadn't quite locked in on it, because her mind was racing, trying to sort the flood of the mixing currents.

And then Kreindia *knew.*

And then she didn't.

—Because almonds and cicadas assaulted her nose and ears, turning her thoughts broadside, and exposing her to just one idea: *The End of Everything.* She linked it with something Lorraine once said, *Wade's not here...here where the Everything is.*

Theodotos' apocalyptic improvisation rippled through Kreindia to raise the tiny hairs on every inch of her body. One hundred eighty years from this day would be the turn of the millennium. The room twisted and snapped back into place.

With the certainty of a vision as proof, Kreindia knew that Wade had skipped the year 820 and followed this same spoor to the much more serious crisis at the turn of the millennium, the year 1000. Again, the little Norseman she'd vowed to avoid was in her hand, and this time back at the pressure point on her ear. She had no choice. The threatened End of Everything was where she had to go next.

CHAPTER 19

Faron and Clara

<u>Twenty-First Century, Jericho, New York</u>

A S CLARA LOOKED on in apprehension, Faron pounded on the living room door, shouting, "Kreindel, let me in."

They heard nothing back. She knew that Faron would not allow himself to be kept at bay by something as simple as a homemade barricade. He would look upon the problem as a fascinating hobby.

Indeed, he sized up the situation and set to work. Employing a skillful manipulation of the door handle, rattling it forward and back with the little play afforded him by the slight opening, he was able to cause enough vibration for small shifts in the blockage that led to a widening crack.

Whenever he paused, husband and wife picked up more of the disturbing silence. Clara hoped her daughter was all right, and dreaded what would happen when Faron gained access, which he surely would. The willfulness Kreindel had exhibited before her paralysis was back with a vengeance that would, in turn, be visited upon her in kind.

Faron interrupted his first pursuit to get a fireplace tool from the den—a frightening wrought iron poker with spike and hook—which he laid aside to stand by. Then he continued his push-pull effort with several more demands and admonishments to their daughter thrown in. By degrees, he gained just enough room to slip the fireplace rod through, hooking and dislodging the tilted chair, and opening their living room door to reveal...

"Kreindel! Why didn't you answer me?"

She only moaned in response.

Clara hurried into the room behind Faron.

With her tilted and drooping head, and the way her hands quirked to the side at her wrists, Kreindel seemed to have regressed to the point before her breakthrough. At the same time, Clara noticed a new look in her daughter's eyes. A look of trauma and scorched triumph, of glimpsed secrets within a terrible loss, and ultimately, of mystery. Clara bit her lip and sniffled. Even though she thought she could read all of those things in the eyes of her only child, she did not have the slightest idea what that collection of ideas could mean. A stray and foreign thought intruded on Clara's mind: *Only a fraction and not even half.*

But her husband studied Kreindel and smiled, fully satisfied by what he saw. Extending his appraisal to the inanimate, he set the barricade chair back in its usual position along with anything else in the room that seemed slightly out of place. Thus satisfied, he went to the den to restore the fireplace poker to its tool stand. No punishment. *Is it possible that Faron had anticipated this turn of events? Perhaps even wished for it?*

As much as Kreindel had been a mystery to Clara—at least as long as she'd been paralyzed—her husband was the biggest mystery of all.

Clara had seen news reports and documentary television shows showing men who were guilty of great crimes—rapists, murderers, and even serial killers. The narrators warned that these miscreants appeared to be like their viewers, normal in every respect, but born missing the part of the brain that housed a conscience. Parricides, matricides, fratricides and slaughterers of their entire family, who forged a new identity in a new place and fooled some stupid woman into marrying them. With that mask firmly in place they sometimes continued their life of unspeakable crime under the new wife's nose.

And sometimes they contented themselves by employing slow torture on their present families. Though Faron said strange, undecipherable things sometimes, Clara couldn't say for certain that Faron fit the psychological profile that they talked about on the shows. She wasn't a psychologist. The mask was always a good one, and she after all, was the person who had been fooled in the first place. For no matter what he was, she knew now that she had at least been the victim of the grand deception that Faron Richter was a good man.

Clara hailed from El Sabado, a Texas "bedroom community" where she had a high school baby with a boy who left town fast. When she started waitressing at the fairly upscale Jinny's Steak House, she began to attract the attention of all sorts of aggressive men, mostly married. They all liked how young she was until the baby aversion kicked in. One visit to her home, one diaper, one stray toy, told them all they needed to know.

Then one day Faron Richter showed up. He told her that he sold medical devices to hospitals, which you could say was the one thriving industry in town if you didn't count everyone's obsession with high school football. Clara's own obsession with the sport was what had gotten her in trouble in the first place. The Grunewald family had disowned her, including her brother, who had been best friends with her child's father. *An awful town.*

Against that background, the older man with the impeccable manners and the bankroll had considerable power over her. As soon as they were married, Faron moved her away from the few friends she had to live in Long Island, New York. Upon making that unilateral decision, he said his first crazy thing: "If it's a good enough place for the Gospel of Judas, it's good enough for us." And there her suffering—and Kreindel's suffering—

began.

The wives of killers were always soft spoken and gentle women who were "shocked and devastated" when they discovered their spouse's atrocities by virtue of seeing his trial and conviction. They'd suspected their husbands guilty of a host of smaller crimes and peccadilloes, many of which they'd witnessed for themselves. The biggest clues, however, were abundant and ignored. All of the murderers had excuses for every domestic curiosity. Blood in the car was because they'd hit a dog in the road and kindly taken it to the vet in their car. In one family, when the son dug up human remains in the backyard, his father said the skeleton came from his uncle's medical practice. Clara had even read that one of the serial killers wives had found a poem her husband had written to taunt the police about one of the killings he had done. Finally she saw reason, only to dismiss it once again.

Clara had likewise one day found a note on her bed that said, "Roses are red, my love, violence is blue." When she got up the naïve courage to ask Faron about it, he explained that all sorts of random things in the world made him see colors. Ridiculous. She hadn't asked him anything since. In fact, she'd been getting more and more timid over the years, fading away to nothing. But Clara had a helpless daughter that she should have been looking after. Why hadn't she remembered that before? More accurately, why hadn't she seen it as her paramount concern? How could she justify the fact that her craven cowering, her complete inability to stand up to Faron on Kreindel's behalf, had triggered her daughter's paralysis? How could she explain that she'd then allowed Faron to strike a paralyzed girl?

When Faron returned from the den and challenged her inquiring look with a withering, "Yes?" Clara said defiantly, "Kreindel needs help. I'm taking her back to the physical therapy place." Then she flinched, preparing to be hit, ready to take whatever retribution her newfound humanity would cost her.

As he turned on his heel, Faron said, "Well, I won't be here. You can do whatever the hell you want."

Again. He'd be vanishing again. He'd stopped pretending to go off to work. She didn't know where his money came from. His absences were never explained, and that included the physical and mental ones. Like the wives of serial killers, Clara had at one point suspected her husband of infidelity. Yet in Faron's case there was never any evidence that he had done anything or been anywhere. He hadn't been seen at a motel. No missing cash, and no credit card activity at all. And in the Richter house there were no hidden or forbidden rooms, no freshly turned dirt on the lawn. He had the ability to act without evidence of his actions and to move without a trace.

Yet how would she even know the extent of his capabilities? Most of the time, Clara would mysteriously forget things he'd done, and then dimly remember them later. Simple as Clara was, and maybe because she was simple, she sensed that if Faron was a serial killer, he was also much more than that. In her wildest fantasies, she wondered if Faron was something that didn't even have the limitations of a mortal man. But like every other wife in denial, she didn't want to believe it. Who would willingly believe *that?*

CHAPTER 20

One Thousand

<u>Syria, 998 A.D.</u>

"THE END OF the world is coming!" the soldier with the wild, black eyes shouted as he struck Kreindia down with his shield. He leaned over her as she lay on the ground and cried, "The days slip too easily and soon comes the End of Everything for those who violate time. Because of you, you, YOU." At last he dissolved his rant to an incoherent scream.

Supine but well-leveraged, she used the hilt of her sword to strike the man in the forehead, much the way she had seen Wade do it, and as he collapsed, she rolled out from under. Her assailant was an older man with an ill-used face on a head shaped like a cup. He didn't look so dangerous now that he was at rest. She stood and dusted herself off. Had she come to the wrong place, the wrong time or both?

The rundown colonnade in which she and a few others sheltered was encircled and partially filled by sand. She wondered where they were yet couldn't ask the soldiers she saw in the distance. The question would seem too odd. The stretches of gold and red between sparse tufts of green could have been anywhere south of Antioch. Heavy smoke rose from a nearby city. There were screams in the distance and purposeless running in all directions. There was indeed a crisis in this land, even if it were only generated by the hysteria of its citizens. This generation had lived all of their lives with their perception of the pending catastrophe near the end of the millennium. Given the words of Theodotos and the context in which they were delivered, she believed her travel was accurate and that the time he spoke of must be near at hand.

For her part, she was fresh from the change in power wrought one hundred eighty years earlier and still disturbed by the brutality of Leo's handsome face relieved of its body. Having studied history from a Byzantine perspective, she knew that all assassinations were overkill whether it be that of Julius Caesar, Caligula, or any of the other dozens of forgotten emperors killed between Caesar's time and hers. As with the others, Leo V's assassins—with the exception of Pammon as the enforcer—consisted of representatives from all walks of aristocratic life. Each was required to stab the imperator in order to get the blood on their hands and so bind them together.

She wasn't present at those butcherings. She didn't order anyone's execution in her version of the plan. Because of her central role in Leo's undoing, the gore stained her hands nonetheless. She had to focus on the life she'd saved and the good that Michael could achieve. If life required a fight for that which had to be done, then the response must be infinitely more robust when a universe was at stake. She was determined to clear her head and do what was necessary here and now.

"Well done," said an officer approaching her from the dusty battlefield in the heat of summer. "I'm sorry he attacked you. Some of our best troops are not right in the head but I've never seen Cnaeus act like that."

"I can take care of myself." It didn't surprise her that violence continued nearly two centuries after her own time.

"There's a lull in battle for repositioning, my lady, but the fight will soon continue." With narrowed eyes, he asked, "How did you get yourself in the middle of it? I didn't see you with the other women."

"No, I've only just arrived. I'm the emperor's niece. I got trapped here on an inspection visit."

"You're Basil's niece?"

She looked at him in alarm. "Yes!" she said. "Korinna." She was so disoriented from the time shift that the lie had started out as a mistake when she thought of Michael. She was stuck with it now. In any event, the unofficial leadership role had served her well so far, providing entrée, tolerance, and a blanket of uncertainty under which she could operate. No other mantle could be better for ambitious women in Byzantine society. Or astral travelers.

"I'm Tullius," he said. As the troops of both camps repositioned with the city between them, he called out several instructions to his men, and said to her, "I'm sorry, Korinna, but I think we're destined to lose this one. You probably saved Cnaeus' life. When they overtake us, he'll be left for dead. We can help him out of his chain mail, and it will complete the illusion. Then you can wear it. The fit won't be that bad. You're going to need the protection more than he will anyway."

She wanted to say, "I'm confused," but she replied, "All right."

As Tullius crouched and struggled with the dead weight, a bold and striking contingent marched by, being shuffled to the rear, and Kreindia regarded these troops in stunned silence. They wore leather and iron-plated *spangenhelm* with prominent eyebrow spectacle guards and extended nose blocks; Byzantine chain mail from chin to hips; splint limb armor; and they all carried the long-hafted Danish axe with the crescent edge. A perfect match for the Norseman figure she held. To her, the coincidence was a confirmation that she'd arrived at the right temporal nexus. She shivered with a sense of relief and happiness that she'd made it to the right time, yet also anxiety and fear that she would not recognize the catastrophe she needed to avert. History could not be her guide. She knew nothing of the era.

"Don't look to them for help," warned Tullius, marking her gaze. "The general doesn't want to utilize the Varangian guards that Basil gave him. He doesn't trust them."

"Who are they?"

"Former Viking raiders. We acquired them in a treaty with the Rus. Haven't you seen them around court?"

"I never noticed them until now." She could always fall back on the overly pampered princess dance. It squared with everyone's expectations of a lady at court. She added, "Maybe they weren't there when I went abroad. But I know one thing. We can't afford to leave a part of our force idle."

"I would use them, but I'm just a simple commander," he smiled.

"Whatever is going on here, I'm prepared to fight."

He studied her with her sword, the one that had knocked out Cnaeus. "I suppose you are. I suggest you stay to the rear all the same. You'll live longer. Defend that position if you must, Korinna. But the enemy's ranks are still swelling. We're going to lose either way."

"Who do I speak to about that?"

Tullius stared at her with his mouth open.

"Who is in charge?" she amended slowly for him.

"Do you know the Dalassenos family?"

"I do." They were a wealthy family from Dalassa who had been around a long time.

"Well, that's Damien Dalassenos over there," said Tullius, still struggling with Cnaeus' limp body. "He's the military governor of Antioch and our general. But you can't speak to him."

She saw the chubby man Tullius had indicated in the distance, and she crouched down to help with the chain mail. "Who leads the opposing army?"

"The Fatimid Caliphate's *Amir* Jaush ibn al-Samsama."

"How did we come here? Our forces?"

"Apamea was afire from some natural disaster. It looked like the perfect opportunity to attack, but it just brought their armies to us. The Fatimids are taking over the world. They have all our former possessions in Africa, including the great bread basket. I think that's what's driving people like Cnaeus mad."

"So you don't believe the world will end in the year 1000?"

"Maybe in the year 2000," he laughed. "How should I know?"

Not then either, she thought with a ghost of a smile.

She knew her history of the Arab lands and conflicts, and she'd never heard of the Fatimid Caliphate in the early ninth century. The Abbasid Caliphate ruled in her time and the Aghlabids were on the horizon. She'd faced the latter as pirates. She had little idea what to expect from the new group, but if they came into conflict with the Byzantines, it was her concern.

"Why can't we retreat?" she asked.

"Al-Samsama would never allow that. We'll be cut down. Surrender and we'll be executed."

"It sounds like the perfect reason to fight well. Excuse me." She started walking.

"No, don't," he yelled after her.

She proceeded to the stout general, calling out, "General Dalassenos!"

"Who are *you*?" Dalassenos demanded when she came up to him.

"My uncle thanks you for your service and asks if you are properly enjoying the benefit of his Varangian guards."

Because she came from Tullius' direction, Damien looked at him with suspicion of treachery and then explained to her patiently, "We're safer with them here rather than leaving them in the hands of the Rus. Other than that, I can think of no use for them. They'll betray us or run away as soon as they get the chance."

"You want a use for them?" she asked the general. The one thing she felt certain of was that Arab nature would not change in two hundred years. In the drawing rooms they were scientists; on the battlefield, all heart. "Use the Varangians as bait."

"In what sense, dear lady?" he asked with a patronizing smirk.

"Send them far around the flank in a long narrow line. Let them attract attention. The Arabs will attack them. If they run, the Arabs will chase them. Then you can attack from the rear." She was absolutely certain the Varangians would not run.

"*Who* are you?"

Giving him a confidential double pat on the forearm, she told him, "Please don't think of Basil as spying on you. He wants to learn something from your leadership."

Damien considered this information with a wry smile, and said, "Yes, I think the Varangians have rested long enough. I will order their disposition."

Kreindia was grouped with Cnaeus, the wounded, and the other noncombatants as Dalassenos issued orders. Tullius and Kreindia bid each other good luck as he went to join the ranks, and she donned Cnaeus' chain mail, grateful that he wasn't a big man.

She looked up and stopped Tullius, calling out. "Apamea is on fire."

"It was."

"No, look over there. It's begun again."

"We're deployed. I have to go." Tullius dutifully ran to face his fate.

As Kreindia predicted, the Arabs were prompted to attack the thin line that flanked them. Whereupon the Varangians fell on them with such glee, ferocity and efficiency that the larger Arabian force actually fled from them and headed for the Byzantine main army where they hoped to make a better trade for their lives on the way to

Paradise.

Dalassenos led the charge to meet them and Kreindia noticed in his swift flight that he was one of those bulky men who was nonetheless active and completely fit for duty. As the forces clashed, Basil's more disciplined troops cut down the first rank of al-Samsama's men. The Varangians continued their successful assault from the rear, grabbing and butchering as they went. At this rate the imbalance between their numbers would soon swing in the Byzantine's favor.

As the action slowed to flow over and around the dead, the wind shifted, bringing the thick smoke from the burning city of Apamea. It drew a blanket over the north end of the field, covering Dalassenos' reserves even as they thundered into it. Before she was blinded entirely, Kreindia could see by those nearest that the drift was halting the advance. Some soldiers were falling to their knees, overcome by smoke.

When the wind finally shifted in a different direction, some recovered and were willing to go forward but as they plunged onward they could no longer see the enemy who was now encumbered by the shroud. The heat and sand made further mockery of their efforts to progress.

As the battle wore on, the smoke varied in intensity and direction, revealing by degrees a front that was no longer an even line but a discontinuous and bewildering collection of salients, oxbows, and gaps. With the disarray increasing, four of the enemy broke all the way through and did not turn to engage again but continued on a pell mell course toward Byzantium's noncombatants.

"Arms," Kreindia called, and some of the wounded sluggishly took up their weapons. As she helped to brace up as many of the fallen as possible, she called to the able women among them, "Rocks."

There were two dozen in her group. After a few stunned moments, they gathered the abundant stones in reserves around their feet.

When the Arabs drew close enough for even a feeble throw, such as might be expected of her charges, Kreindia called to the women, "Fire." And then immediately, "Reload!"

Most of the sallies were of poor aim and many of the small rocks fell short or did nothing. One managed to fly true and stuck an attacker on the chin, taking him down. A stone from the second batch struck a knee. The barrage was enough to give their foes pause, but that only served to make them more prudent in their approach.

One of the wounded Byzantine men lurched to his feet and stood beside Kreindia to fight the remaining three Arabs, one of whom was limping.

Cnaeus' eyes popped open. He took in the situation and closed them.

Three Arabs moved in on Kreindia and the wounded man as the other women fell back. Two Arabs got there ahead of the third and fashioned an energetic attack. Kreindia's newfound reflexes kept up, and though she tried her own attacks those too were parried. As she used the last of her strength, she could not see a way to end the contest. When the hobbled attacker came within his range, Cnaeus jumped up to strike the injured leg. Once that one was out of commission, he tipped the balance, first for Kreindia and then for his wounded companions by helping dispatch the other two, who were taken very much by surprise to see his vigorous recovery.

Kreindia was equally amazed. Apparently, Cnaeus' madness had passed. She didn't want to think about what would have happened had it not.

The city's fire had burned out only to be replaced with a rolling wall of battle dust. When Kreindia was able to see again, the small number of Arab survivors were on the retreat and the Varangians were mopping them up.

She winced at the pain in her cheek and remembered the sword tip that nicked her in this fight with the little spray of blood. She'd been insensate during the rush of battle and unable to attend to the wound, just grateful that it was no closer to her eye. Touching the fingertip-sized gouge of flesh, she realized it corresponded to the scar on her double. The idea that she and Amynta could be the same person became slightly more comprehensible but only in the way that an ocean becomes slightly more full when a pebble is thrown into its vastness. It still left her wondering how Amynta had picked up the Syrian accent, and such an unusual one at that. Kreindia didn't intend to stay in Syria that long.

After a while, she spotted Tullius in the distance directing post-battle traffic. Dalassenos, who had suffered a leg wound, was being helped back by a man on each side of him as the heat of the day lingered.

Without the battle to distract her, the pain in her head and side renewed and seemed to worsen. The jagged cut had opened again.

Another engagement is over, and where is Wade?

She sat in the colonnade and shook soot out of her hair with the inexplicable feeling that all she had done was built of no more than the dry Syrian sand. And not only because Wade hadn't appeared. Her swirling thoughts touched something deeper at work. Like the gaps in the smoke, she began to sense in herself a mental haze that alternately cleared and fogged. Cnaeus, in the throes of his temporary insanity, had said it was *the end of everything for those who violate time.*

From the billows of dust, a tall man came running up to her, and seeing him first from a distance, her heart leapt. She scrambled to meet him. On close approach, her thrill melted to disappointment. Perhaps some expression, some mannerism or even a trick of the light had reminded her of Wade.

He said, "I'm sorry I got here late. I had no choice."

"Who are you?" she asked him.

"A friend."

"Of whose?"

"No matter what your questions, it will all become clear. Are you well?"

"I'm not," she admitted to the stranger. Downhearted as she was, for some reason a seed of trust like hope grew inside her. The need might have emerged from her exhaustion. His voice was like Wade's.

"I didn't want to be the one to tell you this," he told her, "but the battle at Apamea in 998 is one that Byzantium was supposed to lose."

"It looked so, but we didn't."

"That's the problem." His eyes were downcast. "Dalassenos did not survive the battle originally and that circumstance brought Basil in to personally end the crisis. Now Basil will not come and the war will be won by al-Samsama. As a result, the balance of power in the year 1000 will look quite different, and Byzantium will be weakened and fall before its time."

"I don't understand. How could you know?"

"What you'll need to hold onto when you look back on this day is this: Murphy's Law, where I come from—"

"Murphy?"

"Yes, it's the idea that anything that can go wrong, will go wrong. But I believe it's simply a corollary of Entropy Theory, which tells us that a continual breakdown to disorder is the natural state. Therefore, it takes enormous, continuous constructive energy to make life work. And sometimes everything is so completely wrong that it seems like nothing human could ever get thing things right. But it depends on which human."

She had the bizarre idea that the way he explained things made him look even more like Wade. A generation older, but could he be some other manifestation of the Wade she knew?

He could not. He bore no synesthetic signature that she could read.

"I don't understand any of that," she said, and her head flared in pain, blocking all sound.

He spoke through a thick silence, mouthing the words, "I know you don't."

"Are you Allen Linwood?" Wade's father, another synesthete, had once joined Charlemagne's retinue masquerading as Alcuin, but would have moved on at Charlemagne's death. She'd never met Allen Linwood in person. She had only seen him through Wade.

In response, he deliberately tapped her on the shoulder and the box of memory turned over completely, spilling all the rest of its secrets.

~*W*~

The astral plane... the dark ripple... Her life slipping away as she and Wade traveled and were thrown off course...

In that moment, it occurred to her that instead of going with Wade to the twenty first century, she might drag him to the final rest with her, and might not that be a good thing? *End it all at a time he would never suspect. What better opportunity?*

But no. She was horrified. Where did these insidious notions hail from? Even in her dimmest, most vulnerable state, she perceived in that malevolent train of thought a third mind invading the process, trying to influence her to play along. The soul she'd noticed in the ripple. No, not exactly a countable soul, she amended, but a being of great power.

As she began to resist, she heard a buzzing swarm and saw bees attacking a raft in salty, storm-tossed seas. The bees were influenced by an outsider's will just as she was. Nevertheless, she felt them infiltrate her weakened mind to help steer it to disaster. The nudge from the insect attack formed another ripple, spreading a mild current within the stronger heaves. Instead of dissipating, however, the ripple gained strength. It boosted her consciousness and took hold of her at the same time.

She sensed that the manipulator was another synesthete, though against her weakness it was hard to be certain. *Wade has no defenses up*, the Manipulator advised her. *You can take him as you fade away.*

No! The more she held fast, the more the Manipulator redoubled his efforts to pervert her will. *Take him! Kill him! I'll help you.*

Wade kept her close, and made progress, even against the force of the bees. Even though he didn't know what he was fighting. He didn't appear to hear the malevolent voice or feel its malicious presence.

When she glimpsed a strange place that must have been far in the future, the current built like an angry rip tide, threatening to tear her apart. *It's your last chance. He'll die anyway, and more painfully if you resist me.*

In a moment of clarity she understood that her mind was being irreparably poisoned and she realized of her own accord that before she lost all control, the only way to spare the lives of both she and Wade would be if she simply...

... let go. And as she let go, the astral plane turned to foam.

~*W*~

The vision ceased like a curtain torn from its rod and borne off by the wind. Filling that vacuum, revelation slammed into her with the force of unadulterated, heart-stopping dread. The dark ripple was the same as the Beast, the same as the invader of her contemplation forest.

And it was Faron. Yet it was she herself who had caused the separation of her and Wade.

With all of her efforts—regardless of them and because of them—she had played into the Manipulator's hands.

Allen Linwood, if that's who the visitor was, was right. As she sagged against a colonnade pillar in the dust of conquered Apamea, she understood that everything she had done in the years 820 through the millennium's end was an utter waste of time. Much worse than that, it had been a recipe for doom.

Part III

On Time's River

"Every lover is a soldier."

~Ovid

CHAPTER 21

Rome Declined

Rome, 500 A.D.

"HAVE YOU EVER been to Rome?" Egan asked Wade as he set the riding pace toward the Porta Flaminia at a leisurely trot. The Tiber ran faithfully on their right, a murky flood as impenetrable as Wade's escort. *Egan and his "more clever" test. Anastasius and Egan, should not be here in Rome when they were never in Italy in this year before.*

Their presence and interference was an enormous complication while Wade was trying to focus on the impending clash of Theoderic and Clovis, the two most powerful leaders of the western world.

With a steady gaze at Anastasius' chief war counselor, who sounded suspiciously lackadaisical, Wade said, "No, I have not."

"Whether you're from Aquitaine, Africa, or Antioch, you all read the pagan poets and think you know Rome from your dreams. You don't know this Rome."

Egan was right. As a history buff, if there was one thing that Wade always wished he could see, it was the state of forgotten Rome after the city fell into the endless drought before the Renaissance. In astral travel he'd found a particularly dangerous form of tourism. He suddenly remembered what Grimketil had told him when dealing with the Avars: *Do not underestimate the situation.* That wisdom applied here too.

They drew up to the end of the road and waited at the foot of the gate. Even though Wade could be fairly certain he'd be received peacefully in present company, the Aurelian Walls were daunting when viewed up close. With heavily crenellated solid brick buried in concrete rising four or five times the height of a man, the barrier was the definition of impregnable. Near the entrance itself, the great turrets were studded with arrow slits. He could imagine the archers delivering a withering barrage to invaders on his side of the wall. Amazing that the features bore no damage from the sack of Rome ninety years earlier. It made sense though. History said that the walls had not been breached that day but flung open to the enemy by a confederate from the undermanned ranks of defenders. Not even the most ambitious raider would ever surmount these obstacles on his own. Unless perhaps he was an astral traveler.

Somewhere within these walls was Kreindia.

Or not.

Egan drew out of his pocket a folded flag of Byzantium. With a flourish, he unfurled and waved the modest-sized green banner as he called out to the tower. The breeze was strong enough to lift and display the cloth, and the guards must have recognized the thin scholar as well. The great doors slowly swung wide, allowing Wade to cross the portal with Egan to a world long diverged from the Imperium.

As they passed through, he gaped at the wall's thickness, room for two supine Goliaths laid end-to-end within its breadth. In this supreme siege defense he saw, too, the reflected grimness of a world that made such construction necessary. The endless hostility embedded in human nature.

As Wade stared beyond the paved road where their horses trotted side by side, he finally processed where he was going. Cattle grazed in an open field amidst the punctuated sounds of birds and the rising and falling shimmer of insects. Only one man could be seen, bumping along as he drove an ox cart through the ruts of a dirt path. Presently, the driver stopped to inspect a portion of his field. The rows ran marvelously straight, and the crop stood healthy and intact but for a degree of animal pilfering that he seemed to accept with a fatalistic tilt of his head. A tick-seeking bird settled briefly on the ox's back and then took wing as the driver prodded the ox to move again.

"Is Rome much further?" Wade asked.

Egan laughed. "Are you looking for their million people? Nine out of ten have resettled in Venezia, in Ravenna, in Constantinople and other points east if they could afford it."

"This is what the walls are defending now? Farmland?"

Egan squinted at him. "The West's capital has been Ravenna, not Rome, for the past hundred years. This campus, like several others, was torn down and opened to livestock."

"I didn't know about that last part."

"You don't know much, do you? A generation ago, Rutilius said, 'What was once a world, you have left one city.' Now it's a fraction of a city. Why did you choose the Via Flaminia, which led to the only gate that was closed to the public when there are more than a dozen other roads? And where is your horse?"

"Flaminia was the direct route and I was in a hurry, especially after my horse broke a leg."

"So your horse broke a leg?" Egan raised his eyebrows in tacit, if temporary, acceptance of Wade's sparing answer. Wade ignored him and they moved on to another acreage with a different crop. The skyline, such as it was, emerged over the planting fields but remained in the distance.

This, then, was Rome at its worst, a pastoral waste of the Eternal City. *But no,* Wade corrected himself, *this was simply its most mysterious period.* He'd missed the Rome that suffered through the mid-fifth Century of contraction and the Rome that limped under Odoacer's leadership afterward. This Rome had nominally returned to the sway of the Imperium, in care of the Ostrogoths under Theoderic. The new viceroy of Byzantium was already reversing some one hundred years of neglect, corruption and terror. There had to be some of its original landmarks left because he knew for a fact that the Coliseum and some of the triumphal arches still existed in the twenty-first century. *Or at least,* he reminded himself with a tingling rush of concern, *that was true in the world I knew.*

A mottled tan creature sprung through the tall grass with its white-snout leading the way. Wade was fascinated as it loped like an incredibly tall and skinny rabbit, its legs straight out in one stroke, then gathered so close they overlapped one another before repeating the pattern. It circled in this manner, staying close to them even as they moved.

Egan noticed what had caught Wade's attention and said, "Eh, the Laconian's not a popular breed of dog these days. A poor specimen, too. No wonder it's been let go."

Dog? Studying the beast more closely, Wade noticed that this ancient breed best resembled the Polish greyhounds, only without the characteristic neck length and distinctive sweep of chest. From some angles it had the pointy-shoe head but when it turned to look at him, it swung a perfect cylinder of a snout.

The hound ran to sniff out a pale rocky outcrop ahead of them, and Egan reached across to nudge Wade. "Here is a monument for you."

"Where?"

"The Tomb of Augustus," Egan replied, pointing to the lonely territory the dog investigated.

"Really?" Wade would not have thought Augustus was so despised in Rome to have his tomb appear as it did. Weeds grew on top of each terrace, leaving the verticals bare so that the stone seemed to struggle out of the earth rather than the soil heaping on top of it. He discerned hints that there was a great deal more to the structure beneath nature's reclamation project. To that extent, it reminded him of the hidden pyramids of Visocica, left purposeless when the Illyrians were conquered. Augustus' monument came mainly in the shape of massive rings with squat vents. Perhaps the crudest precursor of Byzantine architecture, the center looked like a thousand-ton stone lid built to keep the spirit of Augustus from rising.

"Too ugly and expensive to fix," Egan explained as he led Wade away. "And people are scared to destroy it. Except for stealing the marble panels, of course. The prospect of riches always inspires bravery in some enterprising soul."

The Laconian, who may have been Augustus' only fan, saw them move on, and it hastened to catch up, requiring only a few bounding leaps. As soon as it did, the dog gazed at Wade and raced ahead like the legendary bear on the Danube that came out of hibernation to show the Christians where to go.

"Where were you coming from, Wade?" Egan continued his soft interrogation.

Wade pressed his lips together to remind himself not to speak too hastily until his synesthetic memory faithfully came up with the right map. He saw the outlines of the country, then the cities, then the network that connected them. Nine major roads, and only three of them would have made sense, as those were the ones that traced a long distance from the north. He needed to name a city on the route he had already professed to have traveled. "Spoleto," he said. The Flaminian Way, which he'd found himself on, was the direct road that connected the central city to Rome.

"We would have passed you coming from Ravenna." Egan stayed calm even as he offered the contradiction.

So did Wade. "No, I'm certain that you didn't overtake me until I was near the gate."

More pointedly, Egan pressed, "Supposing I asked you

where this dead horse of yours could be found?"

"Then I would lead you to it," Wade answered with stubborn determination.

"Would you?"As Wade's information was neither contradictory nor particularly illuminating, Egan moved on in silence, reserving whatever challenge he had in mind for Wade.

With the sun climbing, the hound drew them onward in a barking romp to an Egyptian obelisk complete with hieroglyphics spilling down its surface. The incongruous item on top, however, was a sphere decorated with stone flowers, birds and three-dimensional stars. Its globe had been skewered on a pointer, an obvious addition to the stolen relic.

"The Horologium," Egan smiled with a grand sweep of his arm.

"An hour counter," said Wade, impressed by the elaborate display.

Sounding puzzled and more than a little irritated, Egan snapped, "That's what I just said." Its Latin name was a literal one so Wade had literally repeated the term Horologium, forgetting that, with Egan, his words came out as nothing but Latin.

"I'm just surprised to see such a good one," Wade amended.

"It's probably the best in the world," said Egan, finally pleased. "Not only does it tally the hours, but on September twenty-third—Augustus' birthday—the sun points its shadow straight at the altar. What do you have for a time keeper in Aquitaine?"

"Nothing. I once saw a water clock in Constantinople, though."

Egan gazed straight ahead with a superior smile of amusement. "Constantinople has almost everything," he agreed.

Wade hoped his relief didn't show. Every word he uttered was a gamble. He simply assumed that either

Aquitaine had no clocks or that this was what Egan wanted to hear. Egan's method of being part tour guide and part interrogator was wearing Wade down, just as the wily old soldier must have intended. As they continued south on the Flaminian Way, Wade worried about what could be on Egan's menu for him in the miles ahead. The Dark Ages were not in full swing. In Rome there had to be a modicum of Christian civilization after a couple hundred years of the religion being practiced here. The days of crucifixion were behind them and the days of boiling oil yet to come. He'd experienced the horrors of the Byzantine arena in 814, three hundred years hence. What sort of brutal test lay in between?

"What will we find beyond this campus?" Wade asked.

"The bulk of old Rome and some new churches. Theoderic—the man you claim to work for?—has commissioned a survey, but I suspect he will find some forty thousand common dwellings as well as fifteen hundred homes of magnates, and of course the public works. You will see it all for yourself very soon."

The Laconian greyhound stuck with them, demonstrating a particular affinity for Wade, and barking when he thought Wade's interest in him waned. Given its energy and apparent pedigree, it probably would have kept up with them even if their pace were a more urgent one. When they lingered, it raced ahead to an aqueduct that dominated the skyline.

Once they crossed under the rumbling water course, Wade saw a stand-alone triple arch and a chaotic mass of buildings across a wide stretch of wild land as large as the parcel through which they'd already passed. Vast expanses of the dismantled city had been razed to the ground. Sheep roamed in one area, while some further farmland was left fallow.

The Laconian did an eager dance before they entered under the triple arch, and just as the hound turned its bottle nose to measure Wade's attention, Egan identified the structure as, "the Arch of Claudius," as though he were the dog's voice personified.

"It's pink," Wade observed, wondering if that were the original color.

"Rose marble, actually. You're going to have to drive that beast off with a stick."

"The dog? I'd rather keep him."

"Good luck wasting your time with that."

Wade tried to keep a straight face. His actual wish was that he could drive Egan off with a stick.

The emptiness came to an abrupt end in a fully urban, fully peopled environment, concentrated by narrow streets. The arrangement was a familiar one, with shops on the bottom and apartments on top. When they passed a market with copious cuts of meat, Egan remarked, "Perhaps you can find your missing horse here."

Wade pretended not to hear him.

"Capitoline Hill is coming up right in front of us," Egan noted as they approached the stately buildings of government. Ahead, the population on the street rapidly grew so dense that Wade wondered if he must be one of many visitors in Rome that day. The crowd was jubilant, empowered and restless. Had Wade and Egan not been on horseback and dressed in high regalia, Wade doubted that anyone would have stepped aside to let them pass.

They climbed a gentle rise, and Egan expounded, "This was once one of the great Seven Hills of Rome's origin."

"Once?"

"The heights have been reduced in Rome, the valleys mostly filled in. Easier to build that way. How do you come to work for Theoderic?"

"Mutual interest. We both want stability under a benign rule."

"Hmm." Once again Egan let the limited explanation pass and it made Wade wonder whether there was a reason why it didn't matter what he said. Amongst the dense crowds and the appearance of a significant number of soldiers managing them, Wade's mind raced, trying to remember any historical detail that might explain what he witnessed in the streets. His survey on the astral plane had left him long on major developments and short on immediate details. In light of the fact that the Interloper had been hard at work undoing events in the immediate timeline he could trust none of what he knew from before. What was the circumstance that Egan held back from him? What should Wade have known?

"Where are we going?" Wade tried.

"This is Palatine Hill just in front of us. You will dismount and approach on foot."

Wade climbed down and led his horse through the crowd after Egan. The civilians in this section were better dressed, some of them in togas. The women among them looked remarkably modern with dresses of a cut that would have worked even in the mid-twentieth century. As a new set of guards greeted them and parted, Wade asked Egan, "Any particular reason we're here?"

Egan's smile had a cruel edge. "I lied. There was one more gate closed to entrance by the general public. That would be the Triumphal Way."

"Meaning what? The Pope is traveling?" Wade asked, although his heart sank because he thought he knew who had come to Rome.

"As Anastasius told you," said Egan, "I devise the cleverest tests of all. But the secret is to keep your tests simple. If you work for Theoderic as you claim…then you can tell that to him."

And with that, he moved his horse aside, allowing Wade to face Theoderic himself.

The monarch wore a half-century well. The crudely minted coins of the realm never did his Viking-handsome face justice. That very countenance was staring at Wade with supreme impatience.

Wade felt the heat rise to his scalp and he stopped hard, completely unprepared to reconcile the story he had given Egan about working for Theoderic if the namesake of his excuse was there to contradict him so soon. His only chance was to speak privately with the Ostrogoth, and that wasn't going to happen. *And how do I address this man? Is he emperor? Is he king?*

"Is this your mutt?" Theoderic demanded.

The Laconian had made the entire journey, sticking close to them near the end. Wade looked down at the prancing dog and smiled, glad of the diversion. Thus inspired, he said, "I guess so, my lord." The Laconian was crouched by his side as though ready to defend the synesthete, his bottle nose upturned to snarl at Itale's conqueror. Spontaneously, Wade decided, "I'll keep him, and call him Augustulus."

Seeing the shock in Theoderic's face, his skin gone white, Wade's momentary comfort fled and he felt his legs going out from under him. "Did I say something wrong?"

But of course he had. With dread, he realized he'd invited himself to Rome, adopted an animal, and named him "Little Augustus," without ever calculating what effect those actions might have on Theoderic the Great—the supremely powerful man about whom he knew so little and needed so much.

CHAPTER 22

Theoderic the Amal

Constantinople, 471 A.D.

THE KING'S MIND wandered back to the morning of his seventeenth birthday. Theoderic the Amal, as he was called then, thought he spied Strabo on the horizon and tried to will it not to be so… because the day Theoderic received his warhorse and Strabo stormed the court, the Gothic prince's ideal existence in Constantinople was over.

On the last day of that life, he emerged from the stables leading out the emperor's birthday gift to him, the Arabian that became his instant favorite. The horse was a wonder. With a bloom of pale russet on its forward barrel, the stallion's flesh quickly and dramatically blended to a black shine at its extremities. Its forehead bulged with intellect, its tail mounted high and flowing like a fountain. When Theoderic brought out apple slices, the horse looked to him for permission. Once granted, it ate carefully, never allowing its teeth to touch his hand. The prince intended to name the stallion Majid, which meant "glorious" in Arabic, but he was superstitious and did not announce the appellation as soon as it occurred to him.

As usual, Theoderic's older sister, Amalafrida, was with him, enjoying the paddock outside the palace. It was the sort of cool, late summer day that presages the coming of an early, cold fall. A chain of such days had persisted long enough to convince two of the central trees in the courtyard to begin shading auburn at their peaks.

"He's a warrior's horse," Frida observed. "May I take him for a run?" He and Frida were as close as siblings could be, subjected as they were to a common isolation.

"Of course," he said, surrendering the Arabian to her.

The lean horse responded faultlessly to her command as she ran the field. It exuded a confidence that seemed unusually self-aware, even for an equine champion. And it seemed, too, that Theodoric's sister was even more taken with Majid than he was. He had always respected his only sibling and her formidable riding skills. Today she was a handsome woman on a magnificent beast. She could easily take that steed into battle.

As a teenage prince in the world's greatest city, albeit a foreign one, Theodoric enjoyed all of the advantages of a son-at-arms, but Frida too had a warrior soul. Over the years, she'd had him repeat to her his lessons on Roman strategy and tactics. Technically, Theodoric's steed was the captive of a captive, as he was a hostage-guest of the Byzantines, the arrangement meant to keep the peace between his people and theirs. Frida lived under the same imposition without an equal share of inheritance. Did it matter at this point which sibling owned which property? His previous favorite horse would do him well enough.

"Frida," he called out as she passed him in the loop.

She romped ahead, laughing like a young girl and protesting, "No, it's still my turn."

Theodoric was planning to tell her that she could enjoy Majid all she wanted, when the young man he'd spotted earlier galloped toward him and reigned in hard, tempering the Amal's mood to caution. If he hadn't been in such high spirits to begin with, his thoughts would have darkened to outright suspicion. The visitor, who shared with him the common name Theodoric, was known for a while as "the Lesser Theodoric," and he now went by his popular name, Strabo, which meant The Cross-Eyed. The epithet was true, if mildly, and if those who acquired their derogatory nicknames at court minded the slur, they never complained.

Strabo, who did not dismount, told him, "It looks like that horse is not all yours, cousin."

"I know," he answered with little tolerance.

"Fortunately, I have a much better birthday present for you."

"I doubt that, Strabo."

"Oh my present goes with anything."

"Just tell me what you came to say."

"Your father is dead," Strabo replied, his voice suddenly tight with anticipation.

Theoderic stared straight ahead at a monumental Valonia oak prematurely browning at its crest, his mind unable to engage, as though Strabo's assertion were inconceivable. Not that he actually knew his father, Theodimir, but he bore the man no animosity.

"Did you hear me, Amal? I said your father is dead. You've always been the lucky one."

It wasn't the eyes, but Strabo's closely gathered features under a high forehead, which gave him the look of intensity that Theoderic always wanted to strike at when given a reason. "Is this your idea of a joke, Strabo?"

"No," said Strabo, "the messenger from Pannonia was just here."

"How would you know? You're not exactly welcome at this court."

"The message was that you're going back to the Neusiedler See."

"What does that have to do with my father, Theodimir?"

"There's only one reason they send a prince back— when a territory loses its king."

Theoderic knew for a fact that such practices were not written in stone, though this condition was part of the original hostage agreement. He said, "Supposing you are right, what advantage do you see in it?

"Do you remember nothing about Ostrogothic

238

society?"

"No, why would I?"

"The details don't matter. You inherit. You're only seventeen and you get to do what I've wanted to do all my life. Run an empire. If you don't want it, I'll take it. It's as much mine as it is yours. I'm a prince too."

"So you wish to believe, but you're going to have to be satisfied with your Thracian Goths." Strabo, although he might have been a distant relative of Theoderic's, and a noble, as well as a brother-in-law to General Aspar, was not of the Amali line in the royal house.

"At least celebrate that you're not a captive anymore. Be realistic, or I'll strike you with Marcellus' staff until you realize how fortunate you are."

Coming from Strabo, Theoderic realized how misplaced the notion of him feeling like a captive was. Theoderic had never actually been made to feel restricted in Constantinople. Not by the people who counted. He lived more like the gladly adopted son of the emperor. So had Strabo been like a son at one time. The difference was that the Thracian's tenure as a guest began late and ended early due to his relative lack of importance and generally disagreeable demeanor. Strabo's twenty-four years may as well have been fourteen for all the maturity it had given him. As soon as he'd been turned loose from his obligation, he capitalized on real and imagined grievances, causing havoc in the civilian population with his troops in Thrace until he got his way, which was whatever prize he sought at a particular time.

Go back to the Ostrogoths? thought Theoderic as he reexamined the aging oak tree. *I wasn't brought up the way Strabo was, to revere the marauding life.* Theoderic remembered his people only in scraps of childhood memory. Days spent launching sling shot pebbles across a lake that may as well have been an ocean. Nothing of the social, economic, political and cultural context required to make sense of anything important.

Palace life of the last twelve years was all he knew. Private tutoring in languages, math, history and warfare. Fencing with experts within the marbled halls. A hot bath whenever he needed it. The taunts of those who called him a barbarian could reasonably apply to his native people compared to the standard of living he now enjoyed. He dreaded stepping into Strabo's world.

"Instead of focusing on my business," said Theoderic warily, "maybe you can tell me what brought you to court in the first place, Strabo."

"Visiting my kin would be enough, but we're also here in negotiations."

Theoderic reddened. "Between your Goths and the Byzantines? Because you have such a talent for making a nuisance of yourself? You've got your legacy of Aspar, and you've settled your people in the rich lands of Thrace. That should have been everything. Yet you refuse to sign an oath of loyalty to the empire. What kind of negotiation do you expect from that? Instead of rewarding you, they should be dragging you behind a chariot."

"Yes, they should, but they can't. You're a quick study, Amal. Maybe that royal blood of yours is worth something after all. With your return to the Neusiedler See you finally get a chance to be the savage you were born."

"Yes I'm a savage," Theoderic smiled, recalling how often he'd played into his heritage with the native-born Byzantine kids. "See that you remember that when I sneak back and tear your head off with my bare hands every evening. One day I will not use my heathen magic to restore it." Given his new concerns, the jest came across less satisfying than he'd remembered. Neither of them were kids anymore.

Strabo laughed politely, but he was leering at Frida in the paddock.

Due to his years in Constantinople, Theoderic actually equated barbarians with non-Christians. He was in fact a

240

Christian, as was his entire tribe. Since their conversion, though, the centers of Christianity had drifted and now they labeled his people Arians, complaining that they didn't conform to the current church doctrine. How were Ostrogoths supposed to keep up with church doctrine?

So far they had not been harshly punished. Heretics were customarily fed to the Games, but the Arian Ostrogoths ranged by the hundreds of thousands between Itale and Thrace, a force that could not be trifled with. These were wild lands too, with the Huns a recent memory. When his father Theodimir led a confederation of tribes to defeat the son of Attila at the Battle of Nedao, their victory was a boon to the besieged Imperium. No, Byzantium did better to hold onto their tentative friendships with grace than to attack the Arians.

"Marcellus seems in a good mood," remarked Strabo.

"Is he?"

"Whistling all day. He must be happy to lose you to the tribe."

"He's always happy to keep the peace."

"It won't work."

Strabo had a point. Theoderic loved the current emperor, Leo Marcellus, like an uncle but had no illusions that such a man could gain the respect of the Ostrogoths no matter what accommodations he made. If someone could be said to have a weak face, it was Leo the Thracian with his sad, bulging eyes of a hippo and pouchy chipmunk cheeks. Hippos were nothing more than river horses, not much good on land, and chipmunks were the tiny stewards of the animal kingdom, not the leaders. His weakness showed in his policies toward the useless Western emperor Anthemius and his brother-in-law Basiliscus in dealing with the Vandals, as well as Strabo at a time when the Imperium could least afford to be lax. If it was not a cruel Fate that settled the Thracian emperor on Byzantium it was at least an insensitive one.

Before Theoderic could respond to Strabo with a barb

of his own, Frida rode back. She greeted Strabo by name with the sort of strain in her voice that could only be born of the complex dynamic of former lovers.

Strabo replied in similar fashion, using her name as a one-word greeting. Each of them was already married to other people, another circumstance of the present that Strabo didn't appear satisfied with.

"What news do you bring?" asked Frida.

"Your brother is being sent home."

"We're going to Pannonia?" she asked Theoderic breathlessly.

"Not you," said Strabo before Theoderic could formulate a more delicate answer. "You're now the best hostage Byzantium owns."

She leaned against Majid for support and he held her steady rather than resorting to a nervous sidestep as many young or less acquainted horses could be expected to do. Theoderic was stung by the realization that his homecoming was the very reason that Leo Marcellus had given him the Arabian.

"When?" she asked.

"Immediately," said Strabo. "You'll see your brother pack today or tomorrow at the latest."

Theoderic interposed himself as best he could between the mounted pair, coldly remarking to Strabo, "I'll pack right now if you will leave us to go spin your illusions." It had dawned on Theoderic that Strabo was not so fiercely jealous of him as he pretended. If his cousin were to become master of Byzantium's troops, as some believed to be his aim, he would be the second most powerful man after the basileus himself, a far greater prize than ruling the Ostrogoths as king. It could in fact make him emperor. Hoping that he uttered the truth, he added, "You won't find Leo Marcellus such a fool as to fall for your maneuvering."

"Yes," said Strabo, staring at Frida. "A quick study, your brother. A very clever boy." With a pointed glance at Theoderic, he said, "Good luck, Amal," and rode off.

They watched him until he was out of sight, whereupon Frida dismounted and asked, "Have you come up with a name for him?"

Still watching the distance, Theoderic said, "I have many names for him."

"I meant the horse."

"As far as you are concerned, it's Atiya." Both of them had studied Arabic. *Atiya* meant "gift."

She hugged him tightly in silence. The coming days would upend everything.

It was time for Theoderic to live up to his potential. If he had to go home, he would lead his people as his army of proof, police the nations on Byzantium's behalf, and show Leo that he should be *magister militum* rather than Strabo. He would fight the Imperium's way back to greatness before all of their territories were gone.

Yes, he would go home and take his place in the jostling ranks of Ostrogothic royalty. His uncles, Videmir and Valamir, would not be happy.

$$\sim W \sim$$

AS Strabo had predicted, the prince was dropped off by Leo Marcellus' men at the Neusiedler See, where his branch of goths had so far been expected to remain. Theoderic rode into his people's nation for the first time as a man, allowing himself a measure of pride despite the circumstances. He arrived when the day was late and he saw that a few of the chimneys by the lakeside were smoking early in the season. Most of his people were hardy and didn't need heat until winter so the fires should not have been set in the hearths. The work of smiths then. But in his memory, they had a single blacksmith who would be at his craft every day. Was there some urgency to retain more than one smith now?

A team of villagers building a new home stopped

hammering and stared at him and the stunning Majid as they came down the road. Frida had refused to allow him to give the horse to her, saying that he would need the stallion more than she when he started his new life.

Stroking Majid's thick mane thoughtfully, he decided he would trade anything to win Amalafrida's liberty for her. *She won't necessarily want to come here*, he realized, *but she would be better off with her family and the freedom to go anywhere she pleased than remaining at the perpetual twilight of the court.*

Reaching the center of town, which was marked by a mixed wood and stone church, he recognized tall blonde Videmir the Younger poised on the road to greet him. It was a bad sign. He would have expected both of his uncles rather than one. The most junior hero of the Battle of Nedao was now in his mid-thirties, and did not look happy. Theoderic displaced him in the line of succession.

"So you deign to come here," Videmir scowled as though Theoderic had selected his fate by choice, first to be a hostage and then to be released. "Exile suited you well. We did fine in your absence. We flourished in fact."

"Where is your brother Valamir?" Theoderic's uncle Valamir, his mother's brother, had been one of the top leaders in the confederated tribes. That much was in the imperium's history books. He was a man to be respected, someone Theoderic looked forward to meeting whether the feeling was mutual or not.

"Thrown from a horse and broke his neck. *In battle.*" Videmir betrayed little emotion, as was expected of him. Those conditioned to recognize it could see that he shared just a taste of the bitterness while conveying the proud fatalism of honor. Theodoric was surprised at how quickly the nuances of his culture came back to him.

"I'm sorry for that. Congratulations on your victory over the Huns," said Theoderic. "I want to hear all about it. Tonight if possible."

Though the event Theoderic referred to took place almost eighteen years earlier, this traditional offer to hear war stories seemed to please Videmir greatly. "That can be done," he said, stroking Majid above the muzzle. "A fine horse you have."

"Thank you." *He must be happy that I'm not claiming one from the tribe.*

"Are you surprised to see me as well?" said someone behind Theoderic, and Videmir hastily excused himself.

With one of the great strengths of its breed, Majid was able to turn abruptly in response to its startled master.

And there was his father Theodimir in the flesh, his nose broadened by age, extended eyebrows riding high at the corners. Some of his long white hair had vacated his broad forehead and his great smiling white beard stood in contrast to his son's clean shave.

"Strabo lied to me," said Theoderic.

His father raised his eyebrows. "I was hoping for something more like, 'Thank God you're alive. I wanted nothing more than to see you again, my dear father.'"

"In that case, thank God you're alive. I was allowed to have a painting of you. Otherwise I wouldn't have even known what you looked like."

His son's bitterness was lost on him. "When you were a little boy, I appeared as you do now."

When Theoderic mentally pried beneath Theodimir's age, he noticed that they indeed shared the even and angular features that the girls in Constantinople swooned over. What's more, he could see the powerful bloodline of their noble Norse heritage.

"Lucky for us," said Theodimir, "your Thracian lord is a weak one. It took little convincing when I told him that I was retiring and needed you back to safeguard the territories."

"It's not a failing. He likes me," said Theoderic, wondering why he was suddenly defending Leo Marcellus when he was recently decrying the man's weakness himself.

"That's good then. Because the core of my appeal was

true. I can remain king but I'm no longer fit to command in the field. The army is yours now. Make good use of it."

"Against whom?" Theoderic asked.

With a glance at the sun settling behind the cross, Theodimir said, "Come inside."

Directly across from the church was their most popular tavern, a coincidence that no Ostrogoth found incongruous. Father and son strode through the oaken doors, causing the patrons' heads to turn. Out of respect, none dared interrupt them. Theodimir kindly told them, "You'll all meet my son in good time."

Such was their society that the monarch and monarch-to-be could have a private meeting in a public place.

When they were properly acquainted with their two steins of beer, which meant draining them halfway to the bottom, Theoderic asked, "What is the threat that brings me here?"

With another sip, Theodimir said, "You saw the fires burning by the lake."

"New weapons being forged?"

Theodimir nodded. "In defeating the Huns and the Alans, we strengthened ourselves and also liberated the Gepids."

"...who say they liberated us."

"Yes, so they say," he shrugged. "They've taken Sirmium, and so emboldened, they wish to move west onto our land as well."

"I thought you had unified all of these tribes. Marcellus calls them all Ostrogoth."

"I did that with Ardaric, a Gepid himself. He never recovered from his wounds at Nedao. Without him there is no one to keep the Gepids from our throat."

Theoderic shifted forward. "And the Rugians, the Heruli, the Suebi? Are they not cooperative?"

"Don't forget the Scirians. They're all content to be rid of the Huns for now. Only the Gepids, our main ally, turn against us. They are the strongest, and so they challenge us.

246

We stand to lose everything and I can do nothing about it."

"I respect them."

"That's well," said Theodimir. "Then you will be able to kill them."

~ W ~

ALL that mild winter, Theoderic prepared for war, a large part of which involved becoming acquainted with his people and their capabilities. He trained the young recruits in Roman warfare as Videmir schooled them in the Germanic traditions of valor and the rules their fighters lived by. At first, Theoderic had to appease Videmir by letting him take turns, intruding in the same session. The arrangement would only have made sense if his uncle had stayed on the same topic. On one occasion, Theoderic said, "We keep the infantry in the center and the cavalry on the wings. That way the enemy cannot outflank you."

And then Videmir told them, "If you should lose your shield in battle and cannot retrieve it, do not even attempt to return home. You will have no home."

Although both statements were true, it made for an eclectic, almost comedic mix. From then on, he took the mornings and gave Videmir the afternoons, assuring him, "Your work is important and needs to stand alone."

Videmir replied, "I don't care who you are. If you don't destroy the Gepids, I will cut off your sword arm and fix it to my banner, and that will be the only part of you that sees the next battle."

Although Theoderic said nothing of this to his father, Theodimir instinctively chose that juncture to join the training sessions as an observer. Theoderic was glad of it because the presence of so many ranking officers made the troops a little keener to impress them.

One day, as the two Amali stood on the sidelines watching an afternoon drill, Theodimir advised, "I hope you are learning from Videmir as well."

"Of course. He's a warrior."

"The knowledge of our people encompasses far more than the mechanics of battle."

"And more than the threat of retribution?"

Letting that pass, his father pursued, "What do you Byzantines do for an oracle now that Delphi is closed?"

Theoderic was not offended by his father identifying him with the empire. He couldn't help but be the local authority on what Byzantines did, but he wondered, *Is he testing my knowledge of Christian doctrine?* Just in case, he rattled off the standard justification. "Delphi is closed for its blasphemy. There is no higher power but that which comes to us through Jesus. The Church—"

"—the Church tells you so. But I know what the priests say behind closed doors. They say, 'Keep out the competition.' They want no magic. They want no soothsayers. But do you truly wish me to believe that you go from all of those Roman gods down to one?"

"And the saints."

Theodimir smiled patiently. "When Western Rome started thinking that way, they fell to 'barbarians' such as us. The Imperium in the East wouldn't still exist if its emperors believed everything they fed their people. No, the truth is there is a source of influence in every natural and unnatural thing in Midgard and the eight other worlds. Where else does Jesus' might come from? Asgard, Heaven, or whatever you wish to call it, can provide him that strength because Yggdrasil drinks of the Nine Worlds to obtain a portion of each of the powers within them."

Theoderic remembered his people's belief that Midgard was the world that humans inhabited in life, just a ninth of the Universe, and the humblest part. He marveled to hear the incipient accommodation of new beliefs in his father's discourse. "It's true," Theoderic admitted. "The Greek Romans don't believe as you do, but the old ways of Jove are not entirely gone. They're unofficial. Leo Marcellus has his own source to consult."

"Of course he does. And you, my son? What do you believe?"

He is *testing me after all, in a different way than I expected.* Theoderic said, "I'm a child of the court, father. Higher education tells us to keep an open mind. All things are possible."

"The things I speak of are not merely possible, Theoderic, but real. Our seer, Evermud, has been indispensable to our tribe since the Battle of Nedao. It was he who pointed the way when no one thought we would be free of the Hunnic yolk. Do not go into combat without seeing Evermud first. He is the Shaper of Nations."

"I wouldn't think of it," replied Theoderic, his eyes shifting away. In truth, he did not know what to think because his open mind worked to keep conflicting possibilities alive. It could be a grave handicap for him if neither argument ever blossomed into a probability.

Theodimir said, "Even if you are lying to me right now, boy, do go through with it all the same. Evermud will complete the void in your education and turn the course of your life."

Theoderic, who had received the world's finest instruction, could not imagine that there was a gap of any appreciable size in his education, particularly when it came to spiritual matters. He didn't answer.

Seeing his hesitation, his father asked, "Who do you think is prodding the Gepids to attack us?"

"Odoacer the Scirian?"

"No, it's Strabo! And how has Strabo been so successful? Roman methods and the consultation of a seer!"

Theoderic realized that his father was probably right. The Gepid's pressure on the Amalis fit Strabo's plans perfectly. If his cousin could play off the rival tribes he would have a clear field in Byzantium. But Strabo and his deceitful ways could not be allowed any advantage. Come the next season of war, in the spring of his eighteenth year, Theoderic did the sensible thing and went to meet with the Shaper of Nations.

~ W ~

THE seer of the Ostrogoths lived deep in the forest near the sacred tree. Theoderic arrived on foot, having left Majid at a safe distance from this camp, for he did not know what to expect. The tree itself was in a man-made clearing populated with several stumps, but Evermud dwelt at the edge in a heap that looked like debris piled up by a storm. Beneath the detritus, the house was no doubt sturdy, its unwelcoming face a ploy to add to the oracle's privacy.

Theoderic called out instead of trying to enter. He realized that no sacred ritual would be performed indoors. All of the customs were rushing back to him despite his doubts about fitting in with his people.

Evermud emerged promptly, an unusual and small dark-haired man serving a sea of tall, blonde and red Ostrogoths. Outside of the Imperium proper, such talents as his were openly valued, rather than frowned upon. If half of what Theoderic's father said about the worth of his advice were true, any tribe would have sought to acquire such an oracle no matter what his appearance.

"Your father warned me that you would come," said Evermud. His shoulders stood high, while at the same time deep creases bracketed his mouth as though he were equally quick by habit to fight or to laugh. He was not laughing now.

"I have your price," said Theoderic. He'd brought exactly what his father had listed, a quantity of tools and food measured out for someone who would not soon be shopping in town.

"You may want to keep it," said Evermud. "I don't

guarantee that anything I say will help you."

"The reason?"

"I am not a powerful seer."

"Theodimir speaks well of you."

"I am the best he knows. And his mind is better primed to benefit than yours is."

Theoderic tried to be equally humble and patient, though his skepticism was on the rise even while his patience was short. "Please accept what I bring, and I'll agree to listen with an open heart."

"My reward is the success of my people," Evermud said diplomatically.

Your people? "Can you see what will befall them?"

"Give me a chance to prepare," Evermud said. "Give yourself a chance too. Did you bring that goat I see tethered in the clearing?"

"That was part of the deal, yes."

"Gut him then."

"Gut him?" That was one skill that had never been part of Theoderic's training at court.

"Yes."

"If I must." Theoderic reluctantly ventured out to the clearing, and Evermud followed in proximity. With a tentative hand at the hilt of his knife, Theoderic examined the animal in terms of his prospects with it. The goat was fidgety, already aroused, and made suspicious by the scrutiny. Theoderic set his jaw in contemplation, beginning to realize he appeared discomfited both to the goat and to Evermud who had stopped nearby in an observant posture.

Evermud sighed. "If you can't gut a goat, young man, then I need not be a seer to predict failure in your future."

"I can do it," Theoderic said defensively. "I'm just not accustomed to it."

"Different words, same problem. Do it fast."

Theoderic pulled his long knife and approached the goat on its flank. The buck fled more quickly than he could follow and more evasively than he could predict.

With an amused smile, Evermud advised, "They have excellent vision, see all around. You shouldn't have put him on such a long tether."

"I didn't know your plans for him," said Theoderic, chasing the goat and finding it remarkably difficult to trap.

"Well now he knows what you want to do, it won't be easy."

Theoderic stopped. "Do you propose to read the entrails, or will the goat be your dinner?"

"Neither. You'll pull the teeth for me."

"Its teeth?"

"For a bone throw. You didn't think it would sit still for that, did you?"

Theoderic threw down his blade. He could not believe what he was doing. The fate of the Ostrogoths, while not fully his people, was the fate of *a* people, and he believed that the fate of the civilized world depended on them. It wouldn't be settled with this nonsense. He said, "This is not a battle, and I don't believe in animal sacrifice. I won't kill it."

Evermud crossed his arms. "You're an unusual young man, Theoderic. As I said before, this reticence does not bode well. Does your father know of your weakness?"

"My father," he spat, "thinks that you are the Shaper of Nations. He sent me here and I'm here. You've told me that the reading may not work and I'm still prepared to listen. But I will be king, and I tell you to find another way. Those are my orders to you."

"Then I shall, my lord," Evermud said with a smile.

He went back inside his home, brought out a pouch, and spilled a set of small bones on the tree stump.

"You had them already?" Theoderic cried incredulously.

"These are different. I was saving them for a special occasion. You, Amal, are a special occasion."

Mine was the correct response, Theoderic realized. *It wasn't a physical challenge after all.*

They sank into the grass on opposite ends of the stump, and dark Evermud studied him through intense slitted eyes, a twitch raising one side of his lip. "Are you ready, boy?"

"Yes." *As much as I can be for murky arts that the Christian priests have forever warned me against.* "I would learn about the Gepids before I face them."

Without a word, the seer took up his throwing stones in a large open cup that he cradled in his right hand and covered with his left. With distinct double-shakes, he made them rattle nine times in Theoderic's direction. *To represent the Nine Worlds.* Each run chilled the young prince further and seemed to reach deeper into him until he was certain that the crackle that sounded was the shivering of his spine. With the last forward swing, the seer removed his hand and the bones were gone even as their last clatter sounded. Out flew a purple clump of grain that invaded Theoderic's eyes and nose. When he coughed, the sand did not leave him but found yet another way in.

His eyes stuck open and Theoderic gave a startled shout. In the center of his sight, an enormous orb stared back at him with an iris of orange bathed in green. A constant supply of the purple grit appeared to spew from the center in writhing tendrils. Beyond that came gemstone bursts from long sprays of blue that expanded outward to consume the clearing. Highlighting this ever-changing field, small ruptures of lightning flashed, which he flailed at in a useless defense.

While his sight gradually cleared at the periphery, the orb remained. If its function were to drain the fight out of him, it was working, for he could feel the insistence of its pull sapping his vital force. Presently, he became conscious of the pain in his chest and head, which he tried to rub and blink away. Nothing around him looked natural anymore and the lightning flashes persisted even when the orb had finally taken its fill of his strength and departed.

For a fleeting moment, repeated in bursts, Theoderic saw that every last object in the world beyond them was made of seething foam, and he said, "I don't understand what I'm seeing." He did not fail to see the horror of his situation. If the orb had not worn him to the nub he would have run in panic. But its control was not complete. A trickle of unease still roiled the pit of his stomach.

Evermud said, "As long as half of what you see is in Midgard, you will never understand." Just then, Evermud, too, became a being of foam, tiny bits of him growing, dividing and popping in a ceaseless cycle.

Remembering the purpose of his visit, Theoderic coughed, "What will be my future?"

"Your future already happened," Evermud informed him. "As have all futures. Ever the waters of time return to the past as the dew drips from Yggdrasil into the Well of Urd and are drunk again by the tree. Thereby the past—your present—is remade. The future as you imagine it, does not exist. There is only destiny."

"Then why—?" he croaked.

"Because every man in his time has an opportunity to reinvent creation. But destiny can be changed only in proportion to power. There will come a day when you will be known and respected at every turn of the O-Round Sea, that which you call *Mare Nostrum*."

"The Middle Sea? Does that place me at Ravenna?" *Mare Nostrum* was the great sea around which all of the vanishing empire had stretched. Rome was its traditional center, but by this time Ravenna had long been the Western capital.

"Ravenna and Rome. Rome will be great and poor again more than once."

"You have the oracle's gift for not answering a question." Theoderic laughed, though he knew his laughter came to dispel his fear of the orange orb and the changes he'd seen as well as the odd light cast over the clearing now and the lightning that would not cease. Now

Evermud sat across from him looking like Majid's saddle ornament, the polychrome warrior eagle that had been bestowed to Theoderic on his return; his high shoulders curving like wings, his chest bulging like the turtle shell breastplate, his nose stretching to ever-changing beak-like proportions with the turn of his head.

"I answer what the Norns share with me through the Eye of Portents," said Evermud, "and I give you more than naught. I've warned you that my sight has limits. It's up to you to recognize the meaning in good time."

"Do we prevail over the Gepids and Strabo in tomorrow's battle?" Theoderic asked the eagle.

"Only you will."

Now Theoderic laughed deeper at the challenge of getting a proper response, and the lingering powder gave him a sharp pain behind his eyes as though serving a reminder of his place. "Will I restore the West?"

"Do all that you can," said Evermud. "Your efforts will come to nil but for a single strategic move."

"That hardly seems worth it."

"It will be, for that choice will eventually preserve civilization."

"Which choice?" Theoderic asked, trying hard to blink against the dust.

"I don't know, but it will involve Augustulus."

"I'm not acquainted with this person."

"When the time comes that you need to know, you will meet someone of far greater power than mine who will help you to the next juncture."

"How will I know him?"

"You will not know him at all."

"But there will there be a sign...?"

"For those who can read them, yes. Your great Arabian Majid is the first sign of the power that will be yours, yet I see that you leave him in the forest. You must never be so foolish again. Power is to be kept close."

Theoderic tried one last question. "Will I be wise

enough to govern?"

"Your wisdom will come with age," said Evermud, "and age will come, robust years known only by a few."

Then Evermud appeared to be himself again. No longer the eagle, he seemed unmindful and wary of what had transpired. "Did you get what you came for, young prince?"

"You don't remember?"

"I don't."

Theoderic, who still had his wondering eyes full of dust, forgot none of it.

And the long decades passed.

Augustulus. Theoderic had watched all of his adult life for a personal encounter with someone of that name— ever since the Shaper of Nations revealed the truth through the Eye of Portents... *When the time comes that you need to know, you will meet someone of far greater power than mine.*

And this person of power, Theoderic was certain now, would be Wade of Aquitaine.

CHAPTER 23

At First Sight

Rome, 500 A.D.

AUGUSTULUS WHINED. AS Wade sank to one knee and bowed his head to Theoderic, he placed a settling hand on the dog's back. Beneath his fingers he could feel some of the tension melt from the Laconian's shoulders while its powerful muscles hinted at a ready reserve for defense should its new master decide he'd read the situation wrong and require it to attack either Theoderic or Egan.

"So this is Augustulus. Mighty little Augustus," Theoderic laughed. "We finally meet, and he is covered in fur. I wonder if his master is in the mood for an execution."

Wade went rigid and raised his head to gawk at the Ostrogoth even though he knew he violated protocol in doing so.

"You'll need to be," Theoderic continued. "The crowd will not abide the wait much longer."

"I'm not sure I'm properly dressed for an execution," Wade hedged.

Theoderic said, "As long as it's not yours, you can dress any way you please."

"And it's not mine, right?"

Theoderic shook his head. "Why would it be? Not now and not ever, General Wade."

Wade breathed a little easier having answered the most pressing question—whether it would be him in the dock or not. Yet Theoderic's instant familiarity came as a shock. Had they somehow previously met in this alternate universe?

"My lord King," protested Egan as though certain there had been a mistake. He licked his nervous lips and asked, "Do you know this man?"

Theoderic rounded on him. "General Wade is known to me since the Neusiedler See. So, yes, I know him better than I know you, and he is worth ten thousand of you."

Egan's confusion turned to devastation that nearly prevented him from responding, but he managed to say, "My apologies. I brought this Visigoth general to you directly on the orders of Anastasius."

"So noted. Support from the empire is as important to me as it has ever been. But while you do not trust Wade of Aquitaine, a man who you falsely trusted, Count Odoin, has tried to kill me. Now Rome needs to see his fate."

By the way his face creased all over, Egan was beyond devastated. Statements linking him to the accused could lead to his own execution regardless of his high position with Anastasius. He could only reply, "These are unpredictable times, my lord."

"Then I will thank you not to attempt any more predictions. If you have no other foolish questions, why don't you go tally the real estate?"

More than happy to escape, Egan backed away and bowed with only a sidewise glance at Wade. It was not a friendly gaze.

Once Egan was empty-handed and out of sight, Theoderic asked Wade, "Do you carry your introduction?" Wade struggled to concoct a response, but Theoderic changed his mind and waved him off. "Actually there's no time now. You'll give me your papers afterward."

Wade's shoulders drooped. He neither had his papers now nor would he have them later. With Theoderic's remark he'd been put on notice that he wasn't off the hook.

As though remembering his manners, Theoderic asked Wade directly, "Will you and Augustulus join me as my guests of honor at Count Odoin's execution?"

Wade did not want to attend another blood sport, regardless of who the victim would be, and he still hadn't decided whether he had a true reprieve or was being entrapped. Trying to sound chipper, he said, "Of course, my lord."

"Then come, Wade, we are going to the Castrense Amphitheater at the Sessorian Palace." He mounted up and Wade did the same a bit less steadily as the escorts moved to flank them. No one stopped the dog from coming with them as they rode off at a stately pace and Theodoric waved to his admirers. He was cheered by some in the throng as king, and by an especially enthusiastic few as *imperator.*

"It's obvious that this is not your horse," Theoderic said to Wade while scanning the crowd.

"I borrowed it from Egan. He must have been loath to reclaim it."

Theoderic laughed, "I wonder why."

The king added no more until they neared the palace complex, part of which was built directly into the Aurelian Walls as one of its sturdier components. A curious and ancient looking collection of rounded bricks formed the amphitheater columns and arches ringing the exterior under a spill of ivy. To the right was an even more vast construction, equal in dimensions to the circus wall of the hippodrome, a resemblance that fed Wade's sense of dread. *A great many people must have been executed within these structures.*

The air thinned and cooled abruptly, picking up a tinge of must as they entered a vaulted corridor. They continued the slow ride, hoofbeats echoing loudly off the stone walls, flanked by an honor guard lining the ascending route on foot to supplement their armed escort. A rectangle of glaring sunlight awaited them at the end. Now the jubilation that leaked in behind them gave way to this bloodthirsty sound ahead, a restless clamor of the crowd magnified in the great bowl. Theoderic seemed to be carefully monitoring Wade's reactions, particularly how his hands rose and dipped at the reins.

As though he could read Wade's mind, Theoderic said, "I abhor executions as much as you do, as any general should, but I have responsibilities."

"You would prefer to kill him in battle," Wade surmised. "That would come more naturally because he would have an equal chance to slay you."

"Precisely. Count Odoin reminds me fondly of a man I slew in my very first battle. There were few within reach that I did not kill that day when the frenzy was on me." He took a deep breath. "The frenzy and the terror."

~*W*~

Pannonia, 472 A.D.

THE Gepids arrived in force, fanning out to build an overlapping shield wall with deep ranks behind. Once their great numbers settled in place, they clashed the shields, each against its neighbor, to sound a thundering warning.

Their site was well chosen. They filled the empty plain and leveraged the protection of a mountain bounding them on one side and a minor river on the other. A strip of forest, which could provide cover for a retreat, lay two hundred yards at the backs of the last rank. Theoderic had not imagined there would be so many of them willing to face him in battle on a clear day in early spring. But of course it was known that his father was ailing and freshly retired. Eighteen-year-old Theoderic was untested and his rivals had gathered sympathetic allies to make their victory certain.

The field held every tribe of Gepids…

Joined by Odoacer with his Scirians solidifying their right flank right up to the mountainside...

Joined by Strabo and his Thracian Goths guarding the left flank at the river.

Pointing with a pike, his uncle Videmir said, "You know Strabo, and I'm sure you have spotted Odoacer."

"Yes, by his hair pulled into a top knot and by his moustache and chin beard."

"I recognize Heruli tribesmen mixed in as well, and even a couple of hired men among Strabo's force, with Suebian knots braided on the side." He cited the participants as though Theoderic should figure out the implications for himself.

He did. The Gepids alone were not strong enough to prevail, but these four tribes combined in the field, plus mercenaries, were far stronger than Theoderic's Ostrogoths. There was no great pretense at high strategy on the part of his opposition; all the tribes had assembled in plain sight in order to intimidate, and win the battle before it had begun. Their only concession was to cede to the Ostrogoths a slightly higher ground, and thus a better view of their misfortune.

"Good to see them all," said Theoderic drily. "Our scouts will not be tied up finding their strays."

"We run," said Videmir with certainty. Retreat was not shameful in the face of overwhelming force. It was how all of these tribes had survived thus far, avoiding the unfavorable odds.

Theoderic regarded the old veteran. Videmir was no less strong than he had been the day before, probably the fiercest in the entire field of battle. Yet he had resisted the idea of blending the latest in Roman strategy and tactics that could have made the tribe even stronger.

Theoderic set his pike in the dirt. "As of today, that's not who we are anymore."

"If we stay, we will be no one."

"I command," the Ostrogoth prince reminded him.

261

"Then I suggest that you fall back and command from a more defensible position."

"We would do that if we had not a better choice."

"What choice?"

"Right there," Theoderic pointed to his rivals.

"The Thracian Goths?"

"The traitors. They come to our very soil this time and cannot help but be ashamed and weakened by it. That is where we break their line. I will lead our best men."

"If your plan does not work, we will be the ones exposed. A complete slaughter."

"Then we'll have to be right, move rapidly, and win fast."

Before Videmir could raise another objection, Theoderic rode before the lines of wary men in the staging area. His people were the greatest under the Hunnic subjugation, the greatest to triumph over the Huns, yet now they were the hunted. They needed reminding of who they had been at their best. "How do you stand today?" Theoderic called loudly. "We who defeated the Huns at the Battle of Nedao?"

The cheers were modest.

"Did the Imperium do that?" Theoderic shouted.

"No!"

"Did Persia do that?"

"No!"

"Did Clovis do that?"

"No!"

"Who defeated the Huns?"

"Theodimir!"

"Who?"

"Theodimir!"

"Yes! Are we the people of Videmir, Valamir, and Theodimir?"

"Yes!"

"Then prove it! You prove it! We run through the Thracian traitors and strike the soft belly of the rest."

Their shouts thundered in response, pretenders be damned.

Theoderic sent most of his forces to the other side of the river to attack the Thracian Goths at the crossing. The first group made for a spot in sight of the opposing lines so that the Thracians did not fully appreciate the concealed threat. Another group would skirt behind them. The river was wide enough that they had to move at almost chest height for nine excruciating paces, pikes, swords, and shields held high against a smattering of spears and arrows, before rising on the next bank. Men who fell and could not rise were left behind.

To compensate for the loss of speed, Theoderic personally directed a smaller force on the same side of the river with his battle standard raised for the enemy to see. He attacked the flank in a wedge, leaving his own flank exposed, shouting, "Whoever seeks a path through the enemy's ranks follow me."

There was no time for fear and yet Theoderic was filled with it. In the approach he chose, the young prince knew he took a big chance. The wedge formation, shaped like an arrowhead, had some of the attributes of a cavalry charge with its concentrated weight and its speed relative to a static line. Neither advantage was quite the equal of cavalry. Foot soldiers, however, were slightly more often convinced to face mortal injury than were horses. If his formation crumbled without effect, all of the disadvantages of an infantry line returned. To be trapped by the riverbank in a shoving match would be death for him and all of his tribe.

At the point of the wedge, Theoderic went into the fray before anyone, slamming his heavy shield into a clutch of Suebian-knotted mercenaries who stood fast in the strongest part of the shield wall. Strabo, his treacherous cousin, had brought them, and there had to be a reckoning.

His opposite shuddered and gave way a full step.

Theoderic struck aside the pike leveled at him and thrust rapidly at any opening with his sword, the way he'd been trained in Constantinople. The way he'd trained his men. These battles went quickly. Long-established practice, not thinking, was the key. There was no hint of the thrill he would feel until the first spear flew wide of him and the first of his opponent's blows failed to drop him, and then he was invigorated. His first opponent fell and the man behind, a Thracian Goth, tried to take his place but could not advance easily through the press of the crowd as his fellows drew backward. Nor did he seem keen to do so. Strabo himself could be seen directing the splintered action and desperately shouting encouragement from two ranks behind. Theoderic struck with ever more confidence as his housecarls, his bodyguard, flowed into a breach that opened at his sides and covered him from behind as he pushed in further.

The mercenaries were few and the Thracians around them had no taste for this fight. They were panic stricken with a shattered front, and he could see Strabo searching for a way out.

Because Theoderic had changed the orientation of the battlefield with his entire force at one flank—the mountain barrier now to the enemy's rear—the Gepids would be compelled to an awkward lateral retreat that would cut them up greatly. They must have sensed this growing danger as soon as their difficulties began. But by the time the Gepids pivoted their lines to cover their flank, the Thracian Goths had broken and run, leaving no shield wall and allowing the Ostrogoths from the crossing to inflict enough casualties that all of the Gepid's forces were put to flight.

With momentum on Theoderic's side, he released the few cavalry he had to run down the disorganized Gepid-led armies. Galloping through and wheeling for a second and third pass, they made quick slashes to one man out of five in the thinning field. Even before every last one of the enemy could fall back toward the cover of forest they begged for a truce, waving an improvised signal flag. Moments later, the leadership shoved Strabo out from the trees to speak for them.

~W~

Rome, 500 A.D.

THE Castrense Amphitheater rang to the sounds of elation as the accused and already convicted prisoner was marched at sword point with his hands bound. Count Odoin, a Germanic general, was not of the Ostrogoths but one of their shifting allies who had helped defeat Odoacer's Scirians in the war for Itale.

Theoderic and Wade sat in the emperor's Sun-Temple box at a long side of the amphitheater oval with a refreshment table between them, and a bowl at their feet for Augustulus. They could see, and be seen by, a full house of "friends, Romans and countrymen," as the fictional Mark Antony might have called them. In the center of the oval arena, Odoin was being stretched out and staked to ropes. The count had already been stripped of his finery and his hair had been cut, the braid now set beside him.

"He normally wears a Suebian Knot," Theoderic explained. "For some tribes, it distinguishes a free man from a slave, but of course he is a free man no longer."

Wade could not help but feel sympathy and a measure of dread. Not long ago he had been in a similar situation. In his case he was compelled to be part of an elaborate, cruel play staged for the audience at the East's Hippodrome.

"How will it be done?" asked Wade.

"N'Kolo," said Theoderic.

"What is that?"

"Not a Roman method. Times have changed. You

see, the wine I am drinking is from Gaza. But the corridor lamps, their oil, and the tableware in front of us are all from Africa, our new trading partner. N'Kolo is from Africa as well, a gift from my brother-in-law to be. These changes bring excitement. Excitement brings support."

A man rode into the courtyard on a costumed elephant to the cheers of the crowd. The behemoth showed remarkable finesse as he wheeled to recognize each quarter with a genteel dip of his trunk.

"N'Kolo is the elephant," Theoderic remembered to explain as the beast reared up on its hind legs to even louder acclaim.

Wade drew the thick, expectant air through his teeth. "Are you sure that the count is guilty?"

"When I confronted him, I told him that his plot had been revealed to me."

"How did he respond to that?"

Theoderic lifted his sleeve to show Wade the underside of his forearm. "Here is his response, where my arm stopped his knife!" There was a raw six inch wound, rejoined but still ragged. Theoderic asked, "Now what did you say happened to that horse of yours?"

"It broke a leg on the way down here from Spoleto." Having tried the tale once and wanting to stay consistent, Wade repeated his story with more confidence this time.

Still watching the show intently, Theoderic queried, "Did you lose your army too? What makes you think I need a Visigoth general by himself?"

"My troops are tied up fighting Clovis. I bring information."

The elephant picked up a small, red flag with its trunk and began to circle the condemned man while waving the flag merrily, as directed by the handler who sat astride his neck with a crop. Wade ascertained that thoughts of Count Odoin had spoiled Theoderic's trusting mood.

At this moment, Theoderic chose to ask with an edge of pique, "Why do you arrive now, Wade of Aquitaine?

Now, on my first state visit to Rome, at a time when I am rebuilding it, a time when my sister is getting married to one of our African allies, when I have urgent business with the Pope. Most of all, when Clovis is on the march and Anastasius does not trust me to handle it? And all of this during an assassination plot."

N'Kolo stopped where the ropes met the stakes and raised its great flat foot to press lightly on Odoin's chest. The stadium went silent as the pressure elicited an audible groan. Then N'Kolo backed away and resumed the pageantry with his delicate little flag to the approbation of the throng.

By the time N'Kolo was circling back and nearing the prisoner once again, Wade was ready to tell this king the truth, the absolute and entire truth about who he was and what he was doing. All in the hopes that Theoderic would understand. As Wade considered where to begin, the elephant's trainer stopped, looked up to the balcony, and Theodoric nodded. And immediately N'Kolo stepped on Odoin's head, splattering it like a smashed melon.

Wade looked away, but too late. Augustulus growled softly as if to voice the unease he sensed in his master.

"Why does such a merciful execution bother you?" Theoderic asked Wade. "Odoin was a traitor, no better than Strabo is."

"Strabo?"

"You do know who Strabo is, don't you?"

Wade thought he had some conception of who Strabo was. The idea that Strabo could be discussed in the present tense in this timeline disturbed him. According to history, Strabo should not have survived this far.

$\sim W \sim$

Pannonia, 472 A.D.

WHEN chasing the Gepids became a questionable

matter at the tree line, Theoderic granted the armistice and allowed Strabo to make his way to his tent through the ranks of jeering men. He was to remain undisturbed for the course of their discussion.

Videmir had disapproved of the meeting on the grounds that this pause "allowed the enemy to regroup." The scouts, however, said that many of the Gepids themselves had retreated a great distance to the field beyond the strip of forest. To end the argument, Theoderic gave in to his uncle's demand to be assigned to the front with a ready contingent to watch for treachery. It was better than having Videmir as part of the audience.

Theoderic said to his cousin, "I will hear your terms of surrender, Strabo."

Strabo, with his usual irritating cockiness, replied, "I say that the Imperium itself must surrender."

"To whom? To you?"

"You think that Marcellus is some loveable hippo-eyed, chipmunk-cheeked fool."

Theoderic froze. *That was exactly what I thought!*

"But you are the fool." Now Strabo let his agitation show, pacing and gesticulating with ire. "Your loyalty is nothing to Marcellus. Every move he makes is calculated to keep all of us off balance. Keep all the tribes disunited to neutralize us. Why do you suppose he showers me with gifts when you are supposed to be his favorite? To balance against his fear of the Amali royals—to balance against his fear of *you* even as he held you to his bosom. He tries to act as though he doesn't understand your tribe's politics, doesn't he? Yet Marcellus knows the Ostrogoths and the political situation better than you do. He was once tribune in Dacia. He served in the homeland of your birth with Aspar."

"That was long ago," Theoderic insisted.

"Are you dense? He didn't send you home to fight some band of Gepids to please Theodimir, but as a further hedge against me. Out of the same desire to equivocate, he sent the incompetent Basiliscus against the Vandals instead of using Aspar, who was powerful and popular and would have been strengthened by a victory. And Marcellus endorses my fight against you today despite the fact that you witlessly adore him."

Young Theoderic looked away.

Strabo smirked, knowing he'd scored. "You see, Amal, the years between us *do* make a difference."

Theoderic didn't know if Strabo meant the years they knew each other or the gap in their ages, and he didn't care. At this time, he was too well steeped in his Roman upbringing to identify with Strabo, even with the sting of Marcellus' likely betrayal hanging over him like a specter.

Strabo took a deep breath. "I've lost this battle only because my Thracian Ostrogoths didn't want to fight your Pannonian Ostrogoths."

"Because you are inferior."

"But together..." Strabo fairly whispered, "...together we will always win. Ally with me, let me have your sister Frida, and all will be well."

Theoderic saw red. Strabo wanted to bind himself to the Amali line to seal the alliance. His proposal was the furthest thing from unreasonable, something Theoderic would do himself in such circumstances, and Strabo was probably right about everything he'd said about Marcellus. But his dear, already-married Frida going to Strabo? That was the hidden purpose of the present bloodletting? "Never!"

Strabo was dismissed, and in the action that followed, the Pannonian Goths decisively threw the Gepids and their allies out of their territory, making a special effort to punish any lagging Scirians and Heruli for their poor choice of associates. Videmir did not credit Theoderic for the victory, but thanked Asgard, Evermud and Jesus, in that order. Perhaps he was right to reserve his full applause, Theoderic reflected later, since Strabo escaped with his life, as did Theoderic's future nemesis, Odoacer.

~*W*~

Rome, 500 A.D.

A clean-up crew cleared the remains of the late Count Odoin, some of which required scraping and gathering. Two struggling men tipped a large bucket of water over the residue, although the concrete had already absorbed a stain that would take the next rainfall to clear completely. At the same time, preparations for further entertainment were being set up in the amphitheater, a series of banners and props ranging around the oval. Both crews had to run off as a parade of lions began to issue from the release cage to fill the arena. The cheers rose.

Theoderic shouted to Wade, "Don't forget that we await those papers of yours."

"You don't really trust me then."

"I don't."

"Why did you tell Egan that you did?"

"How I conduct my affairs is not for the ears of Egan or his master."

"So why did you accept me at all?"

"I couldn't speak freely in front of the emperor's man, but your appearance was foretold to me by Evermud of the Ostrogoths. He warned me that your powers were great."

"Powers?"

"All the more reason to be wary of you."

Wade took note of the extra guards that had joined them in the Sun-Temple box. "I don't know anyone named Evermud."

"I'm not sure that he knew you either. He was not himself when the visions came on him."

"Then how—?"

"I was asked to await a sign that would be known to me via Augustulus. You brought him."

"My dog?"

"Evermud got his predictions from the Norns." Theoderic's tone warned Wade not to question the Norns.

Everything up to and including the fate of this universe, if not more, depended on what was going on inside Theoderic's head. Right now, Wade thought, he would give anything, even trade away his enormous gifts, if only he could gain the talent of reading minds.

Theoderic continued, "I have no problem with you so far as I know. But I do have a problem with people who should be on my side and turn out to be disloyal. I deal harshly with betrayal."

Obviously.

~*W*~

Ravenna, Winter, 493 A.D.

THEODERIC, now king of his own people and most of Itale, rode with his armies into a starving Ravenna bearing food. His soldiers distributed relief along his triumphant and snow-mantled route to the palace where the besieged Odoacer waited. The people cheered for the imperial insignia, which Theoderic was returning to the city at a stately march, and cheered even more for the bread he brought. Theoderic's smile was thin, as he himself had an appetite only for revenge. General Tufa, the latest man to betray him, was fresh in his mind, and out of reach due to his death at another's hand.

Amalafrida, who rode at her brother's side, her spirits lifted by victory even in the miserable weather, said, "You've studied history, Theoderic. Has anyone ever accomplished what we just did in Itale or anywhere?"

"You mean laying a three-year siege while we ruled the country from a camp outside of its capital? No, Frida. That has never been done before."

She arched an eyebrow teasingly. "And then negotiating a treaty of our enemy's half-surrender?"

"The half part will soon be remedied," he bristled. "If it were not for Tufa and his monster of an overlord, Odoacer, doing the unthinkable together, we would have been in Ravenna long ago."

Amalafrida had been released to him in 487, and she had been a valuable partner for the entire war against Odoacer, gently prodding her brother this way and that when she was not in battle herself. Theoderic had sworn he'd give anything for her freedom from Constantinople, and he'd made it a condition that she join the armies if emperor Zeno insisted on him recapturing Itale. The price was that Frida's son was made *magister militum* of the Eastern Empire instead of Theoderic. It didn't surprise him. That was part of how generals were kept in check. If Theoderic won, he would have the West. Frida had told him not to trust General Tufa, and she was right.

"Remedied when?" she urged softly. "When do we remedy Odoacer's half-surrender?"

"Today, if conditions favor it." With Emperor Marcellus gone, they had proceeded at Zeno's direction. Zeno, who ruled over the entire empire and did not watch Theoderic grow into his might, thought that he alone had the power to decide the fate of the East-West axis. His win-win scenario was to pit two Arian kings against each other. And now Zeno, in his turn, was gone and the emperor was Anastasius. With Theoderic the only point of continuity, it was he who saw the proper high strategy for restoration of the Roman Empire. Odoacer, he had to remember, was a trifle on that scale.

Uncle Videmir, who rode a bit further back, called, "What are you two talking about?"

"The war," said Theoderic over his shoulder. "The war that's not over."

"Yes, and we're out here waving and smiling like idiots."

"Our reward will come soon," Theoderic answered loudly enough for those closest to hear.

The entourage was arranged in order of trustworthiness. Frida came first. Theoderic's wife, Audofleda — Clovis' repugnant sister — rode last. Completing the group after Videmir and before Audofleda, was Frederick, the young king of the Rugii. Frederick had come over to Theoderic after Odoacer kidnapped and murdered his parents. There could be no better recommendation for friendship with the Ostrogoths than sharing a common enemy. Still, the brutal lesson of Tufa made Theoderic hold Frederick at arm's length.

Frederick, though, had been to Ravenna before and he led them to their first stop at Piazzale Anita Garibaldi. The great church, San Giovanni Evangelista, was where the Ostrogoths met with the coincidentally named Giovanni, bishop of Ravenna, looking thin and tired in his humble brown robes and skullcap. His tasseled white stole bore a black footed cross, which was the only thing that Theoderic found pleasing about him.

In a voice tight as a violin string, Giovanni said, "You have returned with your entire army it seems."

"That was the point," said Theoderic. "My point, anyway."

"You agreed to co-rule with Odoacer," Giovanni reminded him sternly. The bishop had brokered the deal that let Theoderic into Ravenna after the three year standoff.

"Did you expect us to shiver in camp when there's a city right here?"

"But we've no food to support ourselves, let alone you," Giovanni complained. "It's been ten days. You promised us a feast at the palace."

"Yes, I know. It took time to gather so many provisions."

Eyeing the wagons with growing avarice, Giovanni said, "Can you leave some of those barrels and amphora at the church before we go to the banquet?"

Theoderic smirked. "You want to be seen distributing

the wealth yourself, don't you?"

"I played an important role in securing it."

"But I'm afraid you'll forget who it comes from. Are you certain that you can accept a handout from yet another Arian king?" Although the prince of the Ostrogoths had been brought up in Constantinople among Trinitarian Christians, he directly represented a people who were Arian. For fifteen years, Theoderic had ridden at the head of his rolling Ostrogothic armies, policing the provinces under his care. Honorable and faithful servant of the Imperium. And yet, the attacks on Arian churches grew. He would not permit the intolerance to spread to Itale.

"You are the least of the heretics," Giovanni joked nervously. "At any rate, the strife with Arians is an Eastern problem. I will be happy to dine with you."

"You want to eat? You want your supply lines reopened? Once I enter the palace at Ravenna," Theoderic warned him, "no one of any religion will be persecuted any longer."

Giovanni swallowed. "I understand, my lord. That's fair."

"Get ready and come with us."

"Thank you, my lord!"

Aside, Videmir asked Theoderic, "Why bring him and his parasitic rabble?"

"Because it will look good."

Gathering all of his ministers and lesser clerics, Giovanni and the rest led the way, cradling crosses, and swinging incense burners or clutching Holy Gospels, invoking the triumph of peace in their songs. The bells of San Giovanni Evangelista rang behind them. Wherever crowds gathered, the holy men conveyed bread from the soldiers to the starving.

They continued as the procession entered the palace and the clergy stepped to the sides to line the walls. Theoderic and his entourage, with all of his surviving nobles, went through, pausing only to surrender their weapons to the master of arms. Videmir posted guards outside and supervised them himself together with Frederick, who was not permitted inside under the old king's instructions.

Odoacer was in his late fifties now and he looked diminished with his top-knot hair thinned, his moustache and chin beard white, but by no means had he joined in his people's starvation. He was rather plump in fact.

"Welcome to Ravenna," said Odoacer with a sly grin. "Did I give you plenty of trouble, I hope?"

"Not too much once I boxed you in here," replied Theoderic, trying to hold his temper. After Odoacer had retreated to the swamp-barrier stronghold, Theoderic's siege camp had to be defended from a number of aggressive forays issuing from the city gates, but the real trouble the Scirian gave him was in the mobile war that preceded it.

Odoacer said, "And this is my wife, Sunigilda."

She was a large, unpleasant woman who shrugged her beefy shoulders at the introduction and said to Theoderic in a prickly tone, "I see that you found your way in. Are you sure you wish to proceed with the feast?"

"And why would I not?" he asked.

"After living in the field for so long it's understandable that your odor precedes you. Perhaps we should postpone until you can bathe in the spring rains."

Theoderic countered, "Perhaps it would be best if you sat at a table that does not offend your exaggerated self-image. Audofleda, show her the way!"

Audofleda, a strong woman herself, stepped quickly to direct Sunigilda away from Theoderic's wrath.

Turning back on her heel, Sunigilda replied to Theoderic, "The only reason that you are in this palace is because my husband is charitable toward vagabonds."

"Please pardon my Gilda," said Odoacer with smug contentment. "She did not agree with our arrangement, smart woman that she is."

The tables were already set, the staff scurrying. The Scirian royals had demanded that the food and a contingent of cooks precede the entrance of Theoderic and his nobles. Now the Ostrogoth king was grateful for that arrangement because it reduced his time suffering the insufferable.

Over the host's objections, Theoderic insisted that Giovanni and his clergy fill the long table where he sat with Odoacer and Amalifrida on either side. The bishop joined them with a self-satisfied smile. The servers came to the royals and clergy first, setting out the initial round of the feast.

As he tucked in, Odoacer said, "I fooled you well with Tufa, didn't I?"

"You did," Theoderic admitted tightly. Tufa, Odoacer's commander-in-chief, had surrendered to Theoderic, saying that unity of the empire was more important than Odoacer's ego and that the Scirian had violated his caretaker role. He claimed that with his special knowledge of Odoacer's operation he could avoid a great deal of bloodshed for men he respected on both sides. Enchanted by those sentiments, Theoderic gave Tufa charge of the elite troops, all of them Pannonian Ostrogoths, to lead them in a final battle that would settle the war.

Tufa lured them to an empty fortification that he said was identical to the one Odoacer currently occupied. To prepare for the upcoming assault, he ordered them to run through a training exercise where the combatants would carry only wooden swords. Once they were in the courtyard, Tufa's men barred the gates and descended on the Ostrogoths with multi-bladed pikes to pierce and chop them to bits. Almost all of the Amali royal family was laid to waste. Only a few, including a badly wounded Videmir had fought their way out of the trap with nothing but the splintered sticks in their hands.

Although a crucial element of warfare was deception,

Odoacer had committed the one unforgivable deception as far as any Goth was concerned. He denied them the honor of battle and slaughtered them like cattle instead.

Theoderic had been thwarted in his revenge on Tufa when the commander died in battle with the Rugii. Odoacer, however, was the mastermind behind Tufa's crime. He ran free to taunt Theoderic while chewing happily on a pork shank paid for by the Ostrogoths, saying, "It's a shame you weren't among the slain. Why aren't you eating? Did you wish to make a toast first? Shall we drink to our co-rule?"

There were no arms permitted in the feasting hall except possibly for the one that Theoderic had ordered fastened to the underside of the table where he sat. His entire plan depended on whether that order had been carried out. If it had not, revenge would have to wait, but there might never be an opportunity comparable to this day at the feast. With one hand, Theoderic felt beneath the table and located the head of a screw, a small brace bar, and another screw. For one dreadful moment he worried that the weapon was bolted in. The brace, however, supported a scabbard, and when he traced along that length he found a hilt well within reach. Theoderic had been patient. Too patient. He would do this thing now or never. One surprise attack deserved another.

Right in front of Bishop Giovanni, Theoderic drew the sword.

The horrified Odoacer saw the only weapon in the hall being raised against him, and shouted, "No!" Helplessly turning to an equally surprised Giovanni, he admonished, "Where is your god?"

Theoderic wasted little time stabbing his co-ruler while crying out, "This is what you did to mine," and repeating the sentiment before he struck the second time and the third. The first blow was already a good one, going in through the stomach and up to the heart, giving the old king just enough time to form an expression of bewilderment. Since Theoderic was not given to excess, by the last blow he was chagrinned with himself, explaining to the blood-spattered onlookers with a crooked smile, "I wanted to see if the fellow had any spine, but there wasn't a single bone anywhere in him."

~ *W* ~

Rome 500 A.D.

WADE could do nothing but watch the continuing spectacle. The lions in the arena were well trained, turning smartly to the crack of each whip, roaring a protest while doing exactly as they were bidden.

The ringmaster called out, "See the beasts, marvel at how we've bent them to civilized use. You will see next how quickly they can return to unbridled savagery."

Theoderic said to Wade, "Now that the business of Odoin is resolved, I will have those papers of yours. Your introduction and your orders."

Unable to figure a way out of this obligation, Wade admitted, "I expect some difficulty in securing them for you."

"Difficulty?"

"Yes, as in—"

"Hold on," said Theoderic. An aide whispered in Theoderic's ear. "Ah," he said to Wade. "Your papers have been delivered separately."

"My... papers?" Wade asked incredulously. "You have them?"

"They bear your name. Shall I read the document for you?"

"Please."

"Let it be Known Hereby and Acknowledged by Whomsoever Shall Read this Missive that the Bearer, one Wade of Aquitaine—" he paused to inspect the red-caped Wade "—is a General in the Visigoth Army who Humble

278

Lends his Sword to Theoderic the Great in Furtherance of Peace and Friendship Between our People."

Theoderic nodded in satisfaction. He held the letter up for show, and said, "It's signed by Alaric himself. Not the first time my cousin Visigoths have lent me their aid in a time of crisis, but I will not grow lax in my appreciation."

Wade was thunderstruck. How could there be documents that confirmed him as a Visigoth general when it wasn't true in the first place?

"I don't see your specific orders here, Wade. Can you explain that?"

Wade could not explain any of it. On guard within his numbness, he answered, "My orders are in my head. They were too important to risk on paper."

Theoderic contemplated that information with a wistful smile. "The oracle Evermud told me that in the end, only one thing will matter. He said you're to tell me what it is."

"Me?"

Theoderic said. "Perhaps you. Tell me what you think."

Wade, who was still reeling from his reprieve tried, "The only thing that matters is the future. Securing the future, to be exact."

"How would you do that?"

"The same way you plan to do it. The legion."

"I believe you are correct."

"Only..." Wade hesitated. How did he tell the king that he believed that someone had stolen information from the Norns and was using it against the timeline itself? Was there any other way to say it that would be understood?

"Only?"

"How do you plant a secret legion when the plan is already known to Clovis?"

"I've thought about this. If he attacks, we wipe him out and accelerate the contingency plan. If the troops are not immediately needed and not seen for a long enough time, people will consider the rumors of them a myth."

Wade thought that plan over and asked, "Why were there so few in the legion reserve to begin with?"

"That part was not my idea. Anastasius insisted they have to be pure of blood and long on tradition, bred in the cold of the mountains. So said Delphi."

"Delphi?"

"The current Byzantine equivalent of my Evermud, and not really Delphi, but whoever was Anastasius' mystery advisor, a Syrian woman, they say. I have to work with what I'm given."

Anastasius' mystery advisor, and even Theoderic who had lived at court did not know who it was. Now that Wade felt on safer ground, he ventured, "Who brought in my documents?"

"That would be Kreindia of Amorium. Here she comes now."

In the greatest shock of Wade's sixth century journey so far, Theoderic beckoned, the guards shuffled back and Kreindia of Amorium stepped forward in a bright swirling gown.

Augustulus barked at her. Her synesthetic signature struck Wade as authentic but she looked...changed? Matured? And with papers proving him a Visigoth general? From what universe had she come?

She smiled sweetly at him and said, "My apologies for being late."

CHAPTER 24

Clarity

<u>Syria, 998 A.D.</u>

KREINDIA ROAMED THE nearest lines, tending to the wounded and wondering if her disastrous role here could be undone if only she could assess the damage fully. Allen Linwood was right. Why had she gotten involved in this doomed battle? Shame struck her like a body blow with each new insight.

Dalassenos, who must have understood his enemy, had nevertheless made two crucial misjudgments on this day. The first was his opportunistic strike on Apamea. He'd arrived with his forces after the conflagration, thinking his work had been partly done for him. Isolated considerations like that were never advisable. Generals who personally led their men into battle had to be right every day, or risk forfeiting their own lives.

The Arabs had also seen the fire that brought the Byzantines down on them. Al Samsama proceeded to Apamea thinking that it was already long under attack, and he undoubtedly expected to drive off the raid and get what revenge he could. If Dalassenos had burned the city himself he would have already gained a superior position by the time his opposition appeared. At the very least he would have been prepared for an orderly retreat.

If that were Dalassenos' only error, Kreindia's involvement might not have been pivotal. The general's second mistake was not knowing the value and loyalty of his supplemental forces, the Varangian Guard. In the original timeline, a pitched battle where personal valor would make the difference for one side or the other, he failed to trust the guard and his troops were routed. Kreindia's assistance kept the inferior general in a theater where he wasn't meant to continue. The stains accumulating on her hands were much greater than Leo's crimes. She may have somehow been responsible for an irreversible schism in time.

She saw the men returning wearily from the front to add a handful of new items to the modest possessions they'd left behind the lines with the women. They must have taken only field souvenirs rather than looting. Like them, she was loath to linger on this battleground, and yet she had to sort through the rubble of her decisions because she had no idea where to go or what to do. If the situation pointed to any options, she hadn't seen them yet. With every soldier she aided, her main objective was to stop their bleeding using anything at hand to bind the wound. As she helped some ladies break off a table leg to use as a splint, she wondered if there was there any way to do the same for the wounds of Time.

She was convinced now that the ruse that had sent her to the year 820 to rescue Michael had been calibrated to make her think that her actions in 998 were also correct. That meant that nothing Faron said could be trusted. She must now favor the alternative that Wade never gave Faron a message to pass along to her and was never intending to meet her in either time period. Nonetheless she suspected that something had happened to propel Wade out of the twenty-first century and into the time stream once again.

Cnaeus, who had gone off to dig bodies out of the sand, returned now, shaking his cup-shaped head, and Kreindia was glad she had waited. She wanted to question him.

"I believe that is my coat of mail you wear," he asserted. "I would like it back."

"Would you?" she flared. "Do you realize that you attacked me?"

"Then it wasn't a dream as I thought. Sometimes I get battle crazed. That was a bad one even for me, but I hardly think of it as my fault. The madness comes on me."

While she found his contemplation useful, the orange scarf he wore captured her attention because it was wrong. The sight of anything dyed from alder bark, as an article of this color would have been, had always produced a synesthetic brackish taste in her mouth, yet this one did not. She had to know why. "I'll give you the mail in return for the scarf at your neck."

"The scarf is from my wife!"

"There's never been a better trade in the history of the world. Tell her you lost it."

Though Cnaeus frowned and muttered at the odd request, he surrendered the orange wrap. His bare neck, the cleanest part of him, showed a Celtic knot tattooed in the shape of a bat in flight. As soon as the scarf was away from the interference of his tattoo, the brackish taste associated with the orange dye surfaced.

"Where did you get that design?" she asked.

"The hand-wing? A drunken binge in Anatolia. At least I suppose I must have been drunk," he puzzled. "That too seemed like a dream."

"Like a dream in what way?"

"Like I was acting in a play that didn't make sense, saying lines that were written for me, describing to the artist exactly what kind of tattoo I wanted even though I didn't know where the description came from. But that wasn't even the strangest part."

"What was?"

"I paid the artist to put something in the ink. I don't even know where I got the jar from. I wasn't worried because I was sure it was a dream, yet I woke with the hand-wing nonetheless."

The ink. Cnaeus' design was remarkably similar to the

tattoo she'd seen before on Dr. Nesky's patient Henry, who appeared to have an affinity to Faron. Faced with this connection, and the fact that the tattoo ink caused an illusory cloak, she wondered, *Had Faron manipulated the twenty-first century Celt, Henry, into helping him separate her from Wade?* Henry had responded to Faron's suggestions almost as easily as those of his doctor. The commonality was Cnaeus' and Henry's troubled minds as well as their tattoos. Then there was the little boy with the wheels on his shoes. He was drawn into scenario as well. *An unformed mind.*

If it was Faron directing these plays and he could affect multiple time periods, then she had to consider that he may also have been the master of Raginpert's actions in trying to cause a ninth century clash of the superpowers, Byzantium versus the Holy Roman Empire. That development had borne the tattered astral marker of an event that had been altered—the choking concentration of driest sawdust—a sign that she perceived easily when her sight was clear. Faron's hand in everything was the only link that made sense.

The question was not why she had such powerful suspicions now; it was why she hadn't seen these connections before. The Norse figurine that took her here was from Faron! It must have acted as a block just as the scarf did!

As Cnaeus helped her off with the heavy coat of mail, she realized that Del's fake father could not only cloak the signs of his manipulation, but also had the ability to mute her perceptions directly. She didn't know who Faron really was or how he had insinuated himself into Del's household, but he was undoubtedly a synesthete far more powerful than either she or Wade. Most recently, he'd used his special knowledge of events to bait her into his scheme that began with Michael. That was merely a mental trick. But what if there was more to it than that? A cut from Zoticus' sword made her hallucinate and become suggestible enough to go to Apamea. If he could control Zoticus, who else could Faron get to?

She wanted to believe that Faron had lessened his effectiveness by having taken the gamble of revealing himself, but by now he must be operating with the confidence of having won absolutely. At the moment, his supremacy certainly seemed secure to Kreindia.

Given these events, she could not go forward or backward. Not just yet. Even though her distance from Faron allowed her to recover her memory by stages, he'd maintained a lingering block. He might engage her with a new device in their next encounter, which she had no doubt would take place. While she was still mentally clear, she needed to ensure that she had a way to determine when she was acting under free will and when she was not. Once she could feel relatively safe from manipulation, she would try to locate Wade.

She watched Cnaeus shrugging on his mail and doing up his laces while the brackish taste of orange dye ran rampant and an idea teased at the periphery of her mind. She badly wanted to go to the perfectly tamed confines of her contemplation forest to work out the answer; times like these were the entire reason she had created it. Yet she dare not go anywhere that Faron could reach her, as he had proven he could do. Neither the Earthly realm nor the astral plane was safe from his predations.

Making certain she was unobserved, she found a dark corner inside the war-torn colonnade. The cool darkness of the portico's shadows reminded her of childhood days hiding in a ship's hold. Her uncle, just a centurion then, had taken charge of her when her father died. When he was shuttled from one command to another, they needed a rigorous protocol to keep her safe from the sailors. That came at a price. In a world where her every action was dictated by strict commands, all she wanted to do was to go and hide where she could exercise her free will to prove to herself that she possessed at least a modicum of that precious commodity. It turned out to be good practice for when she was imprisoned by the usurper Raginpert. Free will was the most fundamental of human attributes, and hers was in jeopardy once again.

When her eyes were adjusted to the dark, she looked for a place to sit and continue her train of thought. Mounds of sand had gotten into the structure. As she sank into one of them to get as comfortable as she could, her senses crossed and a panel of illuminated stained glass appeared in the air. Being a strong synesthete, many things she encountered had an association to them, some so strong that they landed like fists; some so weak that she routinely pushed them below perception to get them out of the way. The sight of the bright beams made her gasp.

This was not the first time that sitting in sand triggered a rich red and blue collection of tesserae above her, but it was particularly striking in the shadowed space, and therefore not so easy to dismiss. What if the entire infinity of her thoughts and actions each had at least a mild association to them that she simply never noticed? If free will, taken for granted as a constant, were linked to a tangible feeling, then she would be accustomed to ignoring it. Even ordinary people became oblivious to things that had a pervasive presence, like the odor of a horse pen to a stable hand. Synesthetes needed to push a multitude of impressions to the background far more often.

Supposing, however, that free will did have a synesthetic link, how could she recognize its marker? Because her ability to suppress was so exercised, the opposite—elevating a hidden feeling—was far more difficult to achieve. Free will—way at the bottom of the infinity that represented the totality of her being—was what she had to find, and she needed an alternate way to go there.

If she were to treat this goal as she did her astral travel, her target could be visualized as directional; the way was down—far beneath her first five senses. She shut her eyes and listened to the sound of the air with its myriad susurrations, and then she let its input dissolve. She smelled Apamea burning and let the olfactory assault float by like the cloud it was. She felt the hard floor beneath her and imagined its pressure dropping away.

She pictured the Boucoleon Palace and imagined descending the marbled stairs to a lower level. At the first turn, the landing was covered with a barrier of orange scarves, their stench multiplied to an unbearable olfactory assault, halting her advance. *The damned scarf from Cnaeus.* Why hadn't she left it outside? How many hindrances must she face?

She could not interrupt the headway she'd made so far. Shrugging away the emotion that threatened her concentration, she reached for a twenty-first century tool—the elevator—the box that could bypass the stairs with a controlled fall. Hers looked like the one in Dr. Nesky's office, silvered, polished and perfect, the only kind she'd ever seen. She entered the isolated space and pressed the lowest button. The machine sealed its heavy doors and started slowly downward. As she relaxed, it sped up, avoiding the alder bark barrier and skipping past her awareness of every worldly matter.

Don't disturb the progress. Don't breathe. Don't think about anything but the elevator.

Suddenly all her perceptions peeled down to her core. And the fragile place inside hurt like it would never stop. The very air attacked her essence as though her unprotected center were exposed to a corrosive element. She screamed, and it felt like that scream was all she was. One blind, disconnected hand found a rock, and her other hand seized upon the Norseman figurine. What had possessed her to facilitate Faron's last hold on her? *The same compulsion I've been under all along.* Through her blind pain, she smashed Faron's totem. One, two, three times against the ground.

Then all the agony was gone. Still naked of her upper

five senses, she could nonetheless view the entirety of the space around her, and what she saw was bubbles. Delicate membranes making up every solid Greek column, churning in every bit of Apamea's rubble, forming and bursting in every pore in her hands, effervescence so tiny that it was impossible that she could discern it, and yet she did. Foam like whitecaps shifting on the sea, every bit of the Everything popping in and out of existence. She was uncannily certain that this was the composition of both life and nonlife at its smallest scale.

Foam, like she saw that day with Faron. Only this was different than what had briefly peeked out during that encounter. His bubbles were stagnant. These cycled like life itself. His was power robbed from his contact with the Everything. But at its root the foam was pure. Without his taint it was reality. If she could see reality, then she had free will. She hoped that's what her discovery meant.

When she wanted her other senses, they returned with ease, only now she had to open her eyes in order to see. She found the Norseman smashed to bits. Its tiny axe had come free. After all that had happened, she still felt a lingering urge to take the remnant and use it. Perhaps just that small piece divested of its power?

She reached for it and then shuddered and drew away. With rationality returning, she knew that she had to shun anything that came from Faron. Just as Wade didn't need a particular totem for astral travel, she likewise didn't need the figurine, only something pointy to trigger the acupuncture gateway. She saw too that her figurine was not the only thing smashed on the colonnade floor. Sifting the dirt where it gleamed, she unearthed a bit of jewelry. It was a dented ring with a naked setting uncorrupted by associations with Faron. The claw talons that once held a stone were bent away so that only one remained. With the warped shank it would fit her small finger. She slipped it on.

Armed with this untested tool, and what she now held

in reserve—her ability to peel down to reality—there was no time to waste. She compelled her mind across the centuries as she had done once before in the bowels of the ship that had first brought her to Constantinople. With ease now, she probed Time and Space for Wade, scanning the centuries in both directions, delving all the way to infinity because nothing could stand in the way of his signature. She sought only his vital indicia, the active signal in the form of little dancing flames that she had originally located to call him to her century.

His unique sign should have been a beacon cutting across Heaven and Earth, yet she found no trace of it.

I cannot break down now. What if Wade is in transit, on the river outside of Time and Space?

So Kreindia searched that flooded concourse as well, again attuning herself only to him so that nothing could stand in the way. That was the easy part. The result was the painful part, for by that method, she found only emptiness. She could stare and stare and there wouldn't be anything else.

No!

It was just as she'd feared—or more precisely, just as she'd kept herself from believing. By all indications, Wade existed nowhere in the world she inhabited, nowhere in the future or past, and nowhere on the astral plane. He'd been erased from the timeline, more thoroughly absent than her friend Verina who had perished in an earthquake. Wiping her rush of silent tears, Kreindia decided that this outcome left her no alternative. Armed with a new defense, the only outlet for her pain before it swamped her was to find and confront Faron. He was a threat to everyone on this timeline and quite likely, Wade's killer. No matter the cost, she would hunt him down, face him, and make him pay.

~*W*~

FARON Richter was supervising the construction of a Wicker Man at Turin in northern Itale when Kreindia smashed his Norse figurine. He could sense its dissolution as a collapsing wave function, taking down a wide swath of possibilities he would have preferred not to part with. Kreindia must have believed it would only be a matter of time before she found him. He laughed at the struggle of those on her level, for Faron was the ultimate synesthete. His crossed senses were unfettered agents of information blending like a unified theory of physics. Like Wade and Kreindia, he could move through time and space. But Faron was not a man. He was free of conventional human limitations and mores, free of mortality too because he fed on weaker versions of himself.

Fortunately, Faron had another functioning talisman in place—a small Wheel of Taranis wrapped in a page of the Gospel of Judas. He used it to influence Clovis' chief druid Morcant. Per his suggestion to Morcant, the destitute would be burned in the limbs of the Wicker Man as a sacrifice to Taranis in order to ensure the success of the war against Theoderic. It was all nonsense to him but the more he made a subject do, the more the victim came under his control.

He had first learned the art of the talisman as a young man visiting a temple at Angkor Wat, although as a frequent astral traveler, Faron had no way to calculate his age. More than the sixty-five years or so that he appeared to be, yes, easily that. Beyond this point, he saw no reason to think about it. Earlier on, he technically qualified as a corporeal being, one rich enough in experience and maturity to enjoy all that life offered for someone of his powers. Granted, he had no equal and he grew stronger by the year. There was a time when he'd begun to wonder if he were something else as well. In those days, he thought it would be easy to fall prey to narcissism, grandiosity, and delusion, so he guarded against them, grounding himself in domestic situations when he wasn't otherwise occupied.

As with his earlier wives, life with Clara and the kid became a habit and then a marvelous way to stay close to his enemies.

Now he understood his place in the natural order of things. Just as mankind in its rise destroyed its rival species, such as Neanderthals, Faron's natural impulse was to eliminate other astral travelers. Wade and Kreindia qualified as rivals, though not of his caliber. Pretenders at best. For Faron was peerless, a creature that no one had ever been.

Nothing so crude as killing them would suit the situation. Besides, it was impossible to end Wade and Kreindia even if he chose that course of action. Not to his satisfaction. They would always be alive at some time and place or in some other universe that they could cross over from. No, it was far more effective and entertaining for Faron to manipulate them as agents of his corruption, to destroy civilization, and themselves in the process. If he damaged Wade's and Kreindia's minds enough, they would become his soldiers. Before he was through, they would doubt themselves and each other, and damage the veil of time in such a way that only Faron could swim through it. Then they would truly be neutralized.

$\sim W \sim$

KREINDIA had not left the solitude of the colonnade, and her plan included no intention of physically leaving. But where could she look for Faron? If she were to seek him out at the most obvious place, at his home in twenty-first century Long Island, then Kreindia was liable to recombine with Del. If she did that, the result would be unpredictable and likely undesirable for both her and her counterpart. Moreover, Faron would be well prepared for a confrontation in that place and time. Kreindia was willing to take any chance in regard to herself, but she did not have the right to endanger Del's life even if they were aspects of the same being.

She had previously ruled out a battle with Faron on the astral plane, a venue where his experience would give him tremendous advantage. Yet she could not go anywhere without following that avenue. She could seek to take an earlier Faron by surprise as he huddled with Raginpert in the ninth century, yet she had to consider that his present form might intercept her along the way. She had to be prepared for everything, including the small chance of astral battle. Gaining a certainty of whether or not the ideas in her head were her own or someone else's was the foundation of her arsenal. Her sense of reality would be invaluable if she teetered on the brink. What would she do about his tools of manipulation, the almonds and cicadas that could rob her memory? She would ground herself in reality, but would that be enough?

She realized that she'd been sitting there clutching handfuls of sand and letting the grains escape her fingers. Now she swiped her palms against each other until the residue was gone. Linwood the Elder had spoken to her of the Theory of Entropy, *a continual breakdown to disorder*, the ineluctable unwinding of everything you held sacred. No one who ever lived was a stranger to decay. The ruins she sat in were a tribute to that principle.

Therefore, it takes enormous, continuous constructive energy to make life work.

This entropy could eat your heart.

Her heart needed to be stronger than that.

For Wade.

Finally Kreindia allowed herself a few minutes to cry. Or perhaps it was an hour. There would be many more tears and some of them had to come out now. Otherwise she couldn't function. With her mental state as fortified as she knew how to make it, she touched the claw point to the trigger spot on her ear.

Her color sequence and ascension went through with only the slightest hesitation. Once on the astral plane, she scanned its dimensions, searching deep up and down the river. She did not find Faron there.

Kreindia breathed a sigh of relief. As much as she wanted to engage in battle with him, her survival instinct ruled the day.

Then a separate passage opened, manifesting to her sight as a peaked door like that of a church. There she saw Faron. He seemed overwhelmed at finding her there. The wattles of flesh on his neck shook with the turn of his head. But when the door opened wider to admit Faron to the astral plane, Kreindia spied a flash of Wade's signature behind him—the flames on crests of water that filled her with wild euphoria. Before Faron could collect his wits about him—and before the portal could close—she gathered every bit of her power and peeled her senses down to her core. Saying a prayer so brief that it could truly have fit on the head of a pin, she used every bit of her angst, need and newfound euphoria to slam into him, shoving him aside and following the sign of Wade... into another realm.

The portal slammed shut behind her, and reason began to catch up to her wild emotions. What if the place had been a trap, some kind of pinched off fold in Time? For safety's sake, she let her senses loose to probe and sample all that there was. The new place had its own temporal river, nearly identical to the one she'd left. Gazing into it, she saw not limitation but completeness. For every part of the astral plane she'd known, she found a counterpart here. She could select just where and when to travel, though she had to choose carefully. Up until a certain point, the historical differences from her universe were trifling. Then, at approximately Wade's location, events branched dramatically, and that made sense.

With her minimal experience on the astral plane, she had never been aware of other portals. She had thought that the changes she'd seen did not go beyond altering the original timeline. These hidden directions were the very reason she hadn't found Wade before. How could there be other infinities?

Now she knew precisely what she wanted to do because the branching showed her the way. Faron's reckoning could wait until she was reunited with Wade. Together they would be stronger.

Wade was very nearly all she could think about as she plunged into that river. Even in her triumph, though, she could not suppress a shudder, for in that awful moment when she'd made contact with Faron with her senses bared to reality, what she discerned of the beast's essence was an ossified housing of elemental evil.

CHAPTER 25

Gaul

<u>Ligugé Abbey, late winter, 500 A.D.</u>

WITH A QUICKENING pulse of new hope, Kreindia materialized in western Gaul. She knew that Wade would arrive in Rome in the coming spring. It drove her half-mad that she couldn't meet him until her crucial errand was done. Given the situation he'd dropped himself into, his success over Clovis, and ultimately Faron, now depended on hers.

The first thing she saw was an ice-mantled tree shedding water in the warm day. When she looked over to find a single dormitory wing of no more than twenty small rooms, she decided that her location was right on target. The dormitory fit into a modest yet handsome design incorporating a great hall and a single spire denoting the church. Ligugé Abbey stood intact even after the Salian Franks had ravaged the land: a state of affairs Kreindia had every right to expect. This first monastery in Gaul had the favor of Clovis, for he credited its founder as being instrumental in his victory over the Alamanni and for his conversion to Christianity.

While admiring the abbey's beautiful reflection in the lake, Kreindia suddenly realized she was standing in the shallow part of the water and hurried to get out of it. It was still too cold out to be wet. As she paused to pour lake water from her shoes, a self-important man leaned out an upper window and asked, "Can I assist you?"

"Yes. Is this the abbey founded by Saint Martin of Tours?"

"It is," he confirmed with his chest full.

"I need to see the Abbot."

"No. No you don't, pilgrims go that way." He pointed to a separate structure just south.

"I'm not a pilgrim. I have an urgent matter that requires I speak with your superior."

"I am the prior here." His voice pitched high with impatience. "You'll tell me your business, woman, and then be on your way."

"My business is not to be shouted from an open field to a high window. Come down and open the door."

He gave the ledge an annoyed slap and ducked inside. She tried to predict where he would emerge so that she could confront him on the spot. A few steps to the side and she found another wing. Through the windows she could see a courtyard with lively activity in progress.

He emerged from the second wing and made a stand outside the door. "I am Guillaume, and your name would be?"

"Kreindia," she said proudly. "Of Amorium."

The prior examined her fine dress with nervous anticipation. "I've never heard of you. Do you even know who our abbot is?"

"Larimore." As a historian she knew both the abbot's identity and his fascination, a secret occupation that meant she must speak only to him. She urgently needed something from Larimore that Wade could not have acquired by his own devices—documents that would provide him safe passage in Rome. She would brook no nonsense along the way. "Now surely you have a locutory where functionaries can meet with the public." As she spoke, she felt a sharp pain inside her head, and there arose around Guillaume's person a shifting blue cloud. Through the pain, she ordered, "Step inside now."

Startled by her tone, he obeyed briskly, and she

advanced as he retreated. His subtle glow did not vanish. A flickering muddy blue enveloped him like pollution, and grew stronger away from the glare of the sun. The only explanation for her seeing emanations must have been her most recent astral crossing; the process of splitting away from one place and time and returning to another, brought changes great and small.

This particular change was as familiar to her as it was odd. A few of her people, the Athinganoi, could perceive the astral bodies of the soul and read them like an illustrated book. Some could not manage the pulsing flow of ideas and it laid them low. On this trip, she too suffered that gift and would have to get used to it. "What are you afraid of?" she asked.

"Nothing," he blurted.

Unconsciously, she rattled off, "Loss of control, falling out of favor, the idea that you may be less than you are. You fear all of those things." The assessment tumbled out of the information stream without her knowing how she managed to interpret the light that surrounded him.

Guillaume now wore his fear directly on his face. "Whoever you are, you'd better leave."

"Whoever I am, you'd better bring me to Larimore. The sooner you do, the sooner you're free of me."

He made haste, and she hurried after him, bypassing the locutory through an inner passage. They rushed past a group of monks, all of them glowing in their own colors and patterns, which she absorbed in the same automatic way that gave her the assessment of their prior. She staggered as the pain that shuttled through her head flared again and threatened to swamp her. This time, however, she took only what she needed and managed to cut off the rest.

Abbot Larimore had his pen in hand when they burst in on his candlelit chamber.

"Abbot, this woman, Kreindia of Amorium, is the devil."

"So you foist her on me?" Larimore's face was gaunt under gray stubble, his eyes bloodshot and circled in shadow, his back bent.

But Guillaume did not stick around to explain himself. By the time Larimore straightened up to the best of his ability, the prior's quick feet could be heard retreating down the hallway.

"Our prior has too little to do," Larimore apologized. "Too much energy and too much imagination. And I'm too busy for visitors. You must leave."

Kreindia said, "He fears me because I read insecurity in his aura."

"His aura? Do you claim to be—?"

"I am an oracle." She knew Larimore's weakness, his eclectic set of beliefs.

"An oracle?" he asked with conflicted wonder. "And yet you travel? I don't believe—"

"I travel if I am sent by the highest power."

His eyes brightened. "And you've been sent to me?

"Directly."

Some of the wind was knocked out of him and the pen dropped from his hand. "I'm humbled. Well, you are absolutely right about Guillaume, though his bluster fools most people. But you might have guessed that. How do I know—?"

"And you…" To her surprise, she could discern the brightness about Larimore's head and nowhere else. "You have a golden halo."

"I do? What does it tell you?"

"That you are truly inspired."

"Is that so?" He raised a self-conscious smile and then lost it, as though remembering to be wary. "Who else have you seen here? Describe them to me."

"I saw a group in the hall." She closed her eyes and pointed to where each stood in relative succession, saying, "The red haired one is shiftless. The tall one is vain, the stout one courageous, the yellow hair loves nature, and the handsome one is dull."

Larimore arched his back as she pronounced their faults and virtues. "Ah." He waved his fists in paroxysms of delight. "You have the gift of sight."

"Astral seeing," she corrected him.

"The best I've ever seen. I prayed for this. A pox on the doubters—God has sent you to me."

"And you to me. My visit is more important than you can know. I need your help."

"Of course, of course. But first I have to show you something." He moved aside a small chest of drawers, knelt on the floor and peeled back an area rug. After some prodding and prying he removed a section of floor and rose again quickly, saying, "This is my own copy." With all of his excitement it seemed for a moment that he'd brought out nothing at all, until he placed in her hand a tiny codex that filled only her palm. "The Gospel of the Lots of Mary," he said reverently.

"Mary?" she asked with a frown. "Are you saying that Mary herself was casting lots?"

"Yes, yes, Mother Mary!" With frantic lifting motions of his fingertips, he urged her to raise the cover.

Turning to the first page, she read aloud, "The Gospel of the Lots of Mary, the mother of the Lord Jesus Christ..." She looked at Larimore.

"Go on."

"...she to whom Gabriel the archangel brought the good news."

"That confirms it. And the charge?" he prompted anxiously.

She read, "He who will go forward with his whole heart will obtain what he seeks. Only do not be of two minds..."

She flipped through the codex and saw eighty leaves, half of which included predictions written in a tight, neat hand.

Larimore held out a set of four sheep's knucklebones,

as though Kreindia would be as eager as he to get started. When she didn't take them, he said, "Please. Ask the book a question about a decision in your life and then toss them in the air."

"Cleromancy," she identified.

"Proverbs say, 'The lot's every decision is from *Yahweh.*' You must be careful what you ask." He put the bones in her hand, unbidden. The four were concave, convex, narrow, and broad, meant to be tossed and caught because they could not land evenly.

Setting aside the bones, she flipped through the pages and read some of the contents aloud. Each of the exultations had its own page. "Have endurance and patience; make haste; do not doubt; God's glory is great; beware your enemies and you will triumph; your desire will come to pass; and, all will become clear." She closed the book.

"You haven't asked anything," Larimore protested. "Surely you know someone with an illness or the need of a good harvest?"

"The method is sound. This set of lots is worthless."

"No, no, it's invaluable. The abbey is funded by what the pilgrims pay us for that information."

"Then let it be so, and let them be happy, but for larger purposes, the book does not suffice."

"But if not this way, then how do you do your divination?"

"I read the random in nature."

"Yet surely our way is random. We throw the sheep knuckles and the values show us the leaf number to choose. There we find the answer."

"Whichever number it is, this is rigged to show mostly good news."

"Yes, it is a gospel after all."

"Exactly. You can't do divination with a gospel."

Crestfallen, Larimore swallowed his reluctance hard. "Yes, I thought so, even as I hoped the other way. I was warned that this method is frowned upon."

"It's forbidden to be exact. You are only supposed to choose this route when God himself calls for it."

"They get away with the practice, even in Egypt," he replied in sullen protest.

"Yes," she said, giving the Lots of Mary back to him, "because they use it for the public good as you do, but the secret you harbor in Ligugé Abbey is that cleromancy is not just for pilgrims. You wish to use it to solve your crisis."

He raised a finger to his lips. "Hush, please. Not for me. For the monastery. The land is seized in madness. I've prayed for guidance but none comes. There has to be a way to unlock the future."

"Charms and books don't make you a diviner, but perhaps I can find your answer if you'll admit your purpose."

Larimore sighed, and stared blankly as though his eyes pointed inward to the gruesome truth. "Our problem is Clovis."

"The Salian Frank Clovis? Your patron?"

"Have you met Clovis? While you're reading auras, you'll want to get a read on his. He's the greatest threat of all time." He lifted his shaking hands to explain. "We survive under the domination of the Franks now, but those he draws out of the rotted wood are not so particular. In Gaul, we toil in the shadow of Franks, Visigoths, Celts, Burgundians, and old Romans in an uneasy truce, and by that I mean constant low-level warfare. You have only to step outside these walls to find yourself at the mercy of brigands. Every day I hear new reports of savagery around us. I stay up night after night worrying about it. And what happens when the next Clovis conquers this land? Or when *this* Clovis runs short of neighbors to kill? If our old protector Rome is forever diminished, what will become of our monastery?"

Kreindia hated leveraging Larimore's secret to get what

she required, and she hated even more that she would pretend to read what she already knew, but her needs were great. "To answer that," she said, "I will need a scraping of the wall...right here."

She chose the section of wall where Larimore had removed the furniture and he looked pleased at the choice, no doubt because it would be hidden when he moved the chest back.

He said, "It's dark on the floor. Shall I light more candles so that you can read it better?"

"No, abbot. Bring your halo close. I must read it by your light."

Larimore threw his head back and clasped his hands, unable to hide his joy at her suggestion. Then he remembered himself, pleading, "Lord, forgive my pride."

With his accession, she used her knife, cutting three vertical zigzags into the plaster. The scraping cast a pale spray of dust on the floor, a random pattern for her to read.

They kneeled down together as if they were going to pray. His halo cast no illumination. No astral occurrence would do so in this world, though Kreindia kept up the pretense.

"Does the random speak to you?" he whispered.

"Wait... yes. By this line among the others—which show great tribulations ahead—I can see that the monastery will long survive."

"How?"

"Its future will be secured... when yours becomes a Benedictine order."

"Change what we are? What is a Benedictine order?"

"From Benedict of Nursia. He will be a saint and the founder of a new discipline. Monasteries in his name will spread throughout this region."

"Of Nursia?" Larimore looked astounded and rushed to his desk. She followed him there. "Romanus of Subaico just wrote to me about a brilliant young man who goes by that name. I have the letter right here."

Kreindia examined the writing by the candle on the desk. The communication was no surprise to her, though it was amazing to see the actual handwriting instead of just reading the accounts. "Yes, this is he. Romanus and Benedict will both be recognized as saints. They are together now, and Benedict is soon to visit you."

"Visit *me*?" His face lit up in joy and then collapsed in turmoil. "But Saint Martin, our founder—"

"—will be revered forever. Your prayers will be answered."

For a moment, Larimore was speechless. When he found his voice he said, "What can Ligugé Abbey do for you? Anything you wish." His relief seemed to lift the shadowed years from his face.

"I'm on a vital mission to preserve the natural course of events against the forces of darkness."

"Indeed, our task is ever so. Charge me as you need."

"I need documents to begin with. Then an unassuming set of traveling clothes, food for a long journey, and a horse. But any certificate that you pen for me must appear to come from the Visigoths."

"Forgeries!" The intrigue thrilled him.

"Perfect forgeries," she insisted, "from your best copyist, and the text will assure the recipient that one Wade of Aquitaine is a Visigoth general lent to the service of Theoderic the Great." She knew that only the monks at a monastery would have the skills and resources to produce such papers. They resorted to clandestine missions such as hers in troubled times.

"Guillaume will not like it," he laughed. "Too bad for him. And the horse?"

"Will be a strong but plain one from your stables." She wouldn't attempt to astral travel to Wade's time and location. Now that she had the gift of auras she might need it again and this aspect of her could easily be lost in her next transit.

"Done. All shall be done." Larimore's eyes glowed in the candlelight. "Now a great deal more of the purpose behind what we do has been revealed. You are like Mary, who shared the good news brought by Gabriel. Our order shall always and forever be at your service."

"I can hold you to that promise," she warned. And she surely could.

He nodded in solemnity.

Yet when Kreindia rode away from Liguge Abbey with her bounty she did so under a burden of misgivings. Pragmatic as she might be, she was not irreligious. She'd given the abbot the truth wrapped in a lie about how she knew it. Although she'd gained an invaluable document and everything she needed to get that support to Wade, she did so at a cost to the core of her identity. The former empress of Byzantium, who Kreindia worshipped as a saint, was the strongest of women, Kreindia's role model since childhood. The sort of thing Kreindia had done with Larimore was unlike Irene and too close to Faron's tools of deception. Rather than hold Larimore to his promise forever, she now swore an oath to Saint Irene that she would never misuse her foreknowledge with a clergyman again.

$\sim W \sim$

NIGHT came early in winter, especially where the road plunged through the trees, which was most of the way throughout middle and western Gaul. Kreindia wore a coarse, hooded robe over pinned hair, and had stopped to apply the lake's mud to her face before heading east and south toward Itale. Although her mare was a uniform brown and its form under a woolen blanket as unexceptional as could be, she muddied it to match.

The leaves glowed their brightest in the low, slanting rays of the sun and then dimmed again. In her eagerness to catch up with Theoderic before he left Ravenna, she'd allowed dusk to settle in before searching for a suitable campsite. Her local map showed everything built by the Romans. A break in the trees was something she had to discover for herself. Too late, she realized that the first clearing was already occupied with men working to start a fire. They looked as though they might have been German raiders from the east and she did not wish to tangle with them. Her attempt to turn around, however, was thwarted by a man who grabbed her reins. Joining him on that side of her was more than half his party brandishing drawn swords. She carried only a long knife.

"Who disturbs the peace of Gunther?" asked the tall one with generous blonde hair and dark blue eyes.

"A courier." She made her voice sound like a boy's and struck a defiant pose so that they laughed. Her reaction to their amusement was to look downcast and defeated.

The role she claimed here was the safest course of action. She could not reveal herself to be a woman and had best not display prosperity. Horse ownership spoke of wealth so it had to have been borrowed and she was obliged to supply a very good reason to have been entrusted with it.

"Well courier, show us what you carry."

"You interfere with official business of the empire," she said with deflated bitterness.

Gunther said, "Well now it's our business. Hand it over." He wanted more than a look. Gunther's aura was silvered with success and murky pink with dishonesty.

"You take that from me on pain of death," she warned.

They laughed again. "You're a filthy and stupid boy. Good luck to your empire finding us after we cross back over the Rhine. Dismount and give it here. And who knows? Maybe we'll return it." The contest between them was so disproportionate that Gunther didn't even bother drawing a blade.

She dismounted, taking only the courier pouch, the

water gourd, and the knife, which she wore on her belt. Although she read deception in his nature and knew that they were a long way from the Rhine, Kreindia had no choice but to surrender the pouch containing the paper she so desperately needed. While she did so, she kept her head bowed as if in subservience.

Two of the brigands went through her saddlebags and grunted in dissatisfaction.

Gunther manhandled the pouch and came upon the letter with the maps. He was taken aback when he saw the personal seal of royalty. "This dispatch really is official. What's your name, boy?"

"Roderick," she said.

"Roderick, is this message from Alaric?"

"My lord and master, Alaric the second."

None of them were laughing any longer. "And you say that the words inside are meant for the eastern empire?" Gunther paused to hear the answer as he was about to tear it open.

"For Theoderic, who serves the empire." Here Kreindia let some of her fear and anger bleed through. "He will gladly hunt you down if the letter is tampered with."

Gunther shrugged. "Maybe so, maybe not." He broke the seal, whereupon the other men gathered around him to try to discern the writing over his shoulder. Someone had begun a fire, so they all moved to where they could see. Kreindia shifted some of the way with them but hung back as if to keep a respectful distance.

Gunther scanned the message quickly and asked, "The Visigoths lend a general to Theoderic?" He could not take his eyes off the elegant sheet. "A general and no army?"

"Do you ask me?" Kreindia wondered in innocent bewilderment.

"Of course not, boy! Shut up."

A hushed dispute broke out among the men as Gunther opened the map with the route marked up as far as Ravenna. While they were batting around possible meanings of the document, Kreindia slowly backed into the trees until she was enveloped in complete shadow. She paused and retreated still further, shuffling her feet, taking care not to trip. Then she made her way slowly around the clearing so that she could be as close as possible to her horse. Just as she felt she stood a chance to reach it, Gunther said to the man next to him, "See what else is in his saddle bags."

"I already checked. There was nothing useful. Just provisions."

"Check again. More carefully this time."

Kreindia had skillfully folded and concealed her dress in a hidden lining. She had not gone so far as to sew the lining shut. The edge was tucked under a flap. If the Rhinelander checked carefully enough he just might find it.

Before he got there, she burst out of the trees, sprinted the last few steps, jumped on her horse, and pitched forward, barely holding on as the beast charged away. Had she not been from a warrior society so renowned that even Grimketil Forkbeard swore allegiance, her stunt would not have had the slightest chance of success.

"Ho! Nice jump, boy," Gunther yelled. "Aren't you the nimble little rat?" The last thing she heard from the camp was Gunther calling out, "No pursuit in the dark. Let the coward go."

She went only far enough to calm and turn her frightened mount as she burned with repressed anger at her own carelessness and at the men who had robbed her. Hoping to recover the document and repair its broken seal, she planned to stay near, and follow the bandits to their next crime, and the one after that if need be. If their performance so far was a guide, they would soon grow lax. She spent a cold, fireless night in view of the smoky glow of her enemies' camp, consoling herself with the knowledge that she still had time to help Wade.

At dawn, the group moved on and found a dirt road

running due south. As a single traveler following many, Kreindia found it easy to stay concealed. Whenever she grew close enough to hear them, she drew back to ensure that they remained unaware of her pursuit. Although it was another mild day, the clouds gathered to supply a perpetual gloom and the path split several times. She'd been happy as long as she could see the signs of their passage, but at some point it got darker than when she started out, and hard to discern their path. Or was it because they had passed through a long while ago? How long had she stared at the clouds? Was she still time blind? She tried to shorten their lead just in case.

When she came to a wall and a gate, it seemed she'd waited too long to catch up. There was no sign of her quarry.

CHAPTER 26

The Mansio

BEYOND THE WALL and high on a hill, rose a beautiful villa fronted with a many-pillared corridor. Square towers with red tiled roofing capped the corners. The occupants—likely Visigoths—would be tribute-payers, spared from Clovis' voracious march by virtue of their bribery.

Kreindia could well appreciate the Franks' perspective in that transaction. Bypassing the villas in return for a payoff, gained them the ample funding needed for their war and allowed for greater speed while keeping their army at full strength. The Visigoths seemed short-sighted by comparison.

Trenches, posts and other improved fortifications stood as works-in-progress at the Visigoth villa, but the effort had apparently been abandoned when the deal was struck with Clovis, for no one toiled at the half-built supports on this day. Kreindia's pulse quickened as she saw a fresh trail of evidence that led off to her right. A group of horses had begun to circle the wall, their riders likely searching for the weakest point of entry among the incomplete earthworks. She backed off to the trees before they completed the circuit, and hoped that Gunther and his crew had not already spotted her.

Marking time's passage with the tapping of her foot, she noted that the raiders had not posted a sentry on the road into the settlement, a mistake that marked them as amateurs. Unless they had given up the idea of an assault and moved on. Was there another route by which they might have already slipped away without her seeing?

She was startled when the gate flew open. Swifter than she could have imagined, out came Gunther's men with their captives on a greater number of horses than had entered the compound. The animals were being stolen from the Visigoths together with the people.

One of their prisoners galloping by wore an elegant dress with silk sleeves, and her cheeks burned with a young, angry glow. She struggled to rein in her horse.

"Move," yelled Gunther at her hesitation. "Who do you think you are?"

"I'm Princess Eloflora," she warned him in a shout.

"You're what?" His surprise betrayed his dismay.

"Visigoth royalty!"

"Shut up," he burst in frustration. "You're a slave now." Then they were too far away for Kreindia to hear.

So the dawn raid was for human plunder. This Gunther apparently hadn't known or cared exactly who was in the house or who was visiting. Six women captured made for a profitable day. Would Eloflora's noble status become a bonus for the raiders or a liability they would have to terminate? Kreindia mounted up and followed them with caution.

When the dense thicket opened wide to the main thoroughfare, the party rode west. With her synesthetic memory, Kreindia remembered the map well, its lines fairly written in the air. Their course would soon bend north. In order to follow them to their destination, she had to accept that in doing so she would be forced even further out of her way with no likelihood of getting the document she wanted. If Faron's depredations were to be stopped, however, her task began with the kidnappers.

Now her objectives were to recover Wade's letter of introduction, and possibly to rescue Princess Eloflora, providing Kreindia could figure out the effect of that action on the timeline. She hoped the marauders would go to ground soon, before things grew any more complicated.

In the course of the day, the bandits compelled their bounty along Roman roads just seventeen mile markers long; not much progress in returning to Germanic territory, if that's where they were headed. The place they arrived at had been shown on the map as property of the western empire. In fact, the landmark was once a designated *mansio*, a fee-based pilgrim stop on the long journey to the Holy Land.

The old waystation had been transformed into an even more sumptuous villa than the Visigoths occupied. Small turrets and battlements shaped the wall so that the periphery resembled the bounds of a fortified town. There were springs nearby and a well-maintained gravel road leading in. Would they attack this place too?—such a secure location?

No, someone on watch threw open the gates to them immediately.

"Hail Alpinus," cried the so-called Gunther as he rode in. He sounded quite different now that he greeted the guard in unaccented Latin. "We have guests for you."

Gunther, in turn, was greeted by the watchman as "Gaius Lucius," and welcomed warmly.

Eloflora exclaimed, "You Roman filth."

Yes, these were Roman nobles coming home! That explained why they didn't bother seizing Kreindia's provisions from her saddlebag. They had no need of them so near to their base of operations. Their pose as German raiders was a calculated deception.

She pulled back and let them disappear behind the walls. A Roman demi-palace was no place for the boy, Roderick. Kreindia visited one of the springs beyond the perimeter of the estate and suffered the cold water to wash herself and her mare. The scrubbing took some time, but that was good. Using her makeup kit, she painted a light tan star on her horse's forehead as further disguise in case it might be recognized. Then she put on her dress, unpinned her hair, and used the bell pull at the front gate as she thought about how the returning marauders had cheered their successful mission, slapping each other on the back. Kreindia began to realize just how brazen was their attack on their Visigoth neighbors. That level of aggressiveness fit what she knew of the desperate era she visited. Witnessing the depths of greed for herself was another matter, for the last of the Gaulish Romans living in their isolated enclaves no longer grew their wealth by conquest. Despite the fact that the days of expansion were gone and slaves did not flow from abroad, the aristocracy would be damned before they would diminish their lavish lifestyle.

One of their number came to the gate to inspect her, and asked, "Who goes?"

She adopted an aristocratic tone, dripping with privilege and worldliness. "Kreindia of Amorium, wife of Quintus Valerius." Once again, she had no need to trouble with pseudonyms in a time and place that wouldn't know her name. The false background was quite enough to remember.

"You travel on your own?"

"My husband and I are part of an embassy from Ravenna. I am sent ahead, and ask your hospitality."

"Do come in."

"Thank you," she said as she rode through the arch and paused to speak with the man. "Quintus is nearby and anxious to meet your lord."

"I am Alpinus," he said. "You are an embassy to whom?"

"To the court of Clovis of course, and I bring news."

"Then welcome." Extending hospitality to a Roman embassy was mandatory, and news was always valued. All so civilized now. It made her sick.

"The honor is mine," she said with a polite smile.

"Forgive us. Our old stable hand has died, and our new one is... not yet trained." No doubt he meant that the replacement would come from among the newly captured slaves.

"That's quite all right. I was going to ask you to allow me to stable my own horse. She's skittish."

"Be my guest," he smiled. "Join us at the main house when you are ready."

"I will." Kreindia had no idea how to get anything of what she needed from the villa. For now though, she was inside the grounds and unmolested. For people who had just robbed their neighbors, these Gaulish Romans were not as suspicious of her as they might have been. In this place they were secure; the great masters wallowing in their ill-gotten riches while giving solace to a fellow power broker.

After putting away her horse, and getting a good look at the layout of the stables, she went toward the main house, taking note of where the slaves' quarters would likely be, on the outer corners.

Once inside, she held back in the corridor listening to voices echoing in the atrium. As she slowly drew closer, the first one that she could hear distinctly was clearly an old patrician.

"Most extraordinary," he mused. "You were right to wake me, Gaius. What an unusual day. I thought it would be an auspicious one because a rook entered my room last night on gentle wings. He circled the room thrice and left me an unblemished feather."

"A rook. That's fine, but what does our captured letter mean?" asked Alpinus.

At that, the senior man quickly lost his good mood. "The letter is a show of contempt for Theoderic."

"Contempt?"

"Of course. Theoderic must face Clovis. But to fight Clovis, Alaric sends Theoderic nothing but an advisor, this General Wade of Aquitaine, who I never heard of. So he can't be much of a general. Commissioned on the spot, I'd say. Ergo, Alaric must be sick of the Ostrogoths and ready to let his fellow barbarians fall."

"Do we return the letter? Send it on?"

"Of course not, Alpinus! That would lead the Visigoths straight to us, and we have the man's daughter. You're not a fool, are you?"

"No, I see that. It's not our quarrel anyway. I just thought—"

"Get rid of it," the patriarch ordered.

Get rid of the parchment? Kreindia bolted into the room, but was too late. Her letter sat in the blazing hearth, curling as it collapsed inward, little sparks drilling the air around it. She stared at the flames a bit too long as the wax seal melted to liquid.

"What are you doing in here?" shouted the man formerly known as Gunther.

"I thought I had the hospitality of the house," she answered coldly. "I bring news of Ravenna."

"I didn't realize we had guests," said the old man, sitting up and smiling.

"Just the one," said Alpinus. "Flavius Festus Catalinus, this is Kreindia of Amorium, wife of... someone."

"Quintus Valerius," she supplied cheerfully. "I'm honored to meet you, lord."

Flavius crooned, "You look lovely. What news do you have?"

"Well," she warmed to the attentive audience, "it's not my place to say, but since you asked, the Italian court is in an uproar."

"Is that so? Why?"

"As you may know, Amalafrida is to be wed. Well, she is not pleased with marrying the African king—you did know he was African, didn't you?"

"Yes, yes, anything else?"

She took a deep breath as though she had a great deal to say. "Of course there's more. Audofleda is having an affair and Theoderic could not care less. If you ask me—"

Flavius covered his ears. "Marriages and affairs! You

babble, woman. Gossip is not news."

"It's disarray," she said defensively. "An empire is only as good—"

With an impatient wave, he said, "Go with the women. They're off having wine, and they'll welcome your nonsense."

Looking properly offended, she blustered, "Do you at least have a slave that can help me freshen up?"

The men went silent in their irritation.

She added, "I will of course pay for my visit, whatever is your usual *mansio* fee."

"Yes, fine," said Flavius tightly. "Go to the slave's quarters down that hall. Show them what to do."

Thus dismissed and alone in the corridor, Kreindia balled her fists in angst thinking of Wade's letter of introduction, first taken from her, and now destroyed. Time was running out. She could not ask Larimore for a replacement. As a practical matter, she did not want to inspire doubt in the abbot. There was no guarantee he would cooperate a second time, especially under these circumstances. But most of all, another imposition on Ligugé Abbey would violate her solemn promise to Irene. This was the hard reality of promises. After Apamea, and her earlier visit to the abbey, she had to make up for her damage and cause no more.

Her most immediate concern was the Visigoth princess and her servants. In Kreindia's timeline, Eloflora had never been a slave. If she was one now, then Kreindia had somehow been the cause of it.

Once in the slaves' quarters, she searched every face to see which belonged to the princess. She followed the sound of sniffling to the youngest of them, who was not even of marriageable age. The young lady's fine dress with the silk sleeves was gone, her eyes red from sobbing. "I'm a friend, Eloflora," Kreindia assured the frightened girl, "here to help you if I can. What happened at the house?"

"It was awful. We had just arrived when the raiders

came, and I had only just dismounted. Had I come a few minutes later, or the Romans a few minutes earlier..."

"What were you doing traveling at that hour?"

Eloflora's fair skin flushed deeply. "It was only a short way to my friend's house. I had a fight with my father, Alaric. I took my servants and left him a note telling him that I could get by on my own. Obviously I couldn't."

That explained enough.

The burned letter gave Kreindia an idea. The rooms were heated via the hypocaust, a furnace system that ran beneath the floor tiles. The boiler that drove it would supply a ready source of fire. "Listen to me. I can get all of you out, but you must do exactly as I say."

Donning ragged linens and blackening her face like a charwoman, Kreindia made the women go over her instructions, and then ventured into the slave tunnel that led to the furnace. Her heart raced. She had to get in and out before she was missed. The heat of the hypocaust was staggering, the square columns left narrow spaces that limited her view, and she had to weather a coughing fit. She found everything in the wrong order. First, the piles of charcoal, then the tongs, then the brazier, which was already filled, and lastly an unlit torch which she had to set ablaze despite the already scorching heat. Although the bronze vessel and its pilings were remarkably heavy, she felt compelled to bring it along in case the torch went out.

Drenched in sweat, Kreindia emerged in the corridor with her eyes downcast like a proper slave. The hallway was empty at the moment. She tried to walk briskly even though the brazier grew heavier with each step. Ten more paces and she'd be outside.

"Where are you going with that?" He'd emerged of a side corridor, a big man with a lumbering gait.

A thrill of fear went through Kreindia. This man had been one of those in the woods the previous day, and he was making a very close inspection of her.

"I was told to light the rubbish pit." She said it softly

and then flinched the way she'd seen Faron's wife, Clara automatically flinch in anticipation of a beating.

The man laughed and his aura was rank with perversion.

She walked away quickly. One, two, and soon five steps away from him. Then—

He pulled her by the hair and slapped her face so that she staggered, just managing to keep the flames clear of herself.

"You almost dropped the brazier, you stupid girl. Since you're no good at that, why don't you light my fire instead?" He exposed himself to show what he meant.

Then she did spill her burden and deploy the only weapon she had, using the torch to light him up at the face and the gut. That mercy would end his misery as soon as possible. He screamed, twisted in place, and then rushed toward her. She had to hit him in the head with the bronze container. Finally he fell and burned peacefully.

From there, Kreindia took the torch outside. The only way her trick might work was if the householders thought they had a chance of dousing the flaming timbers. While it was a shame to burn the beautiful villa, it was her pleasure to "disturb the peace of Gunther." Gaius be damned. Dashing outside, she set several small burns at the far end of the structures and finally tossed the guttering torch on a woodpile to send it flaming brightly again in the mound of fresh fuel.

Kreindia plunged back inside and ran the length of the villa, hollering, "Fire! Save yourselves! Get out!" In the atrium, the men were still discussing their affairs when she burst in screaming, "What's the matter with you? Your house is on fire. Where is the water? Where is the sand?"

Almost everyone she'd seen in the atrium and several others ran to attend to the matter in the direction from which she'd come. She tried to keep going in the opposite direction when Gaius grabbed her wrist and fixed her in an iron grip.

"Where are you going?"

"To warn everyone."

"That *was* everyone," he said dangerously. "How did it start?"

"That's not my business."

"Your business is whatever I tell you."

"Let go of me," she said with a desperate, ineffective yank.

"Wait, you're not one of our slaves. I recognize you. You're our visitor today. You're Kreindia! And with that dirt on your face, you also look like the boy, Roderick." Confused now, he asked, "Are you also Roderick?" He pressed painfully on her wrist.

"No, I'm not him," she explained patiently. "Roderick's right handed."

"So?"

"I'm left handed."

"What—?"

That was as much as he could say before the knife in her left hand was in his throat. He gurgled, released her, and fell.

She acquired Gaius' sword, held it naked and high, and felt complete.

Eloflora and her entourage were already in the stables with the stalls and main doors flung open. Handing Kreindia a large wet cloth to clean her face and hands, the princess said, "I've saved your dress and found mine too."

"Thank you."

Kreindia led them out swiftly, bearing up as best she could under her loss. At least she hadn't suffered a catastrophe as complete as the one at Apamea. Was this to be an empty outcome then? Had she made promises she could never keep?

They'd passed only five mile markers, hiding and dodging at every sound. They were about to take flight again when they found soldiers combing the woods, looking everywhere. Kreindia got her charges under cover and kept them silent in the gathering shadows.

"Wait, they're Visigoths," said Eloflora proudly. "And that's my father over there."

The glimpse of Alaric in his regal attire renewed Kreindia's hope that she might get the letter of introduction after all. He knew nothing of her earlier machinations. Of course, if anyone from the household was caught and questioned, he might find out about the forgery she'd created under his signature. If she pressed him for help she would be playing a dangerous game.

"Here, change your clothes behind that tree," said Eloflora. "Let him see that you're like us."

"What about you?"

"My father will know me however I dress."

Father and daughter were tearfully reunited, and the group made their way slowly back to Alaric's people, Kreindia looking over her shoulder the whole way.

Eloflora recounted what she and her entourage had been through.

Alaric frowned in thought. "We were nearly done here and going to move our search to the east next, to follow the so-called German raiders. We would never have thought to visit the Roman villa."

"They wouldn't have admitted to anything if you did," said Eloflora with downcast eyes. "The Romans made me a slave. Not for long, of course, but the thought of it was horrible."

"The men of the *mansio* will be dealt with summarily. My soldiers are hunting them now."

"I was ready to take my own life, Father, when Kreindia saved me," Eloflora gushed, pulling her new friend close.

"—With the assistance of Wade of Aquitaine," added Kreindia.

Alaric scrutinized his daughter's companion as though seeing her for the first time and asked, "Who are you? Why did you do this?"

"She's from Amorium," Eloflora said with wonder, "an ambassador from the court at Constantinople."

"Yes," Kreindia confirmed, "and we're ashamed of these people who call themselves part of our empire. General Wade and I witnessed the Romans carrying off your daughter and felt compelled to help."

Alaric folded his arms. "They'll pay for it, but it's Clovis who caused this turmoil. He remains our objective." His aura was a deep-red, survival oriented.

"Naturally. He threatens all of Europe," Kreindia agreed. "Wade and I consider ourselves at your service until the crisis has passed."

"And where is your companion, this General Wade of Aquitaine?"

"Tending to his injuries. I've sent him ahead to a doctor in the next town."

"My people are in your debt."

"I need your help, and we haven't a moment to lose. Wade and I are *en route* to Ravenna."

"No," Alaric said peremptorily.

"No?"

"We'll send no troops to Ravenna, if that's what you were about to ask."

"But that's where Clovis is heading next. You've aided the Ostrogoths before."

"We cannot assist Theoderic directly because we have our hands full fighting the Frankish tribes that Clovis united. If we stop them here, they will not reinforce his Salians in Itale, and that will be your solution."

"We've pledged to you, my lord, and won't break that pledge, but if you cannot help directly, please lend us to Theoderic, and let him see that you are doing something on his behalf. The only cost is two letters of introduction. I'll dictate them to your scribe."

"That we can do."

"Thank you, my—"

"My lord," called a soldier. "We've killed the Romans

and caught one alive. He's only an old man."

"I would see him."

The detainee was dragged before Alaric with a sword to his chin.

"Who are you?" Alaric demanded.

The captive fell to his knees, exhausted from the hunt. Kreindia identified him as, "Flavius."

Flavius leveled a crooked finger at her and moaned, "You. You're that woman who came calling at my house. Kreindia of Amorium, the wife of someone. Is that even your real name?"

"Of course it is."

"You were interested in the burnt letter about Wade of Aquitaine. They got me out of bed to see it. You set my villa on fire!"

"It had to be done."

"But the rook! The rook said I would have good fortune today."

"And you shall, I promise." She took Alaric aside and said, "He's raving, poor man."

"You mean, he's not the master of the house?"

"No, just an old servant. Have mercy on him, my lord."

Alaric turned and ordered the soldier, "Keep this man alive if he settles down. Otherwise, kill him quickly."

"Yes, my lord."

"And someone fetch us a scribe!"

Once Kreindia's new documents were secured, she rode hard, never stopping to glance back. Although she could no longer reach Theoderic before he left Ravenna, she would now be able to salvage her plan. *Enjoy the victory*, she told herself, and she tried to picture the look she'd find on Wade's face at their reunion.

Yet her joy was clouded as she rode south, recalling the ossified evil that awaited them both. Time blind she may have been, but she felt the confrontation with Faron ticking inevitably closer.

CHAPTER 27

Clovis: Glory by Combat

<u>Frankish Gaul, Winter, 500 A.D.</u>

HOLD HIM," CLOVIS said evenly.

His men grabbed and held Clovis' cousin Cerobaud by his naked arms. Like much of his tribe, the captive had fought mostly bare, even before the spring thaw. The company that captured him remained outdoors, using only a few torches and a bright moon for illumination. No bonfire warmed the clearing, but the vanquished king had a great deal more than his lack of preparation for the cold to regret now.

"No good," Clovis complained as Cerobaud squirmed. With a languid wave to the man at his side, Clovis said, "Galchobhar, take that soldier's place. I know *you'll* hold him still."

The soldier Clovis indicated stepped out, but sturdy Galchobhar dismissed the second minder as well and took their places, pinning Cerobaud firmly as he gathered both arms. Someone had already removed the elaborate gold torc from their captive's neck and the short wrap about his shoulders covered little.

Gone half to fat, his defeated cousin appeared disgusting to Clovis. "Oh, look at you. How can you live with yourself?" His hand curled about the hilt of his weapon.

"Don't, don't, don't, don't," begged the wide-eyed Cerobaud, shaking his head. He grew louder when Clovis drew out the short double-edged scramasax, the metal glinting blue in moonlit counterpoint to the firelight.

"Not that," Cerobaud pleaded. The rival chieftain had himself been the proud owner of a very similar knife just a short while ago. He well understood what it could do.

Clovis told him, "Don't complain, you coward. What happens here will be good for you. You may be king of your tribe, Cerobaud, but this will help you be a man. Finally."

"You can't do this to me," Cerobaud screeched. "You're a Catholic."

"Not tonight. Tonight I'm a Celt."

Carefully watching Cerobaud's eyes, Clovis took his long knife and slipped it in by a knuckle's length just under the center of the rib cage. He poked it upward, slowly twisting and easing it deeper and deeper to see what would happen.

"Don't—" Cerobaud let out a hideous keening as he danced against the blade, which only made the cut expand.

"The Celts among us say you can tell the future," Clovis lectured to those assembled, "by the bleeding of a man with a cutting edge at this juncture at the top of his belly."

Galchobhar murmured his appreciation of the lesson as he clamped harder to pinion the arms of the shaking prisoner.

As the official Celtic sage in residence, Morcant arose reluctantly and said, "It's true that you can read him in that manner, my lord … though you have to let him fall."

"Ah." Clovis nodded and Galchobhar released the sufferer, who promptly dropped to the ground in thumping agony with the blade caught in him. Though unrestricted now, he didn't try to escape, and he knew better than to remove the blade and increase his loss of blood. All he could do was slap the ground and endure.

"Settle down," Clovis warned him.

After more pounding and half a dozen swipes in the

air, Cerobaud grew feeble from the escape of his life, and simply clenched his fists.

"There," said Clovis. "That's a little better. So what do we have, Morcant? What can you discern from this... mess?"

The druid, who had studied his art for two decades, squatted close in the gore, unmindful of his pristine white cloak. He actually used the cloth's corner to catch the spurt of blood, and then sniffed the bouquet like heady wine. "It smells of war, my lord."

"All blood smells of war," said Clovis impatiently. "We just *beat* his tribe in a war."

Ignoring the interruption, Morcant opined, "His life sprays to the south and east of here." The senior advisor straightened up and dripped stripes, looking like a scholar trying out a butcher's trade. "The message is that you must march against Ravenna and Rome."

"Itale? Against my brother-in-law Theoderic?" Clovis poked a fingernail through his great, coarse moustache and beard, and chewed in contemplation. "I was saving that attack for later."

Cerobaud's pale hand twitched in the direction of the spray as if to frantically reinforce his message, and Morcant was quick to point to the motion. "Oh yes. See? South and east again. Your cousin confirms the way."

Clovis watched the blood carefully. "That's curious, though. A small, turgid stream points back toward Aquitaine. What does the opposing signal mean, diviner? Visigoth uprising?"

Morcant examined the second flow from where he stood. Folds gathered at the bridge of his nose, and his eyes glistened under his lime-bleached brows. Uncomfortable at what he saw, he nudged the blade deeper, pressing the tip of his shoe against the jeweled pommel to increase the rupture, and watched until Cerobaud settled into weakened resignation, and finally, release. At last, the druid concluded happily, "Nothing, sire. There's nothing to fear from Aquitaine at all."

"Anyway," said Clovis, gesturing at his dead cousin, "this one notwithstanding, we aren't finished with our Frankish kin, nor with the Burgundians."

"Sire," said Galchobhar. "The remaining opposition is only a technicality, to be cured in a blink. You *are* the Franks. They must all bow down to you in the end. Burgundians too."

"Franks? Are we not also Gauls, though?" Clovis proposed in a lecturing tone. "Are we not Celts?" From his father, Childeric, Clovis had inherited the wet pocket of lands deeded to the Salarian Franks, the marshy river-twined high ground of the far north bulge. From that small corner in proximity to England, Clovis had swept south nearly to the Roman's great Middle Sea, and southeast nearly to the Alps to form a horseshoe kingdom dominating the center of Europe. Most of that land had, in Caesar's time, been the stronghold of the continental Celts of the Roman Republic, a people known to the Imperium as Gauls.

"My Lord, your sense of humor is legendary." Galchobhar himself had adopted most local Celtic practices in his appearance with his hair cut in small, thick chunks and a clean shave but for a moustache. He hadn't indulged in the lime bleaching yet.

"I know," said Clovis. "Answer the question all the same. And fetch my scramasax back."

Retrieving the prized knife from the corpse by its blonde wooden handle and admiring it, Galchobhar said, "Plenty of Gaulish blood in some of us, I'd allow. Gallo-Roman to be exact. Plenty of it on this blade. But the Frankish part of us dominates, and washes the rest clear." As if to demonstrate that pronouncement, he mopped the blade clean with Cerobaud's wrap.

Clovis took his scramasax and sheathed it. "You always say what I want to hear, Galchobhar." With a raw, almost wounded look, he added, "See that it stays that way."

He usually admonished Galchobhar to "steer clear of Celts" to cap off his advice, since he didn't care how he spoke around Morcant. But he had to admit that the priest's otherworldly guidance had greatly accelerated his plans of late. Defeating his numerous Frankish cousins should have taken the better part of a lifetime, yet mysteriously it had not. Maybe he ought to begin treating his druid advisor better. Take his counsel to attack Ravenna early? Perhaps.

He asked, "What do you say about Morcant's idea, Galchobhar?"

"Signs are beyond my ken. As a matter of policy, though, an attack on Ravenna this coming spring would be unexpected, and therefore more likely to be successful. So I concur with the priest."

"Do you?" Clovis sneered. "You agree with Morcant altogether too much." Clovis suspected they shared ideas in advance of airing them in court. He didn't know from which of them a particular piece of advice originated, but their alliance made him uneasy. If the two were plotting something, their habitual deference to him was nothing but a mask.

Galchobhar grew uneasy under the scrutiny. "My lord, I will, of course, consider the matter further."

"Do that," said Clovis without any lessening of his rancor. "And remove this filthy corpse."

$\sim W \sim$

WITHIN a fortnight, Clovis, Galchobar, and his other advisers stood on a hill supervising the gathering and redistribution of tribute from the conquered. Items of silver or gold were brought to him personally. The rest was handled by subordinates. Clovis was frowning over a dent in a silver tea set when he said, "I've decided to disregard your terrible idea, Galchobar."

"*Which* terrible idea would that be, my lord?"

Clovis snorted. It had only taken one day to clamp Cerobaud's head safely in a bragging jar. Once the ornament went on tour the following week, his cousin's tribe came into Clovis' gathering fold without any ill will. The Franks loved a winner. Thanks to Morcant, there were only a couple of minor Frankish holdouts left. Conquering the Burgundians, however, would be a chore. "Your idea about turning our vulnerable backsides to the Burgundians, of course."

"By leading our armies to the south? We're not that vulnerable. The Burgundians have no desire to attack us if we are not attacking them. They've never done so."

"They will find a sudden desire to do so as soon as we are tied up with Theoderic. My every instinct screams that we must consolidate our gains in this region before moving on to another."

Wisely, Galchobar said, "You are right, lord, and I shall say no more."

"Good. Now why am I getting so many dented pieces? You should fix them first."

From their vantage on the hill, they were able to see a horseman churning dust from a half mile down the road.

"Who's that, Galchobar?"

"I believe that would be Morcant, my lord."

"What is his haste?"

"I don't know, but he can tell us himself in a moment."

Shortly the horse and rider were upon them. "My lord Clovis," said Morcant breathlessly on arrival.

"Stop breathing on me like that," said Clovis.

"I have news of the utmost urgency."

"Then perhaps you should have sent ahead someone more fit."

"I didn't trust—"

"Since you've already made that mistake, do tell us what excites you."

"Theoderic gathers a Roman legion."

"You mean Roman-*strength*," Clovis corrected.

"No, native soldiers."

Patiently, as though instructing a child, Clovis said, "Native Italians have spent the last hundred years forgetting how to fight. There were only a handful of good ones when Odoacer took over, and they had to run for their lives. So how do you get a whole Roman legion out of that? You don't."

"They will expand."

"From where, Morcant?"

"From the loins of the survivors. Theoderic will breed them for the long run."

"You have signs?"

"No, I have my priests secreted in their ranks."

"What would priests know about military units?" With a half turn to confirm that Galchobhar shared his doubting sneer, Clovis challenged Morcant, "Help us understand how this can be, druid."

"The originals are older men now, yes. But they bring their families, and a few old soldiers might still be capable of fathering more children. Their numbers are bolstered by half-breed Ostrogoths housebroken to loyalty like Theoderic himself."

"Not fully native then. I said as much. And what threat are these reserves to me?"

"I'd say it's a threat to the legacy of your empire," Galchobhar put in. "That sounds like their intention at least."

"But you say that this information reaches us from priests."

Morcant said, "The facts are corroborated by Strabo himself."

"Theoderic Strabo of the Thracian Goths? The rival of Theoderic the Great?"

"Yes, my lord. He is more determined than ever to get even with his cousins. And he will join us."

"That changes everything." Clovis turned to

Galchobhar now. "If this development is true, what do you suggest?"

Galchobhar did not have to think about it. "Stop the Kingdom of Itale in the coming season when they are least ready."

"In what order of action?"

"Break their army in the field. Then hit Florence before the legion is concealed. That will draw them out."

"Why Florence, of all places?"

"That's where retired soldiers and their families live. The legion will be in a frenzy to defend it."

"And Ravenna?"

"Save it for last like Theoderic did in his campaign against Odoacer. In the meantime, smash this future legion and they will never threaten our Frankish confederation."

Nothing, from the day Clovis was born, was more important to him than acquiring the heartland of the Roman heritage as well as its provinces. It mattered not that the West's empire was already dismantled. The question was: Who would be the one to reunite it? Momentum made it increasingly plain that only the Salian Franks stood a chance. Fate made it plain that Clovis would found an empire.

Sounding a rare note of caution, Galchobhar added, "The first stage will be the most difficult. Even if we engage him in battle promptly, Theoderic will be loathe to risk the embryonic legion. We'll face his Ostrogoths and whatever Visigoths he can muster."

"That I don't fear," said Clovis. "We are better than them."

Clovis' mouth watered at the idea that he could be the one to permanently annex Itale to his own empire rather than that of the East. He'd been only a young boy when Odoacer, the first non-Roman to succeed, wrested the throne in Itale from the remnant of empire. And once again he had been too young and unready when Constantinople reached out to restore the peninsula to friendly hands in the person of Theoderic. But now... now could be *his* time. Itale was within his grasp. That glorious conceit was the sole reason he'd allowed his wife to convince him to take on the trappings of a Roman Catholic. Given his new station, his fellow Arians must see that he alone was fit to wrest the entirety of the Western Empire from so worthy an opponent as the Imperium Romanum out of Constantinople.

Galchobhar prompted, "What are your wishes, my lord?"

Patience, Clovis thought. *All my life I've stood on the threshold of the world's greatest prize.* Ambition tempered by patience, that's what had separated him from the monarchs whose kingdoms now bowed down to him. Now that he had most of Aquitaine, he possessed an ample path around the Burgundians. The idea of a hidden Roman legion waiting to attack his descendants and undo his rightful legacy chilled him. This possibility of a hidden threat decided the matter.

"Bring Strabo of the Thracian Goths to me."

"And then?"

"Prepare to fight."

CHAPTER 28

The Sword in Fire

H ER MARKER WAS *exact in every detail. Blue powder on ice in a plane of infinity.* Wade could scarcely believe that he found the "real" Kreindia of Amorium in front of him, rather than one of her universal counterparts. But her synesthetic signature did not lie. The reason for the trifling difference in her appearance did not matter at this moment. She was the best thing he'd ever seen, the single most important person in his life. In front of forty thousand howling spectators, he cut across the emperor's Sun-Temple box to go to her, unmindful of what Theoderic might have known about their relationship, or thought about decorum.

She rushed toward him with equal urgency, pulling up the hem of her gown to race across the gap. As they pressed their lips together and encircled each other, Wade felt a dizzying shift in reality. With the dislocation came a multiplicity of embraces, as though he shared those sensations with every version of her and him in every time and every timeline across the multiverse. As with his early glimmerings of synesthesia, he had to wonder whether he should ascribe the peculiarity to a spectacular imagination or accept the marvel as reality.

When she kissed him deeply, his perception of these myriad passions expanded as quickly as he could absorb it. The effect was as if both of their souls were transported up to Time's river and distributed across the temporal waters to partake in an astral communion with their counterparts. And Wade came to the same conclusion that he had reached when acupuncture first unlocked a hidden portal in his brain: that feelings have consequences; they bring tangible change in the real world. For hadn't he been willing to remake the universe for her? And hadn't she already done the same?

"You've never been more beautiful," he whispered.

Her eyes were shining with tears.

"You are like Goths in your passion," Theoderic declared, "competing well with the performance in the arena. The crowds scarcely know where to look."

Augustulus bounded over, barked for attention and took an exploratory lick of Kreindia's hand, and then her face the moment he could reach it.

Breathless, Wade said to Theoderic, "Kreindia and I need some time alone."

"Your needs must wait. While you were so occupied, I received word that Clovis is about to be engaged in battle and therefore distracted. Now is our chance to settle the legion in its hiding place. Mount up. We leave immediately."

"But it will be dark soon," Wade protested, "We can't move an army now."

"The legion is not in Rome, and we go to them without foot soldiers, just cavalry. We travel under battlefield conditions. You're with me, and Kreindia goes with my sister."

Bereft, Wade turned to Kreindia, but she nodded to him in acquiescence with eyes that promised, "Soon."

"Yes," he agreed. He understood her better than ever.

~ *W* ~

THEODERIC had been right about the balance of the day being sufficient for their needs. Wade saw that the sky was clear and the avenues wide, giving them the maximum daylight for their travels. Once they were on the Via Cassia and had slowed their furious pace, Wade was directed to ride next to the king, and he had the good sense to thank the monarch directly for the opportunity.

Theoderic replied, "The arrangement is only provisional. I brought you up to this rank to make sure we know each other well enough to fight side-by-side in the coming days."

Searching for a trace of a smile somewhere in that statement, and not being sure he caught it, Wade tightened his hands on the reins. He did not utter the phrase, *Ask me anything you want.*

But Theoderic went on. "What is your earlier history in Aquitaine? Or before that time, if there was one."

With a wandering smile, Wade thought about how much to tell him. It would not be a story of twenty-first century Long Island, and pretty much anything else would be incompatible with the legend he was trying to create. Finally, he reached for something so minimal that he supposed nothing could be made of it. "Before Aquitaine... I was called Wade Linwood."

Theoderic laughed with pleasure. "You possess a woodname?"

"Yes. I suppose I do."

"Do you know the significance of such an appellation among your people?"

"I don't."

"I am called Ansis and Aesir," said Theoderic proudly. "You do know those, don't you?"

"Not the meaning, I'm afraid."

Now Theoderic was fired up. "These are the woodnames of the Goths and Celts, for even the Celts know me. It means that I am of the wood used to carve the gods, and therefore not purely human." He looked serious, or wanted Wade to think so. "My people, the Ostrogoths, are older than Woden. We are descended from Hunuil, who was invulnerable to magic. We once ruled a Gothic kingdom from the Baltic to the Black Sea.

My lineage—the Amali—is older than that of the Black Sea Goths."

Wade was stunned by Theoderic's embrace of pagan mythology, and he asked his next question carefully. "Do you find that you are invulnerable to magic like your ancestor Hunuil?"

Theoderic stared at him for a few uncomfortable moments and then laughed at his unease. "When I grew up in Constantinople, I knew little of my heritage and believed even less. As I grow older, I find that the world is more complicated than that which you can see from any Roman road."

"So magic…?"

"It's real all right. And I don't trust that I'm invulnerable to it."

"So what do you do to combat such a force when it turns against you?"

"I proceed as best I can, with caution and awareness at the fore, and do what I feel is right. Yes, even kings and emperors must go forward in that groping way, given the invisibility of life's plan."

Wade thought about that. "If we don't know what's meant to happen, shouldn't we refrain from any big decisions?"

"Decisions that might tempt Fate?"

Wade nodded.

"No. Half of life is fate, and the other half is free will. If you don't exercise the latter, all will be the former."

"This conversation is more suited to Kreindia than me."

"In good time. Right now she will do fine in Frida's company."

Wade noted that their detachment numbered twenty-five combatants, not including the king and his guests. The rest were support staff. They rode two abreast, with the exception of one point man well in front. Wade checked behind them to see Kreindia in animated conversation with a woman he supposed was Theoderic's sister. Amalafrida's marriage to the African would be her second, and that element was true in Wade's timeline as well, but he believed that her diversion to the north with Theoderic represented a potentially unsettling change in history. "If you don't mind my asking, my lord, why is your sister not with her new fiancé? Has something happened?"

"This business with Clovis, of course. Designing her wedding ceremony can wait. My sister is a warrior by birth. In Africa, Frida will be a peace weaver; in Gaul, she will be hellfire."

"And on the way to Gaul, she will be Kreindia's minder," Wade finished for him.

"Yes."

"It's understandable that you don't trust outside advisers like us."

"Constantinople tries to give me advisors too. Egan was offered to me when I first took power. You may have noticed I dislike him for good cause."

"He wouldn't be my first choice either."

Theoderic allowed a perfunctory smile. "Why shouldn't I be on guard? The empire in Constantinople would make of me a puppet. All of my efforts and those who shed blood for me would be for naught. That will not happen so long as I live."

Wade asked, "Will the legion and their families be safe before we get to them?" He had personally lived through the results of Theoderic's plan, a battle for civilization that took place three hundred years hence. With Clovis suddenly willing to wage all-out war with Itale, Wade feared that the legion and all that it meant for posterity would never come to fruition.

Theoderic closed his eyes in what looked like a moment of solemn prayer. "I've given the legion every chance to survive by moving them two or three days north of here to a location where no one would ever go. The

Place of Bones… by the River of Blood. Most people would just as soon venture to Hell."

Wade's flesh crawled. "Some catastrophe must have happened there."

"The greatest ambush in history, when young Rome was humiliated; an entire army destroyed by Hannibal Barca in the heart of Itale."

Wade had not known at what stage were the plans for gathering and secreting the legion. "So why put the new legion there? Wouldn't it be demoralizing?"

Theoderic fixed Wade with an unyielding stare. "Every sword begins in fire, and the Carthaginians were our bladesmiths. The hardening event that led to six hundred years of Roman supremacy must be commemorated— never forgotten." And with that, the descendant of Hunuil urged his mount faster against the setting of the sun.

~ W ~

WADE stirred at the sound of a birdcall on the move: *ee-oo, ee-oooo,* keening repeatedly in the darkness. The cry seemed like the voice of something that had once been human, rising and falling in a plea for help, and finally echoing eerily against the trees as it passed into the distance. As the first one faded, it was joined by a whole chorus of weepy supplications in constant flight. All the while, the whole collection of night insects supplied an undulating background of hisses. Every time Wade got used to the participants, another mimic of distorted humanity would join in the calling, making him wonder fearfully what the new beast was and what foul business it had in the night.

"Jordanes? … Hello? … Am I the only one awake?"

No answer.

Wade had already been quite saddle sore by the time the cavalry unit picked out a field for its camp well away from the road. Helping to pitch the tent he would occupy

336

had pushed him further toward exhaustion, and yet his mind churned ceaselessly among the still men. From his knowledge of maps, Wade worked out where they must be going. With any luck, they would reach Lake Trasimeno by late morning and somewhere around those shores was the dreaded place they would celebrate. It was obvious that Theoderic did not fully trust him as he was kept at a distance in camp and paired with Commander Jordanes who was too bored and tired to speak with him. Jordanes had fallen asleep instantly despite a sharp nip in the air.

Wade pulled his spare blanket on top of the first. The campfire had been smothered at dark lest they reveal their position, giving free rein to the evening's chill. He wished he could have stood under the prickling heat of a shower and spent at least one full night wallowing in his soft, warm bed at home when he had the chance. Those luxuries might have made him intolerant of his many privations here, but so what? He'd never meant to return to the brutal life of the Dark Ages.

The sudden howling of wolves made his hair stand on end and roused his companion. Jordanes rustled in the dark, listened a bit to the variety in their communication, which ranged from a smooth blend like an orchestra of horns to emanations whiny and rough. Unperturbed, he commented, "Interesting night."

"Do you think they're close?" Wade asked. "It sounds like we're surrounded." To him the wolves' piercing calls-to-action sounded dangerously nearby, equally unnerving when they sang in chorus as when they "spoke" individually.

Jordanes said, "We probably are, if that matters. Near or far, though, the cry of the wolves is a sign of impending disaster. Heh, so they say."

"Disaster for who?"

"Ha! A good question, and I'm too drained to worry about it. If the wolf-demons come while I sleep, I'll thank you to pick me out of their teeth." He went back to his slumber as easily as he had the first time.

A single howl cutting above the rest, like that of a leader calling the others to attention, scared Wade the most. He could picture its thick neck, tilting its large head and powerful jaws to the dark sky, and then its luminous yellow eyes focusing on prey as it lowered its head to attack. Wade told himself that the wolves were probably frustrated that man was abed in their territory, and they had no chance of dislodging him. That would explain why Jordanes didn't mind. Naturally, they would call to each other and assemble to consider the threat, to smell the numbers that opposed them.

No sooner had he made that assessment than it grew altogether quiet. The birds did not return. Instead, the chirping refrain of crickets took over. Wade would not have believed relaxation possible on a night like this, but with the benign and familiar sound easing his mind, the rigors of the day finally sapped him enough to drag him into a groggy state.

Whenever Wade passed into sleep, regardless of the century, he experienced a modest sinking as subtle as the gear pop of a downshifting transmission. But when sleep extended its downy grip to Wade that night, a vision snatched him away with the all the power and speed of rock-strewn rapids, and resolved into nightmare.

~*W*~

His keen reflexes took control before he even realized what was happening. Wade stood in the throes of battle, the tang of blood and sweat filling his nostrils, the clang of sword on sword reverberating down his arm. Every jolt and insult to his tendons feeling incredibly real. And wearing.

Striking high or low, on the inside or out, he made no headway against the indistinct figure in opposition, matched blow for blow as if he were fighting a mirror self.

Yet he realized they differed in one key aspect. While Wade grew fatigued, his opponent appeared to bristle with boundless energy. After a while, the sword impact shrieked like a metal bat meeting a pitching machine ball at top speed. Instead of a baseball, however, Wade faced a long deadly cutting edge, which he dared never miss. He fought on adrenaline-pumped reserves, but his body did not have the conditioning to match.

The next clang drove the pain through his back and numbed his entire upper body. *Is this really a nightmare*, he wondered, *or is it a vision?* So far he'd felt like both a participant and a helpless witness. Dreamlike qualities. At the same time, it was all too real and he was too awake. And losing.

Though Wade still doubted the predictive value of his visions, he was loath to die in one. Even as he kept the long sword high, he reached across his body to unsheathe his short sword for close fighting. Trying to locate the smaller blade's grip and unable to spare a glance downward, he touched the hilt first, which meant he'd reached too low. Aching for relief now, he pulled back to settle his palm on the crosshatching and tried to close his hand. Instead of firmly encircling the grip, his curling fingers drove what felt like four spikes into his wrist. At the same moment the attacker finally began to slow.

Startled, and thinking himself beset with stinging insects, Wade shook his hand out and tried grabbing the short sword again with the same shocking result where he stung himself. Together with that pain, every joint in his hand ached. If those were his fingernails jamming him up, they must have grown as long as his throbbing fingers themselves. The sword escaped his grasp, clanging back to its sheath.

And within that prolonged ringing sound, the battle froze all around him, dirt suspended in air, droplets of sweat trailing his opponent's dark face like a curved string of Aleutian Islands. In the stillness, Wade uncurled his painful hand and raised it to his astonished eyes for inspection. His extremity resembled the forelimb of a bat but for the lack of webbing; the winged portion of a bat skeleton clad in a gaunt glove of human flesh. In amazement, he swiped the thick air, his long digits cutting a whooping sound. *No wonder I couldn't get hold of my gladius.*

His spatha hand, however, retained ordinary size and shape.

Without warning, battle resumed. Sweat raining, a flake of broken armor plate spun past his nose. He'd done nothing to prepare for the coming strike. Before Wade could recover, his opponent's blade rose and ran through his guts to stick in his spine.

~*W*~

Wade sat up gasping in his hard bed in the early light, blinking at the new day through the open tent flap. The thumping, dull barrage of sword hilts clubbing shields came from the other side of camp—the wake-up summons to a challenging day in which he must clear his troubled mind and help plan the clash with Clovis. Cicadas splashed their shimmering call across the trees, and he waved off the flies landing on his brow and buzzing loudly in his ears. The sting in his chest was not a stab wound. It was extreme dehydration. He must have been panting throughout his ordeal. He reached for his water gourd and took quick gulps, thinking that if these nightmares kept up, he would be in a terrible state in which to enter battle.

Jordanes and the others had already gotten up and left the tent, but apparently they hadn't gone far. From outside, came the sounds of trickling water streaming and splashing in the dirt, changing in pitch the way it would if the water filled a small trench. Wade pressed his hands together for comparison, aligning them with the greatest care to even out the bottoms of his palms and see where

340

his fingers met—the sort of effort people make after a bad dream to remind them that dreams don't change reality.

Yet his extremities did not match.

His left thumb and pinky stood taller than his right, though his right index finger had an even better height advantage over his left, perhaps a quarter of an inch. The other differences were tiny one way or the other. His recollection was that right-handed people often had bigger right hands. Not exactly so in his case. If these discrepancies in digit size were his normal state, he had never noticed it. *And I damn well would have noticed it*, he thought in frustration.

Still, he couldn't swear that one or the other part had grown, not if he was being honest. Now he gathered two fists. Both hands closed to snug balls without any injury to his palms. Naturally they could do so at their right size. Wade thought back to his dangerous encounter with the Avars and the vague warning of a dream waterfall that had presaged the appearance of the real-life waterfall and the outcast warriors that hid in wait under the water's surface. His rare night visions, solid as they felt, were not entirely accurate dispatches from the future, but not wholly dreams either. Truth lived somewhere in the mix.

His left wrist, with its carpel tunnel syndrome, had begun his journeys through the application of acupuncture. Now the fingers on that same hand ached the way his reaching limbs sometimes did as a kid. His mother had called that feeling growing pains. Only now the place where he perceived the existence of joints did not correspond to where he saw them.

He flexed his left hand and felt pain in the void beyond his fingertips like the throbbing of phantom limbs severed in war. As though his body's blueprint demanded the missing parts.

As if he'd acquired a ghost wing like the one in his vision. The blood drained from his face. Wade's post-nightmare reassurance routine was not working. It didn't ease his concerns at all.

~ *W* ~

THEY mounted up and rode north towards their rendezvous at the River of Blood. *The greatest ambush in history.*

The point man went down the road on his lonely way first, and perhaps also an unseen scout or two had set out even earlier. The king and an advisor went next, followed by Amalafrida and Kreindia, and after them a contingent of housecarls to see to their safety. Wade was happy she would be in his sight as they moved forward on this last leg of the journey.

Wade was paired with Jordanes, who observed cheerfully, "I see that you have the good fortune to be with us another day."

"What do you mean?"

"The wolf pack did not choose last night to carry you off."

Wade worked out a smile as best he could. "If they come for you one day, Jordanes, remember to thank them for last night's kindness to me." While he didn't feel comfortable enough with Jordanes to tell him what actually did happen in the night, the big laugh he got from the commander in response to his comment meant he was blending in reasonably well.

He wished that the spark of comradery was more than superficial though. As the low eastern sun beamed across their path, Jordanes rode with his head high and his eyes shining with a singularity of purpose. His skin had a natural red flush to it, but on him it looked like a very private joy. It troubled Wade that he was not at all certain what Jordanes' purpose was.

"You seem awfully confident that we'll be all right."

"Oh, the opposite," Jordanes averred. "Disaster is nigh." His eyes were large as he spoke.

"I wouldn't be so happy about it."

"More like content. I've avoided the misfortune of a common life. A man must die in battle, not in bed, and not at mundane work. There's nothing that could ever be done with a plough or a scroll that could satisfy me. We will go to war, the hammer will fall, and it will be glorious to be amidst that cataclysm, the storm of man."

From the even tone, Wade could not tell if Jordanes were putting him on or was just as crazy as he seemed. Given the look in his eyes, the commander may as well have been a wolf himself, taking on the guise of a human form. Even Grimketil did not crave war this much. *Did he?*

Wade became aware of how his left hand—or rather the air beyond his fingertips—throbbed, reminding him that he could not afford to love war, not with the gifts he held and the far more terrible power he might have at his core, straining to be unleashed. Perhaps Theoderic had paired him with Jordanes in order to teach him a passion for armed conflict that he, as a general, should have. Whatever the intention, the arrangement had instead the opposite effect, making Wade abhor destructive engagement more than ever.

But there was Kreindia riding out ahead of him. With a boost of lightness that felt like drinking pure oxygen, Wade saw that his brief moment with her had changed him even more profoundly than had their earlier encounters. They were bonded in a way he could never explain, and somehow that connection came from a time before they had even met. Now, though, he had tasted the infinity of life in her embrace, and however much destruction might be a central facet of the cycle of nature, he rejected that negativity. Most of all, the thought of annihilation of an entire timeline, such as the Interloper was fashioning, made him physically sick. If Jordanes understood the maelstrom into which Itale was truly headed, he might reconsider his position.

Or maybe not.

The cavalry settled into the cautious routine of a long trek where the horses could not be exchanged for fresh ones. Those who approached to pass them from the north had to move to the side of the road and wait. Those few who overtook them from behind were turned back to their origin. All who they encountered were given erroneous information about the king's destination and were charged with a warning of silence. At midday the cavalry abandoned the paved roads for less-direct dirt paths where they would encounter fewer travelers on the last leg of their journey.

By nightfall, their scout reported seeing individual smoky blazes lit in the distant hills. Wade could barely make them out as pale dots in the inky green slopes. He remarked, "Those must be the campfires of our legion."

"No," said Jordanes. "The fires you see are much further ahead than the legion. We call these Hannibal's lights."

"Why?"

Jordanes smiled crookedly. "You'll find out in the morning."

The night was no worse than the last. Better, in fact. If any dreams or visions came into Wade's head, he remembered none of them. By first light, they were swaddled in intermittent fog and leading the snorting and squealing horses in a cautious march. Some of the legionnaires finally joined them on foot, looking disoriented and out of place as they each emerged from the swirling mists. Resplendent silver, red and gold of an earlier era adorned tired, gray-bearded men burdened by enormous shields they could barely lift. Their uniforms could not hide their bare, wizened knees and the veins that showed through their frayed sandal-boots as they fell in step.

"This is perfect," Jordanes told Wade. It didn't quite sound like a sarcastic complaint; more of a wary and disappointed observation.

Wade was no happier. "I'd like to find out more about this army we're trying to hide."

Jordanes warmed to the topic. "Legions have names, you know. Not just their official ones made up of dry numbers and their regions. My grandfather told of the glory days, when they had sobriquets such as Thunderbolt, Victorious, and Steadfast. My favorites were Rapacious and Lightning Hurler."

"And this one?"

"This one," said Jordanes with wolfish satisfaction, "is called Vengeance. You see, by the time they are called to serve in future generations, something terrible will have happened."

Wade sealed his lips to hold his tongue, thinking, *I know that part better than you do.*

They came upon the lake they sought from the west and began to trace its muddy shore. Trasimene opened like an ocean and their path ran around its northwestern lobe in a strip of beach. The wooded hills loomed on their left, causing them to march in a narrow file, and at times, fairly pushing them into the water. Wade could occasionally see a small island that appeared out of the haze, its flora nudged about by whatever creatures lived there. No one sailed the desolate lake in the foul conditions.

When they had traveled some miles along the northern stretch under increasing protest from their equine companions, they stopped.

"The Place of Bones..." Theoderic called out in his best stentorian voice.

"... by the River of Blood," the troops chanted in reply. There was indeed a creek running from their left to feed the lake, one of many brooks they'd crossed. It flowed clear and fresh, though as Wade examined it, he saw footprints running north along its edge and into the hills.

Wade's left hand grew hot like a warning, and a chilling scream issued from the woods all around before the soldiers came running at them from out of the trees.

CHAPTER 29

The Witch of His Time

WADE INSTINCTIVELY RAN east and upslope in order to rally with the command structure where Kreindia could also be found. He drew his spatha in horrified wonder. It felt light and looked pale and dull as though someone had replaced his steel with a wooden training sword. With the enemy bearing down, he didn't have time to think about it; he had to move.

Jordanes saw Wade's intention in his uphill drive and came with him, rushing ahead with confident athletic strides to take point. They made contact with the lead cavalry only to find the way forward blocked by another contingent of opposing soldiers on a stationary front east of them. Incoming spears flew crosswise from two directions. A missile knocked Wade to the ground and fell with him. He picked it up and examined it as he rubbed at the pain in his left shoulder. It, too, had a point made of blunted wood instead of metal.

As he regained his feet and hurled the spear back at his foes, Wade grasped the significance of Trasimene. It was the inspiration, if not the prototype, for their mission in the Italian Alps where the legion intended an ensnarement of their own. This was no mere celebration, but a war game. Just as he thought so, Wade was shocked to see the river turn deep red, its rapid froth gushing pink over the rocks. *It must be pig's blood*, he assured himself, but he felt a twinge of fear for Kreindia, having nearly lost her forever in the Battle of Brenii Pass itself. His main objective, as he tracked through the lower slope's thin cover of trees, was to ensure that she was all right.

He turned around to find her and Amalafrida fighting back-to-back, surprising their attackers by making their training swords nearly lethal with the right combination of jabs and leverage. Two warrior souls. He watched long enough to see Kreindia take a man down with a blunt strike to the back of his knee. Then Wade had opponents of his own.

The mock battle raged all day, during which Wade and the leadership broke through, escaping with some of the elite defenders in his company.

"Just as it happened in real life," Theoderic remarked as they passed into the dark of the woods.

At the end, Wade witnessed the "dead" rise to join the living on the banks of the lake. He enjoyed the spectacle as they reenacted their swearing allegiance to Romulus Augustulus who was deposed and sent into exile. They presented arms, their spears thrust high, as Theoderic himself recounted the story of Odoacer's treachery. A boisterous young actor with a great mop of hair played "Romulus," and even at that he was several years older than the actual teenage emperor. There were separate rites included for Trinitarians, Arians, and Mithrasians, the latter complete with a bull slaughtered on the spot. The priest filled a large goblet with its blood and passed the chalice to his right. Wade stuck with the Trinitarians. Kreindia and Amalafrida were off on their own.

Frankincense spiked with a musky and bitter resin rolled past them in clouds from giant burners and sat heavily in the humid air. As Wade watched the end of the ceremony, where spear struck spear, the world spun around him. In bright flashes, he re-lived the multiplicity of embraces; his bat wing; his hand burning like fire at the first sign of trouble.

When they finally raised the tents, Wade abruptly suffered a bout of claustrophobia and couldn't bring himself to rest under cover. Even when his phantom limb did not throb or burn, he could feel its extra burden dragging on his left side and aggravating his bruised shoulder. He felt every bit like a restless animal that needed to be outdoors. In a flash of insight reminiscent of his vision-sense, Wade recalled the bat wing tattoo on Henry, the man who seemed to kotow to Faron in the parking lot standoff all the way forward in the twenty-first century.

Most people, he was sure, would have found it a useless exercise to give any weight to the idea that the two images—one of which was merely a tattoo—could be anything more than an idle coincidence. Even Wade, who lived so far from a normal human existence, found the idea problematic. Nonetheless, he had to consider that the events might be connected. The possibility that the bat wing was associated with Faron in both cases weighed on his mind.

He watched the sky in anxious anticipation as the others laid down, a good number of them joining him outside. The clouds that concerned him hung in knotted, serried ranks like an army of the gods crowded to the horizons, as though Heaven had called out all of its forces in the twilight of the day to oppose their mission. Wade was certain of a coming storm despite the fact that Theoderic had told him the weather for their journey would continue to be fine.

If a deluge did in fact come, it would be miserable to sleep in the rain. Wade rested beneath the impending cloudburst like a Boy Scout come late to the camp grounds, abed with a lumpy collection of boulders and roots. His armor lay in a random heap at his side, creating a vaguely menacing impression. He deliberated putting the plating back on for defense against the ground if nothing else. Sitting up once more, he even considered going back to the crush of the tents. He would not do that; above all, he did not wish to admit his fears.

That night the wolves came again, baying their supremacy. The beasts were everywhere. Perhaps they howled their defiance at the shifting thunderheads. The outcome of the evening's show was near and it turned out to be a startling mystery, for the cooling night struck the original players from the stage so completely that every part of the hemisphere's zodiac lay exposed to interpretation. As fatigue pinned him, there was little to do but stare into the Heavens where the greater and lesser magnitude stars shined like the blazing suns they were. But for a fragile rag of cloud come to trouble the north, the night was clear enough to bring the universe to the empire's doorstep.

Wade sensed that if he were a reader of portents discerning the astrologer's chart, here was the rest of his story writ large in the form of pictograms. The way matters stood now, he dared not attempt to interpret the depiction.

This wasn't Wade's first venture into the wilderness. Far from it. It was his first in the year five hundred, where the seven points of the Big Dipper loomed over him in a discomfiting new version. Stars did not stay put over a long period of time. Familiar as he was with the Great Bear's tail, it struck him that the dipper had a slightly greater regularity in this era, a fractionally straighter handle and cup than it would display in the fifteen hundred years to come since two of those stars didn't move in the same direction as the others. The fact that he could discern the minute change was an unsettling reminder of how many centuries he was from home.

Peering into the fulsome void, Wade had the stomach-churning impression of a myriad heavenly witnesses among the Dipper stars and in the other configurations of the night. Irrationally, he felt that they were sitting in judgment of all he'd ever done and would do.

And none of these locations, including his, were truly

anchored. As he watched the hypnotic twinkling of those deceptive lights and listened to the howling wolves, Wade drifted into the grip of an absurd fear that he was being drawn toward the distant points of light. In the steely grip of his panic attack, he seemed to be falling upward. Still on his back, he clawed the ground, splintering his nails against the stony dirt. Convinced that he could not last much longer, he found the tree roots beneath him and clutched them tightly enough to anchor his imagined negative weight.

Gritting his teeth, he squeezed his eyes tightly shut then wrenched them open.

The suns became fixed points above him again. The cooling air began to dry his sweat. In starlight, the people around him enjoyed the sleep of the indifferent. None of them madly clutched roots to keep from rising into a hostile sky.

While he had begun to have visions lately—the painful early visitations of a novice seer—he preferred to interpret this latest episode as only a bad case of vertigo.

At least the ordeal was over. Even as his thoughts grew fuzzy with the illogic of sleep, he drew a mental image of Kreindia. When he tried to call to her, he kept substituting her name with the repetition of a set of syllables he didn't recognize: *Ah-min-tah. Ahmintah. Amynta.* For a moment, the question of *How did Kreindia equal Amynta?* nearly forced him fully awake. If his subconscious meant to form a word, as opposed to drowsy nonsense, that word made no sense to him either. His gift for languages held no purchase in his dreams, and he was very close to slumber.

"Wade!"

Wade bolted upright and reached for his sword.

Kreindia put a hand on his shoulder and kneeled beside him. "I felt you calling to me in the night. I'm sorry we weren't able to talk sooner."

"You made it," he said, drawing her down with him.

"That's all I care about. When we kissed in the Sun-Temple Box, did you also—" he broke off, wondering if she could understand any explanation that involved the multiverse.

She said, "I sensed it on the astral plane, like being everywhere and every*when*."

"It seemed as if you...somehow caused that."

"It felt that way. I peeled my senses down to reality to make sure I wasn't dreaming."

"And that experience was the result."

"I'm not exactly sure how, but for me, our separation has been months and I've gone many places with multiple jumps. My education in the astral arts has been increasing the whole time."

"For me, you reappeared after only a day. One very long day."

"Each time my spirit splits and recombines, my abilities are re-made."

"Re-made?"

"Fashioned differently, for better or worse."

Wade subconsciously touched his phantom limb. "I didn't notice any changes in myself in the transition to sixth century Rome." He wasn't ready to tell her that he felt like he was turning into a monster.

"It was Faron," Kreindia blurted out. "My fears held me back from saying it, but I was trapped in his illusions and couldn't see what he was—the cause of every disturbance from Raginpert to Clovis and our troubles in between."

"Faron," he agreed with a sigh. "I came close to the same conclusion. But I'm struggling to figure out the extent of it."

"To every extent, and for reasons he's not sharing. It's a long story of hidden truths, or more accurately, layered lies."

Wade took her hands in his. "I wish this conflict could end here and now, just the way things are, with you and I never moving from this place and time so that nothing can interfere with us any longer."

"You know that's not an option. Faron is out there, sowing lies to turn everyone against each other. His threat is even bigger than when we faced the loss of the *Pax Nicephori*."

Now the sky was light and Wade saw and heard the men stirring. It was time for them all to face a very difficult day.

~ *W* ~

CLOVIS led his troops south through the subdued territories on his way to clash with Theoderic's army of Ostrogoths, all the way thinking of the glory that could be his. Even if he died in this engagement, Clovis, in his horseshoe empire, would have left a deep mark on the history of Europe. If he succeeded even halfway with the remainder of his plans, the memory of his conquests would endure for a thousand years or better. And if he succeeded fully, a trembling world would writhe beneath his heel.

Before his forces could engage Theoderic, they were blocked by an army of Visigoths, the largest they had seen in a long time. Since his divination with cousin Cerobaud, he'd felt some trepidation about an Aquitainian attempt at aiding the Ostrogoths. By their banners, however, these were mostly the more distant Visigoths who came from Spain. That meant that Morcant had been right. There was nothing to fear from conquered Aquitaine. If that contingent was coming at all they would have arrived first.

Now Clovis smiled broadly. The modern, Romanized Visigoths in their armor and shields stood in stark contrast to the nearly naked Salian Franks armed with angons and axes. Underneath, Clovis' troops, and the rivals who faced them, were not too different in background. He knew about armor but didn't use it. In what most generals would think a counterintuitive move, he had begun to revolutionize how the Franks fought by stripping them down completely. Lack of armor brought out real bravery as well as speed and maneuverability that an armored soldier could never match.

"For glory!" he cried as he waved them on. Both sides ran towards each other and in just minutes they would close the gap. Clovis knew that his troops felt fear and needed reassurance. He never led them with the battle cry, "For Jesus." It wouldn't have meant a thing to them even though he had one man carry a banner with a cross. His faux Catholicism was not adopted for their sake but for that of the East, as well as for his rival chieftains, and of course for his figurehead wife, for she made an incompetent liar. She had to believe that his faith was true or she would give him away. One day, when he ruled the world, he would shout in irony, "For the Pope," and laugh at those who thought him loyal to the church.

Clovis saw the enemy arrayed against him and he knew the time had come. "Ready the angons!" he told his commanders, and they repeated his order. It was not necessary that he tell his well-trained men what to do next, but he took no chances as battle nerves might get to the best of men, especially the new ones. "I want you to throw, run, and step," he shouted. "Now throw!"

They took their barbed lances, their angons, and hurled them all at once so that the air was black with their missiles. The projectiles made a perfect arc into the enemy's shields where they landed with a satisfying staccato impact. Angons, once embedded, could not be removed. The burden made shield arms sag from the weight.

Before long, the far ends of the angons were slung low to the ground. The Salarian Franks stepped on them to lower the shields, which allowed them to sink an axe into the defenseless soldiers. All the rest was a frenzy as his naked soldiers fought to kill before they could be wounded. The slaughter was thorough.

"Take their silver and then leave them," Clovis shouted. "We travel light."

Having utterly destroyed this first opposition on the road to Itale, Clovis' chest swelled. Yes, he long had the hang of killing Visigoths. That was how he'd acquired Aquitaine. Now he ached to slay some Ostrogoths.

"My lord Clovis," called Galchobhar before he even reached the king. "The Burgundians gather behind us, only a few days lagging. I'm sorry, but you were right."

"Perfect timing. Tell all the men it's a close pursuit, and let us continue on our drive to the south," Clovis instructed with a gleam in his eye.

"I didn't hear you correctly, my lord. Surely we will discontinue?"

"No. Our men must know there is no turning back. We succeed or die."

~W~

"LOYALTY is everything to me," Theoderic avowed to Wade as he assembled his troops on the battlefield near the city of Florence. Clovis had been spotted bearing down on the homes of the legion's families, and given what he'd done to the countryside, his intentions to ravage the city were unmistakable.

By now Wade understood that Theoderic's loyalty extended equally to his Arian Ostrogoths and to the Imperium. He wasn't a member of either group.

"As a young man," said Theorderic, "I preferred to offer blind trust rather than become like the people I hated. But after two betrayals, where the second one led to the mass murder of most of my relatives, any trust extended to my allies is entirely provisional"

"I am loyal," Wade swore.

"Then I want you to understand that we must not allow Clovis to retreat."

Wade's eyes widened in alarm. This was the most distressing opinion he had heard Theoderic express so far. "I understand the importance of dealing with him quickly, but—"

Theoderic poked his forefinger at Wade's chest. "The last thing the oracle Evermud said to me was, 'One rich in gold who harbors a demon, cannot hide his demon.'"

Faron.

"He meant that admonition to be the last sign for me to observe, and the last danger to guard against. Clovis has taken the illogical step of leaving the Burgundians at his back thinking that he can destroy me quickly and then turn to battle them. Given his miraculous gains in Gaul and limitless confidence to do what should be impossible for him, only a supernatural force can be behind his success."

Demon or not, Wade could not allow Theoderic to change the course of events so completely. "I see it too, but because of his unnatural assistance, Clovis will have perfect knowledge of us. He wants to force us to defend Florence."

"I was more afraid he would not engage us in open battle. As a tool of evil, Clovis needs to be destroyed utterly."

"He will be, but you have to allow me to face Clovis myself."

"Why you?"

"I'm personally familiar with the unnatural power you speak of, and I'm the only one who may be able to match the threat."

Theoderic closed his eyes and frowned, clearly struggling with a difficult decision. He was slowly shaking his head, "No," when Jordanes reached him.

"My lord, Strabo has taken the field and he leads an army of his Thracian Ostrogoths. They are burning the Catholic churches so that the Arians will be blamed."

Clenching his fists, Theoderic struggled to master himself. "Thank you, Jordanes. Stand by."

When the king looked at Wade again, he said, "That settles it. Strabo's support of the Franks has been crucial for them. I would punish him first and remove him from the field. Very well, you may approach Clovis before I do. Jordanes goes with you. But I will stand ready, and you must destroy him. If you prove disloyal to me, I swear by the Nine Worlds, I will be the strongest enemy you ever face in Midgard."

Wade hoped Theoderic could not see him blanch. He fully intended to go against Theoderic's wishes by sparing Clovis and did not relish the prospect of that fallout, but he had larger considerations and he had to face one enemy at a time. The king of the Franks was his first problem.

"Now bow your head," Theoderic commanded. The king's lips moved in a silent prayer as he settled a loop of chain over Wade's head.

Wade looked down and saw a footed cross settled on his chest.

CHAPTER 30

Hunting

KREINDIA TOOK A deep breath and sought out Wade one more time. No matter what, she had to let him know of the confrontation she planned for Faron and why. Coordination was essential if her ploy stood any chance of working.

She waited until Wade finished listening to an update on the disposition of Clovis's troops. New concern etched his face upon hearing her news and he sounded grief stricken. "You're going to face Faron? You said that he's more powerful than both of us. You barely got past him the last time."

Kreindia's eyes stung with the memories of all the pain Faron had caused, including her recent scare that Wade was forever gone. The anger of that close call drove her, even though she knew Wade was alive and with her now. Faron could never be allowed to keep that power over them. Then she thought about Faron's role in the Longobard uprising, and more recently with Clovis. The whole timeline was at stake, if not more. "Faron has succeeded so far," she theorized, "because of his ability to involve himself in the affairs of the powerful. It's crucial that we keep him off the battlefield and unable to interfere any further. I have to distract him."

"Then I'm coming with you."

"No, you need to stay here to see to it that Clovis retreats before either he or Theoderic are killed. Without

Faron to control and assist the Frankish advance, Clovis will see the futility of the conflict and go back to his plans from the original timeline."

Wade sighed. "You don't need my consent, but I don't want you to go."

"Can you think of an alternative plan?"

"Yes, we go back to an earlier time when Faron doesn't have us at this disadvantage."

"Then he goes back to an earlier time and where does it end? At least now we know all the players and the situation. So far we've had the good fortune to survive. Another scenario is a whole new set of risks and for all we know, every other time in history is worse."

"This is crazy," said Wade, rubbing his scalp. "The fate of the multiverse is on our shoulders, and there's only two of us foolish enough to be on this team."

"Good, now you've got it," she said, and kissed him for luck.

~ W ~

FARON watched the battle preparations from a hill near the Frankish forces that he'd set into motion. With a satisfied smile, he sensed the comforting power of his talisman radiating inside the king's treasure box they carried everywhere. Even with the Wheel of Taranis though, Clovis' mind had proven too strong to be mastered. Nor, with his suspicious nature, was he easily manipulated. His lieutenant Galchobhar and his chief priest, Morcant, also had sturdy minds, subject only to small influences. With the proper planning and effort, Faron might have broken them all, but the timeline itself balked at such a direct approach. That's why he had fed Morcant his gifts of information gradually through Strabo and had to prove the value of his whispers about the Gaulish countryside at each stage. What made the manipulation a challenge even for him was that the sister timelines with their own closely related versions of the three men tended to reinforce the integrity of this one.

Strabo, though, was corrupt in this and every neighboring timeline. That made him a suitable choice to steer Faron's pawns. And Strabo had done well at the task.

Although Faron knew how to conceal his hand in the alterations of history, he could not work in secrecy forever. Nor did he expect to. The strain would show and his influence would be revealed sooner or later to all who cared to oppose him. And the more he pushed, the more the fabric of space-time would resist.

Let it be so. I'm up to the challenge. If Nature abhors my ambitions, then Nature itself will have to change.

His problem right now was that Wade Linwood of Aquitaine could not be driven forward like a wild horse. Those possessed of the ancient woodnames were robust and constant. In addition, Wade came from a lineage of ancestors with an affinity for the multiverse and all the resources that might avail him. With Kreindia at his side, he would not act in the reckless manner that Faron had counted on thus far.

That's why my new plan will work. Destroy the Kreindia that Wade knows. Let him see her die. Linwood will never be able to control himself then.

~W~

KREINDIA stood tall on a hill north of Florence and opened her perception to search for Faron's detestable signature in the region. She shivered in the morning sun. In engaging Faron, the stakes were considerably higher than they had been for Dalassenos at Apamea. Here she was a general leading the whole timeline into battle. Yet there was no sign of him.

He must be here at this place and time, she assured herself. *He cannot miss the clash of Clovis and Theoderic.*

She knew that there were circumstances where he could hide his signature from her. He'd done it before. *But he doesn't know to hide his aura.* Since she didn't know what his aura would look like, she opened herself up to the signals from every individual as she allowed a narrow sweep of her awareness across the hills.

When she reached the hill directly behind Clovis, the pain struck her and knocked her to the ground. Faron's aura was black, a darkness that swallowed every other aura in its proximity.

She shut herself off from the loudest part of his input. Having found his location, she could discern his hidden signature, a stagnant perversion of the multiversal foam from which all things were built.

Now her guard was up, as the act of finding him would point him straight back at her. Indeed, she could feel his immediate attempt to neutralize her with his tools of almonds and mechanical cicadas: the scent that dampened awareness, and the clicking and hissing that went with the tug on her memory. If he were successful, the illusion that all was well would soon follow.

Her encounter risked everything. It was essential that she make choices that were not influenced by deception. She focused on diving beneath her upper senses, attempting to ground herself in reality, which meant opening a window on the world of the extremely small. As before, she used the silver elevator, and the process of reaching the very bottom came more quickly and easily for her this time. She nestled deep below corporeal distractions. From this new perspective, she looked past his ossified bubbles that were a mockery of life to the effervescence of raw Nature that constantly appeared and disappeared in a churning film. And in that beautiful jitter and fluctuation, she defeated Faron's first assault.

In his second assault, she wasn't so lucky. She restored her upper senses a beat too late. *The bees are here and they're real.* While she was unseeing and unhearing, the swarm was able to approach and envelop her. Unlike the iconic bees that Faron had used to attack Wade on the astral plane, these could do harm directly and there was no time to get out of the way or divert them. Only one of them stung her as she ducked to protect her head. It got her in the ear in precisely the right spot. She felt herself deprived of her control and forced up through a quick sequence of colors to the astral plane. Here she was far less experienced.

Faron manifested close to her with his red-rimmed pebble eyes. She remembered when she first saw him and noticed even then that his face had aged unevenly—the peppered stubble on otherwise smooth, younger skin; the drape of flesh that hung on his neck. *Was that one of the signs of his true nature that I was blind to, a consequence of long-term time travel?*

Kreindia studied all that she could see on the astral plane to find some option for escape. Faron blocked the portal that led back. The river beckoned to her with its infinite possibilities. *Is that what he wants from me, to abandon Wade? That will never happen.*

Her heart sang when a tall man joined them. Wade's father, Alan, appeared and stood firm. His aura was resolute like that of Alaric's, the deep red of survival.

There's not just two of us on this team anymore. I do stand a chance.

Faron seemed to anticipate the interruption even as Kreindia screamed a warning. At a quirk of the Beast's patchy, callused hands, Time's river itself rose against the would-be savior. The elder Linwood raised his arms instinctively and turned to run before he was washed over by its great wall and borne away.

~ *W* ~

Twenty-first century

CLARA felt her determination rise. *This is my home and*

my daughter is in danger from my husband. I have every right to defend her. She couldn't remember ever having felt this way before, but with her memory gaps, she had no way of knowing for certain.

After declaring that he didn't care, and seeming like he was quite satisfied with the state of affairs inside the house, Faron appeared to change his mind, an angry frown creasing his brow. Now he lapsed into a trance the way he had in Nesky's office. The way he had done many times before. Only this time, he didn't come back from it so quickly. He twitched and flared like an orchestral conductor gone mad. A standing lamp on his left was dashed to the floor.

I need your help, said a voice inside Clara's head. It wasn't some interior counsel that reached her, but rather the sound of a young child. Even at that, it wasn't an entreaty but a declarative statement. The pronouncement sounded so far away, so fleeting, and yet so absolutely certain even in the space of four little words—*a voice like Wisdom itself*, she thought. But Clara had no idea how to answer it.

Faron snapped back awake. Now he strode purposefully past Clara and toward Del. What would he do to her when he got there?

I need a distraction, the young voice suggested. Now it sounded less certain than before and edged in fear.

What distraction?

Get the gun.

Faron was the proud owner of a Glock 19, which he spoke of often. He didn't secure it well; in a household like his, he probably didn't think he had to. Still, she hesitated. Her father liked guns too and she found it awful when he forced her to shoot—the kick and the stink of it, the sound that ripped through her ears. The utter destruction.

DON'T HESITATE.

At the mental shout, Clara ran for the gun and brought

it back to where Faron was, standing so very near her Del.

When he saw her with the weapon, he examined her with keen curiosity as he stroked his daughter's hair.

Pointing the weapon squarely at Faron's chest with two hands, Clara warned him, "Back away from her. Never go near my daughter again."

Faron smiled in amusement. "What has gotten into you, Clara mouse?"

Where is that voice in my head now?

Faron said, "I really haven't got time for this and you really don't know how to fire that."

With tears streaming from her eyes, she charged a round, pressed the center blade evenly to enable the action, and shot accurately against the kick until the gun was empty. Faron fell.

The room twisted in a bizarre disdain for reality, and went back into its place.

It's different somehow. Faron was up before and now he's down, but it's more than that.

When Clara was sure the blood on Del was not her own, she looked up and asked the child in her head, "Did I do the right thing? Was this what you needed?"

I'm scared, replied the voice of Wisdom. **Kreindia is gone.**

Kreindia?

~*W*~

FARON attacked Kreindia by the muddy banks of Time's river on the astral plane—the river that had washed away her only ally. *Alan was more experienced, more powerful than Wade and yet he never even stood a chance.* The Beast again unleashed his mechanical cicadas on her with their grinding clicks and searching hook. In the null space she did not know how to anchor herself to fundamental reality. This time she could feel the tug of the spool he held drawing out her memories.

She saw herself slipping away, remembrances torn from

her. They were not being neatly stored in the memory box this time—the one that had tipped to reveal memories secreted away. No, hers was the unwinding of someone who faced death with a high degree of certainty that the event of their demise was imminent: a review at the end of yourself. Kreindia the Strange; Kreindia Athinginoi; Kreindia of Constantinople. *All going so fast.*

I have to reach out to Wade.

Only fragments of awareness left.

He needs to know.

She felt someone reaching inside her very essence, plundering what he found there and poaching savagely.

Her sense of self fled. There was a distant struggle against high pressure, then a sudden pop, like a bottle uncorked.

Then nothing.

Worse than tabula rasa.

Kreindia of Amorium, and every other title she'd held, was no more.

CHAPTER 31

Destruction

DESPITE THE CONSIDERABLE distance between them, Wade could see Clovis on the battlefield staring back at him. Some of the Frankish forces were forming up behind their leader, making him and his housecarls the tip of a wedge. Wade had charge of his own small army, fresh and waiting in a defensive position while the rest met the enemy just over the nearby hills. Clovis had split his forces and Theoderic did the same. Wade intended to delay, deny, and frustrate the Frankish king while the army of Itale decimated all of his support.

In that tense moment, Wade found himself locked into the same state of hyper-awareness that he'd experienced in Dr. Nesky's parking lot when he'd had his second confrontation with Faron; then, as now, the mode was triggered by a danger-induced mixture of adrenalin and synesthesia. Distant details of his surroundings crowded to intimate proximity. The scent of carrion drifted on the air, the rush of river water assaulted his ears, and the sight of a fish chasing an air bubble to the water's surface— hundreds of yards away—seemed closer than his boots. Closer than the war that raged around him.

While in that delicate state of harmony with minutia, he was hit by the shock of his life. He felt Kreindia vanish from the immediate time stream, and one-by-one, all of the neighboring ones. Not younger versions of Kreindia, but the *present* embodiment that was in synch with him and went forward as he went forward. Or used to. Her exit from Being occurred as cleanly as a life turned off by a digitized switch; she was "one" and then she was "zero." The sudden loss filled him with supreme agony.

"No!" he screamed as Clovis charged towards him. Rage flowed through his body from the center outward, threatening to burst his joints. When the spreading anguish reached his phantom bat wing, the digits ran riot with power. White hot pain flooded his arm as his fingers stretched to the dimensions of his nightmares. He could see the physical wing forming now, the webbing jumping the gaps between his lengthening fingers before the blaze within them made the transformation too dazzling to witness. His anger and sorrow knew no bounds.

The inflamed limb stiffened and flung outward in the direction of Clovis. Power burst from his extremity, loosing a discharge of purest lightning. The flash cut the air all across the field and struck the Frankish king in his center. The impact made him fly backward by several lengths, flipping over until he was finally driven half into the dirt like a hoe cleaving the earth. Lit by the blue fire of Wade's anguish, Clovis flash-burned in a smoking black instant that left him a twisted husk of charred bones and stinking, vaporized flesh.

Wade's shoulders shook as he sobbed at the magnitude of all that had passed. He had envisioned the potential death of Clovis at the hand of Theoderic as a disaster, something to be avoided at all costs. Now that very calamity had come to pass—but not at the hand of Theoderic. Wade himself had slain Clovis with his mindless bolt.

Clovis, the founder of France. *There will be no founder of France.*

Now Wade could not move, nor could anyone. The smoke drifting in from other battles stood motionless with them.

I've triggered the Quantum Divergence Threshold, changes that spawn a new reality when paths diverge too far.

His mind's eye opened to the astral event horizon where Time was rent in the immediate universe and beyond. The sun went backwards in the sky, gaining speed, adjusting to another reality as it plunged the world into darkness and light again. Hyper-aware still, Wade tried to withstand the crush in his chest, and his every cell screamed when he felt connections severed in his brain. The onslaught of sudden large-scale change and the cascade effect of his actions on the verse he occupied, smashed through its sister timelines like the tipping of cosmic dominoes. In that carnage, Wade sensed the loss of other Kreindias like monstrous mirrors held to his pain. For fragments of her had still lived and were now erased along with the active-creation version of her that he had known directly.

Released, Wade staggered and fell to the ground with his face in the dirt. He realized that with the loss of the only person who mattered, there was nothing left to fight for. He had destroyed it all. The vision of his phantom limb that had taken him like rushing rapids some nights ago along the Via Cassia became clear. There, too, time had frozen and resumed: *Sweat raining, a flake of broken armor plate spun past his nose. He'd done nothing to prepare for the coming strike. Before Wade could recover, his opponent's blade rose and ran through his guts to stick in his spine.*

The shadowed man he fought in that nightmare was himself, ensuring his own demise and playing a central role in the end of all he held dear.

The sun stilled and the battle resumed some hundred yards away from him. Jordanes led them. Wade got up and began to run. He didn't stop until he reached the Arno where it met the city. Losing only his helmet, he leapt into the murky river, not caring whether or not he drowned.

Once submerged, his hyper-awareness fled, to be

replaced by an uncommon dulling of his wits and the memory of a chorus of night birds that wailed as if mourning man's folly. He retained just enough sensation to make his clumsy way to the river's turbulent midpoint. Once in that quickest of waters, he stopped swimming. *No more struggles. There's no point to it.*

He shut down his outer senses one by one as if going on a trip to the astral plane, but he did not trigger the transition that would lift him to its safety. If he was still possessed of any survival instinct, he was numb to its call and open to oblivion's mercy. This then was his own exit from Being.

His red cape spread out on the water's surface as the chain mail pulled him down. Theoderic's cross touched his insensate lips. As he sank limp in the rushing waters, a corner of his mind activated to a song in a gentle young voice, and he was cut off from everything but that sound guiding him along.

Row, row, row your boat...

Yes, he thought with shadow of dark humor, *if I were sane, I would want a boat to carry me along this river instead of sinking in it. I'm rowing without a boat, and the direction is down beneath the water.*

Gently down this dream...

The tune was familiar, the author of the altered lyrics unfamiliar. Not a voice that he knew. It was that of a child with a very old soul, and it carried the lilt of a peculiar long-corridor echo that seemed to drag him along to infinity where he belonged. Yet the song's owner—and here Wade had a weak vision-flash of a wheelchair that was not Del's—had the most unusual synesthetic signature, one that flickered in... and out... of existence...

And as his weary senses fled to the Heavens, he heard one last thing in that same childish, chilling voice: *I'll do Spider for you, Wade. That will make you feel better.*

AMYNTA OF AMORIUM

Wade of Aquitaine Book Three

Prologue

Lorraine was terrified. She stood where the Everything was, closed the eyes of the multiverse as she gathered the threads of life, and yanked hard on the parts she needed. That one violent pull was necessary, and she hoped she wasn't too late since she was only able to proceed after the Interloper let go and couldn't see.

The burst of effort tired her immediately. She was not only worn, but weary like the void that bore witness to the eons. *Not fair, I'm a little girl.*

Yet she did the work of Hercules, of Atlas, of gods unnamed.

The rest of her toil was far more delicate and had to be steady. So much to keep track of, including the noxious one called Faron. It was her singing the boat song that held fast the bits of the shattered multiverse. *The secret is to never stop rowing,* she giggled.

Like Atlas, she needed a place from which to gain her leverage. She found that anchorage in the beauty of Kreindia's contemplation forest. She'd discovered it when she noticed Kreindia and Del living together in one head. Sharing knowledge in order to keep Kreindia sane.

Like the Strange one before her, Lorraine arrived in the refuge among an infinity of trees when the rain had just passed, darkening their trunks to burnt umber. Here she did not need a wheelchair. She skipped along its cobbled ways among the greenest grass where any problem could be solved, and tipped the water off the leaves with a fingertip as she thought. It made a fine hiding place from Faron. The forest just needed some tweaking to make it suitable; compatible with the Everything and invisible at the same time. Wasn't hide and seek a child's specialty?

Soon though, Lorraine promised herself, *I will have help. If I do everything right and nothing wrong. If I'm very, very good, my friends and I will defeat the very, awfully bad.*

But her friends were not awake yet. The hero right now was the brave spider who held all the threads and felt all their tremors over vast distances. But if something very important and strong was caught in the web, the spider had to fight. *Still a little girl*, she protested to the silent Heavens.

Yet the spider was her.

Her shield was Wade of Aquitaine.

And her sword was Amynta.

Terms Used in *Wade of Aquitaine* Book Two

People

Agenor: A priest who supports Michael Psellus.

Alaric II: The leader of the Visigoths during the early 6th century.

Allen Linwood: A version of Wade of Aquitaine's father.

Amalafrida: Sister of Theoderic the Great, and fellow hostage-guest of the Byzantines.

Amir Jaush ibn al-Samsama: The leader of the Fatamid Caliphate's army in Syria, end of the 10th century.

Amynta: The Syrian girl who looks like Kreindia.

Anastasius: 5th/6th century emperor of Byzantium, known for his heterochromatic eyes.

Anthemius: One of the last emperors in the late 5th century Western Roman Empire.

Anthimos: The most powerful eunuch in 9th century Constantinople and friend to Kreindia of Amorium.

Aspar: A general and brother-in-law of Strabo.

Audofleda: Wife of Theoderic the Great.

Augustulus: Wade of Aquitaine's Laconian dog and a signal to Theoderic that a powerful aide has arrived.

Bardanes Tourkos: Leading general of Nikephorus' army.

Basil: A Byzantine emperor at the end of the 10th century.

Basiliscus: Brother-in-law of Anthemius.

Boerhtric: Companion and ally of Grimketil Forkbeard.

Brygos: A soldier sent to torture Michael for information.

Cerobaud: Clovis' cousin, another king of a Frankish tribe.

Charlemagne: 8th/9th century king of the Franks and Emperor of Holy Roman Empire.

Clara Richter: Kreindel's mother and wife of Faron.

Clovis: The leader of the Salian Franks who conquerors all Franks.

Cluny of Pavia: A Benedictine monk caring for the dying Grimketil Forkbeard.

Cnaeus: A soldier who attacks Kreindia in a fit of madness.

Codros: Teenage cousin of Keyx.

Commander Dardanes: A commander in the *Foederati*.

Constantine: Founding emperor of Constantinople.

Count Odoin: A Germanic general; shifting ally of Theoderic and the Ostrogoths.

Cynthia Marks: Kreindia/Kreindel's 21st century physical therapist.

Damien Dalassenos: A 10th century military governor and general of the Byzantine army in Syria.

Davilos: A sailor who captains the *Diantha.*

Dr. Gennady "Nate" Nesky: Wade Linwood and Kreindel Richter's acupuncture therapist.

Du Sian: Taoist lord of Constantinople.

Egan: A member of Anastasius' war council who takes Wade to Rome.

Eloflora: Daughter of Alaric II.

Empress Irene: A former Byzantine empress and Kreindia's role model and icon.

Estela: The receptionist at Dr. Nesky's office.

Eudokia: A shop owner in Constantinople.

Evermud: An oracle/soothsayer of the Ostrogoths who foretells most of Theoderic's future.

Faron Richter: Kreindel's stepfather.

Fedelmid: A Celt who aids Kreindia to capture a dromon.

Foederati: Barbarian tribes in Roman military service.

Frederick: King of the Rugii.

Flavius Festus Catalinus: A lord at a Roman outpost in Gaul.

Galchobar: An advisor to Clovis.

General Honoratus: The leader of the Roman legion in the Brenii Pass.

Giovanni: The bishop of Ravenna.

Grimketil Forkbeard: A Saxon from Swabia, companion to Wade of Aquitaine, supporter of Michael Psellus.

Guillaume: The prior of the Abbey of St. Martin.

Gunther/Gaius Lucius: A Gaulish Roman who poses as a Germanic raider.

Henry: A man with a Celtic neck tattoo in 21st century and a psychiatric patient of Dr. Nesky.

Justinian: The only eastern emperor who made a viable attempt to reconquer the west after its loss.

Keyx: A low-level courtier at Constantinople and ally to Kreindia.

Kreindel Richter: a.k.a. Del, the 21st century daughter of Faron and Clara. Paralyzed in her late teenage years.

Kreindia of Amorium/Kreindia the Strange: The protagonist, oracle, scribe, chronicler, synesthete, and niece of Michael Psellus.

Larimore: The abbot in residence at the Abby of St. Martin.

Leo the Armenian: 9th century Byzantine Emperor who usurped the throne, former ally of Michael Psellus.

Leo Marcellus (the Thracian): Emperor and custodian of Theoderic and Amalafrida.

Lorraine: A young girl Kreindia/Kreindel meets at physical therapy.

Majid: Theoderic's Arabian horse.

Malki Tsadek: A powerful synesthete from days past and putative founder of the Melchisedechian faith

Mark Antony: 1st-century B.C. Roman politician and general, Marcus Antonius is known to readers as Shakespeare's Mark Antony. His famous speech is from the play Julius Caesar.

Michael Psellus (the Stutterer): A general of Byzantium and uncle of Kreindia of Amorium.

Morcant: A druid priest/ advisor to Clovis.

Nikephoros: A former emperor of Byzantium.

Odoacer: The leader of the Scirians and enemy of Theoderic the Great.

Pammon: A.k.a. The One and a Half. A giant and former slave; ally of Kreindia.

Phaedo: The decamarch of the *Phaidra*.

Raginpert the Insolent: The leader of the Longobards.

Rhangabe: A former emperor of Byzantium forced to abdicate by Leo the Armenian.

Roderick: An alias used by Kreindia of Amorium.

Senator Blathyllos: A politician in Constantinople and fair-weather friend.

Snorri: Companion of Grimketil, pledged to him in military service.

Solon of Philomelion: The oracle who foretells Leo's, Michael's, and Thomas' ascension to the throne.

Sosthenes: A teenage sailor on the *Phaidra*.

Starkos: A priest at Boucoleon Palace.

Sunigilda: The wife of Odoacer.

Syrian Girl: Doppelgänger of Kreindia who finds her in prison in Constantinople. [See Amynta].

Tankred: A companion to Wade of Aquitaine.

Taoist Lord Du Sian: Chinese acupuncture practitioner living in the 9th century Chinese Quarter of Constantinople

Thamar: Daughter of Thomas the Slav. Kreindia's rival.

Thekla: Michael Psellus' wife and daughter of Bardanes Tourkos.

Theoderic Strabo (the cross-eyed): A Thracian Goth who is the cousin and rival of Theoderic the Great.

Theoderic the Great: Variously known as Theoderic the Amal, King of Italy, King of the Ostrogoths, Western Emperor, and viceroy of the basileus, as well as by his woodnames, Ansis and Aesir. Once a hostage of Leo Marcellus, he is also the son of the champion Theodimir and brother-in-law of Clovis, responsible for installing the Roman soldiers in the Brenii Pass

Theodimir: Father of Theoderic the Great and conqueror of the Huns.

Theodore of Studion: An exiled leading Studite, iconophile, and ally to Kreindia of Amorium. Later, a saint.

Theodosia: Thekla's sister and Leo the Armenian's discarded wife.

Theodotos I: Constantinople's Patriarch.

Thomas the Slav (Pontus): *Foederati* commander, advisor to Leo the Armenian, conspirator, father of Thamar.

Tiro: A prison guard in Constantinople.

Tufa: A general under Odoacer.

Tullius: A soldier stationed in 10th century Syria.

Valamir: Uncle of Theoderic the Great.

Vanoush: A young commander under Thomas the Slav's Feodorati, distant relative of Leo the Armenian.

Verina: A late friend of Kreindia of Amorium.

Videmir: Uncle of Theoderic the Great.

Wade (Linwood) of Aquitaine: 21st century synesthete, former insurance salesman.

Young Wheelie: A kid who finds himself drawn to a standoff between Faron, Wade and Henry.

Zeno: Byzantine emperor after Leo Marcellus (the Thracian) but before Anastasius.

Zoticus Macroducas: Thomas the Slav's second in command, his former bodyguard.

Places

Anatolia: Also called Asia Minor, part of the Byzantine Empire.

Ancyra: A city in the Byzantine Empire.

Antioch: A city in Ancient Greece and Byzantine Empire.

Apamea: A city in Syria on the Orontes River.

Aquitaine: Southwest region of Gaul/France. Visigoth country.

Aurelian Walls: The city walls of Rome, Italy.

Bosporus: The strait that runs past Constantinople, dividing Europe and Asia.

Boucoleon: A palace in Constantinople named after its bull and lion iconography.

Brenii Pass: Also called the Brenner Pass. A stretch of mountains in the Alps between Italy and modern-day Austria.

Byzantium: The Eastern Roman Empire.

Capitoline Hill: One of the Seven Hills of Rome.

Cappadocia: A cave-strewn area of Central Anatolia.

Castrense Amphitheater: An amphitheater in Rome, Italy.

Chalcedon: A maritime city near Constantinople.

Chrysopolis: An ancient trade city near Constantinople.

Church of the Holy Apostles: A major church in Constantinople.

Claudiopolis: An inland city near Constantinople.

Constantinople: The capital of the Byzantine/ Late Roman Empire, modern-day Istanbul.

Danube River: A large river in Eastern Europe.

Delias: The ship from which Kreindia fought Aghlabid pirates on her first journey to the west.

Delphi: The site of an oracle in Ancient Greece.

Diantha: The ship that ferries Kreindia and Keyx to the Princes Islands.

Gaul: A large Roman division in Western Europe inhabited by Celts. Included parts of France, Netherlands, Germany, Northern Italy, among other areas.

Hagia Irene: A church in Constantinople.

Hagia Sophia: The best known church in Constantinople; once Kreindia's favorite.

Halki: A Greek island in Aegean Sea.

Hicksville: A town in Long Island, New York; a one-time resting place for the Gospel of Judas.

Hippodrome: The sporting center in Constantinople that housed games, races, fights, and public events.

Holy Roman Empire: The conglomerate of territories in Central Europe united under Charlemagne and the Pope.

Itale: Former spelling of Italy.

Jericho: A town in Long Island, New York; home to the Richters.

Julian Harbor: A port in Constantinople.

Ligugé Abbey: An early French monastery founded by St. Martin of Tours.

Mese: The main street in Constantinople.

Neusiedler See: Pannonian birthplace of Theoderic the Great, a lake with no outlet to other bodies of water. Today it marks the Austrian-Hungarian border.

Nicomedia: An inland city near Constantinople.

Pannonia: A province of the ancient Roman Empire, later under the Byzantine Empire, near Danube, remnants of a chaotic zone east of northern Italy and just north of Dalmatia. The name for this area is archaic even in the 9th century but the reference persists because it is an untamed buffer between empires.

Persia: Empire east of Byzantium.

Place of the Skull: The place where Jesus was crucified (Golgotha).

Princes' Islands: An archipelago off of Constantinople, perfect for prominent exiles.

Prinkipo Island: The largest of the Princes' Islands.

Ravenna: The second capital city of the Western Roman Empire in Itale, later the capital city of the Kingdom of the Ostrogoths.

Rome: The traditional capital of Itale and power center of the Roman Empire; enjoyed brief resurgence under Theoderic the Great.

Seven Hills: The hills contained within the city walls of Rome (clockwise: Quirinal, Viminal, Esquiline, Caelian, Aventine, Palatine, Capitoline); also can refer to the Seven Hills in Constantinople.

Sirmium: A city in Pannonia.

Spoleto: An ancient city in central Itale.

Syria: A country in Western Asia whose western border opens to the Mediterranean Sea.

Thrace: Province of Byzantium. An area of southeast Europe now including parts of Bulgaria, Turkey, and Greece.
Tiber River: A river in Itale that runs through Rome.
Venezia: Venice, the Floating City.
Via Flaminia: An ancient Roman road running through Italy.

<u>Things</u>

Abbasid Caliphate: The third Islamic caliphate that stretched from Northern Africa to what is now Iran; reached the height of its power in 850 CE.
Aghlabids: Ruled parts of Africa on behalf of the Abbasid Caliphate.
Anatolic Theme: The military division of Anatolia in Asia Minor.
Angon: A long, heavy, barbed spear.
Armicustos: An arms keeper.
Athinganoi: A.k.a. the Untouchables and the Warrior Class, a religious sect from Phrygia later scattered across Anatolia. Kreindia's heritage.
Barbaricum: From the Roman point of view, all lands and peoples not controlled by them.
Basileus: Greek word for emperor.
Blues and Greens: Byzantine chariot teams with strong social and political influence.
Burgundians: A Germanic tribe that inhabited and ruled parts of the Rhineland and Savoy.
Celts: An ethnic group that dispersed from Western Europe and spread both eastward and westward, with particularly significant footholds in what are now France and the British Isles.
Cleromancy: The casting of lots to determine a deity's will.
Contemplation Forest: A place inside Kreindia's mind, created by her as a safe haven in which to solve problems.
Coptic: The language of the Copts, who were the last of the ancient Egyptians.
***Domestikos*:** An administrative and military title in the Byzantine Empire pertaining to defense of the royal inner circle when they reside in the capital.
Dromon: A Byzantine warship.
Excubitors: Imperial guards under the Byzantine Empire
Foederati **(singular-** ***Foederatus*):** Auxiliary military

378

contingents provided by nations under the empire.

Franks: A general term for several Germanic tribes that lived in what is now France and Western Germany, Switzerland, and Northern Italy, among other areas in Western Europe.

Gauls: The people who lived in Gaul, the Celtic region as identified by the Roman Empire, that we now call Western Europe, particularly France.

Gepids: A Germanic tribe related to the Goths.

Gnosticism: From the Greek "having knowledge." A collection of beliefs defined as heretical (Christian variant), prominent in the 2nd century.

Golgotha: Also "the place of the skull," the place outside of Jerusalem where Christ was crucified.

Gospel of Judas/2nd Century Codex Tchacos: A Gnostic Gospel containing conversations ascribed to Judas Iscariot and Jesus.

Heruli: A Germanic tribe.

Housecarls: Military servants bound only to the house of a particular king or lord of Germanic origin.

Hunnuil: Reputed father of the Amali lineage.

Icon: An image of Jesus, Mary, or other saints who were venerated in the Byzantine Empire.

Iconoclast: One who destroys icons.

Iconophile: One who venerates icons.

***Jing Luo* theory:** A concept in Chinese medicine that focuses on meridians and the flow of life-energy, *qi*, throughout the body.

Locutory: Public meeting area for an abbey.

Longobards: Also called the Lombards, a Germanic tribe who ruled in Itale.

Mare Nostrum: A.k.a. the Middle Sea or the O-Round Sea. Today, the Mediterranean.

Midgard: The "middle earth" of the nine worlds in the Scandanavian/ Germanic belief system. Where humans dwell.

***Magister Militum*:** Latin for "Master of the Soldiers." The highest military rank below the emperor in 9th century Byzantium.

***Meiyǒuguó Rén*:** Ancient Chinese idiom for a synesthete who can bend time and space. It means a person without a country.

***Monostrategos*:** A top Byzantine military general.

Ostrogoths: A branch of the Goths who ruled in Itale.

Pax Nicephori: A tentative peace treaty agreed by Charlemagne and Nikephoros I in 803 CE that resulted in the Eastern Byzantine Empire recognizing Frankish authority in the West. Complications and adjustments continued until 815.

Rugians: A Germanic tribe.

Scirians: A Germanic tribe.

Scramasax: A long knife, variant of a seax, often with runic inscriptions on the blade.

Solidus: Popular gold coin of the Roman Empire, replaced with silver in the 8th century, but continuing in limited circulation.

Spangenhelm: A helmet worn by the Varangian guards.

Studites: A religious order that originated in the Byzantine Greek Church.

Suebi: A Germanic people, not homogenous enough to be considered a single nation.

Swabians: An ethnic group in southwest Germany and those within the defined political boundary known as Swabia.

Tagma: A Byzantine military unit.

Tourma: Regiment-sized division of the *Foederati*.

Tourmach: Commander of a regiment-sized division of the *Foederati*.

Take the purple: Become royalty.

Thracian Goths: A division of the Goths from Thrace.

Three Sneezes: An ancient superstition that when someone sneezes three times it confirms the truth of the previous statement.

Vandals: A Germanic tribe.

Varangians: The Greek name for Vikings/ Northmen.

Visigoths: A branch of the Gothic peoples that sacked Rome.

Wheel of Taranis: A chariot wheel representing the god of thunder in the Celtic belief system.

Wicker Man: A giant wicker statue used by the Druids as a vessel to hold human sacrifices for burning.

Woden: Scandanavian/ Germanic god.

Xylocastron: Greek word meaning, "wooden castle." In dromons, this was the central tower near the main mast used as a platform from which to launch projectiles. It also served as storage for Greek Fire materials.

Yggdrasil: A great tree in Norse mythology that embodies the connection of the nine worlds.

ACKNOWLEDGMENTS

The roots of this sequel to *Wade of Aquitaine* go all the way back to experimental chapters penned when the first book was freshly written and I was discussing theories of the series direction with film director Kevin Michaels. My crit-group beta readers on the first draft of the opening chapters were Amy Lau, Kat Hankinson, Ken Altabef, William Freedman, and Jake Packard. Ken Altabef heroically rejoined the effort several times in progress. Grateful thanks in roughly chronological order to:

Scott Boylan, Kim Olsen Boylan, and Keri Vanucci-Olsen who saved me when I lost my electronic copy by repatriating to me the souvenir draft of the first chapters that I had given them!

David Dunton, for enormous encouragement in comparing my writing favorably to that of the great Joss Whedon; and Jan Kardys of the Unicorn Writer's Conference for accidentally giving the manuscript to David Dunton. Bless you, Jan!

My beta readers on the partial second draft- Eli Fixler, Lauren Freund, and Roxanne Gentry.

Madelyn Fisichella, researcher and error eliminator extraordinaire.

Head cheerleader Hannah Wyborski, for her work on emotions and movement.

Anna Goulart, who found many of the stubborn, leftover errors and obfuscations.

Tina Metsala for finding and meeting the rhythm of my writing.

Frances "Tori" Lear, for small but powerful grammatical changes for clarification, adept line edits, and contributions to details in story logic, especially her clarity in conforming the two books.

Nastassia Velasquez, who notably found the misspelled homonyms and later joined in on formatting. Brittany

Landry and Tori Lear for maps.

Megan Prokott, maps and location list.

Roxanne Gentry, who launched the glossary team effort.

Eveling Cerda and Kevin Michaels, for cover art strategy; and Roy Mauritsen, who did the art for all three covers in the trilogy.

Special thanks to HJMT Public Relations, especially Hilary Topper and Lisa Gordon.

Apologies to anyone I might have missed in the finishing frenzy.

ABOUT THE AUTHOR

BEN PARRIS has auditory-tactile synesthesia and other rare forms of the condition. These cognitive impressions were the primary inspiration for his Kindle bestseller *Wade of Aquitaine*. Parris is the author of four books, the latest of which is *Kreindia of Amorium*. When he is not writing, editing or teaching, he enjoys studying history, hiking, and playing chess. Join his Facebook fan page at: www.facebook.com/BenParrisAuthor.

CPSIA information can be obtained
at www.ICGtesting.com
Printed in the USA
LVOW13s1058270617
539532LV00005B/771/P